WHY NOT US?

NAOMI RIVERS

To everyone who's had to stand in the gap.

WHY NOT US?

NAOMI RIVERS

CHAPTER ONE

Jasmine

"Hey, you!" T stood in our kitchen looking very comfortable leaning against a cabinet and very sexy wearing non-descript running shorts and a plain black tank top. Her locs were coiled on top of her head and she held a coffee mug in one hand—aptly reading "Kiss the Cook"—and a piece of what I assumed was banana bread in the other. She also had the whole house smelling like cinnamon, goodness, and five pounds on my hips.

Sure, when Teresa Butler and I started dating three years ago in 2002, she had said she cooked a little bit. I didn't think much of it. Although really? I had yet to tire of the first simple meal she prepared for me, just salmon, wild rice, and veggies. But damn, she said nothing of her baking skills. Somehow, she managed to keep her body firm in all the right places while I knew firsthand that the weight struggle was real.

"You know you want some!" She slid a small plate with a slice of the delectable creation across the island, already toasted with a pat of butter partially melting on top. *Yes, yes, I did.* The corner of her eyes crinkled— those brown copper orbs she called eyeballs made my heart feel like the gooey condiment on my breakfast.

T pushed herself from the counter and opened the fridge. She called over her shoulder, "Any thoughts about dinner?"

I watched her scan the refrigerator before my eyes inadvertently closed and I took a bite of bread—so good. When I opened them, T was standing with her head unusually close to the open freezer. I wasn't surprised. It was a sweltering Monday morning in late July, worse even than a typical summer day.

I rarely set the air conditioning temperature below eighty degrees, so I assumed her behavior was an indictment on my frugality. I had to admit, it was already warm in the house. There was no doubt in my mind that T would fiddle with the thermostat as soon as I left for work. It was one of many small things that she and I had to negotiate to peacefully coexist when she moved into my house in Mt. Washington, a quiet, leafy Baltimore enclave. Now, it was our house.

"No, I'm open to whatever you make," I replied, finally answering her question about dinner.

"Open to whatever, huh?" T's voice dropped an octave, and her sly grin appeared—one side of her mouth dipping enough to form a cute little dimple, the opposite eyebrow reaching toward her hairline—accompanied by swaying shoulders.

"I'm open to whatever you make for dinner, silly! Can we have a conversation without your mind going *there?*"

"There? Me?" She clutched her imaginary pearls to feign innocence. "I was merely seeking clarification about my girlfriend's dinner requests. What are *you* talking about?"

She winked and opened the pantry cabinet to take stock of our canned goods and the shelf loaded with spices. Lots of spices. She said you could never have too many spices. I swear the DEA would think we were up to something nefarious considering all the jars of herbs with T's handwriting on them.

She had essentially taken over a corner of the backyard and planted a vegetable and herb garden. After I got over the fact that she had dug up perfectly good grass and watched her on more than one occasion meticulously drying herbs, I realized that I loved how they made our food taste. And I appreciated her effort. I mean, I loved my flower garden, but I never considered growing produce. Sometimes I felt she had wisdom beyond her thirty-eight years and her southern roots came in handy quite often.

"You, ma'am, need to get out of here." T's chin jutted toward the wall clock as she handed me my lunch bag and travel mug filled with coffee. She also pointed to the water bottle on the table by the front door.

T was right, I needed to pretend I had a job to be at. T taught art at a local middle school so being here with her now that it was summer and school was out, was especially nice. She prepared my lunch every morning, and dinner was ready when I came home. Simply lounging out back with her and Coco, my beloved Bichon Frisé, in the evenings was delightful. Just the thought of it made me want to linger. I poked my bottom lip out and sauntered to the door. I could feel T right behind me, she wasn't making my exit easy. She turned me around, cupped my face with both her hands, and brushed my lips with hers. Definitely not easy.

"I'll see you this evening," she said and kissed me again.

Dear Lord, what had I done to deserve her?

***

My drive from Mt. Washington to Canton, where ReBuild Baltimore's headquarters was located, was uneventful. ReBuild was a nonprofit organization dedicated to helping families achieve homeownership. I was knocking on forty's door and felt like I needed to do more. More for myself and more for the community. So, I initially started working there as a volunteer, transitioned to part-time staff a year later, then full time a year after that. I was drawn to their mission at its basic level: to help people help themselves, which had always been my life's work. First as a social worker at a hospital, now as the Director of Community Development—a fancy title that meant I screened and met with potential families, ensuring they would be able to contribute the sweat equity required of our clients. I also maintained a list of volunteers whose time was critical to running a nonprofit with limited resources and I solicited suppliers, funders, and overall well-meaning people willing to share a piece of their pie. I found that "nonprofit" really meant we needed some profit to keep the lights on, and the staff paid.

I had opened the box of newly framed photos and picture albums delivered by the cutie in a brown uniform before she had a chance to say, "Have a nice day." The albums' contents reflected the joys and hopes of a better life for the people in them—they were also a part of my marketing strategy. Big smiles, tight hugs, and families in front of their brand-new homes were going to help decorate my office and help me tell the story of our company's why. Why we did what we did and how it made a real difference in real people's lives. Each album was a start-to-finish photo compilation of homes in ReBuild Baltimore's portfolio, and I planned to share them with existing and potential donors.

The chorus from Alicia Keys' "Unbreakable" diverted my attention. Three years in and seeing T's number on my phone still elicited a smile. "Hey, baby."

"Hey, love. I know you said I could make whatever for dinner but just wanted to check, are you okay with grilled tuna steaks?" She could be so sweet.

"Of course, that sounds delicious. But I may be home later than usual though."

"Ahhh, ix-nay on the rill-gay, hah, gay, I made a funny."

Thinking about my upcoming afternoon appointment suddenly clouded my mood. I didn't respond.

"Okay, you're not amused. What's up?" T's tone was more serious.

"I got a strange call from Leslie earlier today," I shared.

"Really? What did she say?"

"She left a message asking me to meet her at three o'clock in what I'm assuming are the outpatient medical towers at Charity Hospital."

Leslie Sharp and I had been friends for the better part of twenty years. Of our sister-friend group, she had the more pragmatic, sensible approach to life. She spoke her mind on the regular and didn't let her emotions get too high or too low. But now I was concerned about her and what she wasn't saying.

Starting to feel anxious, I shifted pictures of families beaming brightly on one shelf and mixed in one of super-photogenic Coco, smiling in the backyard and a Savannah sunset taken earlier in the year. I picked up the framed memory—a blue sky fading to coral, then to a vibrant orange-red, making the silhouette of the Talmadge Bridge look like pyramids above the city's river. Apparently, I was distracted because T used her teacher voice to draw my attention back to our conversation.

"Ms. Charles," T said, using my surname.

"Huh? I'm sorry." I didn't realize I had zoned out.

"Did Leslie tell you what's going on?"

"No, her message just said she really needed me to meet her at three."

Holding the phone between my head and shoulder, I sat down and grabbed my lunch out of the bottom drawer of my desk. I needed the physical support of the chair and something on my stomach. Ever since getting Leslie's message, I'd unsuccessfully tried to keep from ruminating on the range of possibilities. Was she sick? Was my godchild, her nine-year-old daughter Portia, sick? No, it couldn't be the child. If it were, the appointment would likely be at the Pediatrics Center instead of Charity. Another thought came to me. Maybe her sister Angel's cancer had returned. *Sheesh.* That was a mess. She was diagnosed with breast cancer three years before, sending everyone into a tailspin. Leslie, God bless her, had literally upended her and Portia's lives to care for Angel. I wasn't so sure I would have done the same for my sanctified siblings.

"Hmm, I hope she's okay," T said, sounding concerned.

"Yeah, me too. Thankfully, I was leaving work early anyway. Now, I'll leave here shortly, meet her at Charity, and then head home."

"I didn't know you were leaving early today."

"I told you Saturday when we were doing yard work," I insisted.

"You thought I'd remember that?"

"See, that's why we need a family calendar…to keep track of stuff."
I imagined T shook her head in resistance.

"I don't know that we need such a thing." She chuckled and moved
on. "Hopefully, everything is alright. Let me know if you need to change
plans."

"Yes ma'am, will do."

Digging through my lunch bag, I found a little square note stuck to
the top of my salad container. The silly face with googly eyes drawn on
it lightened my mood a bit. Dating an art teacher had its perks.

***

I was grateful I'd dropped more ice cubes in my water bottle before
leaving the office. Between the heat and worrying about my friend, I
was nursing a mild headache and my mouth felt like it was stuffed with
cotton. By the time I turned up Calvert Street the air conditioner still
hadn't cooled the car. Thankfully, though, the trip from my office in
Canton to downtown was short, and the mid-afternoon lull in traffic
made the drive less painful.

As luck would have it, I found an open parking space on St. Paul
Street, but when I spotted a red tow truck come around the corner,
I kept going. *Damn, the vultures had already started cruising the parked cars.*
Parking in downtown Baltimore was always a crap shoot—you had to
read the signs three times. Interpreted incorrectly, you could end up
with an expensive ticket or worse, catching a cab out Pulaski Highway
to the city's expensive impound lot.

Besides, I didn't know what Leslie's appointment was about, or how
long I'd be there. I circled the brick and glass complex and headed to the
hospital's garage. Seeing the tow truck had been divine intervention—a
reminder to set aside my frugality for a minute and spend the extra eight
dollars to park.

The ride down to the main floor of the hospital felt longer than it probably was. I got a visitor badge from a security person at the patient information desk and made my way to the medical office tower. My stomach knotted for two reasons. I always associated the antiseptic, sanitizing smell with illness and I saw Leslie obliviously staring out the floor-to-ceiling windows. On an average July day, all the yellow and red blooming flowers in the beautiful little park across the street would calm my nerves. Now that I was here looking at Leslie, it didn't feel like an average day. Silly me. The slight squeak my shoes made against the overly waxed floor likely signaled my approach because she turned toward me, one corner of her mouth lifted, feigning a smile.

I didn't bother with empty pleasantries. "What's going on?" I asked. "I've tried to reach you most of the morning and the calls went straight to voicemail."

Leslie and I had been through the death of her mother, the ups and downs of her marriage, the birth of her daughter, and the craziness with my ex Toni, not to mention Angel's illness. And yet, I had never seen Leslie's eyes so bloodshot.

"I sent a few text messages too—I haven't heard from you. Is everything okay?" I asked, my words tumbling out faster than I wanted them to.

"Hey." Leslie squeezed me tightly. "Thanks for coming on such short notice. I don't know how this appointment's going to go, so I decided I needed someone to be there with me."

I heard the catch and unease in her voice.

"What's that mean? What kind of appointment is this? Is it for you?" In my head, I sounded more apprehensive than I wanted to let on.

"I have an appointment with an oncologist. It's a follow-up for a biopsy I had last week." Her eyes darted back and forth around the lobby as she drew her lips inward and shifted her weight from one leg to the other.

I swallowed hard, trying to ignore the panic settling in my chest. "A biopsy? I've talked to you three times since last week and you didn't mention a biopsy."

I held back my own tears as I forced questions past the lump in my throat and out of my mouth—knowing I probably wasn't being as supportive as I should be. The range of possibilities and what-ifs raced unchecked through my mind.

Come to think of it, Leslie had been real low key the last few weeks. Not a lot of conversation when we chatted on the phone. How had I not sensed that something was off? In addition to Angel's battle with breast cancer, Leslie's mother had died from metastatic breast cancer less than ten years ago. Luckily, Angel was still in remission.

I grabbed Leslie and hugged her hard, trying to convey my concern. "I'm here and no matter how this goes, I got you."

We rode the elevator in silence, save for the chimes, each signaling the next floor. On the eighth floor we entered a suite, an intentionally calming space adorned in pastel colors, silk floral arrangements, and stenciled affirmations. After signing in, Leslie sat next to me, and I gently placed my hand on her forearm to offer a bit of grounding in the present moment. She covered my hand with her opposite one. The slight downturn of her mouth and the look in her eyes, now softer than before, spoke volumes. I was glad I could be here with her.

"Ms. Sharp? Leslie Sharp?"

We gave each other a look that said, "Here goes!" and followed the staff person through the door she held ajar. We walked past several closed doors to an office with windows high above that same park I had been admiring earlier.

"Please have a seat. Dr. Jordan will be with you shortly."

I wondered if Leslie had noticed that the solemn lady in scrubs wasn't the most engaging, not even meeting our eyes. My friend looked like she was carrying the weight of the world, shoulders slumped, staring again out the window at nothing in particular. Her right leg was shaking, clearly betraying the calm front she was trying to maintain. If it hadn't been for the potentially life-altering conversation we were here for, seeing the dome of Baltimore's Basilica and the nation's first Washington Monument against the cloudless, azure sky would have been awe-inspiring.

To allay my own fear and do something with my nervous energy, I got up and pretended to take great interest in the office's decorations. A wall of pamphlets about breast cancer. Anatomical models of breasts on the mahogany credenza behind the desk. The doctor's ego wall loaded with diplomas, certificates, and a couple Baltimore City Council citations. Whoever Dr. Jordan was, she appeared to be well known. There were framed thank you notes from women who had publicly fought breast cancer—a local news anchor and a state senator. Pictures of various breast cancer events—an annual breast cancer walk, a framed pink souvenir shirt with a pledge sheet. It looked like she had raised some significant money for a breast cancer foundation. Also hanging there was a picture of the doctor and Ms. Gloria, Leslie's mom.

"Wow! Looks like she's done a lot of work in the area."

"Yeah," Leslie said. "I've known Dr. Jordan a long time."

"There's your mom." I pointed to the picture frame and Leslie got up to join me.

"Yep, look at them. They did the walk together. Dr. Jordan is a survivor too and was highly recommended. That's why my mom became one of her patients. She treated my sister too."

When I initially met Leslie, Ms. Gloria was doing a lot of fundraising for local breast cancer organizations. Ms. Gloria was so charismatic and spunky that when she asked for money for support, she always put a positive spin on her requests.

"See how good I look as a survivor," she would say, presenting herself like "Ta-daaa!" People often gave more.

I took a beat. "So how long have you been concerned that there was a problem?" I asked, not looking at my friend. My voice already unsteady, I was afraid I would immediately fall apart if I met Leslie's eyes.

"It's only been two weeks since I found the lump. You know with my family history I don't take lumps lightly. I knew I needed to reach out to Dr. Jordan to kinda get this process started."

"Oh, Leslie, I'm so sorry I didn't know." I squeezed her hand.

She shook her head and shrugged. "I didn't want to share until I knew something definitively. But this morning, when Dr. Jordan called and said she needed me in her office this afternoon, I realized I needed someone here with me. It's not like I haven't been in this exact space already. Twice." Leslie massaged her temple. "I didn't call Angel. I didn't think she'd be helpful today."

At that moment the door opened. Both of us turned toward the sound, and a stunningly beautiful silver-haired woman wearing a white coat walked in.

CHAPTER TWO

T

I got Jasmine off to work and went for a run on the Jones Falls Trail. Although at thirty-eight, I didn't recover as well as I used to, I still liked to get it in.

It wasn't quite eleven o'clock in the morning when Coco and I headed out for the day. We, the little furry ball of energy and I, didn't meet under the best of circumstances. That first time she had insisted on terrorizing me while I was on a run at the Harbor. But now she had become my trusted assistant, keeping me company when I worked in my studio and alerting me to unwanted visitors at the front door.

With Coco fastened into her little seatbelt harness, we were on our way. Jasmine let her hang out the window unrestrained, but I wasn't brave enough to take that chance. Plus, I was afraid of Jasmine where Coco was concerned, rightfully so. As beautiful and kind as she was, Jasmine would probably cut somebody about her dog. Ironically at this point, I would too.

Women pushing strollers with little people in tow and all the children playing at the corner playground were a good indication that school was still out for the summer. Of course, my being free to roam at eleven on a random Monday morning was a good barometer too. One of teaching's best benefits was having summers off. Though many teachers opted to work to make extra cash or continue satisfying their altruistic benevolence at specialty camps or city summer and youth programs, I—after giving thought to such pursuits for half of a second—had chosen to use the summer to focus on my art.

I laughed to myself while passing the hardware store on the right and thinking about conversations I'd had with fellow teachers during the final week of school. Our excitement was palpable. Everyone—students, teachers, and staff—was sick of each other and ready for summer break. Gus, the wood shop teacher and my closest work colleague by virtue of our classrooms' proximity, was giddy when he said he'd found a summer position working at the hardware store. He was even more giddy when he talked about the twenty percent employee discount and all the scrap wood the manager said he could have.

I slowed, checking twice for pedestrians, then turned right toward Northern Parkway to access the Jones Falls Expressway, otherwise known as the JFX. With the air caressing my skin and the sun making it glow a bit, smooth jazz vibrating from the car's speakers, and traffic on the JFX particularly light, I couldn't help but shout, "I love summer!"

It was a quick three exits from Mt. Washington to my old Bolton Hill home. I kept the house to use more as an office, gallery, studio-type situation. And truthfully, a place to have a little quiet time from "family" living.

Petals from the pink dogwood trees lined the street as I maneuvered the car to my block. Parking was easier this time of day, and I found a place right in front of the house.

Ms. Donna, my neighbor next door, peeked outside as Coco and I walked up the sidewalk. I didn't know for sure, but the way the woman surveilled the neighborhood and knew everything that went down, I was convinced she was a retired agent of a three-letter government organization. I'd asked about her occupation on more than one occasion in the thirteen years that I'd owned this place. She never confirmed where she might have worked in the past, and she also never denied my speculation. I appreciated her watchful eye, but I didn't feel like listening to gossip just yet.

I waved and mouthed, "I'll be back," then stopped to untangle two plastic bags that were caught in the hedges.

Once the alarm was disabled, I checked the kitchen and basement to ensure all was well and in order. The kitchen clock had stopped—time stood still with dead batteries. I rummaged through the junk drawer for AA batteries. I was thankful I hadn't had any difficulty with break-ins or yard items growing legs and walking away, but then again, I also didn't leave stuff out that could be easily pilfered. Since I didn't live here on the regular anymore, I relied on the alarm and Ms. Donna.

I took Coco's leash off and put fresh water in her bowl, then put a kettle of water on for myself and searched the cabinets for tea. I found several varieties of single-serving pouches of mint, ginger, and chamomile with lemon but nothing else. I settled on mint, without sugar since I didn't see any. I needed to bring more supplies here.

Sitting at the kitchen table with my paintbrush-styled letter opener, I quickly worked through the accumulated mail, separating it into two stacks—recycling and things I needed to follow up on later. I looked through art supply catalogs and put aside brochures that listed new paints that were available for my art classes. My school was one of the lucky few in Baltimore City that still had an arts program. Most of them had been decimated in support of adding and lengthening math and English classes. Those were important for sure, designed to help students meet state standards. But the arts were important for a child's development too. Thinking about the short-sightedness always made the muscles in my face tighten. I understood public versus charter versus private school funding, or lack thereof, firsthand.

Somehow, both charter and private schools maintained a well-rounded curriculum with arts included, and their students performed just fine on statewide tests. The argument could certainly be made to bring classes like home economics and industrial arts back to every city school. Those classes were instrumental in teaching skills about measurements, ratios, and most importantly budgeting, a life skill for sure. By the end of the school year, students and teachers, me included, were weary of the asinine testing frequency.

The whistling kettle interrupted my reverie, keeping my tight jaw from causing any more discomfort.

I sipped my tea and played back my conversation with Jasmine this morning. *A family calendar? Please, we don't need no damn family calendar.* I barely kept track of my own schedule, let alone Jasmine's. I'd seen her calendar—the woman was always on the go—it was too much for me to look at.

"But if we don't know each other's schedules, it's going to be a problem," I remembered her saying. Now I was curious about what Jasmine had in mind and picked up my phone.

Me: What kind of calendar are you talking about? Something electronic or analog?

She texted back: IDK

I rolled my eyes…the acronyms, ugh. Me: Do we really need one?

Jasmine: Yes, we do.

Me: Okay :(

Jasmine: Design something. This isn't that hard.

Me: Says the person who isn't designing something : |

By the time I had downed the last of my tea and put the mug in the sink, Jasmine still hadn't sent another message.

"Well, that wasn't helpful," I thought. Apparently, I was on my own on this one.

The tables needed dusting, and I purged the magazine rack of dated copies before heading to my studio upstairs to get a little work done. Coco beat me up here, already resting on her bed in the corner. I decided not to completely disturb her rest with heavy bass beats today, so I put a few Keiko Matsui and Candy Dulfer CDs in the multi-disc carousel and stood in the middle of the space that had become my creative cocoon. A safe place that I had cultivated to experiment with new techniques and media, create, and just be me. Feeling Keiko's beautiful piano riffs, I snapped my fingers to the smooth sound and let the energy flow through me.

The other part of my conversation with Jasmine concerned me. I wasn't familiar with the specialties of this and that hospital in Baltimore so I wasn't sure if Leslie's appointment at Charity should sound alarm bells. But my girlfriend's melancholy mood certainly did.

Maybe I should work on this family calendar thing, I thought. She hadn't been very clear. However, I knew if I didn't propose something, its absence would be a constant irritant, like flies at a family barbecue. I found a piece of scrap lightweight plywood, roughly twenty-four by eighteen inches to use as the base of this thing I didn't think we needed. I could just go to an office or art supply store to buy a large calendar, but I had all the materials here to tackle my latest "honey-do" project. And besides, I was an artist. No need to pay someone else.

An hour and a half later, I stood at my worktable admiring the almost cured DIY paint specifically formulated to dry in a slate-like finish, gently testing its tackiness before putting the calendar grid on it. Deep in thought, I didn't hear Coco get up, but she had no problem nudging my leg to let me know she wanted to go out. It was just as well—I needed to take a break. I had become so engrossed in staining the frame and making sure the coats of chalkboard paint were sufficiently even that my fingers were starting to cramp. I suddenly welcomed an unplanned break, which would give the paint more time to fully dry and I could get a little fresh air.

"Come on, girl!"

Coco and I raced each other down the stairs to the back door. A few years back if somebody had told me I would find absolute joy being in a race with a little ten-pound dog, especially this one, I wouldn't have believed it.

Coco finished her business outside and we both had a snack in the kitchen, then I grabbed the broom from the hall closet and went to sweep the front steps. I hadn't been outside a minute before Ms. Donna walked out wearing a floral house dress reminiscent of those my grandmother wore all day when she piddled around her house. House dress aside, Ms. Donna was a regal older woman with a sharply tapered salt-and-pepper haircut, more salt than pepper. Her skin was so smooth it wasn't a stretch to imagine her in an Oil of Olay ad—skin that was only now starting to show a hint of her sixty-five years on this planet.

"Afternoon, Ms. Donna. Do you want me to sweep your steps?"

She gave me a polite curtsy and a flourishing gesture that said, "Be my guest." I walked next door, knowing full well that not only did her steps not require sweeping, but she could care less about me sweeping them. She had probably been itching to talk since she'd seen me two hours earlier. Thankfully, her soap operas or "stories," as people of a certain generation called them, had likely kept her occupied earlier. Ms. Donna plopped a cushion down on the top step of her sparkling white marble stoop, gathered the excess fabric of her dress, and took a seat, ready to provide unnecessary supervision.

"How are you doing?" I asked, moving to the step below where she sat to work my way back down.

"Doing just fine. I wasn't sure when I was going to see you to tell you the couple up the street with the new twins are listing their house. You know, the one with the forest green double door and that beautiful wrought iron on the first-floor windows?"

Why I needed to know this bit of information, I wasn't sure.

"Really?" I stopped sweeping and looked toward the rowhouse she was talking about. "I don't see a "For Sale" sign. I'll be interested to see what they get for it."

"What?" She couldn't hear me over the piercing siren of a passing ambulance.

I waited then repeated what I'd just said.

Ms. Donna shifted her weight on the cushion, getting more comfortable. "I don't think it's listed yet. I saw the wife when she was out pushing the stroller yesterday evening. Are you thinking about selling?"

"No, not really, but who knows? If the money's right, I may seriously consider it. But I like my house. You remember how much time and care, not to mention money, I put into it?"

"Yeah, that's what may make it worth it to sell. You know my children want me to move to Charlestown."

"Really?"

"I've been in West Baltimore for forty years, raised those same children here, and they want me to move all the way to the county." She sucked her teeth.

I leaned against the railing—sweeping and listening weren't working so well together—and tried my best to keep my amusement to myself. I felt myself starting to grin, so I turned away from her and trained my gaze across the street.

"Charlestown?" I whistled. "That's a fancy place for seniors. I didn't know you wanted to do that." I glanced back at her.

"Uh huh, very fancy and very expensive." She flicked her wrist, making a dismissive wave and rolling her eyes. "You heard me say *my kids* want me to move to Charlestown."

I smiled.

"I'd like to keep my money and my independence as long as I can." Ms. Donna's lips were pursed now as she shook her head. "That's our conversation every time I talk with one of them. They won't let it go."

"You could get a nice price for your place—the prices here in Bolton Hill have been going up steadily. Some say they're up thirty percent over the last five years."

She twisted her lips.

I added another unwelcome two cents. "With the square footage and Victorian architectural details, you might not do too bad."

Ms. Donna extended her arms out, like "bring it on." I imagined in her younger days she might have thumped her chest. "I know this. Folks moving here 'cause this is a million-dollar house in DC. My youngest tells me that each time she comes home from Howard, with laundry." She chuckled out loud, more to herself than me.

"And we're within a mile of Penn Station. Think of all the professionals who use the MARC commuter train to get them back and forth to DC," I added.

Ms. Donna blew me off again with her waving hand and stood up, gossip session apparently over. I turned to walk back to my own stoop. "I'll be here for maybe a couple more hours today."

"Okay." She paused in her doorway. "Remember to put your alarm on. Sometimes I see young folks looking at our houses a bit too long for my liking. I stand right here or in my bay window so they can see I'm looking too."

This time I let my amusement show and gave her a mock salute.

"Yes ma'am! Talk to you later."

CHAPTER THREE

Jasmine

I recognized the woman who briskly entered the room as the esteemed Dr. Jordan.

"Leslie, I'm sorry, ladies," she said, nodding at me. "Thank you for your patience. It has been *a day*."

"Dr. Jordan, this is my friend Jasmine."

The doctor extended her hand, which I shook, its softness reminding me I could do better at exfoliating and moisturizing.

"Thank you for being here." She held eye contact with me, then turned to Leslie. "I'm glad you were able to get here today." She cleared her throat. "I won't belabor the news…the biopsy was positive for a malignancy."

Leslie gasped and dropped her head. I instinctively reached for her hand to once again ground both of us. Leslie didn't wait long to jump straight into wanting solutions.

"Cancer, seriously, not now. I can't have cancer now." Scooting to the edge of her chair and leaning toward Dr. Jordan, she added, "We need to do whatever has to be done."

Dr. Jordan nodded. "I do understand, Leslie. I've been here, and I really do understand. I'm here in this fight with you—just like I was with your mom and sister."

Leslie sat back a little, her leg starting to bounce again. "I'd like to get you scheduled for scans as soon as possible. Time is critical, we need to get started right away." Leslie pursed her lips, inhaled, and subtly nodded her agreement. "We'll need to determine what our actual situation is and develop our plan of action from here. You may recall we thought we needed to look at possible cancer studies for your sister?" Leslie nodded again. "Well, I'd like to start that process sooner rather than later for you."

Leslie swallowed. "Do you think that's necessary this early?"

"Leslie, given your family history, we likely need to pursue more aggressive treatment."

"How come?" Her voice was so low she barely whispered the question.

"You are BRCA positive, black, and under forty. I'm going to bring in more support than I did with your mother and sister's treatment."

"Wait, what does that mean? BRCA positive?" If I was going to be helpful, I needed to understand what was being said—and not being said.

"BRCA cells are genetic markers that have a familial component. Cancers that show up with these indicators are far more aggressive than those without them."

I listened intently.

"They've been showing up in young black women with increased frequency and I want to treat you with everything we have. So I took the liberty of having my assistant schedule your imaging tests for Thursday. I anticipate getting results on Monday, Tuesday at the latest."

"Gosh, that's only three days from now." I could see beads of sweat forming on Leslie's forehead as she tried really hard to regulate her breathing. She closed her eyes, pinched the bridge of her nose, then massaged her temple.

"Before you leave, I want you to schedule a follow-up for Wednesday morning."

Dr. Jordan came around the desk and stood next to Leslie. With a deep sigh, Leslie collected her handbag and slowly stood, making sure her legs wouldn't give way. Dr. Jordan took her own deep inhalation and embraced the third member of the Sharp family that she would shepherd through this journey.

We rode the elevator back down to the first floor, its dinging sound seeming more amplified than the ride up in the silence.

"Lobby," the electronic voice announced.

I followed Leslie to a quiet seating area away from most of the lobby traffic. The contemporary soft leather chairs provided comfort I was grateful for. Leslie's entire body seemed to be vibrating as she stared in the direction we had just come from, relieving me from having to think of the right thing to say—because I was at a loss.

"I've always wondered how I would feel if I needed to have this conversation," she said at last. "I didn't anticipate the fear that's swelling in my body like a balloon right now. I heard her say "malignant" and my brain shut off. I wanted to run out of there screaming. Hell, I want to scream right now. But I don't have the luxury of running away. I really need to fight this…for me, for Portia, for Mama."

I grabbed both of her hands. "You know we got you. Whatever you and Portia need, we got you. Food, transportation…we're here."

She tried to smile. "Thank you, I know that. This is not what I expected, and yet it's exactly what I expected. A small part of me thought I would sidestep our family genetics. You know?" Leslie finally looked at me, eyelids barely containing the pools of liquid threatening to spill over.

I didn't know what she was even remotely feeling. How could I? I just tightened my grip around her hands.

"I have a child. I want to see her grow up and find her place in the world. How am I going to tell Portia? Lord, Angel is not going to handle this well. She's been on a "You need to live life every day" sorta "carpe diem" kick since her six-month follow-ups have gone well."

"Angel knows what this process is like—between her, me, Stephanie, and T, we're here for you." The unapologetically audacious Stephanie Stewart was another important part of our sister-friend group.

"T? Are you sure?"

"Oh, absolutely, I don't even have to ask. She's going to help me… help you." I was confident.

"I know you're still all in love." That brought a tiny smile to Leslie's face. "But I think you should at least discuss it with her—she didn't sign up to help your sick friend." No longer able to contain her emotions, tears streaked down Leslie's cheeks. I grabbed a couple of tissues from a box on the side table and handed them to Leslie.

"Thanks." She threw her head back and despite her eyes being closed now, she began crying even harder. "Cancer!" she said just above a whisper, "Jasmine, I have cancer."

I sat with Leslie for another hour before we left the hospital. Over that time, I listened to the stream-of-consciousness taking up space in her mind, mentioning the people most important to her and all the things that needed to be taken care of. Among them was the fact that Leslie had apparently started looking at summer camps too late in the season. She had waited until April—which didn't seem late to me, but what did I know about kids and summer camp? All the specialty camps—STEM, art, and performance—were filled. So, Portia was going to a regular day camp that did field trips to pools, parks, and museums—another thing that seemed perfectly normal for a kid to experience. But I couldn't imagine how the cancer conversation was going to go.

I suggested that Leslie get Stephanie's help to break the news to Portia. Stephanie, our sister psychologist, specialized in working with children. Leslie planned to tell Angel first, then her ex-husband Paul, who, considering Dr. Jordan's initial thoughts about treatment, would need to increase his shared custody time to accommodate pending surgery, chemo, and radiation. We probably would have been there longer, but that motherly thing kicked in and Leslie said, "I need to pull myself together to pick Portia up from summer camp."

After we parted, I eased my car off the Northern Parkway exit, lost in thought. I wasn't sure if I was driving the car so much as mindlessly going through the motions of getting home. So much so that I pulled into the Smith Avenue Grocery parking lot out of habit, thinking I needed to make dinner. The muffled Alicia Keys melody jarred me back to reality and I dug the phone out of my bag.

"Hey, you," T sounded all chipper.

I knew I would probably fail but I tried to mirror her mood. "Hey, yourself."

"Are you close? Just trying to gauge if I should sear the steaks on the grill or the stove."

I had completely forgotten that T was cooking tonight. "Let's keep it simple. Just cook them inside. I'll pick up salad fixings and a fresh loaf of bread."

"Sounds like a plan."

I heard pots clanking and assumed T was digging the cast iron skillet out of the cabinet.

"Okay, I'll be home in twenty minutes or so."

I passed the floral stand and grabbed a bouquet of flowers. I had plenty in my cutting garden, but these were convenient, and I needed some instant beauty. I laughed to myself—*these fast grocery florals would have to do*. But I did feel like I was cheating. I had a little Moscato in the fridge that I was going to have tonight too when I told T what was going on.

After putting more groceries than I intended to buy in the back seat, I sat in the driver's seat without putting the key in the ignition. My shoulders slumped and my head involuntarily moved from side to side as I tried to shake loose the thought of this inconceivable situation. But I kept replaying Dr. Jordan's words over and over. I sobbed for the first time that day. The kind of uncontrollable release that happened when life seemed to be too much. *How many times did a family have to deal with a disease?*

I reached into the glove compartment to get tissues to blow my nose, which had become so stopped up I was having trouble breathing. I stared out the window, my tears making the people going in and out of the store look like fuzzy blobs of humanity. *Dear God, this was too much. I didn't want to lose my friend.*

Leslie and I had been through a lot indeed. Through it all, our sister-friend relationship had survived and thrived. Leslie sometimes got a tad jealous of my friendship with Stephanie, but the two relationships weren't the same. I knew Stephanie from high school whereas Leslie was my first real grown-up, ride-or-die friendship. The three of us played well together…most of the time.

I often ended up refereeing disagreements between the two of them. With varying opinions about…well, everything. Fashion? Stephanie was adamant that wearing white after Labor Day was a high crime and misdemeanor. Leslie wore what she wanted when she wanted to. Music? Leslie loved both R&B and rap. Stephanie thought Leslie had poor taste. Organic food labels? Leslie said it was false advertising, convinced that organic was synonymous with shelling out more money at the store and nothing else. Stephanie, on the other hand, swore by organic fruits and vegetables.

Forty minutes after talking with T, I turned into the driveway. Coco's furry white head popped into view through the glass door. I collected the groceries, her bark welcoming me home. Her wagging tail, swishing back and forth like a fan, made me smile and brought much needed calm after the heavy news of the day. The groceries even seemed heavier than when I'd left the store, so I rang the bell instead of juggling them with my keys.

T came from the direction of the kitchen, opened the door, and took the bags from me.

"Hey, love." She leaned in to kiss me. Looking into my puffy red eyes caused her to pause though. "What's wrong?"

I tried to hold the fresh tears at bay but failed. "Leslie has breast cancer."

"What? Oh no!" As I stepped inside, T rushed into the kitchen with our groceries and came back almost immediately with outstretched arms. "Come here, tell me what happened."

CHAPTER FOUR

T

After finishing Jasmine's latest "honey do" request, which took longer than I anticipated, I rushed back to Mt. Washington with Coco to make dinner. I was proud of myself for not only having finished the calendar so it would be there to greet her when she got home, but I had already mounted it too. Except she walked into the house pretty much in tears. Leslie had cancer. Damn!

Jasmine considered Leslie one of her sisters—they were closer than Jasmine and her biological sister, Robin, for sure. Portia, Leslie's daughter, was even Jasmine's godchild. Leslie could be a bit snarky. But compared to their friend Stephanie, who I always thought was trying to get rid of me—as if I wasn't good enough for Jasmine—Leslie was cool. And Jasmine respected Leslie a great deal for caring for her sister when she was battling cancer. It was Angel's turn to reciprocate—hope springs eternal. It would be the right thing to do for a family member. Knowing Jasmine and her big heart, I suspected she would be right in the mix, helping too.

Thinking about it, I hoped she would pace herself. Jasmine's new job had a lot more administrative requirements. She was bringing work home and often staying late to get her team, in her words, "moving in the right direction again."

Two nights earlier, she had come home with a shiny new hard hat still in the plastic bag. She wasn't excited about the prospect of wearing it and messing up her hair, but she loved the fact that her name was on it. After

I attached the interior suspension to the shell for her, she had sashayed around the living room with it canted to one side.

"That thing should be worn square on your head," I chided.

She was cute though, with the little bit of gray hair forming at her temple poking out. I hoped she didn't plan on walking around construction sites looking like she was modeling a church hat.

"I'm surprised we have to wear them." She straightened it slightly.

"Why?" I asked.

"I don't know, it's just home construction."

"Yes, construction is the operative word."

"Yeah, yeah, you sound like the foreman. He showed me a scar on the back of his head. Said when he was a young laborer, a guy turned suddenly with a bundle of two-by-fours and knocked him out. He didn't even see it coming. Two days off without pay and ten stitches later, he never stepped foot on a site again without steel toe boots and his hard hat."

I scrunched my nose and rubbed the back of my head. "Ouch!"

"Exactly. As if I needed any more convincing, he also let me know that ReBuild took their safety requirements seriously and that he would kick me off his construction site should I consider not following the rules."

"Well, all right then."

I liked ReBuild and had encouraged her to apply for her current position. She took my advice and applied after the previous Director of Community Development had all but been shown the door. I had met him during a holiday function, and he hadn't struck me as a warm and fuzzy person. His people skills were a bit lacking, and that was saying something considering I was an introvert. He should have been engaging and encouraging people who wanted home ownership for themselves and their families. But Jasmine said he was arrogant and dismissive to applicants. In my very biased opinion, she was the exact opposite. There was no doubt the program would flourish and grow under her guidance.

"Look, you've had a long and eventful day. Take a shower while I finish dinner."

"Are you sure? I can wait."

"Stress is written all over your face."

Jasmine tried her best to smile. I felt bad for how distressed she was. "Go. Dinner will be ready when you get back."

She quickly kissed me on the cheek and disappeared up the stairs.

***

"Thank you." Jasmine hadn't eaten much of her dinner before pushing her plate away.

"Is it okay? You barely touched it." I knew it wasn't the food.

"Yes, hon, it's fine. I'm just not that hungry."

I shook my head, at a loss as to what to say. What words could a person provide when the good girl friend of their girlfriend was diagnosed with a life-threatening disease? I didn't say anything. I did, however, get up from my side of the breakfast nook where we were eating, slid onto the bench next to Jasmine, and put my arm around her. She put her head on my shoulder without saying a word. It wasn't long before I felt moisture on my shirt. We lingered in silence for I didn't know how long, until Coco decided to move closer to us to be an emotional support dog. Jasmine, sitting up to work the kinks out of her neck, picked Coco up. Her eyes fell on the new wall calendar—its frame stained to complement the kitchen's décor.

"Ahhhh, T, it's beautiful!"

"You like it?"

I had found an inconspicuous place to hang the calendar. Not too obvious for visitors, but still visible enough to be useful.

"I love it." She hugged me. "This is going to come in handy trying to juggle all of Leslie's appointments."

I could have been pushed over with a feather. Jasmine's response was not what I had expected.

CHAPTER FIVE

Jasmine

"What's your schedule look like today?" T asked as she finished scrambling eggs and dividing them between two plates. She added toast and slices of pineapple and mango before setting a plate in front of me. I was ready to eat since I hadn't eaten much the night before.

"Wait." She stopped, sat across from me, and grabbed my hand. "Lord, we thank you for a new day and new opportunities. And we ask that you use this food to nourish our minds and our bodies. Amen."

"Amen," I added. "Thanks, babe. I have a meeting with the boss to present my vision for ReBuild's growth and then I'm meeting Leslie at Dr. Jordan's office for the imaging test results and to talk about treatment."

T raised her eyebrows. "Sounds like this may be another tough day."

I nodded. "Not one that I'm looking forward to. The only good part is we're gathering the information needed to fight this."

"Well, if there's anyone I'd want on my team, it's the MVP Jasmine C." T threw both hands in the air like she had just made a three-pointer. "I know Leslie is glad you're on her team."

"Silly woman." I swatted at T. "Not just me, you too."

T dropped her gaze. "Me? I was thinking I'd be more supportive on the periphery. Like ask how she's doing, see what I could help you with, or pitch in by cooking a few extra meals."

My brow furrowed. "I was thinking you would have a more active role in this."

"Active like how?"

"I don't know!" My words came out louder than I'd wanted them to. I shrugged. "Whatever we need to do to help Leslie and Portia."

"Umm, I'm confused…Doesn't Portia have a father? It's not like he's some extra babysitter. His daughter's mother—the woman he was married to—has cancer."

"Yes, yes, she does," I agreed.

"Are they divorced yet? Is it wrong to assume he's going to be more active? If nothing else, with Portia so her mother can focus on getting better?"

I loved T to pieces, but her simple logic was, well…simple. People were more nuanced for her liking.

"Yes, they're divorced, so I'm not sure it's going to be that simple. But how about this—Let's not tell the story before it happens. Let's see what gets shared this afternoon."

Traffic was heavy on the JFX down to Guilford Avenue. Despite the congestion every day, traveling this route and heading across Fleet Street to Boston Street was the easiest way to get to Canton, where my office was. Gentrification in the city was continuing east, except now blue-collar workers were moving out and young hipsters able to afford four-hundred-thousand-dollar mortgages were settling around the waterfront. New coffee shops, restaurants, and beer gardens told the story of a changing Baltimore.

Every day I turned into the parking lot and every day I appreciated having a parking lot to turn in to. Not having to pay for parking or fighting the meter enforcement folks were extra bonuses. I didn't have an assigned space but that was okay. I was blessed enough to work in one of the prettiest buildings facing the Patapsco River. I greeted my boss' executive assistant with a smile. She was nice enough and had been helpful in getting me up to speed and integrated into the office's operations.

"Good morning, Ruth."

She returned the greeting and told me Jason, the Executive Director and my boss, was running a few minutes late and wanted to push the meeting to nine-thirty.

"That's fine, just let me know when he's ready."

I headed to my office. Nine-thirty was likely a stretch. Jason Byrne seldom came in before ten. But I wasn't mad because he also rarely left the office before six and even then, the likelihood that he was on his way to press flesh to fundraise for ReBuild was high. The rare combination of his blond hair and light green eyes, coupled with a prominent, angular jawline, made him easy on the eyes. If I played on the other team, he would've been a distraction. But that wasn't my issue. Right or wrong, his attractiveness worked in his favor more often than not, and once people took an interest, he turned up the charm and intellect to ReBuild's financial benefit.

I was relieved that his tardiness gave me a few more minutes to review my presentation. I looked at the notecards and recited the keywords I had written.

1. Establish clear guidelines for recipient eligibility.
2. Ensure volunteer hours are met.
3. Complete Home Ownership 101.
4. Determine mortgage limit.
5. Share recipient stories with future homeowners.

I placed the cards on my desk, closed my eyes, and meditated uninterrupted for ten minutes. Ruth called at ten-twenty saying that Jason was finally ready.

"Are you settling in around here, Jasmine?" Jason asked when I entered his office.

"Yes, I am, thank you. Ruth has made sure of that."

"Awesome."

He dipped a tea bag in a mug that I could clearly see was steaming hot, the minty aroma wafting through his well-appointed office. It was replete with an ergonomic chair, antique desk recovered from an abandoned property, an adjustable standing desk behind that, and matching desk accessories.

"You know that one person who knows everything that goes on at a company?" Jason went on. "The one who knows all because they've either been there a long time or they're strategically positioned to witness what's happening in multiple departments?"

"Yes."

"That's Ruth."

"Good to know."

He didn't have to tell me. From the moment I'd met her, she had shaken my hand with a confident assurance that signaled she was the one who ran the place. And her beautiful silver hair pulled into a tight bun also let me know this wasn't her first rodeo. She had been on this earth for a hot minute.

"So that tells me you've met all the staff too. Any questions for me?"

"No, not at the moment."

"Alright then, I've been looking forward to hearing your ideas. Your volunteer efforts and part-time responsibilities were impressive. Having you on board full time will serve us well."

"Thank you." I smiled and pointed to my laptop that I had plugged into the projector, essentially asking if I should begin. Jason nodded.

I was about twenty minutes into my spiel when Ruth appeared at the door and told him he had an important phone call. Jason looked at me and held up a finger as if to say "one minute" and took the call.

I was treated to a one-sided conversation in which he agreed to things and capitulated to an apparent request to provide documents of some sort. Given his monotone voice and the frowning, it didn't appear to be a pleasant conversation, and it ended tersely when he said, "Yes, I understand. We'd be happy to meet with national staff on Thursday." He stopped short of slamming the receiver in its cradle.

"Good news?" I raised my eyebrows high, trying to appear hopeful.

"Not exactly." He massaged his forehead. "Not for me or you."

"Me?" My hand inadvertently clutched my chest.

"Yes, you. Welcome to ReBuild Baltimore and nonprofit organizational management. Apparently, we're hosting a budget meeting with the national staff on, as you heard, the day after tomorrow."

"Thanks?"

"Consider today a trial run. I'll need you to pretty much tell them what you just told me in a condensed version."

"You sound concerned." I didn't know what to make of this information.

"I am. Every time they 'come to help,'—" He added air quotes with his fingers. "Our budget gets slashed."

"Should I be worried about budget cuts in my department?"

"I would be dishonest if I said anything but 'yes.' Here's what we need."

I prepared to write as Jason stroked the stubble on his chin. "Send Ruth a one-page synopsis of your presentation. Plan to make the presentation no longer than fifteen minutes. And expect questions about available community resources that may relieve pressure on the budget and questions about how you can do more with less."

Sheesh! Not again. I had already had my share of doing more with less at the hospital.

I exited Jason's office rolling my eyes in frustration. *It didn't look like he was doing more with less.*

I spent the remainder of the morning prepping for the national staff's arrival, working until I grew even more annoyed, and my eyes were dry and itchy from staring at spreadsheets in my attempt to cut costs. Even as a volunteer, though, I'd known the budget had very little fluff in it. Each line item was essentially a direct expense needed to renovate the houses in our portfolio across Baltimore. This was turning into a bad dream. As far as I could tell, we didn't use premium materials or top-of-the-line appliances, but we didn't procure cheap stuff either. Everyone deserved a nice place to call home. Incorporating quality materials, equipment, and accessories up front helped keep long-term maintenance costs down for people who didn't have a ton of disposable income.

Finally, I just closed my eyes and put my index finger on the computer screen near a line item, the equivalent of throwing spaghetti at the wall to see what stuck. Photography. Hmmm, okay, photography it would be. I needed a better understanding of why we allocated twenty grand a year for it. I would ask T about photography rates and maybe offer that as a budget reduction. I was starting to get a headache and stiff neck in addition to dry eyes. I needed to move my body from this one location.

"Hey, Ruth, do we have any more tea?" I asked as I poked my head out of the little kitchenette.

"Check the cabinet to the right of the sink," she answered.

"Bingo!" Finding the assortment of decaffeinated teas made me happy. Jason's mint tea had smelled so good. With a steeping tea bag in my mug, I wasn't ready to return to my office. "Ruth, thank you." I raised my mug slightly as I came back to the reception area. "I needed this."

She acknowledged my gratitude with a nod. "Jason tells me we're getting ready for the suits to visit."

In my short time on the new job, I'd realized that Jason's assistant didn't mince words or hide her displeasure.

"Yes, I've been trying to crunch numbers all morning, but it's hard to squeeze blood from a turnip."

"I keep telling the boss that. Before he got here, we went through restructuring after restructuring. Our budget was stripped down to next to nothing. So much so that we could only sponsor one family a year for like three or four years. It was pitiful."

"Wow! I didn't know that." I didn't know, but I wasn't surprised.

"Yep. Do you know how much need is in this city?"

"I do." I wondered where this was going.

"Then you know you have to use that psychology jiu-jitsu of yours, Jasmine, and fight with everything you got to keep the little bit of funding we have."

It was a statement rather than a question I was permitted to answer. So I said the only thing I felt would be acceptable.

"Yes, ma'am."

After talking to Ruth, I worked for another hour, but I was no closer to finding a holy grail in the numbers. I closed my laptop, stuck it in my bag, and left to meet Leslie for another appointment with Dr. Jordan.

I found a space in the garage close to the pedestrian bridge and walked over to the hospital. The pretty, late-blooming geraniums and hydrangeas below caught my eye. I had time before the two o'clock appointment, so I stopped to take a breath and say a quick prayer for Leslie and added a few extra petitions to help all of us. As if the universe were in divine order, the phone in my pocket buzzed, indicating a new text message.

Stephanie: Call me with details after the appointment.

Me: Will do.

I headed straight to the eighth floor and looked around for Leslie and Angel when I got there but didn't see either of them in the waiting area. I had just made myself comfortable, as comfortable as one could be under those circumstances, when Leslie burst through the office door at one fifty-eight like someone was chasing her.

"Hey, Ms. Sharp, you aren't late. It's okay, you can have a seat," the staff person said, recognizing the hurried patient needed reassurance. I watched Leslie mouth, "Thank you" before turning to survey the waiting room.

I waved and she walked over.

"Where's Angel?" I asked, giving her a hug.

"That's why I'm late." Leslie pulled back and hissed, "Angel said we'd ride together, but then she called me to say she couldn't come."

"What!?"

"My sister," she declared with emphasis on sister, "said this was too traumatic for her, and I could fill her in this evening when she came home from work."

Stunned, I shook my head. "I'm sorry. I'll make sure to take good notes."

"You know I was here for her first appointment? All the way through to her last treatment, when she rang the bell."

"Rang the bell?" I asked.

"Yeah, it's a tradition signaling your treatment is finished. You ring a bell in the cancer center."

"I'm hoping she comes around. What's her plan for helping you or being here for treatment?"

"Indeed, I don't know." Leslie threw her hands up. "Hell, I don't know what we're fighting yet."

"Ms. Sharp, you can come back now." The tech motioned through the door.

We both stood. I followed Leslie and the tech and declared, "We got this." But my claim sounded hollow, even to me.

CHAPTER SIX

T

August! I was a bit bummed. Not that I was counting, but I only had thirteen days of summer break left. My trusted assistant wasn't pleased either because I had left her at the house. Coco had certainly gotten used to hanging out with me during the day and vice versa. But I couldn't bring a dog (a description Coco would dispute) into someone else's house, no matter how well-trained she was. I thought about it though. I was headed to the Patterson Park neighborhood in east Baltimore with camera equipment and curiosity, looking for a rowhouse on Linwood Avenue that Jasmine wanted me to take pictures of. She'd said there would be balloons on the railing out front and window boxes with freshly planted flowers. Of course. Rarely was our house without fresh flowers in one or more rooms. The time of year didn't matter. Jasmine said they made her happy. Hey, if she liked them, I loved them.

Although it had taken both of us the better part of a year to take a chance on each other, I was glad we had. Jasmine was good for me, and I would like to believe she felt the same way. Before Jasmine, I didn't put much stock in relationships. Some would say I was pretty bad at them. But ours was a true partnership in that we complemented one another quite well. She wore her heart on her sleeve, mine was safely behind lock and key. Jasmine instinctually tried to fix situations. I tended to let them marinate. We nurtured one another's heart and mind and, for the most part, weathered storms together with symbiotic grace. We traded off who cooked and who did the dishes, she did the laundry, I took care of lawn and house maintenance. Not to mention that I still found her perfectly sized body and shoulder length hair with its light brown highlights hella attractive.

I hadn't planned to work today, at least not on a Jasmine project, but she said she needed a favor. So, who was I to leave my girl in the lurch? It was a gorgeous day with only a few clouds hovering above the city's skyline. There was even a slight breeze despite it being late into the summer. Ugh! Where had the time gone?

Spotting the house with the balloons, I parked and grabbed my camera bag. Compared to the other houses on the block, the ReBuild property stood out. Its façade looked like it had been power washed, and the pop of color from the flowers helped. But I felt palpable energy, a vibration in the air as I heard people talking in the back of a moving truck parked directly in front of the house.

A teenager stood in the doorway of the house wearing low-rise jeans and a sleeveless peasant top with her midriff showing. She took her earbuds out when she saw me surveying the place.

"Hey, can I help you?" Her inquiry was very pointed.

"Hopefully. I'm here to take pictures for ReBuild Baltimore?" I showed her my camera.

The child disappeared into the house. I didn't take offense with her abruptness. My thirteen years working in Baltimore City schools had taught me to have incredible patience with humans experiencing hormonal changes and I couldn't blame her—I would have been skeptical of some arbitrary person wanting to come into my house too.

An older woman who resembled the younger one appeared in the doorway. She, however, wore clothes splattered with paint and a headscarf, looking like she was in the process of moving in. "Hi, my daughter said you're here from ReBuild?"

"Yes, Jasmine asked me to stop by. Jasmine Charles?" *Did I have the right place?*

"Oh, oh, I'm sorry. Jasmine did tell me somebody would be taking pictures today. I completely forgot though. It's been cray-cray around here trying to get settled in."

"You don't have to tell me, rehabbing a home is stressful." I could empathize with her from the personal experience of renovating my rowhouse in Bolton Hill.

"You ain't kiddin'. I'm Ivory." She held out her hand.

"Hi, my name is Teresa. May I come in?" I was still standing on the sidewalk.

"Oh, shit, I'm sorry. See, I'm losing my mind." Ivory stepped aside and backed into the house. "Jasmine has been so helpful in the little bit of time she's been at ReBuild. I applied for the program long before she got there. But it didn't seem like nothing was happening until she called me out the blue and had me come in for interviews. This opportunity is going to change my life, it already has."

"That's some testimony and you're probably right." I smiled a bit as I walked past, but then I stopped in my tracks, my mouth dropping open. I didn't know what I had expected to see but I wasn't prepared to see a house worthy of a spread in *Architectural Digest*. From the outside it seemed like a narrow house but inside was a whole different story. The exposed brick walls, gorgeous oak hardwood floors, and the light, lots of sunlight, streaming in from six-foot-tall windows overlooking the street added tons of character.

"Wow!"

"Right?!" Ivory agreed with me, pride written across her face. "I helped fix this place up, was here almost every day, and I can't believe how nice it turned out. I'm still pinching myself."

"I bet." My eyes didn't know where to land. The stainless-steel kitchen appliances contrasted well against the white Shaker-style cabinets—simple but timeless. A stained barn door was slightly ajar, revealing a pantry, ingenious in a kitchen with limited space. I was impressed.

"So it looks like you're pretty settled on this level. I'll capture your great work down here, then if I could get shots of a bathroom and a bedroom or two that would be great." I could feel Ivory's eyes on me and finally turned back to her.

She looked away, but not before my intuition was confirmed, and pointed to the nearby stairs.

"Okay. My room and the spare room are probably best, the third bedroom not so much. If you've ever seen a teenager's room, you know it's probably a mess."

"I can't say that I have except for my own, some twenty-odd years ago."

"You don't have kids?" Her left eyebrow went up, accompanied by a sly smile and an energy I knew very well. In a past life, I would have walked through that miniscule, flirty opening.

"I don't." I returned the smile to be nice, but I needed to do what I had come here for and get the hell out. Enough with the small talk. "Ivory, I'll be out of your way in a minute, and you can get back to making your house your home."

"I like that."

I ignored whatever that comment was conveying and got busy. I shifted a bowl of fruit, repositioned the knife block, and used some other kitchen items as props to get this over with. I took a few candid shots of Ivory and her daughter, captured the cozy spaces upstairs, went outside to get pics of their front door, painted a bold shade that reflected Maryland's state flower, the black-eyed Susan, and finished up, thanking Ivory for her time.

CHAPTER SEVEN

Jasmine

Three weeks after Leslie's diagnosis and five days before Portia was supposed to start school, I met Leslie and Portia at Stephanie's office, which was located in Baltimore's Govan neighborhood. Leslie wanted, and quite frankly needed, support, not only for herself but also for Portia. Our friend Stephanie was one of the best child psychologists in this town, so who better to help with a complicated conversation?

Diamond, Stephanie's assistant, led us to a spare office instead of the waiting room. "Doc said you all would be more comfortable in here. Can I get anyone some water or tea?"

Leslie nodded, "I'd love some water please." She turned to Portia. "Baby, do you want water?"

I was worried. Normally, Portia was a little chatterbox. Now though, she was wedged into a corner of the couch and only shook her head. The kid knew something was amiss. She wasn't even fiddling with the wooden block puzzle on the table, and she usually liked that kind of thing.

Leslie whistled after Diamond stepped out. "Stephanie's doing well. I didn't know she'd moved locations."

The calming environment said, "children were cared for here," rather than stuffy clinic. The office had cubbies filled with children's games, plush alphabet letters, coloring books and crayons, stuffed animals, and sensory boards.

"They kept raising the rent at her previous office, so she bought into this building. This neighborhood is fairly stable and surrounded by a lot of children's service agencies. This is more or less the same area where her previous office was, and I don't think she lost any clients during the transition."

"Good for her."

I kept on like I was an expert in local real estate. "There are mostly outpatient practices and a few nonprofits in the building too. It's a good location and the rent is supposed to be consistent."

"The lobby was beautiful with all the flowers and affirmations on the wall," Leslie observed.

"Very pretty, and Steph said the arrangements rotate every season. I could do that, arrange flowers, I mean. I may need a job."

"What? I thought you liked your new job?" Very little got passed Leslie.

"Nothing serious." I tried to wave her off. "I shouldn't have mentioned it. But it's the same ol', same ol'. Cost-cutting is expected for everyone except the CEO. He still has a full staff, travel, and a *beau-ti-ful* office with a view of the harbor. It's so pretty, we eat at his conference table when he's out of the office." I got out of the overstuffed chair I was sitting in, moved closer to Portia, and kissed her forehead. "Portia, you're really quiet. How you doing, kiddo?"

"I'm okay." She shrugged and didn't look up, having found her lap more interesting.

Leslie glanced at me and shrugged too, as if to say, "I don't know."

Diamond brought water in and set it on the coffee table. "Does anyone need anything else? Doc should be in shortly."

"No, we're good, thanks," I said, trying to be helpful.

Stephanie poked her head in. "Hey, everybody, I'll be right back. I'm going to run to the bathroom. My last appointment took longer than I thought it would."

My feeling of uselessness was growing. Usually, I was okay with silence, but it was too loud at the moment. "Traffic will hopefully have died down by the time we leave."

Leslie gave me a pensive smile. I felt like I needed to do something with myself—I stood to stretch and returned to my original seat.

After saying goodnight to Diamond, Stephanie reappeared, ready to give us her full attention.

"Thanks for your patience," she said. Then she turned to my goddaughter. "Hey Miss Portia, how are you?"

"I'm okay." Portia shrugged again, her voice just above a whisper. She still didn't look up.

Stephanie took her shoes off and sat on the floor close to Portia. "You okay?" She placed her hand over Portia's.

"I don't know why we're here or what I've done."

Leslie moved closer and hugged her. "Oh, baby, you haven't done anything. I just needed a little help to make sure I explain things correctly."

"What do you mean?" Portia's eyes welled. She sucked her bottom lip inward.

"Remember I told you last week that Mommy was sick and would have to go to the doctor a lot for the next few months?"

"Yeah, yes, ma'am."

"Well, Godmommy and Ms. T are going to help us. You'll go to their house during the week so they can help you get back and forth to school and your activities. Then you'll come home with me and Aunt Angel on the weekends."

"I could go to the school up the street, then I could stay home." Portia's tears could no longer be contained. They streaked down her face.

"I think St. Josephine's is a better place for you," Leslie said. "It has a lot more activities and classes that aren't available in our neighborhood school. You've been going there for four years—I thought you liked St. Jo's?"

"I do, but I like being with you better." The kid wore her heart on her sleeve, much like I did.

"That's sweet, baby." Leslie caressed Portia's cheek with the back of her hand.

"So, this would just be for school days? And I come home on the weekend?" Portia was double-checking the arrangement.

"Yes. Except for the weekends when you go to your dad's."

"Who's going to be home with you?"

I looked to Stephanie for strength. Water was beginning to pool in my own eyes.

"Aunt Angel will be there to help me." Leslie tried to sound confident.

"She wasn't there last night. She went out." Portia bluntly noted.

"That's true," Leslie agreed. She squinted at Stephanie and nodded her head toward Portia.

"Portia, like your mom said—" Stephanie began.

I interrupted. "It's just during the week. We'll get you to St. Jo's, take you to your activities, and help with homework. If at any point you want to call your mom or go see her, we can."

Doctor Stephanie decided to save us. "Portia," she said softly, "it sounds like you're worried. Do you know what worried means?"

Portia nodded.

"What's it mean to you?"

"I'm worried Aunt Angel won't be there to help Mommy, and I won't be able to help if I'm not there."

"I understand. Do you understand that your mom is worried too? Worried that she may not feel well enough to make sure you get where you need to go? That's how your godmother and Ms. T are going to help."

"Am I going to have to sleep in the basement?"

"No, sweetie, why are you asking that?" Leslie said.

"We slept in the basement last time."

"That's because we were all watching *Shark Tale* and fell asleep, silly girl. You'll sleep upstairs in the guest room. Now that will be your room."

"Oh, yeah. I still need to finish watching that movie. The beginning was funny." Portia's voice went up a few octaves. "I get to sleep upstairs with Coco?"

"If you want Coco with you, I know she'd like that," I said. "I know this is hard but it's only until your mom has surgery and finishes the first phase of her treatment."

"Are you going to be sick like Aunt Angel?" Portia leaned her head on her mom.

"Yes, sort of like that. You remember Aunt Angel being sick?"

Portia's eyes filled with tears again, her head bobbing up and down.

God, this was heartbreaking. I needed to help them get through this.

"I'll probably have a lot less hair, but it'll grow back. You can help me choose some scarves and teach me how to tie them like you do for your stuffed bears and dolls."

"Where will I eat? What can I take over there?"

"You'll eat meals with me and Ms. T," I told her. "Just like you do on the weekends when you visit. And you can bring anything you want. Maybe we can get you a box to keep your toys in. You know, make it feel like a…um…a...second home."

Portia pondered my response a bit, her mouth twisting to the side in deep concentration.

"Can I cook?"

Oh, boy! "Um, sure. What do you like to make?"

"Mommy won't let me cook. She said I was too young."

"Got you already." Leslie motioned like she was wrapping something around her finger.

"Well…" I glanced at Leslie. "Maybe we can start with some real easy recipes. How does that sound?"

"Okay." Portia's eyes brightened a bit.

"Portia, I have a few questions," Stephanie chimed in, reminding us why we were in a professional's office. "How will Jasmine and Ms. T know if you're upset or need help? Would you feel comfortable telling them?"

"Yes. Godmommy knew my belly was upset after we ate a lot of candy and popcorn last time I spent the night."

"What?" Leslie's head snapped in my direction.

"Nothing, everything was fine." I sucked my teeth and waved my hand at her.

"Okay, so, Portia, tell me what you understand is going to happen next week."

Damn, Stephanie was good.

"I'm going to live with Godmommy and Ms. T so I can go to school and then I'll go home on the weekends or to my dad's. And when Mommy's better, I'm going to go back home with her and Aunt Angel."

"Okay." I pressed my hands together, thankful this had gone fairly well.

"I have a question." We all turned to look at the child. "When will Mommy get better?"

All of us, every adult in the room, held our collective breaths.

CHAPTER EIGHT

T

Meeting after bloody meeting during my first week back in school had my brain feeling like a pile of sopping wet towels. The same information, packaged in new wrapping, was delivered at the beginning of each new school year, which spurred the same questions from Nervous Nellie teachers. This year, however, I had a bit more incentive to pay attention because I found myself in an unfamiliar place.

Two days earlier, my department chair had handed me his big ring of keys and said to "look him up in Belize" if I was in the neighborhood. His long-running battle with the Board of Education's Human Resources Department about his number of qualified years had abruptly ended in his favor. He was allotted the equivalent of two years of employment time, giving him a total of thirty-five years and the magic formula of time and age to say "adios." He literally threw up two fingers when he showed me his retirement approval and said, "I'm out."

This morning I learned that we didn't have a replacement teacher yet and we might not have one until the second quarter. I tried hard, and failed, to control my eye rolling and irritation. Who started a new job in the middle of the semester? I spent the day trying to reassign classes minus a full-time art teacher. No one in our small department was going to be happy, including me.

So tonight, all I wanted to do was enjoy some delicious chamomile tea, relax in the backyard, and be peaceable. I had come to enjoy simply pouring boiling water over fresh chamomile flower heads that I picked from the garden most evenings. I had just finished sorting through mail and preparing a cup when Jasmine came home.

"Hey, love, how was your day?" I kissed her pillowy soft lips, which always took me back to the first time I had the chance to lean in and confirm Jasmine's lips were as soft as they looked.

She gave me a tight hug and sighed loudly. "We have a lot to talk about." Much to my disappointment, she let go and turned to ease herself into one of the kitchen chairs.

"Yeah?"

I watched Jasmine wring her hands, twisting and turning them before pressing her weight on the table to stand up again. Apparently, she needed to share more than just the details of her workday. She paced for a few seconds and then stopped in front of the family calendar. "Yeah." Jasmine replied without looking at me but she tapped the calendar's wood frame, clearly pondering something. "I met with Stephanie, Leslie, and Portia this afternoon." Her pitch got higher as she continued, "… at Stephanie's office, which by the way, is really nice—"

"Jasmine?" I interrupted her.

"Yes." She finally looked at me.

"What's up?" A little cloud of dread passed over me. The backyard could wait a few minutes. We sat down together in the breakfast nook, and I braced myself for whatever it was I was about to hear.

"Well…" Jasmine's hands were busy again.

I was trying to be patient, but her stalling wasn't helping.

"Stephanie helped us break the news to Portia that because of her mother's illness, she was going to live with us during the week—"

"What?" Severe lightning was released from the little cloud. My chest started tightening because I couldn't believe what I was hearing.

A half hour later, Jasmine was still talking. At some point, I stopped responding verbally. I just raised my eyebrows every third sentence and repositioned my head from one side to the other every now and then. I wasn't sure she noticed while she repeated the same sentiment over and over, using different phrases each time. *We* needed to help Portia and Leslie.

It felt like everything around me was spinning in one direction while I was going in the other. I really wanted to listen and be present. Jasmine was obviously concerned about her friend, but all *I* heard was that her best friend's illness would upend everything I had come to love about our heretofore great relationship.

In the span of a few weeks, we had learned of a terrible, life-changing diagnosis, Jasmine—understandably—wanted to offer support, and now her goddaughter was moving in? This was not what I had signed up for.

As it turned out, Leslie's cancer had been diagnosed as an aggressive stage 3. Jasmine rattled off the course of her treatment—surgery, chemo, radiation, possibly more surgery, and then possibly more chemo. I felt bad for Leslie, and Portia, for that matter, I really did. A diagnosis like that had to be a terrifying and devastating thing. She was embarking on a trial no woman wanted, particularly when your support bench wasn't that deep. But I couldn't help thinking there had to be another option rather than Jasmine and I doing what sounded to me like the heavy lifting of caregiving.

I sucked as much air into my lungs as I could and blew long exhalations on the liquid in my cup. At the moment, determined breathing like that was the only thing I could do to stay grounded. Hell, Coco's schedule alone was more than a notion—feeding her, letting her out, walking her, wash, rinse, repeat. The dog liked her activities carried out regularly by whatever human provided for her. Portia was a child, an actual human. A nice child, I'd determined from the times she'd spent the night. She was well-mannered, very observant, kind of an old soul. Inquisitive and fairly decent with math, a fact I noticed whenever she helped Jasmine measure glue and whatever else for their DIY projects. And any child who liked or played sports, which Portia did, was okay with me.

I didn't want to come across as insensitive or like a complete asshole though. Instead of losing my cool, I just stared at Jasmine, waiting for her to say something that could make me understand why us. Why did we have to be caregivers? Didn't the child have a father and an aunt? But I couldn't hold it in.

"Why us?" I finally interrupted as her steady monologue went on and on.

Jasmine's ten-minute response essentially boiled down to "Why not us?"

In a lot of ways, her question was valid. We were a DINK—dual income, no kids—household with extra space. And we could make time in our schedules. So why *not* us? Intellectually, of course I knew we should help. But practically, in terms of Jasmine's and my relationship, this situation scared the living hell out of me.

CHAPTER NINE

Jasmine

I was so concerned about Portia and Leslie successfully navigating their difficult conversation, I should have asked Stephanie to give me advice on how to break the news about our house guest to T. T listened, or appeared like she was listening, but she didn't have much to say when I told her Portia was moving in. At some point, I felt like I had talked too much. I gave her a peck on the cheek, she gave me a half smile, and I excused myself to wash the days heaviness down the shower drain.

The house was quiet when I finished a quick shower and had thrown on something to lounge in. I peeked out the screen door and saw T sitting on the patio.

"Oh, here you are," I said. "What are you doing out here?"

"Enjoying the quiet." T was staring out into the yard and didn't turn to face me.

"The calm before the storm?"

She huffed, "Yeah, something like that."

"T, it's going to be okay." I was talking to myself as well as my girlfriend.

"Will it? Jasmine, you agreed to let a nine-year-old child come live with us." She still hadn't turned to face me. "And without even talking to me about it first."

"I thought we agreed that her staying here would be helpful so Leslie can focus on her treatments and not have to worry about her daughter while she's trying to recover."

"We didn't agree to that. We—" She pointed at herself and continued, "were all but told flat-out that Portia was coming, which means there'll be a little person here *every* day. Jasmine, I work with kids, it's exhausting. Here? Home is my space to decompress from hearing, 'Ms. Butler this' and 'Ms. Butler that' *all* day, every day."

"You're right, it's a huge change for us. But one I think we can manage. It's a team effort." I sat on the chaise and placed my hand on T's leg. "I'm glad you're on this team. We play so well together." I brushed my lips softly across T's cheek before kissing her.

"Oh, don't try that now." T turned her head away from me.

I moved from T's cheek to her neck. "Try what? I'm just giving you a little late afternoon peck. I tell you what, let's get a little fancy tonight and go out for dinner. My treat. Where do you want to go?"

"So, a kiss and a bribe. You're cute and all, but I'm not falling that easy."

"No, not even a little? What about this?" I grabbed T's hand and brushed my lips against it. She closed her eyes and shook her head side to side. I needed her support, and I needed us to be okay. "Come with me." I reached for her and led her back inside to our bedroom.

Our bedroom. It was still funny to think of it that way because even though my ex had lived here, I always thought of the primary bedroom as mine. Maybe because it was always clear that Toni had wanted space for herself. When T moved in, the way we shared space just kind of happened organically. She convinced me to paint the room and the en suite for a fresh start, added two of her paintings. One of them—*"Two Faced"*—was my absolute favorite. It caught my eye on our first official date.

T sat on the bed and pulled me to her—I stood in between her gapped legs and took off the band that was holding her locs and let them cascade past her shoulders down her back. She liked them away from her face, but I liked them down. I always thought her sun-bleached brownish-red hair complemented her eyes perfectly.

"Now that you have me here, what do you want?" T asked.

She slid her hands up my spine, lifting my t-shirt and unhooking my bra at the same time. Her head rested on my stomach, her breath warming my skin.

I shed my bottoms and crawled onto her lap as she reclined back. T scooched back to the center of the bed and rested her head on the pillows, with me still on top. She bent one of her knees to not only apply pressure between my legs, but it provided a place for me to grind my hips and relieve the throbbing that was building.

I took T's bottom lip into my mouth, sucking it until it was plump, while she massaged my butt cheeks, spreading them apart and pushing them back together. I sensed a cooling sensation every time she exposed me more. It didn't take long before I was wet enough to make T's shorts wet too. With our lips still attached, she rolled us both over, so I could feel the fullness of her body on top of me.

"Why am I the only one without clothes?" I tugged on her shirt to register my dissatisfaction.

So, she propped herself up in a pushup position before moving to shed her clothes. I always loved feeling her triceps—very lean and powerful. Who was I kidding? I loved feeling her body in general since she took pretty good care of it.

"What do you want?" T had folded her clothes over the bed's footboard and returned to lie next to me, our bodies exchanging heat again.

She ran her middle finger from my throat down in between my breasts to my belly, feathery enough to elicit chills, then back up toward one breast, circling it until her spiral ended at my very erect nipple. Not to leave the other breast out, T took the nipple into her mouth, her spiraling tongue matching the motion of her finger.

"God!"

Despite knowing full well what I wanted, T generally asked the same question. What do you want? At first, I found it annoying, feeling like she was low-key teasing me for my lack of variety. One day, I asked why she did it.

"There may be a day when you want to shake things up," she said.

While I appreciated her thoughtfulness, I liked what I liked. "Come here." I pulled her full weight on top of me again and our tongues danced together a bit more before I gently pushed her shoulders, indicating I wanted her and her glorious mouth to head south to give my clit the same attention my nipple had received.

She paused and grinned that sly sexy grin. "You never said what you wanted."

I poked my bottom lip out as far as it could go. She laughed out loud this time then began caressing my skin with her tongue down to the source of my arousal, waiting just for her.

***

"Good evening. Welcome to Seaside." The hostess checked our names for a reservation before leading us to our table on the restaurant's perimeter with a view of Baltimore's Inner Harbor. I was feeling more relaxed than earlier and was looking forward to an evening out until I spotted Leslie's ex-husband and Portia's father seated in a booth. I stopped.

The hostess stopped too, waiting politely.

"Paul," I said. "Hey, how are you?"

Paul Duncan was a former basketball star at Coppin State, and every bit of six-three, two hundred pounds. He sported a bald head and a chiseled body you wouldn't mind encountering in an emergency. The likelihood of which was very possible given he was a Baltimore City firefighter. And beside him was a woman I didn't know.

"Uh, Jasmine, what's up?" Paul said.

"Have you gotten my messages?" I turned to greet the woman sitting beside him. "I'm Jasmine, and this is my partner, T."

"Hello." She responded coolly, barely glancing at me, let alone making eye contact with T. I rolled my eyes, turning my attention away from her.

"Paul, have you gotten my messages?" I repeated. "Portia is moving in with us, and I wanted to see if you could change, or maybe increase, your visitation schedule."

"Visitation?" The lady looked up. "For who?"

Paul had yet to introduce her to us and apparently didn't plan to. He was, however, suddenly concerned about getting more air around his neck and kept tugging his shirt collar.

I looked at the woman again. "We haven't met before. I'm Paul's daughter's godmother. His ex-wife is ill and his nine-year-old daughter needs to be cared for. Paul, we really need to talk. I'll call you again tomorrow so we can come up with a plan." I turned to Paul's date and added, "It was nice to meet you."

I didn't wait for a response, but she was openly glaring at Paul as T and I walked away.

"I'm sorry about that," I said to the hostess as we continued on to our table. In that short period of time, I'd forgotten that she was waiting.

T waited until we were alone. "You know, that was so unlike you. Really kind of out of character." She peeked over her menu, behind which I imagined was her mouth upturned at the corners. "I liked it."

Her laugh confirmed my suspicion.

"I've been calling him for two weeks. Crickets, nada, no reply. Then I see him here with a new honey. She clearly didn't know anything about his kid."

"Well, dinner has been interesting already." T placed her napkin in her lap. "Thank you."

"You think?" I sucked my teeth. "I need a drink now."

***

"Hi, Paul, come on in. Thanks for coming," I greeted him as I answered the door. I'd called Paul the day after we'd run into each other at Seaside. There were better things I'd prefer to do on a Friday evening, but I had invited him over to work out the details of Portia's schedule. He'd sounded amenable so I was optimistic this meeting was a mere technicality.

"Hey." T emerged from the kitchen and jutted her chin up at Paul.

"Come, have a seat." I led him to the dining room. "I figured we'd be comfortable in here. Give me a second, I made a few snacks." As I went to grab them from the kitchen, I asked over my shoulder, "Leslie's news has been hard for all of us. How are you doing with it?"

"I'm okay. I mean, I told her I would help out when I could."

Help out? Did this Negro just say, "help out?" I came back because I didn't think I'd heard him correctly. But T's head cocked to the side told me I wasn't having an auditory hallucination.

"Oh, that's good to know. To make this work though, we all have to pitch in. I'm sure Leslie told you she's going to need a lot of support with Portia while she's undergoing treatment."

"Yeah, she told me. Is Baby Girl here?"

"No," I answered. "She'll be staying with us starting this Sunday, she starts school on Monday you know."

"I thought school started August twenty-second?" Paul said.

"Monday is the twenty-second!" T and I replied in unison.

"Look Paul," I calmly, but firmly said. "It's already been a challenge for Leslie, trying to keep up with school preparation and just daily stuff for Portia. Leslie's illness is aggressive—her upcoming surgery may really tax her, physically and mentally. So, we thought it best that we—you, me, and T—make sure we weren't duplicating our efforts…and understand what we're doing and what you're doing."

Paul shifted his weight in the chair.

I continued. "You probably already know this, but St. Josephine's has a limited transportation schedule, most parents drive their kids to school. Are you going to be able to drop off or pick her up from afternoon sports activities?"

"Ummm, you know my schedule at the firehouse is all over the place. If we have an incident with multiple alarms, I may need to respond. I don't have the flexibility to be nobody's driver right now."

"So…" T drew the word out to four syllables. "You aren't planning to do any more than you're doing right now? For your daughter. Who needs you…like, now." Paul focused on the pretzels in front of him. "Help us understand. 'Cause you were able to make time for a date."

"Yeah, after you two stopped by the table, my night didn't go that well."

"You don't say?" T shot back.

I took a deep breath—I really was trying to be nice. "What T is asking—and we're just trying to figure out—is how are we going to work together?"

"No, I was real clear," T interjected. "I said what I meant—it appears that, since we're going to be taking care of your child, our lives are about to change. I want to know what you're going to do to help us, help her. Your daughter."

Save for Paul drumming his thumb on the table, the silence was profound. The tension thicker than Karo syrup. T and Paul locked eyes.

"Look, I gotta be honest," he started before turning his interest back to the pretzels, "I'm not all that cool with Portia living here."

"What in the Sam Hill, if your schedule is so iffy, where else is she going to stay?" T demanded.

Count 1…2…3 I reared back in my chair and shot T a look. "Really?" I said. "What concerns do you have?"

Before he could say anything stupid, T jumped in again. "How about this, bruh. If you're really concerned about your daughter staying here, you're more than welcome to take her home with you and *we'll* help out when our schedules allow."

T hadn't sat down since Paul arrived and was now dulling the hardwood's shine pacing back and forth, punctuating the air with her index finger.

"I mean, I'm just being honest. Anyone would be concerned having their child living with…living with…"

"Say it." T's nostrils flared. "Finish your sentence." If her eyes were lasers, T would have burned a hole in Paul's bald head. "Lesbian? Gay women? Or do you and your boys use more derogatory terms?" T stopped in front of him.

"Portia could be influenced, and I don't want that for her. I don't know why she can't live with Angel."

T slammed her palm on the table, jostling the bowl of snacks, her face contorted. "Ima say this again and real slow 'cause this wasn't in my plans either. You. Are. Welcome. To. Have. *Your* daughter live with you while her mother is in treatment for cancer."

I could count the number of times on one hand that I'd really heard T's Gullah Geechee accent. Hearing it now though, told me she was blazing mad.

Paul, of course, didn't know that, but he knew enough to try and lighten the mood.

"Look, I know y'all are trying to help. I'm just being honest." He sunk a little further in his chair.

Was that all he had? "Thank you for your honesty," I told him. "So let me be clear as well. I don't know if you've talked to Angel, but she doesn't want to change her schedule either. Despite Leslie changing hers when Angel was in the very same situation. I'm only Portia's godmother."

Paul rubbed his forehead, his head moving side to side.

"As her father, you have the absolute right to care for your child. You can exercise that right beginning immediately. But what's not going to happen is you disrespecting us for stepping in to help." I stood up too. "Particularly since you're choosing to do absolutely nothing different."

"I didn't say that," Paul replied, sitting back up.

"What are you saying? Other than you intend to live your life without disruption?" T was pacing again. "Keep this in mind, Paul…If Leslie doesn't recover, you're Portia's next of kin, not us!"

I figured T was finished with the conversation because she stormed out to the back yard, Coco scurrying behind her. My dog was done too.

"Well, that didn't go quite like I planned, but at least we all know where we stand. I'll see you to the door." I took in as much air as my lungs could handle and slowly let it out as Paul made his way to the porch. "Paul, I'm going to say this with all the kindness I can…Either you're going to help us help your daughter, or you need to get out of the way."

I didn't even wait on a response. I closed the door and went to join my girlfriend on the patio.

"Hey, you okay?" I sat on the chaise lounge with T and Coco.

"Yeah, I'm fine." Coco was playing the role of emotional support animal and getting rubbed. T shook her head and opted for levity. "The snacks were a nice touch."

I laughed. "I put some work into that plate."

"That mutha-f…" T's head oscillated like a fan.

"T!"

"What?! You don't expect me to be nice, do you? He came up in here with a lot of big dick energy. Talkin' 'bout he's worried about us influencing his daughter? What kind of b.s. is that? What about him not taking care of her? The more I think about it, the more furious I get. And since we're being honest, I'm not feeling this situation, Jasmine. How did we get saddled with this responsibility? How did it get to be you and me? We don't have any children."

I paused to try and think of the right thing to say. Anything to avoid further antagonizing T after this evening's awkward discussion. "T, you're right. It doesn't have to be us. But I'm asking for your help." I extended my hand to rest on her leg. "Paul's right to a certain extent though, only he's seeing the situation from his straight male perch. I do believe we'll be an influence on Portia—a good influence—by continuing to show her what family, working together, and love can look like."

I reached for T's hand, not just to touch her, but to let her know we were in this together.

"I'm feeling like Paul is right too. I don't necessarily want to upend my life either, but that sorry sack of shit better be glad that I love you."

CHAPTER TEN

T

The Friday after Labor Day, I sat on a bench near the Trolley Trail #9 trailhead waiting for John. I liked this trail, a vestige of the early twentieth century that snaked through wooded Patapsco Valley. I'd suggested we meet here to walk and talk after he declared—which he did at least once a quarter—that he needed to move more. It was a mostly flat, paved path that started in Catonsville and wound down to Main Street in Ellicott City. Once on the path for fifteen seconds, you forgot that you were less than fifteen minutes from the city line.

John Bonaparte and I had been friends since my first year at Savannah College of Art and Design. He was an architecture major while I was in the fine arts program. I had admired him from the jump when he and I were in an Airbrushing 101 elective together. A talented designer, he was adept at code switching while simultaneously speaking his mind. I was pretty sure his colorful bow ties with matching eyeglasses disarmed potential critics. I loved him like I loved my biological brother. We knew where each other's skeletons were buried and, thankfully, there was little evidence, at least to our knowledge, of our youthful debauchery. John and my cousin Kevin were the ones responsible for me coming to Baltimore from our hometown in the low country.

I waved when John's sleek, black Audi A6 eased up to the curb.

"Where are you parked?" he asked through his open window.

I pointed to the right side of Edmondson Avenue, watched him tack two points onto a three-point turn, and realized why it was still a skill on the Maryland driver's license road test. He finally parked and headed my way. We had barely hugged before he stepped back to glare at me.

"I wasn't sure I'd ever see you again now that you and Ms. Jasmine are with child. What time do you need to leave to get in the kiddie pickup line?"

"You are so wrong. On so many levels." I tried to jab him in the shoulder, but he was already bent over laughing at his sorry joke. "Besides, it's only been a few weeks."

"You look cozy though, mother-like." He gestured up and down my outfit, a pair of loose-fitting Lycra fiber shorts with cargo pockets and a matching moisture-wicking shirt. Sporty maybe…but motherly? The boy was trippin'.

"Keep it up, call me mother one more time." I shot him a look. "I've tried my best to avoid that daily spectacle. Parents will run over you to get in line. Jasmine complains about it regularly."

"Oh, testy! Let me stretch a minute."

My eyes rolled before I could stop them. We went through this charade every time we walked together, even though our pace rarely accelerated past easy.

"Come on." He tapped my arm with the back of his hand after lunging for thirty seconds. "Let's walk so you can talk this out."

"Me? This was your idea 'cause you think your butt looks big in your new jeans."

"It does!" He poked out his narrow behind, which could be aptly described as petite if he shopped in the women's clothing section. "Let's get this party started."

We headed down the asphalt path that ran through the surrounding hemlock forest, which made for a comfortable stroll without sweating, a plus for early September. Even more comforting, we hadn't encountered many walkers by the time we reached Oella Avenue, the first cross street.

The isolation gave us a chance to catch up and talk as loud as we liked for the first half-mile of our outing.

"What's good with you and Raymond?"

"Nothing much, unless you consider our dates to Whole Foods good—which I do by the way." The corners of his mouth turned up as he did a little bop with his shoulders. Boy had been in a monogamous relationship for the past year and still swooned with goo-goo eyes every time Ray's name came up in conversation. I was happy for my friend—connecting with someone on a deeper level had been a long time coming for him. I suppose everyone, or maybe most people, desired stable, loving companionship, but I missed the juicy tidbits of tawdry debauchery he used to share. I figured he could say the same about my life as well.

"I was kidding earlier, kind of, about your domesticity. But seriously, how are things going?"

"They're going," I sighed.

Jasmine and I had gotten together for dinner with John and Raymond at least monthly before everything changed, so I filled him in on happenings in the Butler-Charles household since Portia had moved in. I knew we could probably still get together if Portia's father really stuck to his supposed visitation schedule. I had little doubt that Jasmine probably knew already, but I hadn't realized how trifling he was. I might have pushed back a bit more had I known.

We reached Main Street, did an about-face and headed back from whence we'd come. When the path began sloping uphill, our chatting took a backseat because our quads and hammies wanted a say for a quarter-mile.

John broke our silence. "What has you so quiet?"

"A few nights ago, 'Pretty Ricky' stopped by the house to drop off a few things for Portia and had the nerve to pretend like he was headed to the firehouse."

"Does Paul look like Pretty Ricky from *Martin*?" John cackled. "You're foolish. So, what was pretend about the visit?"

"Color me cynical, but his leisure suit and sweet-smelling sandalwood cologne suggested he was going to extinguish flames, but not the kind that erupted from oxygen, fuel, and heat."

I thought that would certainly get a reaction, but John wasn't strolling in my peripheral vision anymore. Instead, he was five paces behind me with his hands on his knees, hiccupping and laughing in the middle of the path.

"Daddy, is that man okay?" I heard a little boy asking as he and his father walked past me. *Served John right.*

He was still wiping away the tears that had sprung up from his laughing fit when he caught up to me. "I'm sorry, T, but you know your dry humor kills me. Seriously though, I know you're irritated because things have changed, but have your feelings for Jasmine changed?"

"No, they haven't. But there's more to a relationship than just feelings. The extra responsibilities have been a lot." John nodded agreement and he threaded his arm around the crook of my elbow. I continued, "Parenting is hard. Being present is hard. Trying to make time for each other—me and Jasmine—after doing all the other daily and weekly stuff is hard. You know?"

"I don't personally, but I imagine it is."

"I'm already tired of working hard and it's only been two and a half weeks. I don't know how long we can keep this pace up."

John could be a lot of things, but unsympathetic was not one of them. He listened, asked a few questions, and offered suggestions for staying connected with Jasmine. He also was not known for subtlety, so I was waiting for a witty retort or two, something like, "You can do bad all by yourself," or "Chile, bye!" This version of John, the one sharing tame dialogue and expressing mature sentiments, was new for me.

After pouring out my frustration, peppered with doubts about my relationship, we made it back to our cars. I wasn't in a hurry to leave though, I just stood there with crossed arms providing little comfort.

John pursed his lips, his head tilted slightly. His expression said, "Silly rabbit." He gripped my shoulders, locked eyes with me, and emphatically declared, "T, go home."

CHAPTER ELEVEN

Jasmine

Portia's move to our house was uneventful—the first week at least. Every weekday we woke up on time for our seven-thirty departure for school, check. By three in the afternoon, I was in the pickup line, handled smoothly. I didn't think having a child in our house during the week was hard per se, but now that we were three weeks in, I was developing a whole new appreciation for parenting. It was tiring.

T sequestered herself in our bedroom after dinner most nights. One evening, she missed dinner entirely and stayed at her studio until well after nine that night. The first casualty of having Portia with us was our evening tea ritual. We had been in the habit of making tea, maybe having a dessert, or listening to a little music before heading to bed. It was our time to wind down. But now that time had been replaced with helping Portia with homework, my evening chat with Leslie, and getting ready to do it all over again the next day. I thanked God the child wore green plaid uniforms, one less thing to worry about during the morning rush.

I was tired though from waking up earlier than I normally did and from all the stuff that comes with taking care of a child. Portia was self-sufficient enough for bathing and breakfast, fruit and a toaster being wonderful things, so no concerns there. However, she had more homework than I remembered having even in high school, certainly more than any fourth grader should. T was helpful in this regard, especially with math, but researching maps for geography lessons and various science assignments this early in the school year seemed like a lot.

Our routine was frayed by week four.

Sitting here in my ReBuild office, I should have been reviewing the twenty-page summation Jason had forwarded from the national office, titled "Efficiency Recommendations for Baltimore Affiliate." By the fifth page, I'd already begun disregarding many of the recommendations. Instead of responding to Jason's irritating email that ended with "NEEDED BY THE END OF THE WEEK," I called Leslie. I wanted to see how she was doing after her surgery. And I needed to ask her about an upcoming back-to-school night, of which we had received notification via a note stuck inside Portia's backpack, which T found only by happenstance. I tried not to worry Leslie, she had enough going on.

"Hey, how are you feeling?" I asked after she picked up on the third ring.

"Like I've been hit by a truck."

I winced. "That sounds painful."

"It's okay, trying to get moving around." Leslie's words sounded pinched, like she couldn't get enough oxygen.

"Have you eaten?"

"Not yet. I'm going to see what's in the kitchen so I can take my pain meds," she said through grunts and wheezes.

I tried to tamp down my own fear and make myself sound more upbeat than I felt. "Has Angel cooked? Do you have food?"

Leslie paused a beat. "I'm not sure."

"Okay, I'll grab some salad and soup so you can put something on your stomach. I'm just leaving Canton, so I'll be there after I stop at the market."

Damn it, Angel! I hissed to myself after making sure the phone was disconnected.

***

Leslie buzzed me into her condo building and left her front door ajar. Nudging it with my hip, I watched her walking gingerly back to the living room. She eased herself into a recliner. The further she bent down, the slower her movement. A long audible breath signaled her butt had finally reached its destination.

"Are you off today?" she asked, raising the leg rest and reclining.

I placed the grocery bags on the dining room table. "No, I had a meeting at one of our housing sites to take pictures capturing our great work. I'm trying to update a promotional brochure to include with our grant applications. There was no need to go back to the office and this way, I can get in line for afternoon pickup." Leslie feigned a smile. "Gurl!" I slapped my leg. "That whole get-in-line thing is really a thing, huh?"

"You got that right." With one eye closed Leslie winced then she laughed, grabbing her side. "Don't make me laugh, these chest tubes are a bitch!"

It was a week and a half after Leslie's double mastectomy. After she called the surgeon an ass and refused to let him do the initial surgery, the procedure had been delayed for a week. All had gone well, but the procedure was painful, including tubes being inserted to drain fluid from her wounds. It was only the beginning of this journey.

"Sorry! When do they come out?"

"Tomorrow, hopefully. The visiting nurse has to come check them, then I can go to the office to have them removed. I'll be able to move around better once they're out."

"When's your first chemo session?"

"Not sure yet. They say a week after the chest tubes are removed. So maybe as early as next week?"

"Okay, make sure you let us know. We may not be able to stay the whole time, but we'll make sure you get there and back home." I got up to unpack the grocery bag. "Soup, salad, or both?"

"Soup."

"Coming right up."

"By the way, you will not be shuttling me around. Everybody still has a day job. I can get a cab or something. They have vouchers at the nurses' station."

"We will too. Hush." I placed a bowl of soup on a TV tray, nudging pill bottles to one side. "So, Miss Portia wants special hair barrettes and beads for bracelets. Where should I look?"

"They're probably somewhere on her desk." Leslie pointed the spoon toward Portia's bedroom and I turned on my heels in that direction while Leslie started eating.

"Oh, I need a form signed so that T and I can speak with her teachers at back-to-school night next week," I announced after finding Portia's requests for the week. "I'll email a scanned copy to you. Luckily, T found the notice about it in Portia's backpack. Otherwise, we might have completely missed the event."

"Hmmm, that sounds like my bright yet absent-minded child. I probably have an email from St. Jo's that I haven't read as well. I should add your email address as a secondary point of contact."

"Phew…bracelets, back-to-school night, I know you didn't think this was in your future."

"True that. And we do what we need to do for family," I said.

"Thanks, Sis, I really mean it."

"I know, and you're welcome. I'm out." I kissed Leslie on the forehead and headed for the door. "I need to go and get in this pickup line."

Her cough-laced laugh made me wince and smile at the same time.

***

The following week, I dropped Portia off at St. Josephine Academy, almost forgetting to give her the signed permission slip to join the basketball team. I was hoping that participating in an after-school activity could give her an outlet from the heaviness of her mom being sick. Stephanie had also recommended Portia participate in a support group for kids whose parents were battling cancer. I hadn't heard back from the group's social worker yet, which reminded me to add another task to my "to do" list. But now, the next thing on today's list was getting Leslie to her first chemotherapy treatment.

I pulled into a space at her complex and found Leslie sitting alone outside on a bench in front of the building.

"Good morning. Are we waiting for Angel?" I asked, looking around for Leslie's sister. I wanted to make sure I phrased the question positively since, in my opinion, Angel had already shown herself to be an unreliable supporter. She wasn't helping with anything…grocery shopping, cooking… nothing. In a short amount of time, I'd gotten in the habit of cooking more food than T and I needed and bringing extra plates to Leslie's.

"It's morning? Yes. Good? That's debatable. And no, Angel decided to discuss the events of the day with me this evening." Leslie clenched her hands together and shrugged a bit before standing up.

I paused to make sure I'd heard what Leslie wasn't saying. *No use dwelling on the negative.*

"Okay, let's get you to the first day of getting this behind us."

Neither of us talked much on the way. Years of friendship had a way of filling in gaps—long enough to be comfortable with silence. Small talk wouldn't have made this situation any better and would have highlighted both of our anxieties. I approached the hospital. "Do you want me to drop you off out front and meet you there?"

"No, park in the garage. I'll walk with you. That way you'll know where to go if I'm not with you."

My biological sister and I weren't particularly close, but I couldn't imagine Robin not helping if she was able if I were in a situation like this. Leslie deserved to be cared for.

"I remember, I came with Angel during one of her visits. Remember? Something was going on with Portia and I covered for you."

"Right. I forgot about that."

"Yeah, Angel had support." *It would be nice if she returned the favor.*

"I have support too," she said, linking her arm through mine.

"Yes. Yes, you do." We walked arm-in-arm to the cancer center. It hadn't changed much except for the fact that there were more chemo bays, ten in all now, that folks could draw a curtain around for privacy. As I understood it, during the first few appointments people drew the curtains. But as they became more comfortable with the staff or other patients, particularly if they ended up on the same chemo day schedule, patients talked amongst themselves and developed their own community of sorts. Nurses had all their supplies on wheeled carts that they moved around to each bay area. I remembered from before that it had been a very efficient process.

Leslie registered at the desk while I walked around looking at colorful displays of information, an events calendar detailing ongoing activities, and support group notices. A harpist played here weekly, and patients could work with an artist to create artwork as keepsakes or donate them to the hope wall—a large collection of work created by cancer patients. Once Leslie changed into the coral-colored wrap gown, a tech took her vital signs and we headed to the bank of chairs.

A nurse in teal-colored scrubs with matching clogs, a gown over her scrubs, gloves, and goggles stopped midstride in front of us. "Hey! Long time! How are you? How's your sister? What are you doing here?"

I watched the joy of seeing Leslie drain from the nurse's face, replaced with the sudden realization that she had a new patient.

She pulled her goggles off. "This can't be happening again. Oh Leslie, I'm so sorry I didn't know. I haven't looked through all my patient charts yet. But you know you are in good hands, right?"

Leslie sighed. "Yes, I know, that's why I'm back here at Charity. I appreciated everything you did for my family—Mom and my sister."

"And I see you've chosen chair five?" the nurse asked.

"My mother had dibs on this chair. Angel couldn't have cared less but I'm going to sit here with the thought that Mom's keeping me covered."

"Ms. Gloria was larger than life."

That thought made me feel a bit lighter, because indeed she was.

The nurse continued, "I bet I've treated thousands of patients in the eight years since she passed. Hands down, she was one of my favorites." This made the corners of Leslie's mouth turn up. "I never met a woman who commanded and held people's attention in such a sweet way. No patient ever closed their little privacy screen when she was here. They didn't want to miss anything. Ms. Gloria." The nurse sighed and put her hands on her hips. Her dimples said the walk down memory lane was a good one.

"Thank you. That means more than you know." Leslie took the blanket from the back of the chair and placed it in her lap, the nurse taking that as a cue to move along to another patient.

"I watched the same park through numerous seasons of chemo treatments," Leslie said, pointing out the window. "I never expected that I'd be sitting in this chair myself. I know the routine. Hell, I know many of the staff members. Thankfully they don't have a lot of turnover here. I brought treats last Christmas because I've kept in contact with some of the nurses. She's one of them." Leslie jutted her chin towards the chatty nurse. "I'm praying for the same outcome as Angel."

I really didn't know how to respond, so I just reached to grab her hand. Leslie placed her other hand over top of mine. I told myself I was going to be strong. This right here was a lot. Pools of water appeared in Leslie's eyes. It was only a matter of time before I could no longer mask my own tears, and I had trouble swallowing the lump in my throat. We were a weeping mess by the time the nurse came back with the tray set up to start an IV.

"Are you ready?" she asked after taking a deep breath.

Leslie nodded and undid her gown so the nurse had access to her port-a-cath.

"I'm ready to get this over with."

***

We didn't talk much during the actual treatment. I read magazines and checked and responded to work emails. Leslie napped and around three that afternoon we were finished for the day. According to the nurse, she did well for her first time—no fever spikes, no immediate nausea, no physical symptoms to speak of. Maybe too well if you asked me. I expected a little more emotion, but I was maybe projecting my own shit onto her. She was right, she knew the routine.

The nurse reminded Leslie to stay hydrated, provided other care instructions, and a schedule that included vigorous biweekly rounds of chemotherapy that scared the hell out of me. Leslie would be getting chemotherapy every two weeks. The nurse explained that when she started to feel remotely better, it would be time for treatment again. Dr. Jordan had recommended five cycles initially, then weekly chemo followed by radiation or surgery depending on Leslie's progress. The plan was also predicated on how Leslie's body responded to the chemotoxic agents and their long list of side effects that could easily halt this process. This was going to be grueling.

CHAPTER TWELVE

T

Luckily, I had avoided the afterschool pickup spectacle—until today. Teachers had half a day off today, and tomorrow we were scheduled for a professional development day that might or might not include sleeping in, a cup of coffee, and maybe an afternoon run to enjoy October's cooler temperatures.

Jasmine had meetings this afternoon and was planning to meet with Leslie and Stephanie this evening for a girl's night at Leslie's, a sort of encouragement visit. So, I agreed to pick Portia up and take her with me to photograph a family that had moved into a ReBuild home in August. This was the third home Jasmine's organization had completed in the Sandtown-Winchester area of West Baltimore. It wasn't far from my studio, and I could swing by there after we finished with the family. My plan was to capture the whole family, a mom and four kids in front of the house, then take a few pictures in various rooms, and maybe some of them sitting around a table with food. Jasmine said the mom had health challenges and it was her family—cousins and siblings—that provided sweat equity to help her qualify for the home. That was love.

"GT, where are we going?" Portia asked as we got in the car.

I wasn't sure when Portia had started calling me "GT." She said it was short for Godmommy T and that it sounded much less formal than "Ms. T." From my perspective, it somehow acknowledged that her real godmother and I were a couple even though no one had told her anything of the sort. Portia was starting to grow on me.

"We're going to visit a family that your godmother worked with. ReBuild Baltimore helped them find a house that needed to be repaired. The family repaired it with the help of other people, like plumbers and electricians, and then the family moved in."

"Really?" She sounded intrigued.

"Yep. I'm going to take a few pictures of them in their new home, hopefully looking happy."

"I can play with the children?"

"How do you know they have children?"

"You said a family." Her nine-year-old logic was on full display.

"Yeah, but you can be a family without kids. Like I consider your godmother my family." *Where was I going with this?*

"I know, but you guys have me!" she beamed at me, the cutest gapped-tooth grin you ever wanted to see. I gave up.

"Yes, the mom has children. But I need you to ask first since I don't know them. It's not going to take me long and then we'll make another stop, at my studio. Did your godmother suggest what you and I should have for dinner?"

"No. So can we stop to get sushi?"

"Sushi?" I laughed. "Most kids want burgers and fries."

"Fast food? Oh no, we can't eat that. Ms. Jarrett at school says it'll kill you."

I struggled not to laugh out loud. This kid cracked me up. "Is that what she said?"

"Yeah. Sushi is better for us. She said we should get oils from fish."

"What does Ms. Jarrett teach?" I was ninety-eight percent sure no teacher at my school was encouraging children to eat sushi for the omega-3 oils.

"She came to our biology class to talk about food biology."

"What grade are you in?"

"Fourth." The high pitch of the child's response said I should know this information already.

"Umm, I'm going to check with your godmother on our way home about your dinner suggestion."

I pulled up to the home on Mosher Street, clearly the diamond on a rough block. Various federal and state grants contributed to efforts to reverse the disinvestment trend in Sandtown-Winchester. But there were still a few boarded-up houses and several in various stages of renovation. City funds for home ownership programs had slowed in the last few years and coupled with rising interest rates, the dream of owning a home was slipping away for many in West Baltimore. ReBuild was leading the way in providing new hope.

We got out of the car, and I knocked on the door. I heard what sounded like little people running and giggling right before the door opened. A lady wearing low-rise, boot-cut jeans and a white crop top stood in the doorway. Two children, about Portia's age and mirror images of each other, stood on either side of her.

"Hi, I'm Teresa Butler. I'm here to take a few family photos for ReBuild Baltimore. This is my assistant, Portia." Portia stood as tall as four feet would allow and nodded as if to say, "Indeed, I am." This kid.

"Come in. Ms. Jasmine said you were coming." The woman extended her hand and sort of looked above my head. "I'm Maya, and this is Quinton and Quetta."

"Nice to meet you. Could we take a few shots outside first? I'd like to get some while it's still bright out."

"Sure, give me a sec." Maya called other names, the rest of the children I assumed, and disappeared back into the house herself. When she returned, she slowly descended the front steps wearing dark, like blackout dark, shades, with Quinton standing close by helping her.

"Quetta, come back, honey," Maya called again, shrugging and shaking her head. "Kids."

I returned the gesture.

"Tabby should be in the pictures," Quetta announced as she appeared holding a honey-colored cat. Maya's apologetic expression returned.

The vast array of colors and patterns in their clothing made an interesting composition, but I set about doing what we were supposed to be doing. I took a few shots outside, the kids posed on the steps and against the house. Since Quetta and Portia looked to be about the same age, I took some of them sitting on the step with a book open on their laps. We went inside and took more photos around the table, in the backyard, and sitting in the living room.

It wasn't until Maya became increasingly self-conscious and started trying to make sure things were straight for each shot—Quinton answering his mother's queries about how things looked—that I realized her vision was most likely impaired. For one pose in the small foyer, she wanted to move all the jackets, purses, and things accumulated on the banister. Portia helped her.

"I need something to hang things up on," Maya explained.

"Like a coat tree? My grandmother had one," I responded.

"Yes! A coat tree."

"I like searching for things like that at thrift stores. There's a good one on Boston Street across from Canton Waterfront Park or this place called Another Life in the Highlands neighborhood."

"Thanks. I don't get over that way often, but maybe I can get my sister to take me."

I didn't know what else to say, but hopefully I hadn't offended her. "After I review these—" I lifted my camera up. "I'll send about ten to fifteen to Jasmine."

"Thank you so much," she replied.

"And I'll mail a few to you as well. A photo collage going up the stairs may be nice?"

Maya's face softened as she drew in a breath. "That would be wonderful. Thank you!"

"No, thank you. You and your family deserve to be surrounded by beauty." Out of the blue, she hugged me. I couldn't even begin to imagine what she endured on a daily basis. The least I could do was use my talent for something good. She walked me to the door. "I'll be in touch." I waved and joined Portia, who was already in the car.

"You okay?" I asked her as we drove. She hadn't said much since we'd left. "Thanks for helping move things around for Maya."

"I've never been there before."

"To their house?"

"No, to that neighborhood," she exclaimed.

"Oh." I wasn't sure where this kid was going with her conversation. Portia was the epitome of an old soul—a little girl wise beyond her years. "Were you worried about something?"

"If they didn't have that house, where would they live?"

"I don't know, Portia. Maybe Maya has family she could stay with."

"Yeah, maybe…" Portia was quiet, staring out the window for a few blocks. "You could make them something."

"Excuse me?" My neck turned so quickly, I thought I heard it crack.

"To hang their coats up. You could make something. You said I was your assistant. I can help make it pretty."

This child was worse than her godmother. I wasn't about to have the two of them giving me honey- or GT-do lists. It wasn't a bad idea though. I twisted my lips at her, and she understood my signal, returning my skepticism with her twenty-six-tooth smile.

"I think I have something that may work."

CHAPTER THIRTEEN

Jasmine

I pulled into a visitor's spot next to what appeared to be Stephanie's Infiniti FX. Yep, there she was, gesturing with one hand, the other holding a mobile phone up to her ear. When she noticed me staring at her, she held up an index finger—I rolled my eyes, the nerve—and stuck out her tongue like we were still freshmen in high school.

It had been Stephanie's idea to check-in on Leslie. It was Thursday and we hadn't done a "weekend eve" get-together since Leslie had gotten sick. I agreed because I needed what I hoped would be a happy and relaxing evening. Our goal was to help lift Leslie's spirits now that her chemotherapy had started.

"Hey, girl." I hugged Stephanie when she finally got out of the car.

"Hey. How are you?"

"I'm good."

"Where's Portia this evening?" Jesus, Stephanie didn't miss a beat as we walked from the parking lot to the building. Leslie buzzed us in, and we stepped into the building's lobby, a clean, mid-century-modern-styled space, and I pushed the elevator call button.

"With T, who wasn't happy about having to pick Portia up from school, but it's not as if Portia needs constant attention. She doesn't need diapers changed and she can get her own snacks from the kitchen. I made dinner for them." I felt the need to defend myself.

"You two will really need to communicate. This whole situation came out of the blue. And you, Ms. Charles, jumped in with both feet."

"I know, but we're a team, and we need to do the right thing by Leslie and Portia."

"I hear you. Doesn't hurt to talk it out."

"Said by the psychologist. Noted for the record, Doc."

"Meow!" Stephanie fashioned her hand into a claw. "No need to be catty."

Upstairs, Leslie opened the door wearing a pair of pink sweatpants and I was pretty sure the same button-down shirt I'd seen her wearing repeatedly in the past month.

"Excuse the mess, I'm too tired to worry about housekeeping and it's certainly not Angel's strong suit." Leslie greeted us.

I tried to ignore Stephanie looking at me with a raised eyebrow as I moved clothes to a chair and made space on the sectional.

"How's it going?" Stephanie asked. She moved more clothes and things in shopping bags to the same chair.

"It's going. First few weeks done. My hair is out and I'm losing my eyebrows." Leslie sighed.

I got close to her for an inspection. "You did a good job penciling them in."

"Who knew all my experience doing Mom and Angel's makeup would be helpful for me."

"True that," I responded. "Have you decided to wear wigs or have reconstruction surgery?"

"I couldn't give two shits about either right now. I'm worried about my daughter. I'm not sure if I'm going to see her grow up." Despite her hair loss and weakness, our pragmatic friend's personality was still very much present. Her shoulders drooped, along with her head. Leslie's sniffles had replaced her sassiness. "I'm worried how my treatments are going to affect her."

Stephanie got up from where she was sitting and put her arm around Leslie's shoulders, trying to comfort her.

"Portia's a good kid," she said. "She's able to self-soothe."

"What?" Leslie scooted back to look at Stephanie and scoffed. "What the hell kind of clinical shit is that?"

"It means she's able to reduce her anxiety appropriately and, most importantly, on her own." Stephanie looked back and forth between me and Leslie. "It's a skill. It's a useful skill that many children and adults I see don't have." Stephanie tried to dismiss us with a hand wave. "I've learned that if people are able to self-soothe, they don't reach for external things when they get upset or feel overwhelmed."

I motioned like I was gagging. I knew Stephanie was right, but jeez, did she always have to be so damn clinical? I inhaled...*She was just trying to help*...and refocused my attention.

"Leslie, where's Angel?"

Leslie sucked her teeth. "I don't know, I haven't seen her in probably two days. All of a sudden, she's infatuated with her body. You know after her mastectomy she had a little more than reconstruction. She had a tummy tuck and a lift or two, so she's feeling fit and fabulous. Or at least that's what she told me. Even made a few profiles on some dating websites." Leslie rolled her eyes.

"What? She needs to be careful with that. She'll have disappeared, and we won't know for two weeks, if at all." I wouldn't consider myself a prude, but you should at least let someone know where you were going to be and with whom.

"I just let Angel talk." Leslie swatted the air. "But honestly, she hasn't provided the support I thought she would've. Or at the very least, returned the support I provided her when she was going through the same thing just three years ago."

"I'm kind of surprised too and sorry she hasn't been here to help you," I said.

"If it hadn't been for you two—" Leslie pointed at both of us. "I'm not sure what I would've done."

"That may be true, but you don't have to find out." I touched her arm.

"To add insult to injury, Paul has been rather stealthy too," Leslie said.

"That's an understatement," I added.

Leslie shot me a look. "I thought he would at least show up for Portia."

Stephanie and I both nodded in agreement.

"As a matter of fact, that fucker told me he has another child on the way."

Was that a record scratch? If "what the hell" was a picture, it would've been Stephanie and me at that moment.

I broke the silence and tried to put a little oxygen back in the room. "When did you find that out?"

"Yep. He told me after I called him yesterday, to see if he was going to be able to watch Portia for the weekend." Leslie threw the tissue she had been holding onto the coffee table. "Said he needed to go somewhere with the new baby mama. It's just as well, next weekend may be better considering my chemo schedule anyway."

"Oh, wow." Stephanie was less clinical now. "I know you're divorced, but that's still hard to hear."

"Does Portia know?" Paul was a piece of work, but I was stunned.

Leslie shook her head. "Not my story to tell." Her eyes welled up again. "If anybody would've told me that I'd end up divorced and battling breast cancer, I wouldn't have believed them. You know what though? That's not true. I wouldn't have believed the divorce. By the time Angel had breast cancer, I knew my odds weren't looking good, but I thought I had way more time for this fight. I'm not even forty."

"Lots of life changes." Stephanie said, then asked, "Are you participating in the group or individual therapy sessions I recommended?"

"I am, but I don't know if I'm in the right group. I need to be in the 'I'm worried about my child' group. I'm not looking for a honey, so I don't care what the hell they're talking about in the reconstruction group or the 'Will I run out of leave fighting cancer?' group. I didn't know there were competing factions in therapy—those worried about their body image after surgery and others talking about estate planning."

We shook our heads.

"I probably sound selfish, but I don't care 'bout none of that shit. Seriously? After my mother's cancer, I lost my glorious attachment to my breasts. You need to wear a bra, 'good foundation' as my grandmother would say, and/or they were good for feeding babies." Leslie smacked her lips. "Other than that, they're just part of my body, like my middle finger…" She threw it up for effect. "Useful but not glorified." Leslie forced a laugh through sobs and virtually shouted at no one in particular, "I don't give a rat's ass about breasts. At this point, my goals are pretty basic …I want to live, and I want to see Portia grow up." The slow trickle from her eyes became a steady stream of tears.

I tried distraction again. "They talk about sex in the therapy group? Really?!"

"Yes, and again, not my interest and certainly not my priority right now. Who looks for someone in this situation? I want to get to my first six-month-clear appointment—that's the goal." She sucked her teeth. "One of the ladies talking about estate planning mentioned guardianship for your kids. I can't have that conversation yet."

My and Stephanie's eyebrows reached skyward.

"Should I have it? Of course I should. But to me, that's like resigning to a fate that I'm not ready for."

We pursed our lips and bobbed our heads up and down.

"Yes, I need to, but let's not have the discussion tonight," Leslie said.

We shelved the topic, sipped from a pot of fresh ginger tea, listened to music, and gossiped about Baltimore happenings the rest of the evening. An emotionally charged, but pleasant evening. We needed to hang out together for no other reason than to absorb each other's energy. This situation would be way harder if not for my faith and the sisterhood I shared with Stephanie and Leslie. And, despite T's reluctance, she had been helpful in caring for Portia. After seeing Leslie and knowing she was getting weaker with each treatment, my concern for Portia's wellbeing was increasing—it certainly couldn't be easy for her either.

"So, what do you think, Doc?"

Stephanie and I had made our way back to the parking lot. We were leaning on our cars facing each other but not saying anything as the heaviness of the night hung in the air. She took a long beat, inhaled deeply, and folded her arms across her chest. "I'm rarely at a loss for words, but this?" Stephanie pointed back to the condo. "This is going to be hard."

I agreed.

***

Finally, it was Friday! Although I loved spending more time with Portia, I was looking forward to spending time alone with T. Instead of taking her home to Leslie, I agreed to drop Portia off at her father's house after school. It was Leslie's "sick week," the week following her chemo, and it was easier for me to just take her over there since Portia was already in the car.

Paul had already changed the drop-off location twice. First it was the fire station—said he had a meeting—then he changed it to fire station headquarters, as if I wanted to ride into the heart of the city on a Friday afternoon. Finally, he sent a text saying to bring her to his house. Never ever did he say, "I'll come get her." I was beyond irritated with Paul at this point.

I parked in front of the Barrington Road address that he sent. The house looked cared for, a duplex with two doors side by side, a main entrance door and another one that went to what I believed was an apartment upstairs. But my gut did a little dance in an uneasy kind of way. Two guys were out front, one sitting on the porch railing, the other on the steps. "Portia, your dad lives here? Alone?"

"No, he has roommates. Firemen like Daddy, I think."

"Are those his roommates on the porch?"

She peered around me. "One of them."

"Where do you sleep?"

"In his room, or sometimes I sleep on the floor."

Oh, hell no! I wondered if Leslie knew that. *She had to know, right?* "Let's go talk to your dad." I grabbed her hand and greeted the men. "Is Paul here?"

"Yeah." One of the guys pointed to the door to the left.

"Thanks." I knocked on it. Moments later Paul appeared behind a steel security door.

"Hi, Jasmine, thanks for bringing her over," he said as he stepped outside, rubbing the back of his neck and finding something on the ground that interested him.

"Hi, Daddy." Portia caught his attention.

"Hey, Baby Girl." Paul's mood brightened as he bent down to kiss her forehead.

Everything in me screamed, "Don't leave her here."

I didn't like the vibe, but Paul was her father. Why did he have a nine-year-old little girl visiting with other grown men in the house? It could be perfectly fine, but I didn't like it and it didn't feel comfortable. I bent down to hug Portia and whispered in her ear, "You call me if you need anything. I'll be right back to pick you up."

She whispered back, "Okay, Godmommy."

Paul cleared his throat to let me know he had heard me, but I didn't care. I stood back up and didn't know if the reason I suddenly felt light-headed was because of the rush of blood from my head or my heart racing, probably a little bit of both.

"Are you staying here for the weekend?" My awareness returned to Paul. He nodded.

I confirmed he had both my and T's cell numbers and the landline number before heading to the grocery store to get a few things. I had planned to make us a really nice dinner, play a little music, and reconnect. Our chi had been off, so I was looking forward to just T and I this weekend. I hadn't made it to the bread aisle before my phone rang. I saw his name and my pulse increased again. "Hi, Paul, is everything okay?"

"No, no, it's not. I just got called to work."

"And what do you usually do when you have your daughter for the weekend, and you have to work?"

"Jasmine, I have to take Portia home." He hadn't even answered my question.

"Leslie's too sick to take care of Portia and Angel is out of town. How long do you have to work?"

"It depends on the situation."

"Where's the fire, Paul?"

"What?"

"Where's the fire? If you have to go in, it's supposed to be a bad fire, right? Where's the fire?" *What the hell?*

"Jasmine, look, I need to bring Portia back now. I'll be at your house in an hour."

I called Stephanie. If I could get her to watch Portia tonight, at least T and I could still have a nice dinner and night. But I got Stephanie's voicemail. She responded by text, however, saying she was heading to D.C. and would call me tomorrow. Damn! I threw a few more things in the basket, hastily paid for my groceries, and put them in the back seat. I called my mother. She answered the phone and sounded like she was in a rush. "Hey, Mom, are you busy?"

"Yes, I'm on my way to a church meeting."

"On a Friday night?"

"Yes, many of us go to church on Sunday and have activities during the week."

"Okay, I'll talk to you later." If I wasn't in a bind, I would have devoted more energy to her snarky response. Now was not that time. "God!" I screamed, beating the steering wheel.

I needed a plan. Fast. I didn't have anyone else I felt comfortable enough to just ask for urgent childcare. Hell, up until two months ago, I hadn't been concerned about childcare. But I didn't feel good about Portia staying at Paul's anyway, so maybe this wasn't that bad. Except—and this was a big exception—T was not going to be happy. We had already rearranged our schedules for our last two date nights. I couldn't take Portia home to Leslie's. Angel had already told me earlier that Leslie was having problems keeping food in her stomach. She didn't need her child over there tonight. This was not going to be the night I had planned.

We—me, T, and Paul—all arrived at our house essentially at the same time. I pulled into the driveway, T parked behind me. Paul pulled up along the curb. T got out and jutted her chin at me, her eyebrows squished together, but she didn't say anything before unlocking the front door and walking in the house. Paul got out and walked up the driveway with Portia in tow.

"I thought you'd be in uniform," I told him.

He couldn't hold my gaze. "Uh, it's at the station." He didn't lie well at all and I smelled cologne.

"Whatever, Paul." I grabbed Portia's backpack from him and slung it over my shoulder, adding weight to the grocery bags I was already carrying. "Come on Sweetie." I left Paul standing outside on the sidewalk. We couldn't get inside fast enough.

"Here." I reached my arm out. "Go take your stuff upstairs. We'll eat dinner in a little bit."

T came from the kitchen and took the rest of the bags from me. "What just happened?"

"Hi, honey." I gave her a light peck on the lips.

"Hello, what's going on?" In the kitchen, T busied herself putting away the food. "Last time I talked to you, you were dropping the child off," she whispered.

"Yes, I was. Then I went to get a few things for dinner and Paul called. Said he had to go to work."

"Pretty Ricky was clearly not going to work. Damn, Jasmine, this isn't right! I wanted some time, some quiet time. How did his wanting to go on a date—'cause he damn sure ain't going to work with that linen suit on—take precedence over *our* time? Why is this falling on us?"

T stood in our kitchen with her hands on her hips, rightfully asking tough questions that I didn't have answers to.

"We can still have a nice dinner," I rationalized.

"There's a kid here. One who was supposed to be gone all weekend," she hissed.

"Even if he hadn't backed out, where Paul lives is a…" I didn't know what to call it "…a sketchy arrangement at best."

"Still not our problem, Jasmine. And she can't go home to her mother for the weekend?"

"T, Leslie is really sick from the chemo. It's going to be all she can do to take care of herself since Angel went out of town."

"Everybody gets to do what they want except us? I wanted dinner, Jasmine, with you…just the two of us."

"I'm still going to cook for us."

Her nostrils flared and I swore those piercing brown eyes went dark. She jeered at me a second longer. "I'm going out. I need to get some air."

CHAPTER FOURTEEN

T

Well, that went left I thought as I stood outside next to my car, not quite sure what to do. My departure had been a bit hasty. I didn't want to go back in the house though. On a whim, I decided to go to T.K.'s for a little while. It was early so I knew I wouldn't impact their packed weekend reservation schedule.

T.K.'s Jazz Club was a cool spot owned by my cousin Kevin and his partner Terrence. It occupied the top floor of a historic, early 1900s warehouse in Fells Point that had been converted into an architectural beauty overlooking Baltimore's harbor. I had frequented the place quite often in my single days with this girl and that girl…But those days were long gone.

I arrived at the club and valet parked with a young man I didn't recognize but who wore a T.K. polo shirt. The hostess was unfamiliar to me as well.

"Here you are, ma'am." The woman pointed to a table in a section I didn't normally sit in.

"Thanks, but I'd like to sit over there." I pointed to my usual spot.

"But this table is available right now." She gestured again at the table I had no interest in sitting at.

I closed my eyes and filled my lungs with air. "Yes, and I'm Terrence's cousin. And I'd like to sit at table—" The pitch of my voice went up an octave. Just as I turned to make my way to my table, a voice I had heard all my life sounded behind me.

"Forty-eight, seat her at table forty-eight."

I glanced at my cousin, whose pointing index finger said "Behave."

As the hostess led me to the table and Terrence went off to take care of his next bit of business, I assured her I'd be gone before the first seating for the table. I just wanted to, have an appetizer and sit for one peaceful minute.

"I didn't get your name," I said as the hostess handed me a menu.

"It's Bailey," she murmured.

"Hi, Bailey, I'm Teresa, Terrence's favorite cousin." As soon as the words left my mouth, I realized how pompous they sounded, but I wasn't a complete asshole or even a run-of-the-mill asshole. This person was just doing her job. "I'm sorry for being a pain."

"Yes, ma'am. I'll get your server." Bailey left as soon as she had the chance.

Ma'am? I didn't look like anybody's ma'am. Was that what being part of a couple got me? Ma'am? Ugh!

When the server arrived, I placed an order for a tequila sunrise minus the tequila along with calamari and a Greek salad. I was halfway through my spur-of-the-moment happy hour when Terrence hugged me from behind.

"Hey, Lil' Cuz, it's good to see you. Where's Jasmine?" He slid into a seat across from me.

"Jasmine is home taking care of a lot of people."

"Oh? I hear the pricklies in that response. What's going on? What did you do?"

"Me? Why does it have to be me?" A woman with a very fitted, restaurant-logoed shirt stopped at the table to ask Terrence a question about the evening menu. She paused a tad longer than necessary, looking at me.

"Good evening," I said, acknowledging the lookover with a sultry smile and a lift of my drink.

The young woman held my gaze. "I'm hoping so," she added with her own suggestive smile.

Terrence looked at both of us. "Add limited oysters to tonight's specials. Thank you." He waved the woman away. "What the hell was that?"

"Nothing." I laughed coyly. "I was being cordial."

"Yeah, okay." Terrence grinned. "For real, what are you doing here?"

"Man, Jasmine has launched headfirst into taking care of Leslie and her kid. Granted, Leslie is sick—like I don't know if she's going to make it sick—and then what happens to the kid?"

He raised one eyebrow.

I continued. "We're not having no fun or spending time together 'cause all of our time is devoted to other people. It's too much and I needed some air."

Both of Terrence's eyebrows were nearly touching his hairline now. He tapped his chin a few times and nodded. "Take some time, get some air, and stop flirting with my damn staff."

"You got a lot of new people! Where are the regulars?"

"It's the nature of the restaurant business, Boo. You keep treating the ones we have like trash, and they'll be gone too." He stood. "Tell Jasmine I'm going to have Kevin drop off a little food every other week to lighten y'all's cooking load."

"Cuz, you don't have to do that," I plead to him.

"I know, I want to help. I think that may give you a little time to do something else—together."

"I love you, man."

"Yeah, back at you! Now go the hell home, T." Terrence pointed his finger at me. "I mean it." He tapped the table. "I need this table in a few minutes."

CHAPTER FIFTEEN

Jasmine

I couldn't believe T had stormed off and left. Paul had put me in a tight bind. Wearing his knockoff Tommy-Hilfiger-smelling cologne there was no way he was going to a fire. But I didn't want Portia thinking any of this had anything to do with her. I improvised the night the best I could. I got Portia to help me cook the meal planned for me and T and I tried to make it fun for us, all the time wondering where T was. My appetite seemed to have vanished when T did, and I only picked over my food.

Just as Portia and I were finishing dinner, I heard the front door open and shut. T appeared in the kitchen doorway carrying what looked like pieces of wood and a bag of something clinking around.

"Portia, since you're going to be here this weekend, we can work on your project," T offered.

I wasn't sure what was happening, but the child's eyes brightened.

"Really, GT? Okay!" She got up to put her plate in the sink. "Thanks for dinner, Godmommy, it was good."

"Thank you, I'm glad you enjoyed it."

"GT, you missed it. We had fish. Fish is good for you."

"Yeah, you told me that's what your teacher said."

After we watched Portia and Coco head upstairs, I turned to T.

"Where you been?" I asked.

"I needed to get some air before I said something that was true, but wrong, in front of Portia. Are we just going to let him take advantage of us like that?"

"What did you want me to say?"

"Say something. 'We have plans.' 'It's your weekend Paul.' Something. Not saying anything looks like you're okay with him treating us like we're the hired help."

"Do you really think I'm okay with this?"

"I don't know, it just looks like you're trying to do all of this by yourself, without the other support you told me Leslie had. Other help besides you."

"Besides *us*?"

"I said what I meant. You were clear you were going to support Leslie, no matter what I had to say about it."

"Where did you go?" I asked, changing the subject. I didn't want to get into this now, especially with Portia in the house.

"Doesn't matter, I'm back."

"It does matter. But since it doesn't seem like you're going to answer me, I'm going to clean up the kitchen."

T paused a second, clearly ruminating on something, but then she headed out the sliding glass door and into the backyard without saying a word. I realized I would've been worried if she wasn't upset about our not being able to have the nice evening we planned. I sighed—I needed to fix this.

I made two cups of mint tea and put them, along with shortbread biscuits, on a tray and took them out to the patio. The night air had more chill in it, a sign that fall had made a graceful entrance. Crickets singing to each other were the only sounds infiltrating the night's stillness. T looked up when I stepped outside—she smiled the faintest of smiles.

"I'm sorry, I have a peace offering."

She moved a plant off the side table to make space for the tray.

"What's Portia doing?"

"Taking a bath." I handed T a mug and joined her on the cushy chaise lounge.

"Thank you. We haven't had tea together in a minute."

"I know. T, I can't say how things are going to turn out from one day to the next, and I need to do a better job of making sure we have our time."

She concentrated on what I was saying, then replied, "I want our time protected. We need 'us' time just like everyone else."

"You're right," I conceded.

T swirled her index finger over the biscuits as if they weren't all the same. She finally selected one, ate half of it, and held it up.

"These are good."

"They are. Portia made them."

"The child cooks too? Nice. She's funny. The wood I brought in is for her. She came up with an idea to hang coats at the ReBuild house we went to last week to take pictures."

"Really?"

"Yeah, she's a sensitive kid. She saw the mom—I forgot her name—"

"Maya."

"Yes, Portia saw Maya move coats and stuff off the banister. I suggested a hall tree, but Portia said they needed something on the wall."

"Did she now?"

"Very persistent, that kid. Gus, the woodshop teacher at school, worked over there at the hardware store this summer and now has a small lumber department of his own in his classroom. I swear he cut one piece for customers and two for himself. Anyway, he has a lot of wood and said I could have some to try and create Portia's idea. I was going to surprise her with it when she came back on Sunday but since she's here, I may as well let her help me."

"Thank you, baby." I leaned over to brush my lips against T's.

"For what?"

"For being you, and for your patience these past few months. I know it hasn't been easy."

"No, it hasn't, and I am really trying."

"Thank you, I'm glad you enjoyed it."

"GT, you missed it. We had fish. Fish is good for you."

"Yeah, you told me that's what your teacher said."

After we watched Portia and Coco head upstairs, I turned to T.

"Where you been?" I asked.

"I needed to get some air before I said something that was true, but wrong, in front of Portia. Are we just going to let him take advantage of us like that?"

"What did you want me to say?"

"Say something. 'We have plans.' 'It's your weekend Paul.' Something. Not saying anything looks like you're okay with him treating us like we're the hired help."

"Do you really think I'm okay with this?"

"I don't know, it just looks like you're trying to do all of this by yourself, without the other support you told me Leslie had. Other help besides you."

"Besides us?"

"I said what I meant. You were clear you were going to support Leslie, no matter what I had to say about it."

"Where did you go?" I asked, changing the subject. I didn't want to get into this now, especially with Portia in the house.

"Doesn't matter, I'm back."

"It does matter. But since it doesn't seem like you're going to answer me, I'm going to clean up the kitchen."

T paused a second, clearly ruminating on something, but then she headed out the sliding glass door and into the backyard without saying a word. I realized I would've been worried if she wasn't upset about our not being able to have the nice evening we planned. I sighed—I needed to fix this.

I made two cups of mint tea and put them, along with shortbread biscuits, on a tray and took them out to the patio. The night air had more chill in it, a sign that fall had made a graceful entrance. Crickets singing to each other were the only sounds infiltrating the night's stillness. T looked up when I stepped outside—she smiled the faintest of smiles.

"I'm sorry, I have a peace offering."

She moved a plant off the side table to make space for the tray.

"What's Portia doing?"

"Taking a bath." I handed T a mug and joined her on the cushy chaise lounge.

"Thank you. We haven't had tea together in a minute."

"I know. T, I can't say how things are going to turn out from one day to the next, and I need to do a better job of making sure we have our time."

She concentrated on what I was saying, then replied, "I want our time protected. We need 'us' time just like everyone else."

"You're right," I conceded.

T swirled her index finger over the biscuits as if they weren't all the same. She finally selected one, ate half of it, and held it up.

"These are good."

"They are. Portia made them."

"The child cooks too? Nice. She's funny. The wood I brought in is for her. She came up with an idea to hang coats at the ReBuild house we went to last week to take pictures."

"Really?"

"Yeah, she's a sensitive kid. She saw the mom—I forgot her name—"

"Maya."

"Yes, Portia saw Maya move coats and stuff off the banister. I suggested a hall tree, but Portia said they needed something on the wall."

"Did she now?"

"Very persistent, that kid. Gus, the woodshop teacher at school, worked over there at the hardware store this summer and now has a small lumber department of his own in his classroom. I swear he cut one piece for customers and two for himself. Anyway, he has a lot of wood and said I could have some to try and create Portia's idea. I was going to surprise her with it when she came back on Sunday but since she's here, I may as well let her help me."

"Thank you, baby." I leaned over to brush my lips against T's.

"For what?"

"For being you, and for your patience these past few months. I know it hasn't been easy."

"No, it hasn't, and I am really trying."

CHAPTER SIXTEEN

T

That damn trifling ass Paul! What little respect I had for him had dissolved like sugar in hot tea. If he was concerned about lesbians taking care of his child, he sure wasn't acting like it now. Step up, man! Have at it. Do us a favor and take your daughter with you on your scheduled weekends. At a minimum that was all I was asking. But at this point, his daughter was here. Jasmine would do what she always did, help people pick up the pieces, and I, by default, had been relegated to doing the same. I loved Portia, of course, but I wasn't happy about how this was playing out.

It was Saturday, which had once been our day to lie in, have pillow talk, and, if I was lucky, a little morning loving. Not today, because we unexpectedly had a child with us whose father had other plans. I got up, no use staying in bed—I tried to adjust my attitude.

We were expecting decent weather today. I had learned enough about Baltimore's weather to know I needed to take advantage of warmer fall days when they came. I made an aromatic pot of coffee using beans that Jasmine had brought home as a peace offering from a local roaster and went out back to sit a spell.

I was admiring the brilliant orange, red, and yellow coloring of the remaining tree canopy when Portia peeked outside and let Coco out. That dog had abandoned us the second night Portia got here, but Coco was smart. She still came to us for the essentials like feeding and walking. Hugs and treats had become Portia's duties.

"Morning, GT."

"Morning kiddo, you're up early for a Saturday."

"Coco kept whining so we came downstairs."

Coco relieved herself and jumped up on the lounger with me.

"Hey, pup-pup." I rubbed her head and behind her ears.

"When are we going to work on the project?" Portia asked.

"I figured later this morning. Once we've had breakfast and stuff."

"What's for breakfast?"

"I understand you can cook, so what are you going to make?" I teased.

"I can make pancakes or, ummm…" She tapped her little lips. "I can make eggs and bacon."

"Let's make all three."

Portia's eyes grew wide.

"Shall I be your sous chef?" I asked.

"What's that?" Her brow furrowed as she plopped down next to me, her curiosity apparent.

"It's the person who really does most of the work in a kitchen—slicing and dicing vegetables and whatnot."

"Oh." She shrugged.

"The person helps the chef with busy work, cracking eggs, getting ingredients together. How do you make pancakes?"

"I use my mother's recipe cards. She has these little cards from my grandmother."

"Really? My mother has some like that too."

"Does your mother live in Baltimore?"

"No, she lives in Georgia."

"Georgia? Oh, that's far away." Portia tilted her head to the side.

"By car, not by plane."

"Oh." Her lips twisted to one side. "Can we go in to make breakfast?"

"Sure. Is your godmother awake?" I asked a little above a whisper.

"I don't think so." Portia lowered her voice too, her eyes cutting from side to side.

I cupped my hand to her ear. "Let's surprise her with breakfast in bed."

She giggled. "Is it her birthday?"

"No. You know her birthday's in November. Don't you remember when we went to Chuck E. Cheese for Jasmine's birthday because you wanted to go?"

"Oh, yeah!" Portia's bright eyes were back. "That was fun."

"Was it?"

"Yes! That's how I remember it. I just thought you only got breakfast in bed on your birthday."

That kid.

"Nope. It's special to have breakfast in bed, but it doesn't have to be your birthday."

Crinkles reappeared on her forehead as she popped up, turned on her heels, and went inside, followed by her furry sidekick. I wasn't going to fill in whatever blanks her little mind was contemplating.

"We don't have recipe cards, but I have a recipe if you want it," I announced once we both had aprons on. Hers hung a bit too long but she had insisted on wearing one.

"Okay, suzy chef!" She clapped her hands, signaling it was time to cook. "Let's wash our hands."

"It's *sous* chef, and I think I like working in your kitchen already," I chuckled.

Portia stood on a step stool to comfortably mix things on the counter. She carefully added this ingredient and that without too much guidance, was able to make a decent pancake batter, provided me directions on how she liked her eggs—yes, she wanted cheese—and used paper towels to absorb grease from the bacon she cooked in the microwave. I personally liked bacon cooked on the stove, but she didn't ask me.

As Portia finished up the cooking, I pulled a serving tray from the top cabinet and decorated it with a hydrangea bloom from the garden that I put in a small vase. The pancakes looked homemade, and the three strips of bacon plus scrambled eggs completed a pretty plate. I let Portia carry the tray and I followed with a cup of coffee.

"Godmommy, wake up," she sang, broadcasting our arrival.

"What's wrong, what's wrong?" Jasmine sat straight up in bed, her hair bonnet canted to the side like she was a figure in a Picasso painting.

"Nothing, we have breakfast." Portia showed her the tray.

"Look at this! This is so nice, Portia." Jasmine patted the bed and propped herself on pillows. "What's the occasion?"

"GT said we should bring you breakfast in bed. She said it wasn't your birthday but it was okay to eat in bed."

Jasmine looked at me with one eyebrow higher than the other—*really*.

I shrugged. "I figured you might enjoy a little breakfast."

"This is pretty. Thank you, ladies."

"GT was my suzy chef."

Jasmine's expression clearly said she had no idea what Portia was talking about.

I laughed. "I was her sous chef."

"Alright, Chef Portia!" Jasmine lifted a piece of pancake to her mouth. "This is delicious. Tasty…beautiful presentation. I certainly feel like it's my birthday." Jasmine winked at me. "What's the plan for the day?"

"Portia and I are going to work on a coat rack project and then we'll see. What's on your agenda?"

"Nothing, for once. I may tidy up a bit and make a few calls."

This was Jasmine's code for check in with Leslie.

"Okay, enjoy your breakfast. We're going to have ours in the kitchen."

"Thanks again, ladies. I really appreciate your thoughtfulness."

I high-fived Portia as we headed back down to the kitchen. "Good job!"

***

After eating and cleaning the kitchen, Portia and I convened in the backyard.

"Here's the wood we're going to make the wall racks with."

I'd had Gus carve a few different shapes, rectangles and ovals with various beveled edges. Portia didn't understand the concept I was going for until I pulled out some knobs and held them against the wood.

"Okay, GT. We can make them different colors."

Leave it to the child to add something to the design concept. Of course, it was a concept that I had conceived without consulting her. "Colors? I was thinking of using a simple stain to make the wood grain stand out."

"We should paint them different colors," Portia insisted. Pink for Quetta and blue for Quinton."

That wasn't what I'd had in mind, but we could do that too. "How about the one in the hallway near the front entrance having a stain?"

She stood there with her arms folded. I'd forgotten I was talking to a nine-year-old, so I rubbed a small amount of stain on the wood and showed her.

"Oh, okay." Portia lifted one shoulder.

Had she just dismissed me? Portia wasn't impressed with the stain, but I pulled designer's prerogative. I gave her two bottles of wood craft paint, covered the table with plastic, and let her paint the children's room racks while I stained the hallway piece. I knew I could get lost in painting, but my heart melted when I saw her tongue sticking out, intensely concentrating on evenly coating the wood. When she'd finished painting, she carefully rifled through the knobs and selected a glass one, two different metal-toned ones, and a flower-shaped knob to add to the racks.

"You don't want the knobs to match?" I asked.

"No, I like this better."

Portia's eclectic design was certainly different than what I'd initially seen in my mind's eye. I kept the foyer coat rack simple—my four knobs matched.

"These are great. Seriously, I really like them."

Portia and I stopped cleaning our brushes and looked up at the sound of Jasmine's voice. She walked over to where we had lain the wood to dry.

"T, take pictures of these once they're dry and then once they're installed."

I cocked my head to the side—helping Jasmine at ReBuild was turning into an unpaid side hustle.

"Sorry, my assumption," Jasmine said. "Are you going to install these, or will it be Maya's responsibility?" Her voice shifted to a softer tone.

Maya's vision challenges came to mind. "I guess I will. It won't take long. That way she won't have to find someone else to do it, and it'll be done."

"Thank you." Jasmine bumped me with her hip.

"Touch base with her to see when she'll be home," I suggested.

"Cool, I'll let you know and I can go with you. And we may as well take Portia since it was her idea," Jasmine added.

***

"Hey, Gus, you got a few minutes?" I called out as I entered his shop area bright and early Monday. I wanted him to see what Portia and I had created over the weekend with the wood he'd given me.

He emerged from his storage area. "Yeah, what you got there?"

I put the three coat racks on a table for inspection.

"Look here, these turned out nice." He said, turning one of the racks over and running his hand along the grain. "You said you were experimenting."

"I was."

"How many of these are you planning to make?"

"How much wood do you have? I'm thinking maybe twenty. There are a few houses that could use them."

"This is a pretty bold pink."

"Yeah, my goddaughter made that one. She was emphatic that it needed to stand out. This is my work." I pointed at the stained wood.

"Subtle," he teased me.

I rolled my eyes.

"I'm joshing, nice detailed craftmanship."

"Why, thank you. I appreciate your seal of approval."

"You know," Gus said, turning the rack over in his hand, "I can get the kids to cut these in advance for you. It'll help me teach them various bevel cuts using the table saw."

"That would be sweet. Then my assistant, also known as my goddaughter, and I can focus our time on staining or painting."

"I can have the twenty finished in a few weeks. You want them all at once or a few at a time?"

"Whenever they get finished is good. I really appreciate it, Gus. I'll make sure to get your class recognized for the effort."

"Nah…don't want no more attention to anything in my woodshop," he drawled.

"What about pizza?" I laughed. "Do you think your students would accept pizza for payment?"

"Are you kidding? They're pubescent middle schoolers—they're always up for pizza. Five pies and at least one veggie please."

CHAPTER SEVENTEEN

Jasmine

With Portia living with us most of the time, I developed a whole new respect and perspective on parenting. I didn't know how my parents had done this every day with three of us! In the before times, it was one thing to get Portia for a weekend. We did fun things together—visited the Science Center at the harbor, went to an apple orchard, saw a children's play, ate a few meals out—then I took her home to her parents or, for the last year, her mother. Parenting every day deserved an award. You had to parent when you were tired, on twenty-four-seven, even when you weren't feeling well, and still manage your own emotions. Parenting done well was work!

Portia was fairly perceptive for a child. Before interrupting me, she tried to ask if I was busy first. I appreciated that. If I said, "yes, I'll come talk in a few minutes," she was okay with that, provided I adhered to the time frame specified. Otherwise, Miss Missy came back to make her needs known.

The last week in October, she slid into the breakfast nook beside me and asked about *our* plans for Halloween. Caught completely off guard, I gave a non-answer. "Yes, Halloween is coming."

Was it forgivable that I didn't telepathically make the connection that she wanted *us* to do something for Halloween? Free candy, an activity, and a cute costume? Okay, we could do that. I told her I couldn't make her an outfit like her mother usually did. Leslie didn't just sew well, she was an excellent seamstress—taught sewing and everything.

She jumped to her feet. "I can sew," Portia informed me with her hands on her narrow hips.

"You can?" My left eyebrow went skyward.

"Yes! Mommy taught me. If we get her sewing machine from our house, I can make something."

"Oh, sweetie." I touched her arm. "We can get a costume from that store that popped up on Falls Road. They probably have an endless stock of all things Halloween."

Portia stomped her foot. "Ah, Godmommy, that's no fun." Then she got herself together. "I'm sorry, I just like wearing a costume that no one else, anywhere in the world, has."

This child was definitely Leslie's offspring. I was finding that out more and more. Portia wanted what she wanted when she wanted it. And that wasn't all.

Portia's request had a second part, which I hadn't foreseen. Not only did she want to make her own costume, but the costume would be worn to a Halloween party she wanted us—all of us—to go to. It was scheduled for Saturday, just five days from now, and she wanted to attend the party instead of trick-or-treating on the thirty-first. That was a blessing at least.

"I'm in, but you need to ask GT yourself," I told her. I suspected T would say no if I proposed the idea, but this little girl was persuasive and was beginning to wrap T around her little finger.

***

Leslie had been a champ. She came through surgery with few complications and chemo treatments were going as well as could be expected. When visiting, I periodically witnessed her wincing from pain and trying to power through the lethargy. I could see she was physically weak and had lost weight. Her clothes were looser, her skin was a bit more ashen. Her typically manicured nails were bare, no polish, no shine, no nothing, a telltale sign that we were experiencing extraordinary times. Much to Leslie's chagrin, Dr. Jordan advised against getting her nails done to prevent infection. But Leslie had become more open to letting us help her. And she still tried to put on a good face to avoid upsetting Portia.

Now, on a rainy afternoon, Leslie had just finished the last cycle of her initial chemotherapy plan, and I was driving her back to her condo. When a radio advertisement came on encouraging listeners to get Halloween costumes soon to get the best selections, Leslie's voice startled me. She hadn't had much to say as I'd sat with her during the treatment today. "I understand you got bamboozled into a Halloween party with the fancy folks."

I hit the steering wheel. "Gurl, your daughter is something!"

"You don't have to tell me."

"You know she got me with a two-part request—I want to make my own costume and there's a party at a classmate's house and I want you both to go." Leslie let out a little breath. Without taking my eyes off the road, I knew she was smirking. "Come to think of it, that's three requests."

"What did T say?" I could see her grinning in my peripheral vision now.

"To Portia or me?" I giggled. "Portia is smooth, and we should be very worried about that. She roped T in after asking her about her younger days trick-or-treating. T caved."

"I'm surprised. T always strikes me as a loner."

"She's introverted, sure, but I had a feeling she'd give in to Portia. Said she was feeling kind of nostalgic, then Portia hit her with the Halloween party part of her scheme. We couldn't stop laughing at Portia's skills that night. T said she didn't realize we needed to be prepared for Jedi mind tricks with a kid."

Sitting at a traffic light, I turned to look at my friend. Her smile had spread across her face, larger than I had seen in days. I snapped my fingers. "That reminds me. I need to get the sewing machine. Does Portia really know how to sew or will I be up late helping to make a costume?"

"Oh, no, she can sew," Leslie replied. "She can make simple things, an apron or a little bag. I'm curious to see how she brings her idea together. We talked it through last night when she called."

"Okay!" My voice went up a few octaves. I was relieved that I wouldn't have the child looking all jacked up like Denise did Theo on *The Cosby Show* and thankful that Leslie and Portia were still having meaningful conversations.

"Which reminds *me*. She said she wants a princess outfit so I have a bag of scrap pieces I need to give you for that."

"Princess? Hmm, I wonder if we're supposed to dress up too?"

"Chile! You didn't know? Girl, these folks go all out for Halloween. Calling their affairs fancy is an understatement." Leslie raised her right pinky. "Expect games, swag bags, and prizes for costumes…best this and best that…"

"Lord have mercy! I need to tell T. We didn't know about the fancy part."

"Consider where she goes to school—when in doubt, think swanky."

"I do have a question." I got a little serious.

"What?"

"How does Portia sound when you two talk? Does she sound okay when she calls? I don't listen in."

"She sounds like herself, a little concerned, but yeah, she sounds like herself. Why?"

"You'll let me know if she says she needs something? I feel like she would tell us, but just in case."

"I will. Thankfully, she's pretty self-sufficient and doesn't usually have a problem voicing her needs. Hell, at this point, I'm worried about you and T more so than my child." Leslie squeezed my shoulder.

"I know the self-sufficient types—they won't always ask for help."

"True statement." Leslie agreed.

I parked and went in with Leslie to pick up the sewing machine, which looked like a child's machine, much like my old easy bake oven had looked. I was curious to see how this little thing worked.

Later that week, we got a preview of the outfit, which was good because it was two days before the party. Portia had done a great job making her costume and I never had to stay up to help her make it. She attached tulle and sparkly gems to a plain pink long-sleeved shirt and skirt. I draped a mother-of-pearl-colored scarf around her shoulders and pinned it with a ridiculously large broach I'd found at an estate sale years ago. We topped her look off with an old tiara I had.

T wore a white button-down with a wingtip collar, deep jade bow tie, and a black vest that matched her pants, looking sexy as hell. I wore a jade satin A-line dress I thought was understated, but I was delighted when T said it rivaled the princess's outfit.

***

We were way out Greenspring Valley Road in a part of town where the average price of a home was over $1.5 million when we pulled into what looked like a half-mile-long driveway. There were arrows, lights, and ghoulish figures lining the drive, directing us which way to go.

"This is going to be something." T whistled.

"Portia, have you been here before?" I asked her.

"Yes, for Ashley's birthday. She had a circus theme with horses and clowns and arrowbats, people balancing on balls."

"You mean acrobats?"

"Yes, it was just like a circus!" Her high-pitched voice signaled her excitement.

We arrived at the end of the driveway, where a teenaged Dracula directed cars.

T looked at me with pursed lips. "Are you kidding me?"

I shrugged.

After parking, we approached a young Cinderella marking names off a list. She literally had on a pale blue, poofy gown cinched at the waist and white evening gloves. Her blond hair was even swept up in an up-do and she wore a black choker around her neck.

"Hi, Portia," Cinderella said.

"Hi, Jessica." Portia turned to us. "Jessica is in the Upper School— she graduates this year."

The Upper School, I thought. It couldn't just be high school. I smiled at Jessica-Cinderella, trying hard not to roll my eyes.

Jessica turned to us. "Hello, may I have your names?"

"These are my godmothers—they're my attendants."

"Cute." Jessica-Cinderella laughed.

T dipped her head down and covered her mouth. "Did she just call us her servants?"

I almost hollered. "No." I tried to keep a straight face. "She said attendants, not servants."

All night, Portia played her role as a princess, and we walked a few steps behind her.

Every time T looked around, she'd blurt out something to the effect of, "Y'all need to get Portia out of St. Josephine Academy before she starts wanting to ski in Vail and summer in Europe."

The Fishers, the host family, were gracious and inviting. Thankfully, it was unseasonably warm for late October since the festivities were held in a barn adorned with orange, yellow, and red decorations on the walls. Bales of straw provided seating in addition to a few bar height chairs and tables topped with pumpkins and lanterns.

As the party went on, T and I got a chance to stroll around the beautiful grounds of the estate without Princess Portia as she "mingled" —her word—with subjects.

"So, what do servants do when they're left to their own devices?" T asked.

T and I were away from the other guests standing shoulder to shoulder on a little bridge that spanned a pond. She had her arm around my waist and leaned in to brush her lips against my cheek.

"Hmmm…I don't know, but I don't want to get relieved of my duties while I'm out here fraternizing with you."

"Fraternizing?"

"Yes, fraternizing. I'm a good girl." I tried to hide my smile with my hand even as I felt blood rush to places I would have rather not had it rush to, given we were at a children's party.

"Well, let it be known that I did not sign an employment agreement, and you can't look this beautiful and smell so good and not get my attention."

T's nose was buried near the most sensitive part of my neck, and she knew it.

I put some distance between us and laced my fingers with T's. "I smell good?"

"Yeah, you know that vanilla musk does something to me."

"Well, for the record, you are very hot your damn self in that tuxedo shirt and cute tie. But employment agreement or not, we should get back to the party."

A few hours later, as we left the party, I thought again about how amazing it had been. It was well-organized and, to my mind, way over the top, which had made it that much more fun. Our little princess was asleep in the back seat before we had even driven off the Fishers' property.

When we got home, Portia stretched her mouth wide open and rubbed her eyes. "I'm tired," she said with a sleepy yawn. "That was a great party, thanks for taking me." She proceeded upstairs without waiting for a reaction from us.

I let Coco out for the evening, and when she came back in, she promptly left me to join her best friend Portia upstairs. T and I weren't far behind.

We shed our attendant/servant clothes and made our way to the shower together.

"I'm some kind of tired," I managed to say through a yawn as I reached for the soap.

"Me, too. People can be exhausting. Let me help you relax." T reached around me to get the soap. Her breasts pressed against my back and suddenly the tightness in my stomach said I wasn't as tired anymore. Without a washcloth, she rubbed the soap against my stomach, then my breasts, way too slowly for this to be a functional bathing experience.

"Stop." I sounded unconvincing even to myself.

T tilted her head to the side and glared at me with those beautiful eyes. And even though she raised both of her hands in surrender, her sly grin suggested we weren't done yet.

T didn't interfere as I finished bathing, for real, and prepared for bed. In fact, I was comfortably nestled under the comforter before I felt T's fingertips skimming my thigh, which wasn't difficult since I hadn't bothered to put on PJ bottoms. She combined her caressing with gentle kisses on my neck and pressed her body into my butt again. I closed my eyes and let the warmth from her own body envelop me, offering a feeling of comfort and safety and certainty that I was so thankful for. I showed my gratitude by returning the rhythm of her pelvis, thrusting my butt into her. A moment later, I involuntarily gasped, bringing me back to reality. I moved slightly away from T.

"T, Portia will hear us."

"Shhh, then let's be quiet." She pulled me back toward her. "You don't have to say anything."

I turned over to face her. "But I'm beat." The relaxing shower had reminded me of that fact. "It's been a long day." I protested way too softly though.

"Does your body know that?"

She kissed my erect nipples one at a time and then gently sucked each one, giving them so much attention. The ache was too much, I moaned. T moved up to lie on top of me. The weight and warmth of her body felt so familiar and comforting. With everything that had been going on since the summer—Leslie, Portia, work—I had missed this feeling.

I took a deep breath and let her scent, which smelled like shea butter and our first date, tickle my nostrils, then let out a satisfied sigh. Her lips met mine and our tongues wrestled for a while before she slowly eased toward my navel, leaving a wet trail with her tongue. T nudged my legs apart with her own and took her time kissing the inside of my thighs. My breathing grew faster and I clung to the sheets to steady myself.

I wasn't sure if my breathing was audible or if it was just echoing inside my head. Just in case, I put a pillow over my face to mask any groans that, three months earlier, I wouldn't have thought twice about. As T's tongue found my sweet spot, flashes of light behind my eyelids and tight muscles in my abdomen were precursors to the building explosion.

I grabbed a handful of T's locs and rode the wave of pleasure. She dialed back the intensity of pressure with her mouth, but she didn't stop completely. I felt her fingers easing in and out of my wetness with the deliberate speed of a sloth.

Still inside me, she moved the pillow aside with her free hand and joined her lips to mine again. I moaned into her mouth as she moved closer, which I hadn't known was possible, and deeper. I held on tight as my hips arched on their own and fireworks exploded in my mind's eye. The sensation was so powerful it made me feel like I was outside of myself watching our lovemaking unfold.

T kissed my earlobe, my cheek, the tip of my nose, then my lips as I tried to regulate my breathing back to normal. After a final peck, she let me know the night was indeed over.

"Now you can go to sleep," T said with a satisfied grin.

CHAPTER EIGHTEEN

T

"Hey, sweetheart." John stood, greeted me, and kissed my cheek.

"What goin' on?" I responded, using our hometown dialect as we took off our jackets and wedged ourselves into a booth at the back of a restaurant we frequented often. It wasn't much to look at from the outside, a 1960s storefront with windows set in aluminum frames and white paint peeling off the brick below the windows.

The inside wasn't much better, red vinyl covered booths, cracked linoleum tiles, laminate countertops, all that could have used an update. But he loved their chicken tikka kababs, I always ordered the salmon tandoori, and we both ate way too many samosas, always swearing off carbs when our bellies were full.

"Not much, same ol', same ol'…work, hanging out with Ray, work…"

"How is Mr. Raymond? Y'all are going strong."

"He's good, we're good. Yeah, we're good." John couldn't hide the huge grin even if he wanted to. "Last night he cooked the most delicious empanadas. We're going to have to step up our workouts." He pointed back and forth between us. "How is domesticity treating you?"

I stuck my tongue out at him in between bites. "Fine, I guess. I certainly wouldn't have volunteered to take care of someone else's kid, but she's growing on me."

"Really?"

"Yeah." I shrugged, "Portia is very little bother. The kid is smart and inquisitive and funny. It's everything—or should I say everyone else—that complicates this whole situation. Like Paul, the dad? That fool acts like he couldn't care less most days, and he treats us like we're the hired help."

"What do you mean?" John gave me a look, then put more green sauce on a piece of chicken.

"Like, we have to be careful about planning too much for weekends because dude conveniently has fire station emergencies, and the next thing we know, Portia is standing on our porch."

"Girl, you all need to establish boundaries," John offered.

"You don't think we've tried?"

"I suppose," John acquiesced.

"And St. Josephine Academy…that affluent school Portia goes to is something else," I continued. "Well, it's not the school so much as the people at the school. And it's not so much the kids, 'cause, I mean, every kid deserves a great education, right?"

"Right," he agreed.

"But I tell you, there's a level of freedom and expectation and, and…I don't know, I can't put my finger on it…When students aren't hungry, their uniforms are clean, and resources are abundant, they can achieve so much. I wish the kids at my school could get a taste of that."

"I hear you."

John's response was so bland I thought maybe my issues were boring him, so I changed the subject. "Are you going home for Thanksgiving?"

"No, I can't. My team and I are under deadline to finish an RFP submission."

This wasn't surprising. The architecture firm John worked for was involved in one high-profile project after another around the city. "Anything you can talk about?"

"Kind of. We're bidding on a new mixed-use development in Harbor East, a public-private venture."

"Nice."

"In theory, yes. One of the public partners is supposed to be Baltimore City Housing Authority. I could see them being muscled out by the developer because he doesn't need the city, city funding, that is. That area is growing fast. Beautiful views. Hot market. Subsidized housing does not get top billing when location-location-location is a factor."

"See, that's what I'm saying." I wiped my mouth. "Every kid deserves a great education, and everyone deserves a nice place to live."

"Okay, Robin Hood. I get it…I'm just saying that developers and dollars are synonymous."

I looked at John and forcibly exhaled my frustration out of my nostrils. He ignored me and turned my question around. "Are *you* going home for Thanksgiving?"

"Yeah, I'm looking forward to seeing my parents and not being a surrogate parent for a few days. You know my parents love the ground Jasmine walks on—They've been talking about seeing her for weeks. I guess I'm just the chauffeur."

"Hah! I love me some Mr. Harold and Ms. Mary. How are they doing?"

"Fine. Busy as ever even though they're supposed to be retired. Pop goes fishing every other day and Mama is involved in every civic and church organization she can volunteer for."

"Love it. It keeps them sharp. Listen, T." John's tone turned a bit more serious.

"What's up?"

"Make sure you're taking care of yourself and make sure you're taking care of your relationship."

I tried to dismiss him. "I am."

"No, I mean like really." He touched my hand to get my attention. "Big life changes can be hard on a couple. When you're always go-go-go, just taking care of what's right in front of you, especially when the stakes are so high, it's easy to lose sight of the broader picture. I know you remember. I don't want you reverting back to your old ways."

I let my friend's advice wash over me. He was referring to the fact that it had taken me a long while to settle down with one person. I had used my ego and immaturity as excuses until my mid-thirties, when I'd met Jasmine Charles. Now, I enjoyed the partnership I had with the love of my life. And I intended on keeping it that way.

Jasmine

"I'm downstairs at the front door." I was standing outside of Stephanie's office building talking into the intercom and shivering. Yes, Baltimore in November could be a mix of mild and cold temperatures. But I couldn't believe that it was thirty degrees colder today than it was yesterday. I had made poor wardrobe choices.

"On my way down," she answered. It was after hours, so Stephanie opened the entrance door herself a few minutes later.

I held up the bag I was carrying, a peace offering.

Stephanie smiled. "Hey, that smells good…like curry."

"I figured if you were going to fix my life, we needed food." I said as I followed Stephanie back into her office suite.

"Girl, please. Let's eat, I'm starving. I didn't get a proper lunch break."

We settled on the comfy chairs in the waiting room.

"My fault that I scheduled patients back-to-back," Stephanie said. "And they all showed up. Share some good news."

"Well, despite Leslie making Dr. Jordan find another surgeon for her mastectomy two months ago, the medical process—"

"What other surgeon? I've talked to both of you eighteen times since then and neither of you said anything about another surgeon. What happened?" Stephanie asked.

I tried to brush her question off with a wave of my hand. "The medical process since then has been fairly smooth considering how serious and aggressive her cancer is."

Stephanie stared at me, not letting the issue go.

"Okay, geesh!" I resigned. "Leslie refused to have the initial surgeon Dr. Jordan recommended do her surgery—said he was an ass that didn't look at her, made assumptions about her health, and was very dismissive when she asked questions."

"I would have looked elsewhere too," Stephanie agreed.

"Dr. Jordan reportedly wasn't happy with his bedside manner either, but thought he was an excellent surgeon and needed for her treatment."

Stephanie took a bite of her coconut curry shrimp, her eyebrows arched.

"They went with someone else though," I went on. "Leslie said the person hugged her when they finished the surgical consultation, and she felt much more comfortable in her care. She said the surgeon even sent a small vase of flowers to her."

"Flowers?"

"Yeah, flowers. But back to Dr. Jordan. She's mounting a hard-hitting response. I like her, like girl-crush like her."

"You scoping out the good doctor? I saw a picture of her, and yeah, she's kind of hot." We high-fived each other. "So, what's next?" Stephanie asked, reaching for more naan.

"To be determined as we move forward. Thus far, bi-weekly chemo, followed by radiation, with scans, and they may repeat the cycle if necessary. Dr. Jordan is also looking at breast cancer studies. Apparently, this whole triple-negative thing for black women makes treatment challenging, studies are popping up around the country."

"What's that mean for Portia?"

"Leslie and I try to speak in code, but Portia's smart. She sees the hair loss and how weak Leslie is. We're just trying to keep her busy, no thanks to her aunt or father. Angel decided she would 'help from the back when needed.'" I gestured in air quotes. "Angel has always been high maintenance, but I never thought she was selfish until now. Leslie rearranged her life to help Angel when she was going through the same thing a few years ago."

Stephanie pursed her lips and nodded.

"I can see it hurts Leslie when she talks about Angel—lots of four-letter words and agitation. And I can't hide how hot I am with Angel myself. According to her, she's taking Oprah's mantra to heart, she's living her best life."

"How are you holding up?" Stephanie wiped her mouth and put her empty food container back in the plastic bag it had come from.

I closed my eyes and inhaled, becoming aware of the analog clock ticking high up on the wall. "I'm holding. The juggling is wearing me out. If we could get a little more help from Portia's blood relatives…" I held my hand up, my index finger and thumb a quarter-inch apart. "I didn't think we'd really be doing the true day-to-day and weekend care. I also didn't know what to expect until I saw the whole chemotherapy process up close."

"Does Leslie talk to you when you're there with her?"

"Not really. We have a little bit of small talk—we may laugh at something on the news but not a lot of talking. Sometimes I think she wants the company, but I mean what are we gonna talk about when she's in there fighting for her life?"

Stephanie's mouth twisted. She was obviously acknowledging what I'd said but she didn't say anything out loud.

"There are a lot of people in there trying to fight to live. Some topics seem so insignificant, like they no longer matter. All the gossip, nice clothes, and frivolous stuff we used to focus on has taken a serious backseat when you want to see your daughter grow up."

"Is that what she talks about?"

"Mostly, when she does talk. I try to keep her up to date on Portia's activities. I'm also limiting the foolishness I share."

"I imagine that's helpful."

"Did I tell you Paul had Portia for two hours on his last weekend? A month ago, by the way. His trifling ass! There was a fire." I unintentionally raised my voice and winked twice at Stephanie. "He dropped Portia back at our house looking and smelling like somebody's Friday night date." I sucked my teeth. "How did your time go when you sat with Leslie last week?"

"Alright, I guess. I wasn't good afterwards." Stephanie's attention was trained on the coffee table for what felt like a long time before she spoke again. When she did, her eyes narrowed and her head moved side to side.

I waited in silence.

"Not 'cause anything happened per se. But I gained a whole new perspective," she shared.

I nodded in agreement.

"All of those people are sick! I was surprised. I mean, I just thought it was gonna be like one or two people there. But no. All ten chairs were occupied by somebody's mother or sister or grandfather or uncle. One person was sick and vomiting, others watched TV. Leslie just sat there and handed me some earphones to block the noise, like she was completely disassociated from our surroundings. After I took her home, I had damn near a whole bottle of wine that night."

"Damn!"

"I had my own moment of reflection, like…God, what am I doing with my life?"

It was my turn to listen without interruption.

"I had to cancel some of my patients the next day 'cause I kept thinking *What am I doing?* Seriously, it's made listening to parents that much harder. The other day I wanted to tell a child's mother, 'Just stop! Stop complaining, your kid is fine. You're the one who needs to be in therapy.' Plus, now I'm wondering, am I doing all that I want or need to do? When you know the person sitting there going through this experience, and you know their only goal is to live? It made me feel helpless."

"I hear you."

"That's what I was feeling, Jasmine…helpless."

Stephanie sharing her emotions was heavy. They were settling in my chest as an uncomfortable truth. She wasn't done.

"I had a hard time with that. Hell, we may all need therapy by the time this is over. Speaking of which, did you connect with a social worker for Portia?"

"Yes." I was glad Stephanie had turned her attention back to a topic on which I could actually make a difference. "We're scheduled to start in two weeks, after Thanksgiving. The social worker said she and I would meet for about ten minutes, then she'd meet with Portia for the remaining thirty-five to forty minutes."

"Okay, that sounds good." Stephanie switched back to professional mode. "You're going to catch the brunt of Portia's mood changes, so a few things to keep in mind."

"You know Portia…precocious and curious? Sure. Moody? Not so much."

"That may be true right now, but this is all new for her. And she's young." Stephanie wasn't going to let me gloss over the hard reality that my godchild might need more than ice cream to soothe her. "One, let Portia know it's okay to feel sad, angry, or scared. Two, it's also okay to not want to talk about her mom's illness all the time. Lastly, it's important to be honest with her about her mom's illness, but it's also important to reassure her that everything is going to be okay."

I sucked my lips into my mouth, trying to hold back the tears I felt bubbling up in the back of my throat.

"You have your hands full. How's T with all this?"

"Depends on the day. I think she's concerned that Paul isn't and will never be the parental figure that Portia needs."

"From what you've shared, that concern is valid. Have you all had a conversation about what will happen if it comes to that?"

Stephanie's question stepped on my sadness. "What kind of conversation?" I rubbed my palms on my pants. All of a sudden, I felt like I had on a layer too many even though I was only wearing a sheer blouse with a camisole underneath.

"About raising Portia?"

"Oh, it's way too early for that. I can't even consider it." I flicked my wrist, trying to shoo away the thought.

"Why not? That's a real possibility."

"How so?"

"What other family does Leslie have?"

"Oh my God…" *God bless, Stephanie.* "I haven't even thought about it. I mean Portia and T get along very well, but to think we'll be responsible for a child for at least the next ten years or so…" I felt lightheaded. "I can't wrap my head around that."

"Well, when you consider how Paul and Angel are behaving…From where I sit, you two may be the logical choice."

"Stephanie, let's stop talking about this." This was too much for one conversation. I got up and threw our empty food containers in the trash, then snatched my purse off the coffee table and slung the straps over my shoulder. "You're making my head hurt, and you're making it sound like Leslie is already gone."

"No, I'm merely providing a reality check that you need to keep in mind."

Stephanie came over to hug me.

"I'm not thinking about that," I sniffled.

"Lies! Yes, you are."

CHAPTER TWENTY

T

I needed some time with my family in a place that had been instrumental in my upbringing and that made me feel most comfortable. The hundred-year-old oak trees clothed in moss and secrets calmed my spirit. In early November, when I broached the subject of traveling to Savannah for Thanksgiving, Jasmine agreed to accompany me and asked if we could bring Portia too. She presented it as a new experience for the kid, an area Portia hadn't been to that she could write about in her winter break journal—apparently, a future assignment at hoity-toity St. Josephine Academy.

"Sure, Portia can come." I was being a bit facetious when I suggested bringing Coco too and didn't think Jasmine would take me seriously, but karma is a bitch, the boarding kennel was full.

Jasmine's office was closed for the week of Thanksgiving and Portia was out for the entire week as well. I was still acting Department Chair, so I worded my leave slip as "departmental prep," and we left early Tuesday morning in a rented mini-van looking like the two-mommy family that we had become. This was a long way away from my two-door sports car days.

Despite our early start, the ride south was laborious—mile after mile of brake lights typical of I-95 holiday traffic. Car games helped pass the time. Portia was good at identifying state license plates and telling us tidbits about states she'd learned in Geography. I hadn't played car games in decades, but our competition kicked up a notch when Jasmine started keeping score. She tried to use her big heart and kindness to mask her quiet competitiveness, but she wasn't fooling me—I stepped up my game. I came in first, followed by Portia. Jasmine likely could have beat Portia, but she started falling asleep. We arrived in Savannah ten-and-a-half long hours after leaving Baltimore.

We had been in the driveway of my childhood home—a single-story cottage with a modest porch and loads of Southern charm—for only two seconds before the front door opened. Mary and Harold Butler, my loudest cheerleaders and fiercest critics, and whom I happened to resemble, stepped out with the biggest grins on their faces. If I had known they would turn into big softies when I brought someone home that they finally liked, I may have considered settling down sooner. But I met Jasmine when and where I was supposed to. Essentially from the first time my parents met Jasmine, three years earlier, they had treated her like their second daughter, a blessing I didn't take lightly.

Now, with Portia in the mix, these people transformed into insufferable grandparents again. I mean, they always spoiled my nephews, my brother Rod's three kids. They saw the kids all the time since Rod and his wife Vicky lived only twenty minutes away. Portia, though, was completely unexpected and a girl to boot. As soon as she opened the van's sliding door, my mother pinched both of Portia's cheeks, grabbed her hand, and led her into the house, leaving me, Jasmine, and my father to carry the luggage in.

Jasmine and I settled into my brother's old room, which was now a lovely guest suite, and we put Portia's suitcase in my old room. After stealing a few kisses and relishing in the quietness we had been missing, Jasmine and I figured we'd better be social.

In the kitchen we found Portia wearing a pint-sized apron and a wide, gapped-tooth grin.

"GT, I'm helping Mama Mary make sweet potato pie!"

She sounded like she was about to jump out of her skin.

"Wow! You and —" *What in the world?*

"Mama Mary! She said to call her 'Mama Mary.'"

I cut my eyes at my mother, who shrugged with a sheepish smile.

"You and Mama Mary are joined at the hip already huh?"

"Yes! She already said I could come back anytime I wanted."

"She did?" I swallowed a laugh. Jasmine let hers out.

"Yes. We're going to cook collard greens, dressing, of course turkey, some other kind of dressing…" Portia looked at my mother for help.

Mom filled in the blank. "Oyster dressing."

"Yes, oyster dressing and cheese straws," Portia sang. "I don't know what those are, but there's cheese so they're probably good."

I lost the battle of trying to contain my amusement. Jasmine was doubled over at this point, whooping loudly. "Well, it sounds like you're going to be busy."

"Yep!" Portia nodded emphatically, as if to say, 'It is done.'

The rest of the night, I heard them in the kitchen laughing and squealing while we watched television in the family room.

Wednesday evening, my mother announced she wanted to do something different Thanksgiving morning.

"We're not watching the parade?" Jasmine asked, leaning over to me and trying to whisper.

"We're going to 'Thankful Thursday,'" Mom announced, looking at Jasmine with a twinkle in her eyes.

Apparently, a new pastor had recently been appointed at Mom's church. The same church Mom was raised in. The same church my grandfather, her father, had been the pastor of for forty-seven years, and the same church my brother and I were raised in. Mom was eager to hear the new young pastor's message. And she wanted us to go as a family.

"You aren't going to see the parade…at least not the live broadcast," I informed Jasmine after hearing my mother's explanation. Church really wasn't in my plans either, but I knew Mom's pronouncement was a pseudo-mandate couched as a suggestion. It would be easier to go than endure her side-eye and cold shoulder for the rest of our vacation. When Mom said "family," she meant er'body.

Thanksgiving morning, as we approached the church, I saw Rod and his family just stepping into the lobby. He held the door open for us, cocking his head at Mom and rolling his eyes. She patted him on his chest with one hand, guiding Portia with her other. Jasmine and I were next through the door. I kissed my brother on the cheek as I passed. He sucked his teeth—this was probably the last place he wanted to be on a Thursday morning, let alone on Thanksgiving. Dad trailed all of us into the sanctuary, which was filled with light that filtered through large stained-glass windows on either side and rows of painted white pews with red fabric cushions. Both the windows and pews dated back to 1897.

There were more folks in attendance than I expected, but it wasn't crowded. I looked around in wonder at one of the places so crucial in my development. My first speech, church. My first sleepover, church friends. And my first leadership position had been in church, as president of the junior usher board. My upbringing aside, frequenting a house of worship was no longer a part of my regular routine, a truth I imagined causing my grandfather to roll over in his grave. Brunch had become more my thing.

The singing was nice but I was playing tic-tac-toe with Portia when the sermon started—listening a bit here and there. The pastor hadn't met a verb he couldn't split and acknowledged that his sermon, titled "Who Got You?", was likely an affront to educators in the congregation. His scripture reference was from the gospel of Mark about a paralyzed man whose friends climbed onto the roof of a building where Jesus was preaching, made a hole, and lowered the man down on a mat to circumvent the gathered crowds. The pastor went on a bit about many of the works of Jesus and about the gospels themselves, including who biblical scholars believed had composed them. Who would have known this story could be strung out so long?

Portia had just drawn additional grids to start another round of our distraction when I heard sniffling and glanced to my left to find Jasmine digging around in her purse. My mother handed her a tissue. I stopped playing games and put my arm around Jasmine's shoulders as she dabbed her eyes. Finally, dude got to his broader point: The paralyzed man had friends who were innovative and persistent as they sought healing for him. Talk about loyalty.

Between the sermon, music, and everything that had been going on for the past few months, I wasn't surprised when Jasmine went to the front of the church to pray during altar call. What surprised me was that Portia followed her.

I watched as Portia tapped a trustee on his arm and the elderly man bent down and put his ear close to Portia's mouth. When he straightened up, he motioned with his hand to the musicians, who immediately lowered the volume on the tune they were playing.

"This baby," he declared in an attention-grabbing baritone voice, "this baby is asking for prayer for her mother."

"Hallelujah!" someone shouted.

"Amen!" another voice proclaimed.

"She says her mother has cancer."

A few chords rang out from the piano, joined by long high notes from the organ.

"Saints, this baby knows who and where to come to for help."

The musicians only needed three seconds before their instruments were in full swing again, along with somebody's tambourine. Once the double hand-clapping started, I could feel this was going to be a moment. A church mother lowered herself onto her knees to embrace Portia and pray. Jasmine was halfway back to our pew but turned around and went back to the altar. She stood behind Portia crying, with her hand on Portia's back. Then folks started coming to stand behind Portia with raised hands.

My mother stood up and motioned for me to come with her to the altar. Dad followed behind me.

By the time the choir sang three rounds of "God Never Fails," there wasn't a dry eye in the place. I wasn't sure about a lot of things when it came to mystical happenings in the Bible and whatnot. But no matter how long a period in between my church visits, when done right, there was no mistaking the communal feeling of transcendence. This morning was that. Jasmine had long forgotten about the parade and the dog show.

The remainder of the day was a typical Butler Thanksgiving—eating way too much food, sleeping shortly thereafter, and watching football. My nephews had a new friend and confidante in Portia, so Rod let them stay and play together. Vicky, however, left early in the evening to take advantage of a husband- and kid-free house.

***

I got up early on Friday morning to sit quietly outside with a cup of coffee, but my mother had already beaten me to the kitchen and was getting breakfast started.

"Morning!"

"Morning, baby. What are you doing up so early?" Mom laughed. "You can't smell food yet, I'm still chopping."

"It's not that early. From what I can tell, you've been up a minute."

I grabbed a mug from the cabinet, poured steaming hot liquid from the carafe, and let the nutty smell, with a hint of cocoa, tickle my nostrils. *Ahhhh, the benefits of being home.* I could see that potatoes had already been peeled and cubed cheese was piled in a bowl for something, grits maybe.

Mom continued slicing onions. "You never said, are you leaving tomorrow or Sunday?"

"I don't know, maybe tomorrow. We're both back to work on Monday and Portia has school."

"She's a sweet child."

"You two seem taken with each other," I said.

"I like having a little girl around."

"She's a good kid, but parenting is hard."

Mom smirked and placed her hand on her chin. "You don't say."

"I know I'm preaching to the choir." I laughed, joining in on her amusement. I'd never really thought about being a parent. It just didn't seem to be in my DNA or hadn't seemed to be in my future, despite having great parents." My mother stuck her tongue out at me. "You're right, Portia is a sweet kid. But boy, can she talk!"

"I know, it's adorable. I thought my heart was going to burst out of my chest yesterday, her asking us to pray for her mom. Jesus!" Mom held a dish towel up to her chest.

"I'm worried though, Ma. They say her mom's cancer is aggressive. What if she doesn't make it?"

"Hush with that negative talk."

"Her father had the nerve to say he was concerned we would influence his daughter 'cause she's living with us."

Mom's brow furrowed.

"But he certainly hasn't changed his life around to care for her. He doesn't strike me as a doting father, and he's using his occupation as an excuse."

My mother tossed the towel on the counter and crossed her arms, looking at me. Her intensity made me suddenly find the contents of my mug interesting. "What does he do?"

"He's a firefighter."

She shook her head and went back to preparing whatever it was she was preparing. "You don't have no control over that. Stop fussing about the child's father."

"I—"

Mom raised her hand up. "And definitely don't say anything bad about him such that Portia can hear you." She stopped chopping and put her knife down. "She'll learn soon enough. One day in the future, she'll ask him why she wasn't with him when her mom got sick. He'll have to provide her whatever sorry excuse he's got to give."

"But—"

"But nothing. It is not your job, T. Your job is to love Jasmine and love on that child."

I wanted so desperately to suck my teeth and leave the room, let my blood pressure simmer down. Except my thirty-eight-year-old self was terrified my mother would threaten bodily harm.

"How would you feel if I died tomorrow?" she asked me.

"What are you talking about?" I shifted on the stool I was sitting on and stared at my mother.

"How would you feel if I died tomorrow?"

"Inconsolable, absolutely terrible. Where are you going with this?"

"How do you think you would've felt if I'd died when you were in the fourth grade?"

"Lost. Alone and abandoned." I frowned. "I don't know!"

She stared back at me with her eyebrows lifted high atop her forehead.

"I'm just asking why us? Why are we suddenly parents?"

"Baby, why not you? You both have the means and enough love for that little girl to land safely if her mother dies."

"It's her father's job. It's not mine."

"It is right now."

"Oh, Ma, don't say that. I'm hoping those prayers yesterday reached the right frequency for Leslie."

"Do right by this child. You hear me? Do right by this child."

I pushed out a sigh through my nostrils. I loved Portia and Jasmine. Did I think we could successfully raise her? Of course, I was sure we could figure it out. I just wasn't prepared to take on that level of responsibility. Or more accurately, I'd never had that level of responsibility on my life's Bingo card. It was one thing to care for pubescent tweens and teens for fifty-five-minute blocks of time. It was another whole ballgame trying to guide a human on a daily basis, especially one as gifted as Portia.

Jasmine had jumped headfirst into trying to be all things for all people. No one could say she wasn't caring and kind. What made her so wonderful, though, meant that our comfortable coupledom was no longer that. And so far I hadn't had much input into the matter. To make matters worse, Paul was straight up trash. I wasn't used to men not taking care of their children, it wasn't how I was raised. The son of a bitch!

Rather than make a stink about Jasmine's and my current circumstances or come across as selfish as hell, I felt myself retreating inward.

"I pray for you and Jasmine's strength too. You'll be blessed," Mom said.

Dad walked into the kitchen. "T, save yourself from a long, drawn-out lecture. Tell your mama she's right and move on with your day." He kissed Mom on the cheek, which she leaned into. Their affection for each other never got stale. "That little girl is special." He popped a piece of cheese in his mouth. "My grandsons don't listen, but she listens real nice."

"I know, Daddy." My shoulders slumped. There was no sense in arguing with these people. Not because they were my parents, but because they were right.

***

Jasmine and I decided to leave the next day so we'd have a day to rest before returning to work and Portia to school on Monday. The ride north was as congested as always in the same places on 95, basically the entire state of North Carolina, seemingly a perpetual construction zone. When we got north of Richmond, I decided to take U.S. 301 to avoid northern Virginia traffic. Our little detour led to Portia asking a lot of questions about areas or things we passed, like Fort A. P. Hill—questions that turned into lessons about U.S. highways and World War II. But minus the "School House Rock" session, the three of us spoke less on the ride home. If Jasmine and Portia were like me, they were both contemplating the challenges that lay ahead.

CHAPTER TWENTY-ONE

Jasmine

What were you thinking? I smacked my forehead. I was in the basement, trying to pull Christmas things from storage. Who planned a Christmas day dinner after spending the previous four months juggling a demanding full-time job, helping coordinate childcare, cancer treatments, sporadic weekend visitation by Portia's father, and school arrangements? Not to mention I should have started, first and foremost, with maintaining a relationship. I shook my head.

I was not doing anything well. As a matter of fact, my relationship with T was strained to say the least. T hardly had much to say as of late. Our relationship was much different than it had been in July, pre-Portia, when I unquestionably thought we were a team.

Now with the family calendar bursting at the seams, one activity after another, some days T seemed angry. Other days she was aloof. Hence, there was no way I was going to rain on her parade when she told me her parents were coming to Baltimore for the holiday. They said Portia and Leslie could use a little extra love.

The Butlers coming north for Christmas implied that Christmas was no longer going to be a small, intimate affair with just me, T, Leslie, and Portia. No, it meant we would host at least six more people—Terrence and Kevin, John and Ray, and now my own parents, who I invited thinking they could chat with Ms. Mary and Mr. Harold. Added to all this, Leslie was immunocompromised, so she really needed to be careful about being around folks. I was glad that at least the likelihood of my self-righteous sister Robin joining us was slim. According to her, my house was halfway between Sodom and Gomorrah, and my brother J.R. was going wherever his latest boo would be. I just wanted whoever joined us to be joyful and peaceable.

I needed to ask Leslie if she had plans for Portia's Christmas gifts. And I wondered if Paul was going to show up or spend any time with her at all. I was so over Paul, I just couldn't deal with him. He wasn't like the men I was used to. Given his child's mother had cancer, this was the perfect time to demonstrate he gave a ham sandwich. But no. If I looked for him on a Friday…crickets. If he had been taking proper care of his child, I wouldn't be leaving pointed messages on his voicemail. Leslie had even said he'd had the nerve to complain about my messages. But she had rightfully reminded him that if he took his daughter half the time he was supposed to, he wouldn't receive them anymore.

I was trying to be helpful, and Leslie was just trying to live. But I wasn't feeling good about how she was doing. She looked weaker with each passing week. She had a third set of imaging scans scheduled for the first week of January. The scans in early November had looked okay, I thought. I'd come away unsure if we were heading in the right direction though.

I sat down on a storage tub, my thoughts all over the place. I felt confident that Dr. Jordan knew what she was doing because Leslie kept saying she trusted her unequivocally. I just didn't understand the process. Dr. Jordan was keeping the current chemo course and we would review the updated images after the holidays. I sighed heavily.

Once I found the plastic bins with the holiday decorations I was looking for, angels, black Santas, and poinsettia florals, I gathered them together, and pushed the bins into a corner. T would get the tree out and bring everything upstairs in the coming week.

Since our time was limited, she and I had talked about not putting up the full Butler-Charles Christmas display as we had the first year we started living together. That year had been fun though, T and I going all out! We had swirled lights around the hedges, placed big ornaments in baskets on the porch, and tied gold- and silver-painted magnolia branches around the porch columns. The house was beautiful. We stood outside for the better part of two hours drinking hot chocolate and admiring the place like we didn't even live here.

Not this year. I wanted it to be festive, but I was just too tired to decorate like we'd done in the past. Portia asked if we were going to make cookies to welcome her Mama Mary and Poppa Harold. The child really was thoughtful, sensitive, and full of energy.

My cell phone, which I had started carrying with me everywhere, rang as I was about to go back upstairs from the basement.

"Hello?" I answered.

"Hey." Leslie's voice sounded a bit stronger than it had the day before.

"How are you?" I sat down again.

"It's a good day today. Hey look—"

"What's up?" My chest tightened.

"Do you mind if I spend Christmas Eve at your house?"

I didn't think twice. "Of course not."

"That way, I'll be there when Portia wakes up Christmas morning."

"That's a great idea."

"Do you think T will mind?" Leslie inquired.

"Of course not," I repeated.

"How can you be so sure?"

"I know my girlfriend and she loves me and she wants what's best for you and Portia." I tried to sound confident but doubt made my insides quiver.

Leslie's voice rose an octave. "You're not going to at least ask her?"

"I'll tell her."

"Uh, Jasmine!"

"I'll tell her, trust me." I could see my friend rolling her eyes even through the phone. "Anyway, do we need to do anything special?"

"My nurse said I should wear a face mask, wash my hands more than I think I should, and limit interacting with a lot of people to reduce the possibility of getting an infection."

"That sounds reasonable, anything else?"

"No, my white cell count hasn't dipped dramatically, so she said I don't have to completely isolate myself."

"That's good."

"Yeah, I'm ready for a little fun and festiveness. I feel like I've been such a drag since…"

Not wanting to weigh down what had been such a positive conversation, I tried to sound hopeful and not let my fear of the future overtake the holiday cheer.

"Me too, girl," I replied. "I'm ready for a little fun too."

But what if this was Leslie's last Christmas? A month earlier, when Stephanie asked if I had thought about Leslie dying, I had lied and said I hadn't. But Stephanie was too good of a psychologist to not know I wasn't telling the truth. Even so, I couldn't think too long about a negative prospect because I truly didn't know what I was feeling moment to moment. I was just trying to focus on what was right in front of me. I jumped to my feet. *Get through the holidays. Chin up, Jasmine!*

***

Two days after I'd talked to Leslie and ten days before Christmas, T, Portia, and I were getting ready for ReBuild's holiday soiree. Our offices would be closed between Christmas and New Year's Day—for that, I was grateful. I believed if I could just make it through next week, I could get my second wind. But first, the party.

All three of us had our clothes and accessories prepped for the festive evening. The thought of T in her green velvet jacket with its slightly shimmery sheen made me smile. I'd chosen a burgundy satin dress and

Portia was going to wear a dark green jumper dress that she and Leslie had made. The girl was talented.

We gathered in the living room at five-thirty, admiring each other's outfits as we walked along an imaginary runway striking pose after pose. Leslie had come over and took pictures of us and we took some of her with Portia. It felt good to get a little dressed up for the evening. It felt even better to laugh.

***

"My goodness, there are lights everywhere!" T whistled as we pulled into the B&O Railroad Museum's parking lot.

"It's so pretty!" the little person shouted from the back seat.

The decorations were indeed stunning. The museum was certainly one of my favorite places to visit during the holidays because they spared no expense. Swags of garland, huge colored ornaments, and decorated trains helped set the atmosphere outside. We were on visual overload even before we left the parking lot.

We walked slowly through a glittered arch to the entrance of the Roundhouse, an imposing, circular structure whose roof soared over a hundred feet in the air. Even more impressive was the fact that this place still existed at all after a massive snowfall had caused a portion of the roof to collapse almost three years before. The museum had reopened a year ago and ReBuild was among the first organizations to rent the venue because their values were aligned, particularly in preserving history for future generations.

The Roundhouse was even grander inside. I waited to get our wristbands at the check-in table while T went to check our coats.

"You think they left any lights for anyone else?" T said when she returned. She handed me the coat ticket to put in my clutch. "These are our tax dollars lighting this place up."

"Girl, you know it's beautiful in here." I laughed and put the band around her wrist.

"That's the tallest Christmas tree I've ever seen inside a building."

"It's huge, isn't it?" I got a bit closer to her, enough that the lavender and ylang-ylang oil she wore made my stomach flutter, which hadn't happened in a minute. "You looking kinda fine tonight. You got a girlfriend?"

"Yes, I do, so please step away, ma'am." T's mouth twisted in that sexy way she did, then she smoothed her jacket sleeve down, and winked at me.

"You are so silly." I bumped her with my shoulder and held my arm out so she could attach my band for me. "We needed this tonight." I winked back at her, my cheeks warming and the corners of my mouth turning up.

"Here, Portia…" I turned to the last place I'd seen her but she was midway across the room looking at a locomotive. She was with Quetta and Quinton, the kids she'd met when T had gone to do a photo shoot at their mom Maya's ReBuild home.

I motioned for her to come back. All three ran over. *Kids ran everywhere— why can't they walk?* I wondered.

"Stay where we can see you and don't run," I said as I put a band on her wrist.

They weren't sticking around. The three of them speed-walked across the expansive room back to the engine they had them so fascinated.

T had already found a small table and was sitting there, rocking her head to the jazzy holiday music the band was playing. "Can I get you anything, babe?"

"Whatever their signature drink is, but as a virgin, or water's fine."

I headed in the direction of the bar and placed our drink requests. On the way back, I stopped for a few appetizers, trying to delicately balance everything as I walked back to the table, gingerly trying to avoid running kids. At the table T and I relaxed, listening to the music, watching the children, and making small talk with whoever came by.

"ReBuild puts on a swinging party," T observed.

"This is nice, right? The band is good, two drink tickets, appetizers, and we'll get a swag bag. I know ReBuild didn't pay much for the rental, not sure about the food. It's not a sit-down dinner so probably affordable. It's good fun."

"You're off tomorrow?"

"Yes. I. Am." I clapped with emphasis. "I'm going to drop Portia off and go home and get back in bed. I'll look like some of the mothers who drop their kids off in fashionable loungewear."

"Hah!"

"I'll piddle and then start cleaning before we decorate. I want everything done before your parents get here."

"I'm excited they're coming."

"Really? Even though they're staying at the studio?"

"Oh, yeah, they'll be fine. They're self-sufficient and reasonable people."

I raised an eyebrow. "Are you sure? Not about the reasonable part but you seem awfully confident."

"Jasmine, they'll be fine. Plus, our spare beds are already taken, remember?"

I relaxed a bit.

"It was actually their idea." T took a sip of her cranberry-basil sangria mocktail. "Mmmmm…This is good."

That was a relief. I'd been skeptical about the bartender's recommendation, but he assured me it would be delicious.

"Really?"

"Really what? Really, is the drink good? Or really my parents suggested they stay at the studio?"

"Really your parents suggested they stay at the studio?"

"Yep!" T smiled at me.

"Well, that makes me feel a bit better. You never said if Rod and Vicky were coming."

"Nah, I think they're looking forward to a quieter holiday. Me and the peeps will meet for a few dinners and they'll be with us Christmas Eve and all day Christmas. I just hope my mother behaves."

"Why do you say that? Ms. Mary is always the epitome of grace and class."

T rolled her eyes. "Yeah okay, don't let the smooth taste fool you. I have half a mind to apologize to your parents up front."

"They'll be fine. Our parents are about the same age, similar experiences, it'll be fine."

"I hope so. Look at your goddaughter…" T pointed to the dance floor at the center of the room. "Who taught her the Cha-Cha Slide?"

"I don't know, but she's getting it."

"I wonder if her mother knows." We both laughed.

"Who taught you how to dance?" I asked Portia once the song was over and she found us.

"Aunt Angel. Did you see me dancing?"

"Alright, twinkle toes, you were slidin'," I said.

The three of us sat and talked for a bit until Jason made his CEO speech thanking us for our hard work over the past year. It was a great speech in that it was short, he extended appropriate appreciation to our supportive agencies, and he dutifully reminded us that ReBuild's community connections were the cornerstone to our success. He closed by raffling off two baskets, one filled with kid-related stuff, the other suitable for an adult couple to indulge in a little fun.

I said our goodbyes and the three of us walked back to the car all holding hands, Portia in the middle. I wished I had buttoned my coat to block the December wind but the energy emanating among us warmed me enough for the short walk.

"That was magical." T glanced over at me once we got settled in the car.

"It was. We need to get back to date nights in the new year. Okay?"

"Indeed," T said as we got on the JFX. She interlaced the fingers of her free hand together with mine and squeezed. I hadn't anticipated it, but that simple gesture filled my chest cavity with love.

CHAPTER TWENTY-TWO

T

With Christmas coming, I was glad I'd invited my parents to Baltimore for the holiday. Feeling overwhelmed with the day-to-day activities of child-rearing and whatnot, I thought having them here, more specifically, having my mom here, she could help me put things in perspective and offer advice that would keep me from weakening under the strain of caregiving.

After they arrived, I usually picked them up from my studio to do whatever we had planned for the day and then dropped them off there again in the evenings. They were comfortable at the studio, especially since they were familiar with the place. And it made me happy to have them there.

One day we spent a day shopping for presents and then I stayed at the studio with them that night. My mother and I wrapped gifts while my dad watched TV. Truthfully, it felt good to be in my own space. The visit was actually going rather well.

Another day, my father wanted a tour of scene locations from *The Wire*, a television series he watched religiously. While I navigated east and west Baltimore, he provided highlights about characters and episodes. He really enjoyed riding around Fells Point.

One night all of us—me, Jasmine, Portia, Mom, and Dad—went to T.K.'s for dinner then rode down to D.C. to see the national tree display. Portia and my mom loved the decorated state trees. We went to Georgia's tree first so Mom could see the ornaments. Jasmine and my father talked and strolled behind us sipping hot chocolate. We also fit in Jasmine's favorite, riding around different neighborhoods to see the holiday lights.

As we got ready for Christmas, I moved furniture here and there to accommodate the growing list of folks who had said they were coming over Christmas day. With the Butlers of Savannah in town, Terrence wanted to spend time with *his* Aunt Mary. And since T.K.'s was closed for the day, he had promised to bring sides.

And then there was John, who also adored the ground my mother walked on. They had become closer after his mother unexpectedly passed shortly after we graduated from college. Once I told him my parents were coming to Baltimore, he had called my mother and scheduled time just for the two of them to sightsee and have lunch. Not Dad. Not me. I couldn't help thinking, *Ain't that about nothing!*

"Are you ready for tomorrow?" I asked on Christmas Eve, once Jasmine and I were in bed.

"As ready as I'm going to be. How about you?" Jasmine responded.

Having Leslie at our house wasn't as disruptive as I had convinced myself it would be with another person contributing to its energy. In fact, the four of us had a great time putting the finishing touches on our decorations while singing along to holiday classics like Boyz to Men's "Let It Snow" and The Temptations' "Silent Night." Leslie mostly sat but had used her keen design sense to steer this ornament here and that poinsettia there. I especially enjoyed trying, and failing, to taste the deliciously-smelling cookies Portia baked for my parents.

I let out an exhale. "I'm a bit nervous, you know."

"Why?" She stroked my arm.

"It's the first time our parents are meeting."

"Yeah, that is kind of a big deal, huh?"

"Yeah!" I agreed.

"I've been on the go so much, I hadn't stopped to think about it," Jasmine confessed.

"Well, from my limited interaction with your folks…I'm nervous."

Although Jasmine and I had been together for three years, her parents hadn't warmed up to me the way mine had to Jasmine. In fact, our parents were as different as oil and water. Mrs. Charles was the kind of person Mary Butler referred to as "nice nasty," someone who used her feigned piety as a weapon and never missed an opportunity to humble brag about their Ashburton neighborhood, a stronghold for black professionals in Baltimore. Jasmine was silent for a while and her breathing had become deeper, so I honestly thought she had fallen asleep.

"Babe?" she said softly.

"Yes?"

"Who's going to say grace?" she abruptly asked.

I didn't answer. It sounded like a random trick question.

"I mean, it's our house," she went on, "and you normally do the honors—"

"That sounds like the right answer to me."

"But there'll be a lot of testosterone here—"

"And?" My insides began to heat up from irritation. I didn't think we should dim our shine to make people comfortable, especially in our own home. My eyes rolled all the way in the back of my head, making me glad it was dark and Jasmine's back was to me.

Jasmine turned to face me. "Let's flip a coin."

I drew all the air I could into my lungs. "Sure, okay."

But Jasmine meant like right at that moment. She hopped out of bed and came back with a quarter. After several rounds of pitting one name against another, my dad won out. Which was a good compromise as far as I was concerned. With Dad praying, there would be no Charles-style hell and damnation, the food wouldn't get cold, and we were guaranteed not to hear about the rapture. I'd let him know in the morning.

***

Christmas morning we were all up early, excited for Portia to check out what Santa had brought her and to exchange gifts. We were relieved to hear that Leslie had slept well in our house and having her with us was another present for Portia.

Our guests began to arrive a little after two. And everything was going well—until it wasn't. Soon enough, the guys—my dad, Kevin, John and his boo Ray, and Jasmine's father—disappeared to the basement to watch football. If the shouting and trash talking were any indication, they were having a good time. Jasmine, Terrence, and Mom were putting the finishing touches on the food and starting to set it out buffet style. Terrence delivered on the sides too. Boy showed up with foil pans filled with greens, seafood mac and cheese, and candied yams.

Meanwhile, Mrs. Charles sat in the living room with her face scrunched up like she smelled rotting fish rather than the sweet scent of homemade cinnamon rolls that tickled my own nostrils. Needless to say, I had little to say to her other than, "Good afternoon. How are you?" After all, I was a southern girl.

Jasmine, on the other hand, and despite having a house full of people expecting a delicious meal, tried to appease her mother. She paused often with a "Mama, do you need anything?" question, continually concerning herself with her mother's well-being.

"No, thank you," Mrs. Charles managed through pursed lips each time. She remained in the living room—alone—while everyone else enjoyed themselves together downstairs or in the kitchen until dinner.

When it was finally time to eat, everyone gathered in the dining room to say grace. Dad said a short prayer thanking God for Jesus' birth. He ended it with, "In God's kingdom, there is room for everyone."

"You know some people would've still been praying," Terrence kidded Dad.

What made Mrs. Charles think they were talking about her? I wasn't sure, but it was at that point that she started holding her purse close to her chest and making snide remarks about the food, raising a child in a home with two women, and feeling a San Francisco vibe in the house... whatever the hell that meant.

"Is she talking about us?" John whispered to me.

"Ignore her, I don't know what she's talking about," I grumbled.

All the guys except Terrence and John filled their plates with everything on the spread and returned downstairs to their game. Jasmine made a plate for Leslie, who wasn't feeling well, and took it upstairs then joined me, Portia, Mom, Terrence, John, and her mother to sit at the dining room table, where glasses and forks clinking against porcelain were the dominant sounds, along with the occasional audible appreciation for the food.

The vibes seemed pleasant until Mrs. Charles spoke up, addressing no one in particular.

"You know," she said, "the Lord sent Jesus to save us from the wicked ways of the world."

Jasmine threw serious dagger eyes at her mother.

What was she talking about? "What the fuck?" I mouthed to Jasmine, who was sitting directly across from me.

My mother threw her napkin on the table.

Terrence peeked at me with both his eyebrows high on his forehead.

I shook my head and inhaled. *Mrs. Saved and Sanctified wasn't ready.*

My mother had had enough. "I have tried to overlook your insults and your funky mood," she said. "I'm sure Jasmine would have rather you stayed home if you were going to be so uncomfortable."

Mrs. Charles stared at Mom with her mouth gaping.

"You've mentioned Jesus a lot," my mom went on. "As I recall, Jesus said, 'Love God, love your neighbor as yourself...Love each other.' He also said we should treat people with kindness and compassion."

"Jesus—" Mrs. Charles couldn't get her thoughts together fast enough.

"Both have been missing in your tone and conversation since you stepped over that threshold." Mom pointed toward the front door. "We are on this earth to please God. Since you've been quoting the Bible and what thus saith the Lord, I don't need to cite exact scripture for you—"

"You most certainly do not. I—" Mrs. Charles clutched her pearls and glanced around the table for support. She found none.

The guys came charging up from the basement, no doubt alarmed by the upstairs conversation's volume.

"But if it suits you to follow a passive, limiting, and hateful God…feel free," Mom continued. "My father taught us about a radically inclusive God who loves us all. Daddy welcomed everyone into our home, and he financially supported people who needed to leave the confines of Savannah for a lot of reasons, including people who were run out of town because of their sexual identity."

Terrence leaned over to me. "Did you know that?"

I shook my head. "Chile, Mary Butler is teaching up in here tonight." I snapped my fingers softly.

"His church benefitted from out-of-state donations for years. Not because he was some big-time televangelist," Mom continued. "Nope. It was because of the kindness and support he gave to people who needed it."

Mrs. Charles scowled at Jasmine as Mom spoke, undaunted.

"'Nobody can hurt you like family,' Daddy used to say." She rose, stood behind Jasmine, and put her hand on Jasmine's shoulder. Jasmine reached up and squeezed my mother's hand. "My husband and I couldn't be happier that our daughter has found someone so loving and caring. We gladly welcomed her to our home, and she is family."

"Amen!" Dad lifted his glass in agreement, and so did John, Terrence, and Kevin.

Mrs. Charles was seething. Her jaw clinched and her nostrils flared as she flung her napkin on her plate. "I, I—"

My mother was right and yet, this was exactly what I had been afraid of. Emotions had gone from zero to sixty in four point five seconds.

And I felt like running out of the dining room but I needed to keep ten toes down for my girlfriend. All we had wanted was a pleasant day.

Mrs. Charles' fun meter had clearly been pegged because not long after Mom's soliloquy she announced she and Jasmine's dad were leaving.

"Catherine, it's Christmas for goodness' sake. I was having a good time with everybody." Mr. Charles hadn't said much all evening, but I assumed he was now thoroughly fed up. Or embarrassed. Or pissed off. Or a combination of all three. I knew I certainly would be.

"Daddy, would you like a piece of red velvet cake? T made it." Jasmine said, as if to redirect the conversation.

Mrs. Charles looked sideways at her husband. Not only had she spent the day in Sodom and Gomorrah, but now she had found out that one of the chief priestesses had made a dessert. She would have had a fit if she had known I'd made every dessert we'd put out, including that sweet potato pie she devoured like no one was watching.

Mr. Charles glared straight at his wife, as if daring her to make a single retort. Then he nodded at Jasmine.

"Give me a big slice," he said, laughing. He leaned over and kissed his daughter on the cheek. "Your mother is not the boss of me."

The room collectively exhaled when my girlfriend finally closed the door behind her parents. She rested her back against it and groaned, her eyes shut. The evening's overwhelming events had taken their toll, that much was obvious. But she tried to wipe away her tears before we could notice how hard it had been for her. As I joined Jasmine in the living room, Mom followed with outstretched arms.

"I meant everything I said," she said, making an effort to reassure Jasmine.

She allowed my mother to comfort her, then pulled away. "Thank you."

Mom offered a warm smile.

"I really mean it, thank you." Jasmine put her hand over her heart. "My mother was something tonight."

"Truer words have never been spoken," Mom agreed.

"She always has something negative to say, but I think seeing everyone here really embracing us while we're trying to support Leslie and Portia was just too much for her."

"Well, that's her problem, not yours," my mother said.

Now that the fireworks were over, the guys grabbed dessert for themselves and retreated back downstairs. I gave Mom a light kiss on her cheek and led Jasmine to the kitchen. "Come on, let me help you clean up."

Jasmine bit her lip and nodded.

"Sometimes Christians give Christ a bad name," I said.

***

Two weeks after the Christmas nightmare I was with Portia, standing on the baseline at her fourth basketball game of the season, watching her and her teammates go through their layup drill. At the same time, I kept checking my phone.

"Where the hell is Sherman?" I muttered under my breath.

Sherman, the so-called coach of Portia's team, hadn't answered any of my texts. So here I was, on my own. I'd first gotten involved with Portia's basketball activities by simply dropping her off at practice. But one afternoon I'd stayed to watch and made the mistake of yelling to Portia, "Shuffle your feet, keep your hips low!" After that, I'd been roped into doing far more, helping Sherman ever since.

Now, as I stood there, I felt perspiration starting to form on my forehead, not because I was exerting energy either. I could feel the head referee staring at me from the scorer's table. We had yet to fill in the players' names in the official scorebook. He waved me over. I held a finger up at him to buy time.

I got that St. Josephine's only paid Sherman a modest stipend and he needed volunteers to help get the girls going in the same direction, but damn! It wasn't unusual for him to be late to practice either, and I ended up running warm-up drills or even helping drop kids off at home when parents were caught in traffic or had some other holdup. But the lack of communication at the moment was something different altogether.

My cell phone pinged. "Christ." Sherman was going to be late, again. I stuffed the phone in my sweatpants pocket and walked over to the referee, a man dressed in too-tight, black polyester pants and a black-and-white striped shirt, the tensile strength of its threads being tested.

"We need to get started or you'll have to forfeit," Ref said, like he had somewhere else to be.

"The coach just texted. He's going to be late."

"Aren't you a coach?" Ref walked away, hollering over his shoulder as he went, "This ain't the WNBA. I need a decision in five minutes," and making sure everyone in the small gym heard him.

"Damn it!" This wasn't what I wanted to happen. *If you let them*, I thought irritably, *people will surely take advantage of your kindness.*

Portia left her teammates sitting at the end of the bench and jogged over to me. "GT, I mean Coach T, we don't want to forfeit, we can play."

My left eyebrow went up.

"Come on, please?" Portia pleaded. "We almost won the last game."

"Alright, y'all do the free-throw drill." I felt like I had been conned.

"Yay!" She ran back over to her teammates, and they lined up around the free-throw lane.

"Ref, Ref! I got a question," I yelled.

"What's up?"

"Since our head coach is delayed, what do I need to do to get started?"

"Just write your name in the scorebook, along with the team's name as well as the players' names and their jersey numbers." He pointed at the table. "Then we can get this game started."

I rolled my eyes, not at him, but at the situation I found myself in. My same old issue was raising its ugly head once again. Jasmine and I had gone from happy couple with no kids, living life to the fullest, to one kid hassle after another, including me stressing about filling out a basketball team roster. I mean, I wasn't immune to athletics, after all. I'd been a decent athlete myself back in the day. I just hadn't imagined being anybody's coach. But I couldn't let this jacked-up situation impact the girls. After all, they just wanted to play. It wasn't their fault their head coach was trash.

No sooner had I entered the last girl's name, than the loud, obnoxious horn sounded to indicate warmups were over.

I huddled the girls. "Okay, ladies, listen up," I said, trying to hide my nervousness. "Coach Sherman is going to be late, so you're stuck with me for now."

I was glad to see their little faces didn't register worry. I wasn't sure they normally listened to directions coming from the sidelines anyway. Right now, though? Twenty-two eyes were on me, waiting for instructions.

"Okay," I began, "we're going to keep this simple. Portia, Maria, Ashley—"

"Which one?" Portia interjected.

There were three Ashleys on the team. Tall Ashley, Short Ashley, and Pink Ashley. Pink Ashley wore the most obnoxious-colored sneakers I had ever seen but, in this moment, I loved her fashion choice.

"Umm, Short Ashley?" I ventured.

"Yes!" A kid with two blonde braids secured with blue barrettes, no doubt to match her jersey, pumped her little fist in the air.

"Britney and Heather will start. Run that wheel offense we practiced and we'll play man-to-man defense."

"Coach T?" Britney spoke up.

I looked in her direction.

"We're girls."

Jesus, be a fence...I inhaled and put on a faux smile. "Indeed, you are. Okay, we'll play girl-to-girl defense to start the game."

They shook their heads.

"Don't worry if you don't remember everything, just listen to me. Okay?"

More nodding.

"Okay, bring it in." I held my hand out and eleven little hands of varying hues piled on top of mine. "Let's see…on three, let's say 'team.' One, two, three…"

"TEAM!" Their excited squeals were the most high-pitched I had ever heard. Damaged ear drum aside, it was game time.

Portia and the prep girls held their own. The game was close. Portia's team was only down by four points the entire game. In the last two minutes, the visiting team went cold and missed their last three baskets. We were down one point with thirty seconds left. I made a "T" with my hands to signal a timeout and called the girls over. Once again, twenty-two eyeballs were looking at me for guidance. Why was this so stressful? It wasn't like I didn't teach little people all day. I grabbed the dry erase playmaker board and tried to act like I knew what I was doing.

"Ashley!"

"Yes, Coach." Three girls answered.

"Ummm…Tall Ashley."

Ashley stood up, "Yes, coach?"

"Stand on the opposite block, on the other side of the basket." I drew and "X" and I looked up.

She nodded.

"Listen…Portia, I want you to take the ball out of bounds."

"Okay," she replied in a sing-song voice.

"Maria, you're standing on the block closest to the bench." I drew another "X." "You'll turn around and set a screen on Ashley's man—" I heard someone suck their teeth. "I'm sorry, Maria, you're going to set a screen on Ashley's defender, No. 10, I think." I drew a line on the board. "Ashley, wait for the screen then curl around…" I drew an arc. "Portia will pass you the ball, you're going to turn and make the winning basket!"

I looked up and was met with concerned expressions.

"What am I doing, Coach?" Britney asked.

"You're going to stand on the opposite wing to be the pass of last resort."

She stared at me blankly.

I put another "X" on the board. "Stand on the other side of the three-point line."

She gave me a big snaggle-tooth smile and nodded.

"What about me? What about me?" Heather was jumping up and down with her hand in the air.

"Ummm, you stand in the corner on this side of the court." I pointed to where I wanted her to be.

"Okay, Coach." In her enthusiasm, Heather left the huddle prematurely and sprinted to the court. "Oh!" She ran back.

I smiled. The horn sounded—our timeout was over. *Here goes.* I stuck my hand out, they piled theirs on. "Win on three. One, two, three…"

"WIN!"

Oh, my, their excitement made my eardrums vibrate.

I wasn't surprised when Tall Ashley started on the wrong side. I screamed like a crazy person until she got where she was supposed to be. I also wasn't surprised when she and Maria bumped into one another. But Portia still managed to get the pass to Ashley before a five-second penalty was called. Ashley turned and tossed the ball toward the rim. It rolled around twice before popping out with fifteen seconds left in the game. At which point, nine little people converged toward the basket. I swore the ball bounced off every player's hands like a beach ball for a full eight seconds. *God bless!*

Lucky for us, Tall Ashley was taller than every other girl on the court. She grabbed the rebound and, Lord have mercy, instead of shooting it again, she passed it out of the paint. I thought my heart was going to stop—the clock read "00:07." Heather took her assignment seriously and had only moved a few feet out of her position in the corner. Not an ideal place to shoot from, but we didn't have a choice.

"Shoot! Shoot!" I jumped up and down like Heather had earlier.

Heather poked her tongue out the side of her mouth, bent her knees, and thrust the ball in the direction of the basket. Her shot looked more like she was a shot putter than a basketball player. But I be damned if the net didn't snap like she was Chamique Holdsclaw when the ball barely jostled the nylon.

The buzzer sounded, the clock read "00:00," and pandemonium broke out. You would have thought we had just won the NCAA finals the way those little girls squealed and danced and hugged each other. Parents in the bleachers chanted, "We won, we won, we won!"

Portia ran over to me and hugged my waist. "We won, GT! I can't believe we won." I hugged her back. "That's the first game we've won." She skipped back to join her friends.

"What happened?"

A tenor male voice invaded my personal space. Amid our exhilaration, I hadn't noticed Sherman sneak into the gym. But there he was, standing next to me with a goofy, cheese-eating grin on his face.

"Coach Sherman, we won!" All three Ashley's screamed simultaneously.

"What?" Sherman shot me an incredulous look, his mouth hanging open. "That's what's up."

"I just gave them a little guidance." I shrugged. "It's all good."

Considering I had achieved something he hadn't since the season started, Sherman's muted response dampened my mood, and I bit the inside of my cheek to keep my irritation to myself.

"I guess your guidance was what they needed," he said, clearly not as thrilled as the girls or their families.

Was this knucklehead dissing me? Coaching youth basketball hadn't been on my "to do" list for the day, and neither was pacifying hurt feelings or soothing a grown man's ego.

"I did what I thought would help. And we won our first game of the season."

"You right, my bad," Sherman conceded.

"They're all yours, I'm out." I went to get my phone and keys from the bench. "Let's go, Portia." My abrupt attempt at departing should have been a clue that I didn't want to be bothered, but Sherman followed me.

"I been working with them, and the last game was so close."

Why was he still talking to me?

"We can make a good team...and I could use your help."

"Could you now? Thirty seconds ago, you were in your feelings."

"I know. I'm just butt hurt that I wasn't here for our first win."

"That's on you." I was not about to make room for this man's shortcomings.

"I know, I know. Work was a bi—" He cut his eyes at the kids. "Look, I really could use your help, Teresa. You're good with the kids, and they love you."

I shifted my weight from one foot to the other.

"I'll talk to the athletic director, I'm pretty sure we can move you from volunteer to paid staff without too much hassle. Plus, if we win like more than fifty percent of our games, we'll get a little bit of a bonus."

Well, now he was making more sense. "The offer sounds intriguing. Talk to the AD and let's see what we can do about helping these girls win." I turned to extricate myself from this conversation, but Sherman kept talking.

"Let's meet to talk about strategy and whatnot," he suggested. "We don't need nothing intricate, just something that some of these other teams aren't necessarily using to win."

"What we need is consistency...in practice and games," I said, moving back toward him so I wasn't yelling over the background chaos still continuing.

"We practice."

"Yes, and the routine is different every time they walk in the gym, or at least it's been different when I've been around."

He shrugged.

"I realize they're nine- and ten-year-olds, but the kids need to develop muscle memory for the game and playing with each other."

"At the end of the day they say it's the teamwork, right?"

"Yeah, that and learning the fundamentals of the game."

"But ain't nothing wrong with winning too." Sherman chuckled. "I'll see you next week."

Portia and I rode home recapping the game. No sooner than we were in the house, she dropped her bag at the base of the stairs and ran straight to Jasmine in the kitchen.

"Guess what?"

"What?" Jasmine was wiping her hands on a dish cloth when I rounded the corner.

"We won the game today!" Portia squealed.

Jasmine's face lit up.

"GT, I mean Coach T—that's what I'm supposed to call her on the court…"

Jasmine looked at me with a sly grin.

"…She said we're going to win more games too."

"Coach T?" Jasmine smirked as I leaned in for a kiss.

I shrugged.

Portia had her hands on both hips and squatted, imitating me, I thought.

"Listen to me, play your own game," Portia ordered. "We can beat these girls. Be ready! Portia, you pass the ball to Ashley. And Ashley, shoot your shot." She pounded her fist against her other hand.

I was amused listening to her commentary and watching her reenactment.

"What happened?" Jasmine asked me.

"How about Sherman didn't get to the gym until after the game was over—at least that's when I saw him."

"What?"

"Yeah, I coached the entire game."

"Wow! That's huge. Congratulations, you two."

"Thank you!" Portia and I responded in unison.

"That's the first win, right? Alright, Coach!" Jasmine shimmied her shoulders and leaned in for another kiss.

"You know I told you before, Sherman's coaching could use an upgrade. The kids are new to the game. He needs to focus on the fundamentals for crying out loud."

Jasmine pointed at Portia. "That was funny. Is that how you were behaving?"

"The kid is exaggerating." I stuck my tongue out at Portia.

"Nuh unh!" she protested.

"I wasn't squatting. I was coaching."

Portia giggled.

"What are you in here cooking?" I lifted the lid off a pot.

"Girl, if you don't get away from my food…" Jasmine nudged me with her hip, but I didn't move very far. "You haven't washed your hands…now move."

"Oh, my God, we're turning into my parents," I said.

The sudden realization was sobering and hilarious. When Jasmine and I started dating, it was moments like this that I hadn't known I was missing in my life. Moments of levity. Moments of genuine human connection.

"That's not a bad thing, is it? They've been together what, nearly fifty years? They're my ideal couple," Jasmine said.

"Really? What about your parents?" I wasn't surprised, some days Mr. and Mrs. Charles acted like they didn't even like one another.

"Not!" Jasmine scoffed. "Please move, Teresa." Jasmine bumped me again. "You still haven't washed your hands. Or do I have to call you Coach T too?"

"Don't say nothing when you throw your hip out. You got jokes *and* using my government name?" I stole another kiss, because I could, and went to sit in the breakfast nook next to Portia. "We haven't seen you since this morning, how was your day?"

"It was good…busy.

"Hmmm." I didn't know what to make of Jasmine's response.

She turned away from the stove to look at me. "I have a proposition for you."

"Should we be talking about propositions in front of the child?" I wiggled my eyebrows.

Portia giggled. Not much got past her.

"No, silly, it's a work proposition."

I poked my lips out, disappointed.

"Can you take some more pictures for me? I need a few of another family. We're redoing a gallery wall at the office and overhauling the website to highlight our wonderful families more."

"Sure."

"Your name will be on the photographer citation too."

"That's cool. Is this a paying gig or is the promo placement a bennie thanks to my close relationship with the Director of Community Development?"

Jasmine smiled and tilted her head to the side. A piece of hair fell out of her messy ponytail. Yep. It was the simple pleasures for me. "Perhaps I can get approval for a very small stipend. Portia, go wash up."

"Okay." She went skipping off. "I'm going to tell Mommy about our game."

"And then maybe we can see how to parlay that into something else. You should get washed up too."

I joined Jasmine at the stove. "Parlay into something else, huh?" I drawled. "I could parlay this into something else." I held her waist from behind and nuzzled her ear.

"Girl, stop! I'm trying to finish dinner. And have you forgotten we have a child here?"

"You can be quiet—I know you can be quiet." I pinched Jasmine on her behind and left out the kitchen, almost tripping over the pile of stuff at the base of the stairs.

"Portia, come get your shoes and this bag and take them down to the basement where they belong."

"Okay," Portia yelled back.

"And make sure your uniform makes it to the hamper."

"Yes, Coach GT!"

Everybody had jokes.

CHAPTER TWENTY-THREE

Jasmine

It was hard to think of celebrating when there was so much heaviness in the air. Mainly because Leslie was not doing well with her revised course of chemotherapy. But I was determined to have a small birthday party for Portia. After all, she was going into double digits, as my father liked to say. I asked what kind of celebration she wanted, and considering our Halloween experience, I expected an extravagant request.

She didn't disappoint—Portia wanted a tea party. She created handmade invitations with minor assistance from T, and invited two other girls, Sarah, a neighbor's daughter up the street, and, not surprisingly, Quetta. Portia and Quetta had become friends, talking periodically on the phone, and inviting each other to events.

On the day of the party, I picked each girl up and we went to a tea shop in Ellicott City. It was a cute, dainty place and a great location for a ten-year-old's birthday celebration. I took pictures of the three of them decked out in lacy gloves and hats, along with feathery boas wrapped around their necks. The owner was even kind enough to provide a gift bag for each child with bags of tea and honey sticks.

After it was over, I dropped everyone back home, ruefully thinking how it would have been a perfect day for an afternoon date with T. Instead, Portia and I stopped to get matzo ball soup from a local deli on Smith Avenue—I was convinced the soup was good for whatever was ailing you—and we went to see Leslie.

I now had the entrance code to the lobby and a key to Leslie's condo so she wouldn't have to expend unnecessary energy shuffling to the door and I hated to think about the possibility, an emergency. Leslie tried hard to appear upbeat, but she wasn't. Her appetite wasn't good, and I knew she was often nauseated, which meant her face had started to appear gaunt. This was the third week of her every-week chemo schedule and my friend could no longer mask her sickness.

Seeing her in bed and not her usual spot on the couch made my chest feel tight. Her complexion was ashen, her lips looked dry, and she had definitely lost a few more pounds since the last time I had taken her to the hospital for a treatment. That time, we stopped to look around the hospital's gift shop. It was well-appointed with well-meaning gifts like bathing suits with prostheses, special bras, and turbans to protect heads that no longer had hair. But Leslie had nixed all of that. Sick though she may have been, my friend still tried to maintain her fashion sense.

"All the fabric I have at home," she said at the time. "Nope, I'll keep wrapping my head."

Now, as she waved us inside, Leslie had her head wrapped in a beautiful crimson and gray scarf. She had lost her shoulder-length hair back in October.

"Mommy, that's pretty." Portia touched the fabric. "I want to wear a wrap."

Leslie looked at her and tried a brave smile.

"Happy Birthday, baby. You don't have to wear a wrap—your hair is beautiful."

"Thank you, Mommy."

"What have you been putting on her hair?" Leslie asked me.

"You know I'm old school, that bergamot-smelling grease in the blue jar."

Leslie laughed, but that led to a coughing fit. "Portia, go get the handheld mirror under my bathroom sink and bring me the bag on the closet floor." Leslie pointed to the hall closet.

Portia came back with a bag stuffed with fabric and pulled out some pieces she liked. Leslie patiently taught her how to make a simple headwrap. I found some fabric that I thought was beautiful and let Portia practice on me. When she was finished with her creation, I held up the hand mirror.

"I can rock this on a bad hair day," I said without thinking. Immediately I regretted not being able to retract my words and apologized.

"No need, chica." Leslie said. "My bad hair days are due to chemo."

"True."

"They won't all be bad." Leslie feigned a smile.

"Amen. You know it'll come back." I wanted to be hopeful. "Both your mom's and Angel's did."

"Yeah, speaking of Angel…" She patted Portia on the back. "Go look in Aunt Angel's room, she left you something on her bed."

Portia disappeared down the hallway and returned a minute later with a package wrapped in beautiful foil paper.

"What is it?" Leslie grunted as she lifted herself a little higher on her pillows to get a better look while Portia unwrapped her gift, something in a frame.

Portia turned the frame toward her mother. It was an endearing picture of Portia and Angel at a beach, Portia covering Angel in sand with a small shovel.

"Where is Aunt Angel?" she asked.

"On vacation in Belize."

"Belize? She's not slowed down at all, huh?" I shook my head.

I wondered what we were missing in Belize. I thought of T's department chair, who had retired suddenly and said he was going to Belize.

"Nope, said she wanted to go, found some kind of flight and hotel package deal, and the next thing I knew, she was on her way there.

"With who?" I was curious.

"I think she went alone."

"Hmmm…okay. It was nice of her to leave a gift."

Leslie deliberately inhaled but didn't respond.

"Let's take a picture with our scarves on," I suggested, wanting to shift the energy in the room.

All of us posed and posed some more. I even set the timer on my little Kodak digital camera and ran to get in some frames. Taking pictures wasn't my strong suit. All too often, my photos unintentionally included ceiling fans, floors with shoes, and my thumb. But I hoped the photos of Portia and Leslie together, and especially those with Portia holding her cupcake with a lit candle, would be nice. Memorializing this birthday for Portia was more important than my pitiful photography skills.

CHAPTER TWENTY-FOUR

T

The turtleneck, hat, scarf, and peacoat I wore, though practical for late January, were making my skin itch. It was a Friday night in the middle of a Baltimore winter. Most folks hibernated until at least March, including me. But I was feeling lonely and jaded, so I had agreed to meet John at The Gallery, one of his favorite bars. The drinks were strong and reasonable, or so I was told. And people turned up for the extended happy hour.

"Aww, what's the matter, being in a committed relationship is hard?" John said after his second drink. He had been making snarky remarks since we had sat down at the bar, and he wasn't making me feel better.

"Stop, I'm serious. I want to be included in the decision-making, at least be consulted about some of these huge decisions that have turned our lives upside down."

Now that Jasmine and I had taken over major child-raising duties, there seemed to be some new thing to deal with practically every week. But Jasmine all too often moved ahead with things without even letting me know beforehand what was going on.

I hadn't been in a bar in a minute, and I looked around to see who was up in there. I noticed the holiday decorations still up, mainly because it was The Gallery, and The Gallery was festive year-round. Unlike my mood at the moment.

"Would your input be helpful to Jasmine, or are you complaining about things you have no control over?" John signaled the bartender for another drink.

"It absolutely would be helpful and I'm complaining…"

John folded his arms and cleared his throat.

"I should have a say about the little person we're caring for or about a father who doesn't pick up his child as scheduled."

"And then what? Are you going to stop giving care? Are you going to drop the child off somewhere when he doesn't come?"

"I'm just saying—"

"What are you saying?" John wasn't giving me an inch.

"I don't know what you two are talking about…" someone interrupted.

A woman with a blonde pixie cut and a slight slur had suddenly barged into our conversation.

"…but I'm saying…you're cute, and you should buy me a drink."

The woman leaned on my shoulder.

I shifted my body, so she was no longer lying on me. "How about we start with 'hello'?"

I looked at John. *Seriously?*

"Well, helllloooo," she complied. "I remember you."

"Do you now?" I asked, trying to control my irritation.

"You used to drive a cute little car." She ran her finger along my collarbone. I shifted again. "You were seeing a friend of mine, but it's all good 'cause she doesn't live in Baltimore anymore."

Good lord, I thought, *that could have been any number of women.* BJ—Before Jasmine—monogamy wasn't exactly my specialty.

"I'd like a gin and tonic…with your cute self and beautiful eyes." Blondie giggled.

Out of the corner of my eye I saw John tapping his finger on the bar. It was only a matter of time before he was going to read Ms. Buy-Me-a-Drink. He couldn't stand being interrupted in general, but back in the day, it wasn't unusual for our time together to include women coming up and hitting on me.

"Darling," he drawled in three long syllables, spinning his barstool around to face her head on. "This cutie has a girlfriend and a child, and she drives a minivan."

"Wait! What?!" My head snapped in his direction. That certainly wasn't the response I had expected to enjoy.

"I'm sorry…" I held up my hand to the woman. "We're just trying to catch up. Maybe next time."

"Oh, don't worry about it…Mami," she said over her shoulder as she sashayed away.

"You know that was wrong and uncalled for," I whined, still burning a little over John's description of me.

"What part wasn't true?"

I rolled my eyes.

"What did you drive to Savannah?" John took another sip.

"You know that was a rental."

"For real though, I hear you, but what are your options?"

I felt my shoulders slump.

"You love Jasmine." He wasn't wrong about that. "T and Jasmine sitting in a tree, first comes marriage, then comes the baby carriage."

My eyebrows met in the middle of my forehead.

"I think I missed some words, but you know what I'm saying." He was delighted with himself, laughing and hiccupping at the same time.

"I am not amused."

"Okay. I'm sorry." John was still laughing. "Go home, tell Jasmine you two need to make decisions and plans *as a couple*."

"That's it? That's all you got?"

"What else do you want me to say?"

I shrugged and sighed.

"You've been complaining off and on for two hours about something you all have been doing for the last five months," John went on.

"But—"

"And apparently doing it such that the child is still alive, and you still have a girlfriend. You really want to do something different?"

"Yes."

"Then paint! You haven't mentioned any work lately. No commissions, no shows, nothing. Do something that satisfies you."

CHAPTER TWENTY-FIVE

Jasmine

I was feeling pretty proud of myself for a Monday, especially during a dreary February. Everything was firing on all cylinders. I was already in the pickup line to get Portia and my morning meeting with Jason had gone well. The ReBuild Baltimore family albums had been a hit and I heard that other state affiliates might be replicating our efforts.

Half of the credit belonged to T for taking fabulous photos, spurred by ReBuild's budget cuts. Jason suggested that I would likely receive an invitation to speak at the regional directors' meeting coming up in late summer. Office gossip said the summer company meeting was really a vacation for lucky staff members and their families, and I was already thinking how much I would love to get away for a few days—just me and T. But before I could dwell longer on that my phone rang. It was Leslie.

"Hey, chica, what's up?" I asked.

Leslie often called during the ride home or early evening to catch up with Portia. The calls kept her in the loop during real time. She was calling early today though. Portia wouldn't come out for another twenty minutes or so.

"Hola, and not sure what's up. Dr. Jordan's scheduler called and asked me to come to the office today or first thing tomorrow morning."

"I'm in the pickup line. We can come pick you up and head downtown today, but tomorrow morning would be better. Unless there's a chance Angel can drive you?"

"Let's not talk about Angel's incapacity, or unwillingness, or whatever the hell it is, to help me. I can't go there today, that's a therapy conversation."

"Well, I can scoop you up tomorrow, drop Portia off at school, then we can head downtown. Did she say what's up?"

"No, I don't know what the good doctor's going to say, so tomorrow sounds better. It's probably safer if Portia doesn't go to the hospital with us."

"Angel…so noted. Okay, I'll be there by seven-fifteen. What's the story for Portia tomorrow, since we're picking you up?"

"I'm keeping it simple—we're going to the doctor's office. I'm certainly not going to try to tell a story before it happens."

"Okay." I tried to keep my heavy sigh from being audible, but my sweating palms made me realize I was gripping the steering wheel, and the car wasn't even moving. "Okay, God…" I whispered to myself, needing to put this into the universe, "no bad news tomorrow."

***

God apparently hadn't heard my petition the previous day. At the appointment, I tried to maintain a neutral face when Dr. Jordan repeated, "The tumors are no longer responding to the chemo cocktail." She directed our attention to different images projected on a side wall. "This is from August last year, another from November past, January, and…" She pointed to the last one. "The imaging from last week."

"Is there any good news in what I'm seeing?" Leslie asked.

I kept looking at all four images, hoping for a better summary.

"The good news is they aren't growing."

"I know what this means." Leslie pointed to the last scan. "They aren't shrinking yet either. Right?"

"That's right. We need to adjust the cocktail."

"To what? I can hardly keep anything down now and I've lost at least forty pounds."

"I'm proposing we go with a two-pronged approach—we need to start radiation sooner."

Leslie closed her eyes. I wasn't sure she was listening anymore, but she was rapidly twiddling her thumbs in her lap. I realized Dr. Jordan was probably comfortable with me now because she kept talking.

"We'll limit it to a concentrated area to prevent spread and change the chemo to something more tumor-specific."

I shook my head.

"There are two studies at the American Research Center, or ARC, in Bethesda concentrating on immunotherapy and cancer protein cells. Both will be accepting patients soon. I'd like your permission to send in an application for you."

I touched Leslie's forearm to bring her mind back from wherever it had wandered.

"You don't even have to ask—I said upfront that I need to live. So, whatever we have to do."

Dr. Jordan leaned against her desk, focused squarely on Leslie.

"When do I start radiation?" Leslie asked.

"Tomorrow if you can and then for nine consecutive days. It'll probably take you longer to get here and park than the actual radiation session."

Leslie nodded.

"I do recommend that you have support at home after the first few treatments, in order to monitor your radiation response."

Leslie looked at me, asking a silent question.

"You can stay with us…in my office or in the room with Portia or we can get you set up in your own space in the basement."

Leslie sucked her bottom lip in and jutted her chin upwards. I had known her long enough to know she was processing the moment and swallowing back tears. I threaded my fingers with hers as tears rolled down her cheeks and she ran her tongue over her front teeth.

"Okay, we have a plan." Leslie let out the heaviest sigh.

A half hour later, as we were standing in the hospital lobby where this saga had first begun, Leslie insisted on taking a cab back home. She said she hadn't used any of the oncology transportation vouchers the department had given her. Normally, I would have pushed back, but I didn't argue since I was already halfway to work and I needed to talk to T, considering I had just committed us to something else. Surely, she would understand how I'd felt compelled to say "yes" right away—wouldn't she?

CHAPTER TWENTY-SIX

T

I knew something was up when Jasmine sent a text message asking that we meet for an early dinner at T.K.'s. Jasmine wasn't a fan of being out on the roads when the temperature dipped, and these days it got dark around five in the afternoon. Like a lot of people, she just wanted to get home after work and avoid slick spots that could easily turn to black ice.

Jasmine said Portia was going to a classmate's house and she would pick her up from there after dinner. That was my second red flag. Jasmine liked to screen all homes that Portia was going to visit—chalk it up to her social work background. She was a trust-but-verify kind of woman.

Before last August, I wouldn't have thought anything of a dinner out during the week. We liked making dinner together at home, but being served a meal was a secret pleasure of mine. I liked having a well-presented plate of food placed in front of me. If a beautiful woman happened to bring the plate? Bonus!

So I was sitting at my favorite table by the time Jasmine arrived.

"Hey, babe, you been here long?" Jasmine gave me a cursory peck on the cheek before sitting across from me.

"No, just a few minutes. How was your day?"

"Not bad, busy. Are the guys here?" She fidgeted with the menu and looked around as if we hadn't been here dozens of times.

"I don't know, I didn't ask for Terrence or Kevin. I'm surprised you left work on time, relatively speaking."

"Me too." She didn't look up, enamored with a menu she was already familiar with.

"You and Portia left the house pretty early this morning. Didn't you have an appointment with Leslie today?"

"Yes, I did." Jasmine finally looked up and our eyes locked. "About the appointment…but let's wait and order first."

What now? I motioned our server over to take our orders. As the server left, another young man brought a basket of bread and herb-seasoned dipping oil.

"Hmmm…bread is still my weakness," Jasmine purred.

It hadn't been long ago that I would have responded with a sultry, "I thought I was your weakness." Now I just smiled and waited—whatever was on her mind had her discombobulated.

"T, I know the last six months haven't been easy."

"No, they have not," I agreed with a nod.

"The appointment this morning was about Leslie's condition."

"What's going on?" I could feel my heart pumping in high gear.

"According to Dr. Jordan, the tumors aren't responding to the chemo anymore."

"I'm so sorry to hear that, but what does that mean exactly?"

"Leslie needs to start radiation sooner than later."

"Okay…" I still didn't know what that meant for me or for us.

"And they're going to change the chemo medication. They don't want to see the tumors grow any larger, so they need to find a combination that keeps shrinking them."

"Okay, change of plans, radiation." I swished a tea bag around in my mug even though my drink was steeped sufficiently. I needed something to do with my hands.

"Radiation starts tomorrow."

I suddenly felt blood rushing upward, my temples throbbed.

"The plan is for Leslie to use the oncology vouchers when needed to transport her back and forth to the hospital."

"Okay." What was she not saying? "Is there anything else?"

Jasmine was holding onto her mug for dear life, with both hands, as if it were giving her strength.

"The radiation, at least initially, is likely to be harsh."

"And?"

"And she shouldn't be home alone."

"How does this change what we've been doing?" I needed Jasmine to just come out with whatever she was trying to say, plain and simple. And finally, it came.

"Leslie is going to stay in my home office for a few days," she said bluntly.

"Is that a question or a statement?"

"It's—"

"Better yet, have you already committed to this?"

"Yes," Jasmine said, her voice barely above a whisper.

"When is she coming?" The blood rushing to my head made me light-headed. I hadn't thought this situation could get worse.

"I'm going to pick her and Portia up on the way home."

"Tonight?" I raised my voice.

"Yes." Jasmine looked up at the server who put our food on the table. "Thank you."

"Thank you for sharing the information." I pushed all the air I could out of my nostrils.

"Is that all you're going to say?"

"What do you want me to say, Jasmine?" I heard myself retort, even slightly louder this time, which was confirmed by some gawking wait staff and a few other patrons.

"You merely informed me that someone else is moving into our house. And not just anyone, but someone who requires a lot of help."

"You think I should have said no?"

"None of this conversation matters, Jasmine. You already told her yes." Jasmine stared at me. "You're only telling me so that I know she'll be there for breakfast or I notice there's more clothes in the laundry, or when I'm walking around, I need to have clothes on, although I changed that when the kid moved in." I really didn't have any more to say. Or, maybe I did. Yet if I said anything more, I knew it wouldn't go well. I gestured for our server. "Would you bring me the check and a container please?"

"So that's it?"

"I'm not sure what else you want me to say."

"Say something," Jasmine pleaded.

"What? That I don't like it? You've already decided for us."

"Babe, they need us right now."

"I need us too." I threw my napkin on the table—I needed to put some distance in between us before I said something I'd regret. "I'll see you at the house."

***

Leslie had been with us for a week while getting radiation, and in that short time, some puffiness and discoloration had developed on her neck. Although I wasn't thrilled about and at times downright detested all the changes in our household, I wasn't an asshole. If ever I found myself in a position like Leslie, I pray I had someone as kind as Jasmine to help me. But all the extra responsibilities at home and work had nudged my normal routine aside.

I was hoping to get a run in before Portia's game that evening. However, a protracted meeting with school administrators, concerning the still-vacant department chair position, didn't go as planned. They claimed they would find someone soon. To my mind, though, finding someone required action, such as actually advertising the position. I knew full well that hadn't happened. I kindly reminded them that six months had gone by, which meant I expected to be compensated, in addition to shedding the 'interim' title. The temporary bump in pay was nice but I wanted leadership to make a bloody decision. The last quarter of school was soon to begin.

Now, I had just enough time to get home and change out of the slacks and sweater I'd worn to work and into something more comfortable for shouting plays and blowing off steam.

As I walked into the house and rounded the corner to the kitchen, I was surprised to see Leslie sitting in the breakfast nook, soaking up a little afternoon sun. Coco was sitting next to her, which explained why she hadn't greeted me at the door. "Hey, you're up. How are you feeling?"

"Pretty rough. I wasn't expecting anyone home yet. I needed to get out of bed and walk for a few minutes."

"I can't even imagine."

"It's still beautiful outside, even during the winter." Leslie was scoping out the garden in the back.

"Yeah, your friend takes pride in her yard."

"I made myself a cup of ginger tea."

"That tea is great." I pointed to the box. "You know Jasmine, she tries to keep things stocked to make you feel better."

"I appreciate everything she, and you, have done for us."

"No thanks needed."

"Yes, absolutely thanks are needed. T, my daughter adores you."

"Why, because of my pleasing personality?" I chuckled and leaned my butt against the cabinet while I bit into an apple.

"She's adopted you as her godmother too." The corners of Leslie's eyes crinkled. "She calls you GT, for goodness sakes. The support you've provided is seen and appreciated."

"It's no problem, really."

"You've helped her develop more confidence than I've ever seen in her."

"Well, we need to watch out 'cause seems like she had plenty of confidence when she got here."

Leslie smiled through eyes underlined by dark circles.

"Have you ever thought about letting her go to public school?"

"Yeah, Paul and I talked about it, but the scholarship money we get because he's a firefighter is so significant that we thought it would be a good opportunity for her."

"Being at St. Josephine's definitely offers opportunities for exposure."

Leslie nodded. "The kids at St. Jo's get excited about summering in Europe, not waiting for public pools to open. Hell, sometimes I've had to remind Portia that we don't own horses for her to ride."

"That's funny…I believe it. That Halloween party at the estate…" I put my pinky up, "…was illuminating."

"You two aren't slouches…evening tea?" Leslie lifted one eyebrow. "Since being here my child talks about having this very special 'evening tea.' She didn't have 'high tea' at home. It's like her grownup time to talk."

"Ain't nobody expecting high tea in the low country. But come to think of it, last week Portia found a recipe for tea cookies and asked that we make them."

"Right? Y'all got—"

"No ma'am, not y'all…Again, thank your friend," I interjected.

Leslie sucked her teeth. "Y'all got my daughter talking about recipes for tea cookies or as she called them, 'biscuits.'" She said the word with a lilted accent.

"She does have an eye and taste for the finer things in life." I giggled.

Leslie laughed and started coughing, hard, like she couldn't catch her breath.

"Hey, hey, you okay?" I threw the apple core in the trash and moved in beside her.

"I'm not sure, I'm starting to feel dizzy again."

"Okay, let me help you back upstairs."

"No, I'm fine." She swayed when she stood.

"Yeah, okay…not so much."

Leslie leaned on me as we gradually made our way up the stairs. Her face had a sheen and she was sweating slightly from the exertion of negotiating the steps. In her makeshift bedroom, I fluffed the pillows and helped Leslie get settled in bed.

"Do you need anything?" I checked my watch.

"I would like fifty more years please. I'd settle for thirty if fifty is too selfish."

Woah. I swallowed—my mouth was suddenly too dry. "I hear you. I'm on team fifty."

"No actually, I do need a favor. A request really."

"What's up?" My heart lodged somewhere between my chest and my throat.

"I want to take some pictures, and on that same day we take the pictures I want to pen a letter to Portia."

"Umm, like a picture diary?"

"I'd like to think of it as a memory journal," Leslie said. "I need to make sure my daughter knows my thoughts for her as she becomes a young woman, goes to college, has children…all of it."

"If you're talking about memories, does that mean you're not sure about living?" I propped myself against the door jam. I seemed to be doing more of that lately, my body in search of something solid to hold it up.

"Living and dying are all I think about, it's a cancer thing."

I swallowed again. "When do you want to get started?" I asked with a hitch in my voice. "On the memory journal, that is?"

"Another day. I feel like hot garbage today, and I'm sure I look like it too."

"Can I make a recommendation?"

"Sure." Leslie winced and sunk further into the pillows.

"Take the pictures on whatever day you decide is picture day—don't wait until you feel good. Every day is not a great day, but you can make it a bit better depending on your perspective."

Leslie nodded and grabbed a tissue from the nightstand.

"We can capture that. And most of all, you'll give Portia the gift of your own words in writing."

I watched her take a deep breath before blowing her nose. "I'll bring a good camera from my studio and be ready whenever you are."

"Thanks, T, for everything. I mean it."

"You're welcome," I said, closing the door as I left the room.

I had barely made it to my and Jasmine's bedroom before the flood of emotions that I felt coursing through my veins spilled out in the form of tears. I wanted to punch a wall and cower in a corner at the same time. Leslie's and Portia's situation seemed so unfair and it sucked. The pain and despair Leslie was experiencing. The disruption she and Portia had been enduring. The uncertainty. The fragility of life. All of it. Sucked.

CHAPTER TWENTY-SEVEN

Jasmine

Late in February, ringing jarred me awake. I squinted at the clock—it was three-thirty in the morning. Nothing good ever came of phone calls that early. "Hello?"

"Jasmine, you need to come to the hospital now." The panic in my mother's voice made sure I was fully awake.

"What's wrong?"

"Jasmine, come to the hospital now, it's your father. They think he had a heart attack."

"Where are you?"

"Hope Springs…in the emergency room. They just wheeled him out for more tests. Jasmine, he was barely conscious."

"I'm on my way."

"I'm calling Robin and J.R. Hurry!"

"Mom—"

She hung up so abruptly I didn't have a chance to ask any more questions. *Sweet Jesus!* Hope Springs had a cardiac unit so I knew they would be better prepared for emergency surgery, but this could go either way. Although these days Daddy didn't work out like he once had, he walked almost every day. A heart attack? As I grabbed a pair of pants and a shirt that were draped across a bedroom chair, I heard T stir.

"Who was that?" She sat up. "Where are you going?"

"My mother, she's…they're at the hospital. My father had a heart attack, or at least my mother thinks he had a heart attack."

I was fully dressed now and heading out the bedroom.

"Hold up. I'll go with you."

"Let's drive separately in case I need to take my mom home."

"What about you?" T whispered, aware of our house guests. She pulled a pair of sweats out of the dresser.

"I'm fine."

"No, you aren't." T shot me a look. "Your shirt is inside out, and your buttons aren't fastened correctly." She threw the head scarf she had been wearing on the dresser. "Let me drive you."

"Okay, hurry up and get dressed."

T drove with a purpose and, thankfully, there was no traffic and the roads had been mostly cleared of snow from yesterday's storm. We got to the hospital in eight minutes and rounded the emergency room's circular drive.

"I'm going to jump out and go in while you park."

"Okay, I'll meet you in the waiting room."

Before heading inside, my sister Robin came running from the direction of the parking garage. "Have you been in yet?"

"No, I just got here too."

We approached the security desk. "Hi, my father's here, Robert Charles," I said to the guy behind the desk, my voice more rushed than I wanted it to be. "What room is he in please?"

Robin stood beside me, saying nothing.

He finally looked up from his phone, unbothered. "Are you two together?" He sighed.

"Yes, this is my sister," we said at the same time.

He pecked on a computer keyboard, presumably looking for our father's location. Then he leisurely came from behind the desk, told the staff at the triage desk he'd be right back, and scanned his badge over an access panel. "I'm going to take you back to the ED."

My feet felt like they were stuck in ten inches of mud and my knees were wobbling so bad it took all my strength to follow him. I knew I'd be able to see better if I could keep my eyes open but I was also blinking back tears. I thought about T, how she would come into the hospital and wonder where we were, but she'd be fine. At the moment, I just needed to get to Daddy.

Security guy led us down a beige, sterile hallway that stretched forever, till finally he opened the door to a little room that was clearly not the emergency room waiting area.

"No, we want to see our father," Robin insisted. "In the emergency room, or wherever he is."

"Ma'am, please have a seat." The guard motioned to some chairs.

"No. Where's my mother?" I demanded.

At that moment, our mother ambled into the room, escorted by another guard. Aww, hell! My stomach flipped. The presence of another person in a uniform made me even more anxious than I already was.

"Mom, what's going on?" I asked.

"I don't know. I was sitting in an ER room just around the corner. I don't know how long I was in there but they asked me to come in here."

"Was Daddy with you?" My hands were shaking and I deliberately inhaled and exhaled slowly, trying to stay calm—to little avail. My heart felt like it was going to beat right out of my chest, and I could feel a throbbing pulse in my neck and behind my eyes. This wasn't good. Why were we by ourselves in this stale-smelling, dull room coated in 1980s mauve?

"At first he was," Mom answered. "But they rushed him out to work on him, and that's when I called you."

Robin hugged Mom. "What happened? I mean, at home?"

Except for her bedtime headscarf, I wouldn't have known my mother wasn't on her way to teach Sunday school. Emergency or not, Catherine Charles was going to be put together.

"He shoveled the walk around midday yesterday. Afterwards, he said he felt a bit tired so he laid down for a while. But everything seemed fine during dinner and when we went to bed. He woke up, said his chest was tight and that he didn't feel well. I thought he had gas. He went to the bathroom and then I heard him downstairs in the kitchen, getting water, I suppose. I went down to check on him. And…"

Robin and I listened intently—Mom was virtually whispering.

"And next thing I know, he was throwing up and collapsed."

Robin put one hand over her mouth and held onto our mother's hand with the other.

"I called 911 and the operator had me give him CPR until paramedics arrived."

From outside the room where we waited came the sound of shoes squeaking on linoleum. The footsteps got louder, then stopped. We all turned when the door opened. A man in navy blue scrubs and a white lab coat, along with yet another security guard, stepped just barely into the room. It wasn't uncommon for hospital security to be present in certain situations. But now I knew why we were here, away from other people in the emergency room. There was only one reason two people came to talk to us. *Shit!*

"Mrs. Charles?" The man in scrubs asked, surveying all of us.

"I'm Mrs. Charles." Mom stood up from the pleather loveseat she was sitting on. Robin jumped up too.

"I'm Dr. Heche." The doctor stood there a moment unmoving, hands in his coat pockets, then he continued.

"Your husband had an MI, a heart attack." He spoke calmly, as if he hadn't just delivered life-altering news. "He had a blockage in his largest artery."

"What?" both Robin and I blurted.

"We were unable to stabilize him." We all stared at this stranger who, I was pretty sure, wasn't speaking English. "I'm sorry, it happened very quickly."

"No!" Mom let out a high-pitched, blood-curdling scream that I would only describe as the physical manifestation of her heart breaking. It made my own heart drop into my stomach. Her body swayed slightly as Robin tried to hold her up. I ran to her other side and we both lowered Mom back onto the loveseat before she had a chance to crumble to the floor. "I need to see him," she sobbed.

"We'll take you back to spend some time with your husband. The nurses will want to talk to you as well about Mr. Charles' remains. But take all the time you need." Dr. Heche said, before backing out of the room along with the guard.

We followed the doctor to a room where Daddy was lying on a bed. He looked at peace, like he was sleeping. Mom laid her head on his chest, perhaps checking for a heartbeat because…why wouldn't she? But Daddy didn't move. It was surreal to not see my father at least reach to comfort his wife. We eased her into the bedside chair where she stayed, with us alongside her, until she became limp and her sobs grew softer.

Finally, Mom was ready to leave. The three of us walked back to the lobby, Mom still supported between me and Robin. When we had arrived at the hospital three hours earlier, I had been in such a hurry that I hadn't noticed the frigid air or how eerily quiet it was for an emergency room. It was nothing like the ERs depicted on television shows, which made me feel all the more numb. But there was T, waiting for us. Tears pooled in my eyes when I saw her, and a sense of relief washed over me.

"What happened back there?" T asked as she approached and stroked my arms. "The guard said only family was allowed back there, so I've been unsuccessfully reading two-year-old magazines and worried sick."

"He's dead!" I cried. "My father is dead!"

"Oh my god! Jasmine, I'm so sorry." T hugged me tight.

"He died. He had a heart attack." The tears I had been trying to hold back slid down my cheeks. T pulled me even closer to her, the familiar comfort of her warmth and the smell of shea butter grounding me. I found the breath to continue. "A nurse told us that the kind of blockage my father had was so large that survival is usually unlikely. It's a condition they call the "widow maker.""

"Baby, I'm so sorry."

I sank a bit deeper into T's embrace.

After only a few seconds of solace, I was startled by my mother's screeching.

"What are you doing here?" Mom demanded. She had been mute as Robin and I had practically carried her out to the waiting room. Now she was pointing at me and T.

T's body tensed but she didn't respond.

"Lower your voice, Mother," I hissed. "She brought me here."

"She has no right to be here."

"Are you seriously questioning why T is here?"

"Indeed I am."

"You called in the middle of the night from the hospital. I didn't know what was what, whether you'd need a ride or not, or even if I should drive myself. Shouldn't my girlfriend be with me?"

"Well, I'm not riding with you." My mother hiked her purse up on her shoulder and pulled her coat tighter around herself. "Robin will take me home."

"That's ridiculous, that's not on her way home," I countered.

"I'll take her." Robin threw up her hands. "We don't have to do this now or here. Where's J.R.?"

"He didn't answer his phone," Mom replied, but she wasn't done projecting her ire at T. "This is a family situation, Jasmine."

I looked at Robin, my lips pursed. "I'll try to reach J.R. on the way home." I appreciated T being there and respected her even more for not reacting to my mother's disrespectful outburst. But I was not T. "She. Is. My. Family."

T put her hands on my shoulders and gently pulled me away from a confrontation I was stunned to be having. A confrontation my mother was focused on having— about my relationship. In a hospital emergency room. And only an hour after her husband of fifty-plus years had died.

"Come on, let me get you home," T whispered to me. She hugged me to her body again and led me toward the parking garage before a bigger scene unfolded. But I was incensed.

"Mother," I shouted over my shoulder, "you are shameful!"

CHAPTER TWENTY-EIGHT

T

The dreadful week that Jasmine's father died was unreal. Jasmine initially tried to maintain the schedule she had created between Leslie's treatments, Portia's activities, and work, but when I found her curled up in bed in the fetal position one night sobbing, I knew something had to give. It was all too much. I encouraged her to request a few weeks off from work to help her mother with the countless details required to arrange her dad's service and deal with so much else. Her boss Jason didn't hesitate, which was incredibly helpful. So, Jasmine stayed at her parents' house for the remainder of the week.

Over that week, I stopped by there a couple of nights to check on her and to bring a few items, like her phone charger. Her childhood homie, Stephanie, and I worked in the kitchen and on cleaning duty the nights we were both there together. Surprisingly, considering Stephanie wasn't a member of the Teresa Butler Fan Club, we made a good team, keeping the living and dining rooms tidy along with juggling the massive amounts of food neighbors and friends brought over.

When Jasmine and I had a chance to talk late at night, I heard about the latest arguments she and Ms. Catherine had had, mostly concerning the details of Mr. Charles' homegoing service: who would speak, the design of the floral casket spray, the casket cost. I personally had never experienced planning a funeral and didn't know the difference between a casket spray, a standing spray, or a casket insert. I just listened.

From my vantage point, the biggest argument they had was about where I would fit into the family processional. On its face, this minutia seemed rather trivial. Jasmine wanted me close, rightfully so, and I wanted to be next to her to offer support. But honestly, I didn't need to sit on the front pew. I let Jasmine know that I was absolutely okay sitting behind her or wherever she wanted me to sit. My exclusion in seating arrangements was completely on brand for Jasmine's mother. Whenever an occasion arose for me and Jasmine to gather with her family, you could count on death, taxes, and Ms. Catherine invoking God, Jesus, the Holy Spirit, the Virgin Mary, and Pontius Pilate as excuses to debase our relationship in general and me specifically.

A year after Jasmine and I had started dating, Mr. Charles retired from the Baltimore City Police Department. Ms. Catherine didn't want me at the celebration at all, even initially refusing to allow me to sit at the "reserved" table. She acquiesced only after Mr. Charles stepped in and pointed out a glaring hypocrisy. J.R.'s girlfriend of a whopping three months would be sitting next to him. I found two things baffling though. One, Jasmine had been gay a long time—her ten-year relationship with a woman before we met was exhibit A. And two, she was forty-one years old. This wasn't a phase.

But to the matter at hand, Mrs. Charles wanted a small funeral at their church. Jasmine wanted a ceremony that would honor Mr. Charles' three decades of service both to the BCPD and the church family. Each stood fast in their determination to see their funeral ideas fulfilled. Meanwhile, Jasmine's siblings were caught in the middle and didn't care either way. They just wanted to bury their father in peace. Ultimately, the BCPD chaplain and their pastor provided a celebration of life program that satisfied both strong-willed Charles women.

I was feeling a little overwhelmed. Mr. Charles' death had brought up too many uncomfortable feelings for me about life's fleeting nature, family bonds, and social barriers. And save for brief conversations with

Leslie and Portia when I took them here and there, since Jasmine was otherwise immersed with her family, I was alone with my thoughts.

"Hey, Ma," I greeted my mother when she answered the phone. I hadn't talked to her since the morning Mr. Charles had died.

"Hey, baby, what's the matter?"

I didn't stand a chance not telling the truth, but I tried anyway.

"I'm just tired is all." That was truthful.

"And how's Jasmine?"

"Worn out, but she probably wouldn't admit that," I replied.

"Probably not, but you need to be there for her."

"I know, I think I'm doing the best I can."

"You need to be there for her and Catherine."

"Wh—?"

"T!" Mary Butler cut me off before I had a chance to protest. "Lord knows the woman can be a bit terse—"

"That's putting it mildly…"

"But she just lost her husband. I cannot begin to imagine what that feels like."

I was not surprised to hear my mother taking up for Ms. Catherine. Mary Butler was the walking embodiment of "turn the other cheek." She wasn't a pushover, but she routinely extended compassion to people who didn't necessarily deserve it.

"Hmmm…" Tears welled up in my eyes and my mouth went dry just at the thought of losing my own father.

"I hope people offer some measure of grace in my time of need."

"True." My mother had a point—she usually did. "I tell you one thing I've learned…"

"What's that, T?"

"There's a thin veil between life and death. You're here one minute and gone the next."

"Ain't that the truth." Silence fell in between us until Mom inhaled. "Time is filled with swift transition." Her statement sounded more like a reminder to herself than wisdom for me. Maybe it was both.

"Do you want me and your father to come?" Her question put my gratitude for my loving, biological family in sharp relief considering Jasmine's current circumstances.

***

Jasmine's father had opened countless doors, held several positions where he was the first African American person to occupy the post in the BCPD. And he had mentored many officers who were still on the force.

The decision about the funeral seating arrangements was settled by the police chaplain. Considering they expected a large turnout, he recommended limiting the front row to immediate family as folks not used to the pomp and circumstance of a police funeral were often overwhelmed by it all.

Before the funeral, during a family hour at the funeral home, Jasmine had a light moment, wondering aloud how she could get all the beautiful floral arrangements back to the house. On a more serious note, fellow officers and friends reflected on Mr. Charles' community service and the pleasure he had taken in helping others, whether it was for church or an event at work. Since retirement, many noted, he had gotten a kick out of presenting at grade school career days. Jasmine had even been trying to incorporate him into a mentor program for young men moving into ReBuild homes.

The next day, compared to family hour, the wake and funeral were intense. The mournful yet hypnotic sound of bagpipes, impressive sea of blue uniforms, consistent throughline of "I can't believe he's gone," and voices repeatedly breaking when speakers stood at the lectern were all palpable reminders of death's finality.

Even with the chaplain's advice, I sat next to Jasmine during the service after all, she said I was her family. "We're at my father's funeral," Jasmine mumbled. "Two weeks ago, I was making him a sandwich in their kitchen and talking about young officers seeking his counsel. Today? We're at his funeral."

It was the third time in the last twenty-four hours she had repeated this statement or something similar. The night before, Jasmine had told me one of the officers said, "Sarge was going to help me with the sergeant's exam. We were supposed to meet for lunch this week." I overheard similar stories during family hour too.

During the service, the songs were both beautiful and sad to me. When offering their reflections, no one adhered to the allotted two minutes and almost everyone openly wept. Mr. Charles' unexpected death had seemed to throw the earth off its axis a bit. The pastor gracefully eulogized Jasmine's father, as graceful as a eulogy could be, capturing his servant's heart and love for his family and friends.

When she had come into the church, Mrs. Charles needed the attendants to literally lean on. Heartache was etched deeply into her face, the weight of her grief virtually mooring her to the ground. As if everything before hadn't been enough, the moment the funeral director started adjusting the bed of the casket so Mr. Charles' body lowered further inside, and then finally closed the lid, something inside Mrs. Charles broke. She flat-out fainted, and it took a good five minutes of fanning and waving smelling salts under her nose before she came to.

I rode in the family car to the burial site holding Jasmine's hand and doing little else. Because what else could I do at that point? I had never been with anyone long enough to even think about final arrangements, though Leslie's situation had lodged a silent "what if" scenario in the back of my mind.

A police escort ensured a smooth processional from the church to the cemetery. Even though I'd lived in Baltimore for thirteen years, I still wasn't used to the differences in customs between here and home. People in the South still pulled over for funeral processions, no matter how many cars were included, and they wouldn't dare think about cutting in line as I'd seen drivers around here do. Luckily, the police motorcycle escort prevented any such foolishness.

After entering the cemetery, our limousine moved slowly in between columns of police officers posted on both sides of the narrow drive leading to the Charles family plot. They were four rows deep and wearing heavy overcoats to shield themselves from the biting wind to render a final salute to Sergeant Charles.

At the gravesite, the color guard and bugler were exceptional in their precision and playing. And despite her outward stoicism, Jasmine's hands trembled in mine when the officers played what I considered the saddest tune ever written in history, "Taps." When it was all over, the somber mood still hung over everyone. Stephanie, Leslie, Portia, and Angel had stood firm with the Charles family throughout all the proceedings and before getting back into the limo, Jasmine and I stopped to hug them. They all looked as miserable as we felt.

"You got her, right?" Stephanie whispered to me.

"Indeed." I wasn't sure of much at the moment, but that was one question I had no problem answering.

After the repast back at the church and once night fell, I headed home. Jasmine planned to stay at her mom's for a few more days to make sure she didn't waste away from not eating or sleeping. Or until either of them had had enough of the other.

My phone rang a little before midnight.

"Hello?" I answered. I had been lying face up, alone in our bed, in the stillness that blanketed the space without Jasmine's energy.

"I wasn't sure if you'd still be awake." It was Jasmine.

"I let Coco out and just locked up the house for the night. How are you, love?"

"I don't know, numb I think."

"Understood. Where have you been sleeping?"

"In my brother's old room. You know Mother turned my room into a reading room."

"So you've told me," I responded. That fact always irritated Jasmine.

"How's your mom?"

"Angry. She said something earlier about how she'd always worried about Daddy not coming home all those years he was on the force, and yet a heart attack killed him after he retired."

The irony didn't escape me, but I didn't know what to do with that. I changed the subject. "What are you doing tomorrow?"

"I know it's early, but I'll probably try and take her to get banking and pension paperwork done. Chaplain reached out to the retirement benefits staff to make the process easier for her."

"Hmm, not sure about easy."

"That's true, smoother maybe." The weariness in Jasmine's voice tugged at me. If she were with me, I could just hold her. The distance from our house to her parents' Ashburton neighborhood, though only fifteen minutes as the crow flew, felt immense.

I didn't tell Jasmine I was having trouble sleeping too. My mind kept circling around the suddenness of her father's death and the emptiness it left for Jasmine and, by extension, me. Not that trying to talk about a protracted illness like Leslie's was any easier. Either way, there was so much I wanted to say, to confide to Jasmine, but I couldn't. She was already juggling a lot, and this sudden terrible loss of her dad just compounded Jasmine's heavy load.

CHAPTER TWENTY-NINE

Jasmine

I returned to the office three weeks after my father died. It wasn't easy, despite Jason and the rest of the staff being extra supportive. The first day I got back, Jason stopped by my office and, from one side of his mouth, told me to take all the time I needed and, from the other, said he was confident I would get my work done. *Yeah, okay.*

Even with everything going on in my personal life and not physically being here in the office, I had managed to keep National off his back and we'd gotten a little recognition for our region. We used the family photo albums to promote and market all our work and had given them to ReBuild families as gifts. Not to mention they were great decoration around the office.

In addition to the albums, T had designed wonderful collages that now hung in our offices and hallways to remind us of why we did what we did. Although I was very biased about her stunning work, she had managed to capture the unmistakable emotional component of homeownership. It was hard for a snaggle-toothed eight-year-old to hide their excitement when they saw their own bedroom for the first time.

I needed a break after sitting at my computer most of the morning, still catching up with email messages and reports to read. My head throbbed and my shoulder muscles were tight, probably because I was starting to feel emotionally overwhelmed. Not panicked, but restless.

"Ruth, I'm going out to grab a coffee," I told Jason's assistant as I headed downstairs. "I'll be back."

I walked up Boston Street bundled up in my coat, a hat, scarf, and gloves, but I still felt chilled to my bones. I knew maybe it was too cold to be out walking, but I needed to do something that would make me feel some emotion other than numb.

"Grief is the price we pay for loving." Queen Elizabeth had spoken these words after the 9/11 attacks, to pay tribute to the victims, and now they brought me a small measure of comfort when the grief of missing my dad became too much. As shameful as my mother could be, I knew she loved my father. He had been the force that kept her parsimoniousness in check, reminding her of their days before she discovered Jesus. As he would say, "Woman, we had fun."

I was worried that in losing him, I would lose her too, especially since I wasn't that close to the rest of my family. When they found out I was "that way," many of them either damned me to hell or simply became very superficial in our interactions. I could go months without having a real conversation with my biological siblings, whereas I talked to either Leslie, Stephanie, or both almost every day. They were my sisters, my true family. The unexpected loss of my father cut so painfully, and an unwelcomed heaviness was still taking up space in my chest.

Those of us in people-oriented fields were well aware of the stages of grieving, but it felt different when reality was more than an academic exercise. I wanted to call my old professor and ask how long the denial stage would last. How many times since my father had died had I instinctively picked up the phone to call him with a question? I saw the most mundane reminders of my dad everywhere. Like that afternoon, as I waited at an intersection to cross Boston Street, a busy four-lane divided thoroughfare, I saw a middle-aged man filling a pothole. The man was maybe ten years younger than Daddy, but even that worker somehow reminded me of him.

I vowed never again to repeat the empty platitudes I had heard at his funeral. "He's in a better place." No, he was not—I wanted him with us, on this side of the divide. "God knows best." Really? I was already salty with God about Leslie. Like seriously, another family member with cancer and then my father drops dead of a heart attack after three decades of fighting crime and all the "isms" of the police force? Yeah, I was questioning a lot right now.

At a small café, I ordered a tuna fish sandwich and chips along with my coffee and found a table nestled in a corner. I was hoping some nourishment would help lift my spirits, but my mind was still ruminating.

The whole situation with Leslie and Portia had just gotten more complicated because before Dad had died, they were the only thing I really needed to focus on—obtaining resources, coordinating care, and I had become exceptional in getting to the pickup line at St. Jo's on time. My social worker background had prepared me well. I could plan and coordinate with military precision. And since Portia had been with us, I had learned to breathe, read emails, and write my to-do lists all in the pickup line. I even got in a chapter or two of whatever book I was reading.

I put my head down, trying to blink away the tears. I had to admit, life felt overwhelming at the moment, but I didn't need to sit here crying. *Deep breaths, Jasmine, keep your head.* I closed my eyes momentarily to let the grief washing over me subside but the jingle of the bells on the café door got my attention. In walked a young BCPD officer, filling out his uniform in all the right places. I remembered when Daddy looked like he could be on the recruitment ads too. Mr. Police Officer smiled easily and nodded hello at me as he walked to the counter to place his order. And he was nice too? The lump in my throat was making it hard to breathe. If I didn't get out of there, I knew my unchecked emotions would likely cause a scene. I peeked behind me and saw that he'd gone to the back where the restrooms were. I quickly made my way to the counter, paid his tab, and left. Daddy would have liked that—I saw him do the same thing for many younger officers. That genuinely made me smile for the first time all day.

CHAPTER THIRTY

T

On a brisk March Saturday, I went for an early morning run on the Jones Falls Trail to boost my *ojas*. After all, I had been feeling a bit sluggish and unmoored as of late. But once I stepped outside, the air making my skin prickle, I felt better, more awake, even though the weather was still raw and gray.

As John had reminded me some months back, I hadn't completed any commissioned artwork in a hot minute. Nor had I submitted any applications for art shows or participated in any of the gallery events that Kevin hosted. With everything going on with Leslie and Portia as well as Mr. Charles dying, I felt like I had little time to myself and even less mental capacity for creativity. I decided this was the day. In fact, I decided, this whole weekend I was going to actively focus on myself.

Not surprisingly, Paul had backed out of his scheduled parental visit via phone call the night before. But I couldn't keep putting my own obligations, as self-imposed as they may have been, aside because he was a shitty father. As for Portia, neither Jasmine nor I made excuses for his failure to show. We simply told her the truth. As my mother continued to remind me, Paul would have to answer to his daughter when she was old enough.

I came back from my run about forty-five minutes and seven miles later, exhausted but invigorated. The house was still quiet, so I grabbed my phone, put a note on the family calendar that I'd be at the studio most of the day, and bounced.

Just as I turned onto my block I noticed another for sale sign, and I knew Ms. Donna would soon fill me in on the particulars of that transaction. I had been occasionally toying with the idea of renting my house but still didn't feel like it was worth the hassle. The market had slowed considerably over the last six months, but the houses in the neighborhood were still yielding a nice return for sellers.

I did a quick safety check once I got inside, showered, put on clean clothes, made a pot of tea, and hit play for a little jazz music to keep me company. Then I sat in front of a blank canvas and stared. I couldn't get out of my head. The canvas felt too big. Only one time before in my life had painting seemed so hard to do—in college, after my heart was broken into pieces by a girl I thought was *fuh true*. Until she wasn't.

I closed my eyes and meditated on a color that was indicative of my mood, a technique I had learned to employ during that awful time. Then I squeezed a bit of acrylic on my palette, grabbed an inch-wide brush, worked in a little fluid medium, and painted the entire canvas black. I snorted in amusement. I squirted a vivid ultramarine blue on the palette and used a different brush to flick splotches on the canvas, creating a nice contrast. That was about right—an adequate depiction of what the last few months had felt like. Irregular and unpredictable moments engulfed by a dark, unsettled mood.

What I was looking at didn't speak to me just yet, but I was going with it. Could I simply add a bleeding heart in the middle without making the composition look like it was painted by a five-year-old? Nah. I sat cross-legged on the floor and stared at the canvas until my legs started to feel numb. I went downstairs and walked through the living room and kitchen, down to the basement—I needed to get a dehumidifier, it smelled old down here—then all the way up to my old bedroom on the top level. Jasmine was the only other person who ever spent any appreciable time up here. I considered it my sanctuary—I supposed that was still the case.

Jasmine was hurting. On second thought, grieving was probably a more accurate term. Both things could be true though. To say that her family relationships were strained was being generous. It was safe to say Mr. Charles was the yin to her mom's yang and had kept Mrs. Charles from morphing into a live Cruella de Vil most days. Without him as a check valve, Jasmine vacillated between trying to be a supportive daughter and getting into screaming matches with her mother. A few years back, Mr. Charles told me the two of them fought because they were so much alike. I didn't think too much of it at the time. Now, in hindsight, his observation, or rather, his declaration, seemed prescient. Over the past few months, even before Mr. Charles' death, Jasmine's bluntness and abrasiveness had left little room for any decisions but hers. She was her mother's child. That harsh reality, I realized, wasn't sitting well with me.

Returning to the studio space, I changed the music to the Zen station. If it started sounding like whales moaning, which was the opposite of Zen for me, I would flip it back to smooth jazz. I went back to the canvas, and since the paint had dried, painted a series of shapes over the splotches until I realized the silhouette was starting to resemble a butterfly. I scrolled through pictures on my camera and found one of a tiger swallowtail flittering about in my mother's garden in Savannah. I used it as a model. I didn't paint butterflies often, but I needed to keep the creative juices flowing. Butterflies transformed. And wasn't that what the past few months had been…a metamorphosis of sorts? Like a larva transforming into a butterfly, Jasmine's and my family structure had changed because of Leslie's illness. Mr. Charles, as we knew him, had left the physical realm.

I had been lost in perfecting the details of the painting when my cell rang. "Hello?"

The call was coming from the house landline.

"GT, it's me." Portia sounded like she was in an undercover operation. At least that was the image that popped into my head when I heard her voice.

"Hey kiddo, why are you whispering?" I found myself whispering too.

"GT, Godmommy's been outside all day—"

I put the palette down. "All day? How long exactly?"

"Yeah, like three hours. And it's cold. I can see my breath and I'm inside, so I know it's cold."

"What's she doing out there?"

"Just sitting out there looking in one direction," Portia replied.

"In one direction?"

"Yeah, like it looks like she's been staring at the same tree."

"Oh…"

"I think she was crying, but she covered her eyes so I wouldn't see when I went out there."

"What does she look like now?"

"She looks sad."

My fingers tightened around the paintbrush. Hearing Portia's concern, my muscles tensed. I'd been in a nice creative flow, but now I was being dragged back to our difficult reality. "Really?"

"Yeah, she keeps wiping her face with tissues. Coco sat with her for a long time but Coco wanted to come in."

"I guess so. Spring hasn't hung around that long this year yet."

"What should I do?"

"Does she have a coat on?"

"Her housecoat and slippers."

Lord! My girlfriend was going to freeze to death. "Okay, take the fleece throw off the couch in the living room and put it around her shoulders. I'll be home soon."

The human mind and body could only take so much. You either cared for them or they would start shutting themselves down and force you to. Every time I asked Jasmine how she was doing, she always responded, "Fine." But she was not fine. Her father had died unexpectedly. The thread that held their family together had been abruptly severed and their threadbare relationships unraveled. Not to mention, one of Jasmine's best friends was seriously ill. My girlfriend was not fine.

I looked at the canvas again and sighed…transformation.

As I cleaned my brushes and palette and put everything back in their designated jars and labeled drawers, I mentally planned my route home. Soup. Jasmine liked matzo ball soup. But was that Jewish deli open on Saturdays? If they weren't, I'd go to the gourmet grocery across the street to get a few prepared entrees. Jasmine wasn't really eating well these days. Actually, she wasn't doing anything well. I ignored the sinking feeling in my stomach and headed out. Maybe a smorgasbord of food options would jumpstart Jasmine's appetite and help me bring her back to life.

CHAPTER THIRTY-ONE

Jasmine

T was so sweet, bringing soup home this past weekend. The thoughtfulness led me to wonder who, if anyone, had been caring for my mother. Our recent phone calls were strained. She was mad at God. She was mad at my father for dying, as if that was the path he had voluntarily chosen. She was mad at everyone. According to my sister, my mother was furious with her church friends who hadn't invited her to the recent Couples' Ministry retreat despite her having participated for ten-plus years. But, as painful as it sounded, that made sense to me. She wasn't a part of a couple anymore.

On a whim, I stopped by my parents' house to bring my mother some flowers before heading to St. Josephine's to pick Portia up. I knocked on the door of the stately, foursquare home where my parents had raised us three children and waited. She didn't answer. I knocked louder but still no answer. Both cars were in the driveway. I called the house phone, no answer. Her cell phone went straight to voicemail. I didn't want to just use my key, but I was also feeling a little nervous. This was silly, I needed to go in the house. I unlocked the door, peeked in, and immediately gasped. *What in the hell?* The thermostat seemed to be set to like 85 degrees or something.

"Mom?"

My question was met with the ticking kitchen wall clock and silence. Her purse was on the bench near the door and keys were on top of it. I felt my core heat up even more as fear started to seep in. The kitchen was in disarray, which was unlike my fastidiously clean and organized mother. There was little food in the refrigerator. The basement door was open, also unlike her. It was usually locked since there was an outside entrance door to the basement. I turned the light on and slowly went down the steps. Nothing looked out of place except for the clothes on the floor near the washing machine. I checked to make sure the locks on the basement door were secured and came back upstairs. The dining and living rooms were as clean as always, as if she expected company at any minute. I headed upstairs, the wood creaking under my weight. The pounding of my heart seemed to intensify as I peered into my parents' bedroom. Although the curtains were drawn, making it hard to see, I could make out the small mounds of clothes on the floor and shoes spilling out of the closet. Papers lay all over the side of the bed my father had slept on—and my mother was next to them on hers. I apprehensively stepped further into their room to see her better. Her eyes were open and she was looking in my direction but not necessarily at me. It was more like she was glaring through me.

"Are you okay?" I asked.

"Yes." My mother's response was flat and monotone.

"Did you hear the phone ring? I called the house and your cell."

"Yes."

"I used my key because you weren't answering, and I was worried."

"I'm fine."

"Are you sure? I can't remember—"

"Jasmine, I'll be okay. Thanks for coming over." She looked past me.

"I can't remember you ever being in bed in the middle of the day unless you were sick."

"I said, I'm fine. Don't ask me again."

"Can I get you something to eat? I didn't see a lot in the refrigerator."

"So you came over unannounced and are surprised to find there's no food here?" She raised her voice—the first sign of emotion that let me know Catherine Charles was still very much alive.

"Mother, I noticed a few things around the house that are unlike you, and I wanted to make sure you're okay."

My chest expanded as I sucked in all the air I could. The strangeness of seeing my mother like this made me feel a little faint.

"Thanks for coming by," my mother said, her tone softening a bit. "I will be fine."

"Okay…"

"Please lock the door on your way out."

I realized I had been clutching the flower bunch to my chest like a shield since entering the house. "I brought you some flowers." I hesitated, wondering if leaving was the right thing to do, but damn, I had to pick up Portia really soon so I did have to get going. "I was thinking about you."

"Place them on the kitchen counter when you leave. Thank you."

"Can I turn the thermostat down before I leave? It feels really warm in here, especially here upstairs."

"No, thank you."

"Okay, I'll check on you a little later." I didn't know how much later, this impromptu visit was painful.

Downstairs, I quickly arranged the flowers in a vase with water and, against my better judgement, did as my mother asked and left.

What the hell was that? I wondered as I got back out to the driveway, finally breathing more easily. The stark contrast between a cloudless, blue sky, trilling birdsong, and children squealing with delight on the playground down the street and what I had just witnessed in my childhood home was jarring. Before I could even get all the way in my car, I called my sister and left a message and texted my brother to ask him to check on his mother.

Somehow, I managed to maneuver my car from my parents' house to the pickup line. By the time I got there, I couldn't even remember the drive. The sobering realization that I couldn't save the world despite my best efforts overtook my thoughts.

"Jasmine, you're doing your best," I whispered to myself. "What is meant to be, will be."

I took a few deep breaths. Intellectually, I knew my mother's pain was not about me, but that didn't mean her words didn't hurt. My father had been right, we were a lot alike.

Neither one of us was doing well. My eyes were closed when I heard the rear passenger door open.

"Godmommy, are you sleep?"

"No, baby, of course not." I turned to see a ray of sunshine hopping into the car.

"Good! You gotta get us home safely, you know." Portia was grinning at me.

"Yes, ma'am." After my rotten afternoon, I needed her childlike optimism.

CHAPTER THIRTY-TWO

T

I heard slippers shuffling across the floor, and looked up from my newspaper, in which I'd been reading a feature about Kristi Toliver, the standout freshman in last Tuesday's NCAA women's basketball championship game. It was a Sunday morning in early April.

"Morning, sleeping beauty," I said.

Jasmine came into the kitchen, moving slower than normal. She had dark circles around her eyes, and I was surprised she still had her pajamas on, not even halfway dressed for church as she might normally have been.

"Morning." Jasmine kissed my forehead. "It's quiet."

I patted her on the butt as she turned around and headed toward the coffee pot. She responded to the gesture with a faint smile. "The quiet before the—"

"Morning, favorite godmothers," Portia said as she came bounding into the kitchen with Coco on her heels.

"Never mind, the storm is awake," I said.

"Do you have any others?" Jasmine questioned Portia.

"No, but you two are my favorite." Portia offered a slightly fake, cheese-eating grin and threw her arms out toward us in a "ta-da" sort of way.

"I feel like we're getting ready to be charmed," Jasmine said to me.

"Yep, I feel a setup coming," I agreed.

"Guess what today is." Portia did her best to look like she wasn't scheming.

We both shrugged. "Sunday?" I said.

"Yes *and…*" she sang, "…the farmers' market opens today." Bubbling excitement replaced her fake grin as she hopped up and down.

"Really?" Jasmine and I asked in unison.

"Really! We should go."

"How do you know it opens today?" Jasmine asked.

"Some of my friends' parents make a big deal of it so my friends do too." Portia said.

"Is there something at the market in particular or are we going because everyone else is going?" I wanted to know.

"No, nothing in particular. But I like to see all the stuff there."

"Portia, I'm beat." Jasmine shook her head. "I really had no plans to change out of my pajamas. I honestly don't have the energy to do anything today."

Jasmine's tired eyes were now welling with water, which she tried to hide with a yawn and one sleeve of her pajama top.

The course of my day had just taken a turn. "I tell you what, how about the two of us go for a little while?"

"Yay!" The hopping started again.

"We're not staying long though, and I need to make a stop to take pictures at a ReBuild house on our way back home."

"Great!" Portia shouted like she was Tony the Tiger, even giving her little fist a pump.

"Go brush your teeth and—"

Portia ran back upstairs before I finished giving directions. I turned to Jasmine.

"Take a little time to yourself."

I folded up the paper and slid it to the corner of the banquette bench, put my coffee cup in the sink, and lightly kissed the woman I deeply loved on her ever-so-soft lips. "Why don't you do absolutely nothing while we're gone."

"Thank you, baby." Jasmine hugged me. Something we hadn't done in months it seemed. I felt her chest rising as she exhaled against my neck. Perhaps it had been too long.

***

There were still a lot of cars parked under the overpass for supposedly the last hour of the market—first weekend excitement perhaps—but I found a space in the closest parking lot. I held Portia's hand as we navigated throngs of folks walking in the opposite direction to their cars. One of Baltimore's largest outdoor markets lay in the shadows of the JFX. Its opening signified growth and new beginnings, a time when the air still had a slight nip, but a jacket wasn't required.

The atmosphere was still festive. Brightly colored, opening-day balloons were tethered to poles at one entrance and Shakira's "Hips Don't Lie" was playing somewhere close by, its reggaeton beat poppin'. Newly painted signs indicated the food merchants were to the left and the market bazaar was to the right. I figured many of the vendors would have already started to break down their areas, but several others still had tables full of produce. Usually, vegetables and other produce had already been picked over near the close of the farmers' market at noon. What did this say about the prices and or the quality?

We moseyed along looking at tables. "Can we buy Godmommy flowers?" Portia asked.

What was I going to say? No? We stopped at the first flower booth we saw and Portia picked out a bouquet of brightly-colored tulips.

When we came across a few kids from St. Jo's, I did the quick greeting with their parents—a sort of "Good to see you, yes, we love the market, and fresh vegetables are wonderful" thing, then we headed to the bazaar side, where Portia stopped in front of a man selling recycled wooden windows.

"Did it take you long to set up your booth?" Portia asked the man.

I thought it was an odd question.

He was polite though. "It did. It took about an hour and a half to load all my windows, secure 'em in my truck, unload 'em here, and then make sure they looked nice enough to buy."

"They do." Portia agreed before she skipped off.

I shrugged, mouthed "Thank you" and went to catch up with her.

Two vendors after the windows, Portia was standing in front of a woman selling handmade goat milk soaps.

"Do you have to pay to sell things here?" Portia asked the lady, sniffing at a blue-green bar of soap, then another.

"Not yet. The city allocated us space for a pilot project." The woman looked at me. "Do you have something to sell?"

"We make coat racks," Portia answered.

I almost choked. "What are you talking about?"

Portia looked up at me with a wide, expectant grin. "We could make some more and sell them here at the market!"

Portia's observation was a statement rather than a question.

"Oh, Portia, no, no, no." I ushered the little swindler away from the soap, wagging my finger to emphasize my disagreement.

"You have yourself a young entrepreneur," Soap Lady shouted through her laughing.

Portia looked at me and smiled. "GT, we could sell them for the kids in the ReBuild program. Then we can buy stuff they need."

Lord, what have we started? "We'll talk about this later. Let's get to the ReBuild house so I can take a few pictures of the block and take advantage of the sun angle and shadows."

***

The rowhouse was on Lorman Street in the Sandtown-Winchester neighborhood, around the corner from Quetta's house. I peeked in the narrow window and saw that demolition was underway, and I was surprised to see a crew of workers on a Sunday. So I knocked on the door and waved.

"Can I help you?" A guy asked, wiping his hands on his coveralls and lifting safety glasses onto his head. He took a green handkerchief out of his back pocket and wiped his brow. The man looked to be in his mid-thirties with strong hands that weren't afraid of hard work.

"Jasmine Charles asked us to take a few progress photos." I told him. "I just wanted to let you know we'd be around."

He gave Portia and me the once-over. "Cool. Make sure you get my good side." He laughed, so I figured we had passed the sniff test. "I'm the super."

He disappeared back into the gutted house and soon returned holding what looked like the tapered legs of a side table.

"We never know what to do when we run across stuff like this. They're table legs," he said, confirming my opinion. "It'd be a shame to just trash them. Any ideas for what to do with the tables? The tops are all inside."

He set them on the marble steps outside so I could get a better look at them.

"We should take them," Portia said, bright-eyed and eager.

"What? And do what with them?"

"Paint them. They'd look nice."

The foreman laughed. "Little princess is right. These Mission-style tables are simple to refinish. You could easily sand and stain them. I wouldn't put paint on wood this nice though."

"Mister, please don't encourage her."

"Okay, but come in and look at this other stuff too while you thinking. It was some real nice things in here. We added extra plywood to the windows and doors to keep things from disappearing." As he started to head back inside, Portia began to follow him but I held her back.

"No, ma'am." I shook my head. This was not what I had planned.

"Come on, we don't bite." The super gestured us to follow him.

"I need to get a few shots outside first, then we'll see about the furniture."

"Deal. We're done with demo on this level, let me get the crew started upstairs and you do what you need to do."

"Great," I agreed.

In about fifteen minutes I'd gotten the snapshots I wanted. I even took a few of Mr. Superintendent directing his two guys, all of them covered in plaster dust. Sun rays streaming through the windows backlit the particles, and I knew these pics would be nice in black and white. I loved seeing people working with their hands.

When it was time to go, I found Portia waiting patiently near the furniture, now stacked by the front door. We had amassed the components of seven side tables and a coffee table. "Okay, let's see if we can get all this stuff in the car," I groaned.

Despite my initial unwillingness to want to take on more projects, the furniture wasn't in bad condition. And as the super had pointed out, it wouldn't take much to make them look nice again. I decided to take the items to school the next day and see what Gus thought. Maybe his woodshop students could sand them faster than I could and get in some practice. But I still hadn't wrapped my head around vending at the farmers' market. My artwork was displayed in local galleries for goodness' sake. Nonetheless, I was sure it wasn't the last I would hear of Portia's grand idea.

CHAPTER THIRTY-THREE

Jasmine

It hadn't taken me long to discover that driving alone was the only time I could cry or scream with abandon—except at a stoplight. I learned that screaming and crying at stoplights attracted too much attention. Instead of repeatedly eliciting unwanted stares or strangers asking, "Ma'am, are you okay?" in mid-April, I made the adult decision to go to a grief support group.

The police chaplain had helped me come to that conclusion when he called me because he was having a hard time connecting with my mother. Mom hadn't answered his calls or responded to his messages at all. In his experience, he explained, wives were often angry for months, years even, and didn't often immediately accept their new roles of being widows. He said he'd left her messages recommending various grief support groups, which spurred me to ask him for suggestions for adult children. He had obliged me by sharing contact information for a few hospice and hospital support groups, and soon after I found one that wasn't out of the way for me.

Now I was on my way there for the first time, knowing I'd have time to make it between work and picking Portia up from school.

I found my way to Clara's Room, a grief support group that met in a local hospice center. Posters with family member testimonials lined the soothing periwinkle-colored walls. Large paned windows allowed in a lot of light and framed the colorful barberry shrubs outside. Before I could talk myself into leaving, a woman with auburn hair pulled back in a neat bun, dark-rimmed glasses, and a warm smile introduced herself as Natalie, the social worker who ran the group. She assured me grief was hard enough, and the fact that I scheduled time to be here at all, was notable.

Natalie invited me to sit in any of the available armchairs that were arranged in a circle. The whole vibe was comforting, from the schedule time to accommodate working people to the plush chairs that said "Sit a while" rather than "Let's get this over with." Apart from Natalie, our small group of four included two ladies who had lost their mothers a few weeks apart the previous year and a young man who had lost the grandmother who raised him.

Natalie was kind and asked subtle questions of everyone. Like during my introduction I shared that my family, especially my mother, was having a difficult time. Natalie reframed her question to ask me, "How are you doing?"

I hadn't expected any such thing before I arrived, but I felt lighter, more unburdened. It was a relief to talk about how I felt about losing my father without being judged. I talked enough to realize that the reason I felt his absence so acutely was because Daddy was the only person in my family whose love or actions never changed toward me. His love had never been predicated on my sexual identity. That revelation brought a whole fresh set of tears. And if the boxes of tissues that sat close to every single chair were any indication, Natalie was used to tears. Not surprisingly, I used a fair share during the sixty-minute meeting.

***

When I got to the pickup line and Portia hopped in the back seat of my car, she was being all Portia. I thought about how I would have loved to have had her energy, world perspective, and self-confidence when I was ten.

"Hi, Godmommy!"

"Hi, sweetie."

"You okay?" She didn't miss anything.

"Yep, I'm okay." Hell, at forty-one I sometimes struggled to lift my voice to be heard in certain situations. I had gained a new perspective from my godchild since she moved in eight months ago.

Portia questioned everything, but not in a disrespectful way. She was very thoughtful in the ways she phrased her questions, but she basically wanted answers to inquiries we adults were too chicken to ask. Why were the girls' basketball crowds smaller than the boys? Why did her math questions include grocery shopping word problems but not business questions like the boys got? And why didn't any of the word problems have names that sounded like hers? The kid was going to be a force to reckon with. She slyly listened to adult conversations, shared what her classmates' parents told them, and saw herself as an exceptional student who wasn't bound by anyone else's notion of what an exceptional student looked like.

In the past, Leslie and I had had conversations about how to maintain Portia's level of curiosity before society attempted to shape her views of herself. But Portia rolled with whatever scenario she encountered without pushing back too much. We asked her to live with me and T for a while, and she got right onboard. When we told her to be mindful of how her skirts fit so as not to draw attention, she told Leslie that she wasn't responsible for what other people thought of her. In that conversation I gave her two snaps before Leslie cut her eyes at me. Leslie was talking about safety—Portia was demonstrating self-assuredness. For Portia, the two could co-exist. We were better people because this little human made it so.

"Godmommy, are you listening?" Portia said, drawing me out of my reverie.

Maybe? Really, I had no idea what the child had been talking about. "You have a big weekend. How did you convince GT to sell furniture at the farmers' market?" I asked.

"It wasn't hard," she said with all the confidence of someone four times her age. "The proceeds are—"

"Proceeds?" I felt my eyes roll but that made me smile at her in the rearview mirror.

"Yeah, the amount of money left over after we subtract furniture and supply costs." She was staring back at me like "duh" but quickly turned her attention to the landscape whizzing by. "The proceeds are going to help kids like Quetta and Quinton. Like, last Christmas, there were a lot of kids at the party, maybe they need help too." She shrugged.

I loved this kid. She made some things seem so simple. "I don't have a dinner plan yet. Any thoughts?"

"Let's get Indian food."

"Indian food? You eat Indian food?"

"Yes, my friend Saria and I share lunch sometimes. It's good." She sang the word good.

"Well, okay, I love Indian food. T likes tandoori salmon, and I'll get saag paneer. What do you want?"

"I'd like chicken pakora and veggie samosas please. Can we get extra naan too?"

This kid was unbelievable. Exposure mattered.

CHAPTER THIRTY-FOUR

T

Four weeks after she broached the idea, why had I let Portia convince me to vend at the Baltimore Farmers' Market? There were a thousand other things I could've been doing at seven o'clock on a Sunday morning. But truth be told, this kid had become my muse and inspiration. Sure, our lives had been turned upside down and I quietly seethed over that. Or maybe not so quietly—John certainly got an earful when we talked. But the flip side of Portia and Leslie living with us was unexpected moments of pure delight and being surrounded by a child's boundless energy.

"Good morning, team," I announced to Leslie, Jasmine, and Portia as I walked into the kitchen. "Are we ready to get this party started?"

Only the youngest crew member appeared to be energized about the day's adventure.

"Yes, GT, I'm so excited!" Portia left her bowl of cereal and ran over to me.

"Me too." I pretended to be enthused. "Finish your breakfast so you have lots of fuel to charm the customers."

Jasmine looked at me, rolled her eyes, and smiled. Ideally, she would have another Sunday to rest and just be, but I needed another adult to take money, be there when I needed to get snacks and a bathroom break. I anticipated a long day ahead of us.

"I think we'll do okay." I poured coffee into a mug and leaned my butt against the cabinet to face my crew. I was nervous about this whole thing.

"But I don't think we'll sell everything, we'll probably come back with a few tables and coat racks."

Leslie was snickering behind her hand. "I know my child." One of her eyebrows rose. "I doubt you come back with anything."

"You don't think so?" I questioned her.

"I don't think you know how competitive she is."

"Oh, I know. I've seen her play basketball."

"Yeah, and this is next level," Leslie said.

"How so?"

"I give St. Josephine's credit in helping reinforce the idea that she can do whatever she sets her mind to."

"Yes, I can," the little peanut gallery interjected. Leslie kissed her on the cheek.

"I saw her hustle Girl Scout cookies that one year she agreed to participate…for a prize," Leslie added.

I laughed out loud. "I can see her doing that."

"So, I got ten dollars that y'all come home empty-handed." Leslie proposed a wager.

Jasmine had been watching and listening to our whole exchange with amusement and finally chimed in. "Empty-handed like we sell out of everything?"

"Yep," Leslie said with tons of confidence.

"Ohhh…you're selling wolf tickets. Don't make no bets you can't cash 'cause I *will* take your money." I rubbed my fingers together.

Leslie got up and disappeared into the living room. She came back with a ten-dollar bill.

"I'm going to leave this here on the table." She secured the money with a saltshaker. "I'll take yours when you get back." She laughed louder than I had heard in a while. The fact that Leslie was even in the mood to talk trash said something about her resilience. Her voice and personality were much stronger than she appeared physically.

The cancer treatments had taken a toll on the once vibrant woman I had come to know. Leslie's face was gaunt, she had probably lost about thirty or more pounds. I saw a slight tremor as she lifted the coffee mug to her lips. And the only thing I ever noticed her eating was soup, some kind of healing broth of chicken, vegetables, ginger, and lots of turmeric Jasmine whipped up every Sunday.

"I see where she gets her confidence—it ain't the damn school." I pushed myself off the cabinet and downed the last bit of my coffee. This stuff wasn't going to sell itself. "Well, let's get the cars loaded up and head downtown."

Just schlepping stuff like pack mules from the parking lot to the area on Guilford Avenue where vendors set up shop along the sidewalk was a test unto itself. Technically, we were taking a risk and could be run off for loitering or vending without a permit or both, but I didn't want to invest too much money into this just yet. As I understood it from my informal poking around trying to prepare for the day, law enforcement left folks alone for the most part.

We set up fairly easily, with just two standalone steel frames to display the coat racks, and we placed the tables in front of those with ReBuild Baltimore brochures on them. We had twenty-five wooden clothes racks in various styles and finishes along with eight side tables.

Before we settled in good, Portia said she would be back and ran off. I shrugged when Jasmine looked my way. I had let this little girl talk me into vending on a public sidewalk and now she had abandoned ship. Clearly, she didn't know that I produced art-gallery-quality pieces. I had work hanging in prominent people's homes locally and abroad and here I was unloading homemade—no, not homemade—handcrafted woodwork to raise money for a children's program.

"I knew you'd be back."

I looked up to see Portia and the hand soap lady standing in front of our setup rubbing her finger along the grain of a table.

"Uh huh…How'd you know that?" I asked.

"Hon, I can spot an entrepreneurial spirit a mile away."

"Well, I don't know about an entrepreneurial spirit, but she—" I jutted my chin toward Portia, "She's definitely a hustler."

"And that's not a bad thing." Soap Lady handed Portia a twenty-dollar bill to purchase the first rack. Portia beamed with pride. I took a picture of them to memorialize our first sale.

Portia was good. She had the gift of gab, eloquently making her pitch to passersby and getting a few extra donations in the process. Not only that, Jasmine recruited two potential volunteers. The day was a win for everyone.

I was amazed the tables sold so quickly. They were simple, some painted outrageous colors, some stained because Gus said the wood *wanted* stain and he had to honor the wood. I was pleasantly surprised that he came to the market to see how we were doing. He took a brochure and talked to Jasmine about his students visiting a reno project. We all agreed that, although it would be a pain in the butt to get permission because of insurance, safety, blah, blah, blah, it would be great for the students to wear hard hats and go to an actual construction site. ReBuild's mission intrigued Gus. I suspected he would end up volunteering too.

True to Leslie's prediction, Portia was almost guaranteed a sale if she could engage a potential customer. And it wasn't just her bushy ponytails or cute purple overalls. She talked to everyone—kids with their parents, people with produce who clearly weren't furniture shopping, unsuspecting people who happened to make eye contact.

"Look what I made," she'd blurt out.

Those four words forced people to at least slow down. Then she would hook them with her spiel about raising money for children.

Around eleven-thirty, we had one end table and two racks left.

"GT, we only have to sell the racks you stained and we'll be done."

"Yes, Portia, I see that." I gave Jasmine a raised eyebrow…this kid. Jasmine tilted her head and smirked in return.

Thirty minutes later, a man with salt-and-pepper hair made a mistake by waving and doing the closed-mouth-smile thing at Portia.

"Good morning, sir," she greeted him. "We saved these for you."

She made a Vanna White gesturing flourish toward the last of our inventory. Before we knew it, the man had walked away with everything, grinning like he had won the lottery. This last encounter, after we'd entirely sold out, made me wonder if our prices were too low.

Before we'd left for the market and thinking we might not sell that much, I had planned a speech in my head for Portia. I was going to suggest we donate the refinished furniture to children in ReBuild homes. Silly me.

Hand Soap Lady saw us packing up, high-fived Portia, and said she had an open invitation to vend with her anytime. *Hah! Lady, you created a monster.*

Portia, totally thrilled, rode with me on the way home. "GT, tell me again how much we made."

"This is the third time you've asked."

"I know, I know, but today was soooo good."

"I'm going to say this for the last time. You raised four hundred and fifty dollars for the ReBuild Baltimore Children's Fund."

My response made Portia more psyched and eager to vend again. When she began spouting out her next plans, I had to put on the brakes.

"Oh, no. No, no, no. We're going to have to shut the operation down until the fall, when the new school year starts. Gus and his students are wrapping up their final projects for Industrial Arts Night."

"Well, can we go to that?" Portia asked. "I want to thank them."

"Sure, we can see about that." I smiled. Mama Mary would call that "good home training."

Once we got back to the house and unloaded the carts and stands, I lifted the saltshaker and put a ten-dollar bill on top of Leslie's.

***

"Portia!" I heard Jasmine calling upstairs from the front of the house.

It was the Tuesday after our farmers' market adventure and I was cooking for three people again since Leslie had felt strong enough to return home and give us space, her words. Jasmine however, was still taking her to chemo and checking in on her.

I stopped chopping carrots and, wiping my hands on a dish towel, came out of the kitchen to see what the fuss was about. Jasmine was holding a cake box from our favorite bakery, Azucar Bakery and Café, which I took out of her hands and brushed my lips against hers. I loved every cake that place made.

"What are we celebrating?" I asked.

"Wait until Portia gets down here, and I'll tell everyone at the same time."

"It's somebody's birthday?" Eagle-eyed Portia saw the cake box before she reached the last step.

"It's not anyone's birthday." Jasmine led us into the dining room and did a drum roll on the table with her hands.

I put the box down.

"We're celebrating great things today," she announced. "We were on our weekly national call and I talked about your fundraising efforts this past weekend." Portia and I stared at Jasmine, waiting on the rest of the story. "Guess what?"

"What?" we asked in unison.

"The national office is matching your fundraising. So, Miss Portia Sharp, you actually raised a thousand dollars!"

Portia's eyes grew as big as saucers, then after a pause she said, "Wait. Matching means double, right?" She looked puzzled. "The total should be nine hundred dollars."

"You're correct, double would be nine hundred dollars, but we got an anonymous donor who likes big, round even numbers," Jasmine assured her.

"Yay!" Portia jumped up and down, her hands in the air, just as I had come to expect.

Jasmine continued, "And T, they're going to officially thank your school principal for the ReBuild partnership. And we can expect an article in the national newsletter—both of you will be interviewed."

More jumping and screaming from the little person.

"Wait, one more thing…" Jasmine teased. "It'll be work on my part, but I'm going to put you two in for one of ReBuild's highest honors."

"And what's that?" I asked.

"A national award that recognizes exceptional community engagement."

More jumping—the child did not need sugar. "I'm going to call Mommy and tell her the good news!"

"That's why we have cake tonight," Jasmine declared, happier than I had seen her in a minute. This was much needed good news for a change.

***

Jasmine had told me the social worker from her support group suggested she should give herself grace for the first holidays and special events after a loved one died. So, as the third week of June approached, she asked that we grill some food in honor of Father's Day, which seemed reasonable to me. I didn't have to work the next day, school was out for the summer and the art program I agreed to run didn't start until after the 4th of July. But it felt like I was in a bit of a quandary since *my* father was still alive. I wanted to be supportive and also honor my father.

On the morning of Father's Day, I told Jasmine our charcoal stash was low and left the house, not just to shop but, more importantly, to call my dad. I was grateful to talk to my father, but felt a little awkward, since I'd seen up-close how quickly life could change unexpectedly.

I parked in the grocery store lot and, before going in, I sat in my car chatting with Dad for a bit. All the while, I could hear my mother in the background trying to be part of the conversation. Dad finally relented and I wished him a nice Father's Day before we said goodbye. I imagined him rolling his eyes as he handed Mom the phone.

"Hey, baby," she greeted me.

"Hi, Ma." I smiled. Those two.

"How's Jasmine?"

"As well as can be expected. She's been tearful but got out of bed this morning."

"Has she spoken to her mama?"

"Not to my knowledge. Ms. Catherine hasn't answered Jasmine's calls as of late."

"That woman is a piece of work."

I didn't have to be in her presence to know that my mother had just taken a dish towel—a permanent fixture when she cooked—off her shoulder and put it on the kitchen counter to direct her energy somewhere. "She's grieving too, Mom."

"I know, because I certainly would be."

I changed the subject. The thought of losing either one of them wasn't on my to-do list. "What did you make for dinner?"

"Your father's favorite, oxtails."

"Oh, I know he's happy."

Thinking about the tender meat submerged in a heavenly brown stew made my mouth water, even though I had stopped eating red meat years ago.

"He was napping when you called."

"I was not! I was watching the NBA finals, the series is tied up," my father shouted.

"He was sleep," Mom whispered.

I laughed. "Y'all have a good Sunday."

"Thanks for the tie," Dad yelled again before Mom disconnected the call.

I made haste in the grocery store since I had talked to my parents way longer than I'd planned to. I knew there likely wasn't much I could do to lift Jasmine's spirits, but I wandered the store looking for something tangible. Flowers were too easy—she had a yard blooming with pretty flowers. I walked up the seasonal aisle and my eyes fell on little toy cars. There was an old-fashioned black and white police car in the pack. A police car! It may have been cheesy, but I didn't care. I thought she would appreciate the sentiment.

Back at the house, I grilled an appropriate Father's Day dinner—turkey burgers, chicken wings, corn on the cob, and slightly charred vegetables— for us, including Leslie who had come over to be with Portia because Paul chose not to. When Jasmine, Leslie and Portia came outside for dinner on the patio, I placed the toy car on Jasmine's place setting. She picked it up and held it to her chest.

I couldn't begin to imagine what Jasmine had been feeling since her dad died. I felt melancholy too. But who knew a little toy could cause such an intense reaction.

CHAPTER THIRTY-FIVE

Jasmine

I felt like I had been sludging through mud since the beginning of June. Thankfully, T hadn't given up on me. While the ad campaigning wasn't as over the top as Mother's Day, I couldn't escape store ads for barbecue grills and designer watches or commercials reminding me of who taught me how to ride a bike. I couldn't figure out how to honor my father and not be immobilized by the disconnection I attempted to hide. I knew grief and grieving were normal, but I wasn't prepared for the numbness. I had trouble recognizing if something hurt anymore. I had bumped into the dresser the previous week and when I saw the bruise two days later, I couldn't even remember hitting it in the first place. I had been rushing to answer the doorbell. When I opened the front door, my mother was standing on the porch and pushed a box toward me.

She said, "these are for you" and left.

The box was full of odd mementos that no one else would care about except my father and me. Ticket stubs to a father-daughter dance. Pictures of us during family outings and vacations. My prom picture with a staged snapshot of him looking at his watch while my prom date smiled at me. There were some old pictures of us wearing sombreros at "South of the Border" the year we drove to Disney World. His promotion to sergeant. I recalled most of the events, except for the early childhood images, and I cried harder with each picture I pulled out. I realized how much I had missed my father. His absence illuminated how estranged my mother and I were.

Her behavior suggested that she was in pain, and I wanted to bridge the gap, but my mother had become distant. She would call and leave short messages. I'd invite her to dinner or ask if I could come spend some time with her. Each time she refused. My brother and sister, however, talked with her at length. I felt like she was targeting me, and I didn't have the energy to fight it.

My mother was very clear in her grief. She was angry, and it would consume her until she got to the acceptance stage. But I knew that process wasn't linear. For me, feelings changed all the time. One minute I was mad, the next I was resigned to our new reality without my father. In the three months since his funeral, my mother and I continued to argue about donating clothes, probate, and establishing a scholarship in his name. One day, she exploded over how I had rearranged the pillows on the sofa, something so insignificant, at least to me. I had faced the pillows in a different direction. She went ballistic about every change I made. After I calmed down, I realized it wasn't about me or the pillows. Mom needed to grieve in her own way.

"I don't want to talk about my husband's death," she declared. "And you don't get to tell me how to grieve."

She just wanted to be left alone, so I obliged.

The days after my father's death had been a blur. In the intervening months, I kept replaying the days leading up to his heart attack. He shouldn't have been shoveling heavy snow. It wasn't a lot, compared to previous February snowstorms, but he had always insisted on doing it himself.

Daddy was old school. He cleared the sidewalk in front of the house within a few hours of snowfall. It was neighborly and helpful to mail carriers, he would say. The last time I saw him, he was sitting in his favorite chair, reading the newspaper, talking about what the Baltimore Courier got wrong on the police beat. I had no idea that would be the last time I would ever see him alive.

A few days before Father's Day, knowing that it was a "first" occasion without him, I asked my siblings if they wanted to get together. Both told me they had plans. But on Father's Day I texted my brother and sister photos of the four of us one Christmas. Robin responded with a sad face emoticon. My brother sent a picture back of him and Dad at an Orioles game. That was the extent of my communication with them the whole day.

I was struggling to carry my own sadness, and T was worried. The day before, she had found me sitting in our bedroom with the phone in my hand.

I simply said, "I was getting ready to call my dad."

I felt fragile, sleepwalking through life. Hell, I was worried about me and the pace I was unsuccessfully trying to keep up.

Sitting at the table in the presence of my chosen family, tears welled in my eyes as I reached for T's hand and mouthed "thank you" to the woman I loved but hadn't been very present for. The toy car she gave me was thoughtful and perfect.

***

I couldn't convince her otherwise, so Leslie had been staying at her condo for about two months. And as if I needed one more thing to worry about, I talked to her one day at the end of June and she sounded lethargic. I asked Leslie questions the nurses told me to ask, about hydration, fever, or any uncontrolled bleeding she might be experiencing, but she said she was okay. After we hung up, I tried to reach Angel, hoping she could really give Leslie a once-over, but she didn't return my calls. I didn't know if she was checking on her sister or not. Hell, Angel may be out of town again.

The next day after we talked, I pulled up to Leslie's building to take her to chemo, but she wasn't outside as usual. I called and she said she was having a hard time getting ready. As a matter of fact, to my ear, she sounded loopy. I let myself into the building.

Upstairs, the place was a complete wreck. An odd stench attacked my nostrils. Paper and trash were everywhere. I opened the refrigerator and pantry, neither of which contained much food. What the hell was going on here? Leslie was in her bedroom sitting half-dressed with one pant leg on. Her port-a-cath had dried blood around it and her skin was discolored.

"I'm calling 911," I said.

"No, I need to get downtown. All my records and things are there." Leslie's speech sounded garbled. "Get me downtown."

I searched for a few minutes to find appropriate clothes for her to wear, brought her a warm washcloth for her face, and used a hospital basin bowl so she could brush her teeth. I was initially afraid she had had a stroke. But she could walk and she leaned on me as we went down to the car.

I drove downtown with purpose, ignoring Leslie's protestations, and parked in the ER's circular driveway—"No Parking" sign be damned— and rushed inside. A staff person grabbed a wheelchair and followed me back outside.

I told them Leslie was a patient of Dr. Jordan and that I had come to the ER instead of taking her to chemo.

"Okay, she'll likely be a direct admit under Dr. Jordan. I'll go back upstairs and page the doctor to the emergency department once Ms. Sharp gets registered."

Leslie covered her face with her hand for the ride to the emergency room. While she got checked in, I had the staff look at her port-a-cath, and they quickly triaged her. Leslie was wheeled to the back and a tech helped her get into a gown and onto a hospital bed. I stepped out while she disrobed. When I saw the tech leave, I went back in and sat in the chair furthest away from the bed so I would be out of the way. The tech came back with a blood pressure machine, took her vitals, and recorded the numbers in a computer. Next, a registered nurse came in for an assessment. She looked at Leslie's chest area and asked her, "How long has your catheter been clogged?"

"A day or two, I think," Leslie said weakly.

"How can you tell?" I asked.

"She has a fever, her vitals aren't stable, and there's dried blood. I suspect that's why her arm is swollen," the nurse replied, then directed her attention back to Leslie. "Is this new swelling or from your initial surgery?"

"No, it started swelling yesterday."

"This is serious. I'm going to get an IV started and wait for your doctor's orders. Someone should be in here shortly." The nurse stepped out.

I cleared my throat. "Leslie."

"Don't say it." She turned her head away from me.

"Leslie."

"I don't know what I was thinking." She was looking at me again. "I kept waiting for Angel to get back from wherever the hell she is."

"When's the last time she's been home?"

"I have no idea."

"This could have turned out much differently, you know?"

"I thought I could handle this." Leslie stared at the ceiling.

"You have an infection. Your immune system can't handle an infection." Now Leslie was crying. "I'm not sure what's happening. What is going on?"

"I thought I could handle this," she repeated between gasps of air. "This has been hard."

I scooted my chair closer and put my hand on Leslie's arm.

"I don't know why I thought Angel would be there for me. I have no idea why she's been such a bitch." All things considered, my friend was still a straight shooter. "You saw the house. The few times I have talked with her, she claimed she's going to help, like take me to chemo or get groceries. But…"

I shook my head in disbelief.

"Then last week, she told me that my being sick was bringing her down."

Leslie was sobbing now, but then Dr. Jordan walked in, her brow furrowed. And if ever there were someone I was glad to see, it was her.

"Now, now, what's going on? I hadn't expected to see you here." Dr. Jordan pinched Leslie's arm, looked at her legs, and listened to her chest with a stethoscope.

Leslie shook her head and choked out a response. "I didn't expect to be here."

"I'm going to admit you, we're going to need to remove the catheter, and figure out a replacement."

Leslie closed her eyes, nodded, and sighed.

"I saw your numbers," the doctor added. "We'll postpone chemo today. The good news is that if you're here on the oncology unit, we can run chemo any time."

Leslie feigned a smile. "I didn't expect to hear good news today."

"I'll have them insert the right-sized IV for what we need to do. We must get the infection down because you are heading toward septicemia. I'm going to put orders in and get you transferred." Dr. Jordan gently touched Leslie's shoulder, as if transferring good energy to her. "I'll see you upstairs."

After she had gone, I said, "Did you hear that? Sepsis?"

"Yes, Dr. Quinn, Medicine Woman, I heard her."

"You know sepsis will take you out quicker than cancer." I inhaled deeply and forced the air out of my nose.

"Don't tell Portia I'm in the hospital," Leslie demanded.

Her kid was too astute, so I wasn't committing to flat-out lying to Portia. "You can't go back to the condo until we have a conversation with Angel. I don't know what's going on, but I can see you've lost more weight, Leslie. I don't know if that's related to your appetite, side effects, or if it's that there's no food in the house. Either way, this can't continue."

"Good luck," Leslie said. "I believe Angel has lost her mind. I can't get her to help me with anything." She started bawling again. "I don't know why my sister hates me."

I grabbed the tissue box from the counter and returned to hug her. "Hate is a strong word."

"Her behavior is fu—"

"Okay, okay." I didn't need Leslie working herself into a lather. "We'll figure something out before you're discharged. She repeatedly sniffled into my shoulder, undoubtedly trying to calm down. "Now that I know you'll be here, I'm going into the office, and I'll swing by on my way home."

"Okay," she said, resigned to her fate of at least one night in the hospital.

"Leslie?"

"Yeah?"

"Two things when you get upstairs?"

She raised her eyebrows.

"Eat and bathe."

She stuck her tongue out at me and, as if that wasn't enough, she added a middle finger. That small, crass gesture gave me a modicum of hope.

CHAPTER THIRTY-SIX

T

Monday was hellacious. The kids in the summer program were out of control. The temperatures in July were in the upper nineties and my school, like many in Baltimore, didn't have air conditioning. Thank goodness we only met until one in the afternoon before the heat peaked and it was the final week of a three-week program. I was encouraging the students to focus on their paintings—their projects for the city art festival were due the coming week. They wanted to be children and paint each other.

I left work well beyond my typical two o'clock departure time after stopping by the front office to talk to the principal about the upcoming term. A whole school year had passed, a new one was upon us, and I was still the department chair. There was no doubt in my mind that the principal and Baltimore City Public Schools figured they had bigger fish to fry than find a replacement for one measly middle school.

I was irritable and I knew it. And I didn't feel like going home because it had gotten a bit too crowded for my taste. After three nights in the hospital, Leslie had moved back in with us. So I picked up a few sushi rolls from a new spot I had noticed one afternoon on the drive home and detoured to my old house in Bolton Hill for a little "me time."

By eight that night, I was comfortable, my belly was full, and I didn't feel like leaving. I wanted to not be needed, no "please, can you" requests, I needed some space. I called Jasmine and told her I was spending the night. Her response was terse, but she asked no questions.

I really had planned to go home after work the following day, except I didn't do that, neither on Wednesday nor for the remainder of the week. I called home every night to say goodnight, but Jasmine didn't say much during our calls. And on Thursday night, she didn't answer at all.

I knew better than to just show up at the house Friday like everything was okay. Because Jasmine and Stephanie were thick as thieves, I suspected Stephanie would know about this whole thing and have an opinion about my behavior. Despite that, I swallowed my pride and called Stephanie to ask if she could watch Portia for the evening. "Yoda" immediately anticipated what I was up to, and to my surprise, she only made one sarcastic comment. She asked where I was taking Jasmine for dinner. I told her Koi in Fells Point.

"That's a good place to apologize," Stephanie agreed.

I felt my eyes involuntarily roll completely to the back of my head, making me glad we were on the phone. I called Jasmine and, truth be told, was thankful she didn't answer. I left a message without fumbling for words, asking her to meet me for dinner to talk.

It took longer than usual to get ready for dinner. I tried on several shirts and pants only to remember that I didn't have any shoes in the house that I would have worn with any combination. I finally started with shoes and went from there.

I was nervous getting ready for dinner. Jasmine's one word text response to my invitation didn't help. It merely said, "Okay." I knew I had messed up, but I really had been just enjoying quiet time, peacefulness, and no conversations about cancer. I needed to be clear about what had driven me to leave for so many days, and figure out how to make Jasmine trust that, in the future, I would talk instead of running.

Four years before, I had taken a leap of faith, jumping into a committed relationship with a woman I wasn't expecting to fall in love with. Now, I was fearful of what the future held for us, which included possibly raising a child, since Leslie looked like she was disappearing in front of us. This wasn't the scenario I had envisioned for me and Jasmine. I had initially thought a child would upend us as a couple. Sure, things were different. Our routine was different now, but we had an extended network of support that, at the beginning, I couldn't see through my narrow lens, clouded by fear of the unknown.

When I arrived at the restaurant, I was immediately seated and fidgeted in my chair as I waited for Jasmine. When she arrived, I rose and leaned in to hug her, even though I really wanted to kiss her supple lips. I caught the slight shake of her head, along with how flat her eyes looked. No sparkle, no smile. I paused and straightened back up, and we sat down.

Jasmine was cordial, as if she were at a business dinner. I tried to explain, in three different ways, why I hadn't come home that week. She listened like I was trying to sell her a vacuum cleaner. As if she wanted to be anywhere else but there with me.

Jasmine was noncommittal about everything I said. Once I stopped talking, she thanked me "for sharing" and said she needed to relieve Stephanie. I had hoped she would say something, anything really, to give me the slightest inclination that she wanted me to come home with her. But I didn't get a thing. When she finally bade me goodnight, she only advised me to be careful getting home.

The drive back to Bolton Hill was painful. If I wasn't steering a car, I would have kicked myself. I knew better. Jasmine could hold a grudge like nobody's business. I had gone about this peace offering all wrong. Jasmine had always been really clear that she wanted to help her friend and her goddaughter. And I hadn't lost anything per se. I had the time and ability to help. Opening our home and our lives for a friend who was closer to Jasmine than her own family was a blessing. I had seen firsthand how well we all, my cousins, Terrence and Kevin, Stephanie, and my bestie John and his partner, came together to care for someone in need.

I walked back into the studio, tossed my keys on the foyer table, and stood there listening. To the humming refrigerator. To the floor creaking under my shifting weight. To my thoughts. It didn't feel the same. I hadn't expected I would be back here this very same evening.

Before heading upstairs to my bedroom, I did my own security check to make sure the house was secure, a habit I had picked up from Jasmine. The text notification pinged on my phone. It was from Jasmine.

"Check your email."

I went back down one level to where I had left my laptop and powered it up.

T,

I listened tonight and didn't want to respond for fear we would become a scene. I have way more emotions bottled up than likely good for me or you, so it was best to just listen.

I heard you and it sounded like you have to make some decisions. From my point of view, it was rude and disrespectful to just NOT come home. The amount of juggling that I had to do! Who does that?! Not giving me a heads up? Telling me "I need a break" would have been the adult thing to do. I know you weren't anticipating or prepared to parent or do extra stuff that comes with being a caregiver. I understand, it's hard.

And read this twice…you don't have to help us. I incorrectly assumed that we were in this situation together to support Leslie and Portia. My sister/friend is doing her best to stay alive for her daughter. My goddaughter needs to be cared for while her mom is fighting for her life. I thought you understood that. No, you don't know them like I do but I see this as no different than if John were ill and had kids or your nephews needed care. How can we justify not helping when we have the ability and resources to do so? I'm not going to offer surface platitudes to someone in need. I believe you know that's not me, and unfortunately in this situation, I've come to realize it's exactly who you are.

This year has been hard already. And we don't have a clue as to how it's going to end, but what I know for sure is I'm going to stand in the gap for anyone that I love and can help.

Again, I understand if that's not where you are and I'm grateful to have found out sooner rather than later for us. I plan to continue to operate as if love is a verb. It requires action, it compels us to do what needs to be done, to do uncomfortable and inconvenient things.

After reading Jasmine's email twice I went back upstairs and crashed with all my weight onto the bed. Sure, I should have told her how I felt. Sure, we had the means to help. Sure, sure, sure. Sure, she was a kind and loving person. But "I've come to know exactly who you are." What the hell did that mean? What was she implying?

I threw myself back against the pillows and punched the air.

CHAPTER THIRTY-SEVEN

Jasmine

I wasn't happy. It was five days after I wrote that email to T and she was still staying at her studio. I went to Stephanie's office, hoping for a listening ear before heading to the afternoon school pickup line. Instead, Stephanie handed me my ass.

"It's not all her fault, you know."

I scrunched my eyebrows and my mouth twisted.

"You moved two people into your home…twice."

"But—"

"Did you even give her an option?"

"I—"

"Did you ask T if she wanted to take care of Leslie and her daughter? You made some really big assumptions. Then Daddy Charles died unexpectedly, and the stress escalated."

With the mention of my father, I wanted to both scream and cry. I grabbed some tissues. "Are you going to let me answer?"

"Of course." Stephanie didn't stop though. "You assumed she would just go along to get along. You assumed you didn't need her consent—"

"I did not," I protested.

"And, you assumed your relationship was stronger than it apparently is."

"Aren't relationships about compromise?" I wasn't pouting, but I was pretty close.

"Relationships do require compromise at times—they also require communication."

"That's what I'm saying, she didn't communicate."

"I don't disagree with what T did to get your attention."

My mouth fell open.

"Girl! It was a big ask! T, would you please change your life because I want to rescue my friend?" Stephanie used her index finger to punctuate the air.

Before Stephanie could say more, I pleaded my case. "It's not like we have the luxury of time here. We weren't deciding to buy a sofa. We're talking about life and death. I jumped in with both feet thinking she would jump with me."

"But you made an assumption."

I rolled my eyes. "I don't see how giving her an option was the right thing to do."

"Say that again into this recorder please." Stephanie slid a mini tape recorder in my direction. "I want you to hear yourself. T isn't a five-year-old that you're persuading to eat her vegetables. When you don't give an option, it's an ultimatum."

"I don't see it like that." I crossed my arms, feeling a bit exposed.

"Of course you don't, you gave the ultimatum. Listen, Jasmine, you know I'd call T out if I thought she was wrong, but I don't think she's entirely off base."

"Chile, please." My eyebrows scrunched up again.

"She had every right to take some time to figure out what she wanted. In your mind you were clear about what you expected her to do, but you didn't ask. That's not how you treat someone you respect and love."

I propped my elbows on my knees and cupped my chin with my hands.

"This has been a very challenging thirteen or fourteen months for sure."

"You're talking to me like I'm one of your clients."

"Really? That's funny, they listen," Stephanie quipped.

"Wait a minute."

"No, seriously. You came here with this 'woe is me' story because your girlfriend is having a hard time keeping up with your decisions to take care of damn near everybody. Your godchild, her mama, your mama. The only two people you haven't taken care of is you and T."

"Ouch!" I loved my friend, but damn.

"That's all you have to say? 'Ouch'?"

"Fair." I held up my hand to Stephanie. She was coming in too hot.

"How about, 'I hadn't considered that'? or maybe 'I understand why she's spending more time at her studio, her refuge where nobody is sick or needs something from her.'"

"I need something from her," I said, raising my voice more than I intended to. To her credit, Stephanie didn't come back at me with the same ire.

"Have you asked her or just assumed she would pull out her crystal ball and magically meet your needs?"

"Isn't that what you do in relationships? Make assumptions?"

"Absolutely not. Not if you want to keep them."

"So now what do I do?" My shoulders slumped as I wiped my eyes.

"Go get your girlfriend. 'Cause based on how Leslie's doing, you could easily be a single woman taking care of your godchild and fighting with her daddy."

"I don't even know what to say to that."

"Is she doing better, Leslie that is?" Stephanie asked.

"No, not really. As a matter of fact, our friend smells sick…like…like soured fruit." I sighed.

Stephanie let the description sink in. "Wow! So back to T, let me help you. 'T, I was wrong. I'm sorry.'" Stephanie made a conciliatory gesture with her hand. "That should get you in the ballpark."

"This fancy office gives you the license to tell people they're wrong?"

"Don't do that, Jasmine. We call that projection and deflection. Most people don't do it in the same sentence though. But since you're a high achiever…" Stephanie snapped her fingers. "There you go."

"Ouch again." I looked down at my hands and the wad of tissue. "I feel like you're being mean now. Do you think I need therapy?"

"Who are you talking to?" Stephanie threw her hands up in exasperation. "I think everybody could use a little therapy. Perhaps you're feeling a bit sensitive 'cause I'm not saying, 'Jasmine, you're right.' I think we've been friends for over twenty years precisely because I don't lie to you."

I nodded. She was right on that point.

"Look, you know I was not a fan of Teresa Butler seemingly dropping out of the sky almost four years ago and sweeping my friend off her feet. I gotta admit, I was skeptical, but T has been good for you, and y'all are good together."

I opened my mouth to respond but nothing came out. Stephanie's perspective was new information.

"Jasmine, you are not right in this instance," she went on. "I mean, I get where you're coming from. I understand. You have stood flat-footed in support of our friend as she's going through what's been a life-changing illness. Don't let that support cost you your relationship."

I certainly didn't want that to happen. The dreadful thought made me light-headed. I had been tending to other people's gardens while mine was withering away.

"My final observation?"

I motioned for her to continue. I was ready for this session to end.

"It's your relationship that has allowed you the freedom and flexibility to provide the care that you have."

I closed my eyes and inhaled. "I'm not sure what I should do," I said in a barely audible voice.

"That's not true, you know what to do. You know who's supported you on this journey." Stephanie smiled slyly. "Other than me, of course."

"Heifer."

"I love you too." Stephanie blew me a kiss.

CHAPTER THIRTY-EIGHT

T

Before being bamboozled into teaching in the summer program, I had told myself that I didn't want to teach camp. I didn't want to teach summer school. I didn't even want to pass by a school. I simply wanted to paint. That was it. After the past crazy year, I wanted some peace and to paint. It was early August, the summer program had ended, and Jasmine and I were taking a break from each other. What that meant for our relationship in the long run, I didn't know. However, being back at my house, I was finally in a routine of rising, working out, eating breakfast, and painting. Wash, rinse, repeat.

I decided to enjoy a nice day outdoors in my long-neglected backyard. It wasn't comparable space-wise to the yard in Mt. Washington, but I had to work with what I had. I planted herbs in pots along the fence line—I didn't know how long I would be in couples' purgatory and thought I might need them here—and I cleaned months of grime off the outdoor furniture before breaking for lunch.

I had just finished a delicious ensemble of summer ripe tomatoes, a thick slice of mozzarella with basil on toasted bread, and low-salt chips when I was surprised to hear the doorbell ring. I wasn't expecting anyone, and the mailman had already delivered the Shoppers, Giant, and Safeway advertisements that were going straight in the recycling bin. When I looked out the sidelight by the front door my heart began pounding against my ribcage.

"Portia, what are you doing here? How did you get here?" I asked when I opened the door. I looked toward the street and saw a driver tip his hat and pull off.

"Ashley's driver brought me from camp," the kid said as I stepped aside so she could come in. "Her mom said it was okay."

"Uh huh. Did you ask your mom or godmother?"

"No, I was coming to see you and thought it was okay."

"Portia, you've obviously lost your ten-year-old mind. Do you think your mom or godmother would be okay with Ashley's driver bringing you here without their knowledge?" I heard my mother asking. It was my voice, sure, but the inflection screamed Mary Butler.

"Everybody is so sad at the house, I didn't think they would mind."

My heart had slowed down from moments before, but now it sank a little lower. "Come on, you know better." I guided her to the kitchen. "We're calling Jasmine, so they aren't worried to death looking for you."

Portia looked quite dejected, but I had to let Leslie and Jasmine know where she was.

I called the house first, then Jasmine's cell phone, leaving messages both times to let her know that Portia was here with me, and I'd bring her home. Then I turned to Portia and tried to not sound like my mother again. "I'm glad to see you, but you should have talked to your mom or Jasmine first."

"Do we have to leave right away?" Portia almost whined. "Can't we visit for a little while? We could plan something else to sell."

"We will not. I'm not vending with you ever again—you work people too hard."

She poked her little lips out.

"You know what, that's not true. I like your initiative and persistence to get things done, that will serve you well in life. I'd just like to add that you need to have a good solid team—"

"We make a good team," she interjected.

I huffed. "Should you plan to continue your entrepreneurial project in the future. And for the record, little Miss Sharp, I'm not your employee." I laughed.

"GT, we sold everything."

"Yes, we did. And it was a lot of work. I'd like to enjoy the rest of summer instead of vending at the farmers' market."

Portia eyed my apron. "Are you painting?"

"Not this morning, but I have been painting quite a bit. I want to have a fall art show and I was painting a few new pieces."

"Can I see them?"

"Yes, right before I take you home."

"Can I have something to drink?"

I sighed, I felt like the child was stalling for some reason. "Is everything okay at home?"

"It's okay." Portia shrugged looking at the ground.

"Tell me what's going on?" I lifted her chin to look into her eyes.

"Mommy's still sick, Godmommy is sad, and I haven't spoken to Auntie Angel."

"Hmmm, that sounds hard…" I paused a second. "How's camp going?"

"It's fun, we do a lot of activities."

"Like what?"

"We do stuff outside, arts and crafts, and go to museums."

"All of those activities sound fascinating."

"They are. Can I see your pictures?"

"I thought you wanted something to drink."

"I do. Do you have some snacks?"

I cut an apple and a few blocks of cheese and gave her some sweet tea. Once she finished, I showed her the paintings in the studio.

"GT, these are pretty. I've never seen butterflies like these."

"Thank you. I like them."

"Will people buy them? I can help you sell them."

"I've seen you in action, I'm sure you could. I hope people buy them," I said, chuckling. "I need to pay for the paint."

"Do people come here to buy them?"

"No, I'll sell them in an art gallery."

"They don't look like the old pictures in museums."

"That's a good thing, right?" We both laughed. "Okay, get your things so I can take you home."

"Am I going to be in trouble?"

"I don't know. I'm sure your mother and Jasmine will have something to say. You made a one-sided decision to come here on your own."

"I didn't want to sit in the house."

"You should tell them that. They don't know how you feel until you say something."

"When are you coming home? This is like when Daddy moved out."

Could she have hit me harder with a hammer? "I'm sorry. Your godmother and I are talking things through." *Now that was a straight-up lie.* I had only talked to Jasmine a handful of times since her pointed email. It wasn't for lack of trying. I invited her a few times to meet me to walk and talk, anything to keep some conversation going. But nada, zilch, crickets.

I changed out of my gardening clothes into a presentable outfit to drive Portia home. I even took the scenic route to chat a bit more with her since I sensed she was feeling lonely. When we arrived at the house, I was going to let Portia walk to the door and then just leave, but I thought better of that idea and walked in with her. I really wanted to see if my key still fit. When I discovered it did, a wave of relief passed through me.

Leslie was sitting in the living room, and Jasmine came around the corner from the kitchen. Both started talking in raised voices.

"Ladies, ladies," I said over them, "I know you were both worried. She was in a safe place and now she's home. So hear her out." I put my hand on Portia's shoulder for reassurance.

"I'll hear her out when I'm not mad," Leslie said through clenched teeth. "Go upstairs Portia."

Portia turned to hug me before heading for her room. Coco tipped slowly through the tension and ran upstairs too.

"Why did she come to your place?" Jasmine's first words sounded harsh to me.

"Hello, Jasmine." I shrugged. "You'll have to ask Portia. I was home minding my business and was surprised when the bell rang. I called you soon after she got there."

Leslie was less coarse. "Thank you for bringing her home."

"You're welcome. It was good to see you both." I turned the doorknob. I realized I hadn't taken my hand off of it, I'd only stepped partway inside.

"Are you serious?" Leslie looked at me and Jasmine. "That's it? You two are something else. Stubborn as hell, both of you!"

"Take care," Jasmine said and turned back toward the kitchen.

Leslie looked at me. I raised my palms in surrender. "That's your friend."

CHAPTER THIRTY-NINE

Jasmine

I felt like things were falling apart. Stephanie had provided wise counsel I had yet to follow despite having the perfect opportunity two days earlier when T had brought Portia home. I found myself speeding across Aliceanna Street. I was late dropping Leslie off to treatment because Portia couldn't seem to get herself together for camp. She hadn't packed her bag the night before as I had asked her to, which left us all scrambling this morning. I knew that if I had taken more time to question what was going on, she probably would have told me, but I had a meeting that I was now trying hard not to be late for—I just couldn't deal with her this morning. But we needed to have a conversation. *Portia wasn't being Portia.*

The new school year was only a few weeks away, and I wondered if that had anything to do with Portia's behavior. She was returning to the same school—we would have to get geared up for that next, even though I had yet to see or hear about back-to-school information. *Note to self*, I thought, *ask Leslie.*

When I pulled into the parking lot at work, not yet late, I was glad to see Jason's car wasn't in his assigned spot. I grabbed my things and headed into the building.

"Morning Ruth!" I greeted Jason's assistant.

"Morning. Jason is running late. Said he needed to meet with Councilwoman Wagner about a home in Irvington."

"Oh, nice. They have a lot of Victorian homes over there."

"Yes, and Victorian homes can be expensive to rehab."

"True, but they're so pretty when done well. Call me when he's ready."

"Will do." Ruth paused. "Are you okay?"

I hesitated—my spirit wouldn't let me utter "I'm fine." I managed a more honest response. "I'm fair to middling."

"Oh, my, I haven't heard that term in a long time. Grab you some sugar in the kitchenette. The bakery across the street dropped off some day-old pastries."

"Yeah, I could use a little sugar."

***

At ten-twenty-five, Ruth rang my phone. "He's ready."

As I came up to Ruth's desk and was about to head into Jason's office, Ruth put a hand up. "His phone rang as soon as I hung up with you," she said. "Sit here for a minute and chat with me."

I manufactured a smile and leaned against the wall, papers spilling out of the portfolio I had pressed to my chest as if it were a shield of armor.

Ruth looked at me with soft eyes. "Are you okay? I mean really, okay?"

Ruth was sharp and very little missed her purview. "I'm tired. I've been juggling a lot and I'm tired. It's just nice to be still without planning anything or making a list of what I need to do next."

"Jasmine, when you're taking care of everyone else, make sure you take care of yourself. I learned that when my beloved Nelson was sick. I couldn't help him if I wasn't well."

At the mention of Ruth's husband, I blinked back tears. A reminder that T and I were not in a good place right now.

"Make sure you and your sweetie have date nights, go get a massage or your nails done. Do something for you. You hear?"

I had been called out. Ruth was the second person in recent days essentially telling me to slow down to take care of myself and my relationship. At least that was what I heard. I heard Jason end his call.

"Thank you, Ruth, I hear you," I sighed.

Sadly, "my sweetie" hadn't been home in a while. But I walked into Jason's office with my shoulders back and chin up. I didn't have time for emotions right now.

"Morning!" I said. "Are we doing a Victorian next?"

"Hey, news travels fast." Jason chuckled and nodded toward his open door, beyond which Ruth sat. "I don't know, it would be a lot of work from what I could see from the exterior."

"Oh, you actually met at the house? What's Councilwoman Wagner's angle, that a house was already picked out?"

"Not sure yet. That's what needs to be figured out. But let me focus on what I wanted to ask you. You've done great work this past year, Jasmine. I know you have a lot on your plate, so I wanted to know if you'd like to join National for their annual conference in Orlando the last week of August? It's supposedly the happiest place on earth."

"Oh, wow! They're going to Disney? This month?"

"I know it's short notice, it took the suits a minute to decide if they'd try to have a 'conference'," he added with air quotes.

I was sure he could see that my expression likely read as doubt.

"Looking at the conference agenda, there's a morning meeting that will last about an hour, but the remainder of the day would be yours."

I paused. "Jason, I am so appreciative that you offered, but I just can't."

"Really?" The expression on his face said it all. Most people would have packed their bags before their boss finished talking.

"I have so much family turbulence right now and school starts that same week. I think you know I'm caring for my goddaughter, the one who helped raise money for our children's fund, because her mom is ill. Her mom, one of my closest friends—more like a sister, really—has also moved in because of her health challenges. A vacation, I mean a conference, is much needed but logistically it would just be an added burden."

"Nope! No burdens. This was supposed to be joyful. I really understand and empathize with your situation. If there's anything we can do here, let me know, Jasmine."

"Thanks for saying that. I've tried to maintain a consistent schedule for being in the office, but I may need a bit more flexibility for early morning or late afternoon appointments. I'll certainly make sure my time is appropriately accounted for."

"No need to even say that. I know your time and effort exceed your contract at ReBuild. I'm sorry you won't be able to join us though. Can I at least offer some tickets to a night at the aquarium?"

I managed to smile. That sounded more reasonable.

"We have special tickets for a private event there. It should be a great time with food and special demonstrations. Could be a good night out for your family."

"Thanks, Jason, I'd love those tickets."

"Great, I'll have Ruth get them for you. Anything else I can help with?"

"No, thanks again for the generous offer."

When I got back to my office, I picked up a picture from my bookcase. It was me and T at the Rehoboth Jazz Festival two years before, a spur of the moment trip, but we had big fun. There was music—jam sessions in unexpected places—good food, October walks on the beach, and lots of loving that weekend. The memory brought a warmth that settled in my chest. *Should I have declined Jason's offer?* I wondered. *Some fun could have been good for us.* I put the picture back in its place. I had a lot of work to do.

CHAPTER FORTY

T

I was in the backyard again, not doing a whole lot except staring off into space, soaking up vitamin D, and enjoying the few remaining days of summer break. Despite focused attention, my backyard looked sparse and unattended. But I needed to give my hands a break from painting. It wasn't too humid—the slight breeze made my outdoor respite pleasant. Not bad for August. I knew the Mt. Washington backyard would be blooming with all the saplings I had helped Jasmine plant before foolishly leaving. I hadn't thought through my protest and Jasmine had gone silent since I'd been over there to bring Portia home.

I connected a piece of chicken wire to the fence to keep out whatever was turning over my pots—probably cats, or at least I hoped it was cats—when I felt a vibrating against my right thigh. I dug my phone out of my pocket. Leslie?

"Hey, is everything alright?" I asked without saying hello.

"I'm okay. Still in the land of the living, thank goodness. I need you to come to the house please."

"Today?"

"Yes, please, as soon as you can."

"What's going on? I can be there in an hour or so, three o'clock at the latest."

"That's fine. I'll see you then. Thanks."

I tried to get more out of her, but that was it. No other explanation. Just a dial tone. I stared at the phone. *What was she up to?*

I made the trek to Mt. Washington and got there a little past three. Jasmine's car wasn't there, which made me all the more suspicious. I peeked through the glass storm door since the main entrance door was open. Leslie was sitting on the sofa and waved for me to come in. Unlocking the storm door, I realized it was the first time I had used my house key in a couple of weeks, when Portia and I had come from my place.

"Hey, what's going on?" I asked. I threw my keys in the bowl as if I still lived there. Wrapped in a flannel blanket and wearing a terrycloth turban covering her head, Leslie's sunken cheeks and eyes suggested she had lost another ten pounds. "Are you okay?"

Before she could answer, a car door closed, prompting me to look outside. It was Jasmine.

"What's wrong?" Jasmine asked Leslie when she came inside, but didn't wait for a response before turning to me. "What are you doing here?"

"Leslie said I needed to come over."

"Leslie! What are you up to?" Jasmine was addressing Leslie but gazing at me. "She called me at work and told me the same thing."

"She asked me to come as soon as I could." I cocked my head to the side. "Um, what's happening? Are you okay?" I asked Leslie.

Leslie took a gulp of air before responding. "I'm as fine as I can be given my current situation."

"Then what's going on?" Jasmine's voice went up a few decibels.

"I'm meddling," Leslie said, her lips pursed and one eyebrow raised.

"What?" Jasmine and I said at the same time.

"I'm meddling. You two need to work this shit out. Tomorrow is not promised." Leslie brushed her hands together as if she were dusting them off. "We need a resolution, 'cause y'all acting like your messiness is only affecting y'all. But you don't live on an island. You moping around." She pointed at Jasmine. "And you." Now she pointed at me. "Talking to Portia on the phone instead of at the dinner table."

"Hey." I put my index finger up. "Portia calls me. Speaking of…where is Lil Bit?"

"Up the street at her friend Sarah's. She won't be back for at least ninety minutes," Leslie responded.

"That's a pretty specific timeframe," Jasmine pointed out.

"Because that's exactly how long you all have to fix this." Leslie made a circle with her finger.

Jasmine stood in the middle of the living room, arms crossed and brow furrowed. I could easily imagine vapor shooting out of her ears. Leslie paid her friend no mind.

"T, let me *paint* you a picture. I'm not sure I'll be here to see the end of 2006," Leslie went on. "That's hard for me to even say. But I can't wait for you two knuckleheads to figure this out on your own. I need to know that you two are okay together and will continue helping raise my daughter once I'm gone. I am absolutely being selfish about this." She stared at me and Jasmine without so much as a blink of an eye.

"So, you going to bully us into talking?" Jasmine shook her head.

"I'm not proud, nor beyond taking advantage of a circumstance." Leslie folded her arms to mimic Jasmine's defensive posture.

"Oh, Leslie, I can't promise anything right now." Jasmine tried to dismiss the whole idea with the wave of her hand.

"Why can't you just agree to talk to me?" I asked Jasmine.

"'Cause you keep running away." She squared her body directly in front of me.

"Because you keep making decisions without me," I protested. "You can't make all the decisions for us. Even if I disagree, we can maybe compromise. You should talk to me, not shove decisions down my throat."

"Decisions needed to be made," Jasmine said, waving her hand as if trying to dismiss me too.

"Every decision, even in a crisis, does not have to be made in a hurry. Like you didn't trust that you had time to at least talk to me over dinner or something?" I said. "Yes, Leslie is sick but moving her in here a second time warranted at least a conversation." I turned to Leslie, adding, "No offense."

She dipped her head slightly. "None taken."

"And I'm a teacher, for God's sake. I work with children every day. Don't you think I'm responsible enough?" I didn't give Jasmine time to answer. "Look, Portia is a great kid. My nephews aside, Portia is the first child I've had the opportunity to care for on a personal level. I want what's best for her too, you know."

"You don't want to be a parent," Jasmine said.

"Is that an assumption or a question? Because you certainly never asked me."

Rather than respond, Jasmine found a spot in the distance to focus on, probably wishing she were anywhere else except here.

"Yes, Jasmine, maybe in August of last year I had no intention of being a parent. This situation came out of the blue and I didn't think parenting was my lot in life. At all. But you can't tell me that, prior to Leslie's illness, you seriously thought about being a parent. Yes, you stood up to say you'd be a godmother, but you didn't expect the mother to die." I shifted my eyes toward Leslie to see if I had gone too far. "I'm sorry."

"Trust me, T, I swear I'm trying my best not to," Leslie conceded. "Look…" Leslie rose from the sofa with considerable effort. "I need you two to work this shit out so that I know if I close my eyes much sooner than I want, my child will be cared for in a loving home. Go talk." She shooed us from the living room like we were feckless teenagers being banished to our rooms. "Go to the backyard or something—it may be too hot out there though. Just go somewhere and talk." She gestured upstairs. And don't come out until you've made a decision. You got seventy-five minutes."

"This is ridiculous, you can't make us talk!" Jasmine shouted, but she was already stomping upstairs.

"Indeed, I can, and I am," Leslie countered.

"Jasmine, I'm already here. Let's have a peaceful conversation." I said, following her.

"I'm feeling ambushed," Jasmine said as she walked into our bedroom.

I sat in a chair opposite the bed, where Jasmine had plopped down.

Rays of afternoon sun filtered through our sheer curtains, landing on the hardwood floors I had refinished not long after moving in. I wasn't sure how we'd gotten here but I missed this part of my life. My entire chest rose as I took in as much air as I could.

"How are you?" I said at last. "I've missed you."

Jasmine cut her eyes at me. "That's what you're starting with?" She crossed her arms across her chest like she had downstairs.

"I figured I'd start with what I've wanted to say for the last few weeks. You haven't exactly answered my calls. And I should add that I'm sorry."

"Don't let Leslie guilt you into saying something you don't mean." Jasmine was looking out the window rather than at me.

I loved this woman deeply, but her stubbornness was next level. "I've meant everything I've said. I know Leslie has a different agenda based on her perspective, but that doesn't mean she's wrong. We do need to figure out what we're doing."

Jasmine sucked her teeth.

"I don't like living in limbo."

"What do you want to do?" Jasmine asked. "I didn't think you wanted to be a parent."

"You ask me a question and then you answer it for me? Despite anything you've told yourself, I want us to work." I motioned my hand back and forth between us. "That's it. And because I want us to work, that includes whatever may come our way. We can work together as loving godparents." I paused to let my revelation sit in the air unabated. "I also want you to trust me enough to be involved in important decisions. Human dynamics is your expertise. Are you telling me that unilateral decision-making is good for a healthy relationship?"

"I want things to be right," Jasmine barely whispered.

"Only your decisions are right?"

"Don't twist my words." She finally turned to look at me, revealing tears streaking down her cheeks. "That's not what I'm saying."

"Then what are you saying?" I leaned forward.

"I'm saying that if I can keep decisions tight, it keeps me from unraveling."

"And by tight you mean you have better control?"

"Sometimes, yes. Especially if I think something needs to be acted on quickly."

"And there's no room for us to talk before you commit us to something involving our joint resources, time or otherwise? If that's what you're saying, then we have bigger problems. I happen to think I make pretty sound decisions…most of the time."

"But why did you leave?" Jasmine was staring at me. "Why did you leave *me*?" She plead through gasps, holding her hand to her chest.

I took a beat as tears welled in my own eyes. My chest tightened. "I don't know. I was being selfish, I guess. I felt like my concerns were being ignored."

"How do I know you won't leave again if something does happen to Leslie?"

"Listen! All I can give you is my word, which I realize isn't worth much right now. Yes, I need to do better."

Jasmine inhaled and I saw a hint of a smile.

It took me a minute to think of the appropriate words to say next. "I need to do better for you…for us, communicate more…" I continued. "And I like you. I don't just love you. I like talking to you. I like doing nothing with you. We're family and I've missed our family."

"T—" Jasmine was rocking back and forth now, trying to hold herself together.

I paused and then answered her cautiously. "Yes?"

"I can't do this alone," she admitted. "I tried. But I can't. And I know that now. I need you."

I closed the distance from the chair to the bed in one step and wrapped my arms around my girlfriend as tight as I could. I felt the tension in her body ease as she hugged me back. The warmth coursing inside of me was the physical manifestation of missing Jasmine.

"I need your help, and I want you here with me." Her words sounded muffled against my shoulder. "I want us to help Leslie and Portia together because it's the right thing to do and it's what families do to support each other."

We held onto each other for I didn't know how long and just breathed each other in. I kissed her on the temple and inhaled her vanilla musk fragrance. The candles I burned all over my studio to remind me of her didn't come close.

Jasmine and I walked downstairs holding hands to find Portia and Leslie sitting on the couch looking at us with unspoken questions. Jasmine kissed my cheek and the two of them cheered like the Ravens had just won the Super Bowl.

"You two!" Leslie looked at us and shook her head. "All this damn emotion will wear a sista out!"

"Mommy, I was worried about Godmommy and GT. I was going to fake being sick like I saw someone doing on the Romance Channel to get them back together." Portia laid across Leslie and coughed dramatically.

"That's your daughter!" Jasmine laughed.

"And your goddaughter," Leslie replied. Then, turning to me, she asked, "When are you coming home?"

"What's your schedule like tomorrow?" I asked Jasmine, rubbing my thumb across the hand I was holding.

"It's light. A few folks are out of the office for the national conference."

"Why don't you come with me to my studio? We'll come back early tomorrow morning."

Jasmine looked at Leslie for confirmation.

"We'll be fine overnight," Leslie said.

Jasmine giggled. "Okay." She went back upstairs, presumably to get a bag together. I mimed "thank you" to Leslie. She patted her chest and mouthed "you're welcome."

***

It was about six o'clock when we walked in the door of my place. Jasmine hadn't said much on our way here—I wanted her to relax for a change.

"Make yourself comfortable up in the bedroom," I said. "Do you want something to eat or drink?"

"Hot tea if you have any," Jasmine answered.

It always amazed me that she drank hot tea all times of the day, in every season. Luckily, I had straightened the place up. I wasn't a slob or anything, far from it. But while I'd been gone from the other house, I had spread out and left things out and about like I had when I lived by myself.

"I do, mint, chamomile, or jasmine?" I wiggled my eyebrows up and down.

She returned the gesture with kind eyes that I hadn't seen in a minute, along with her warm smile.

Having her back here in my space, not just the physical space but my personal space, I realized just how much I had missed my girlfriend. Missed being tethered to another human being—not just any human though. Jasmine kept me grounded and settled. And I had missed waking up next to her warm body and not so accidentally touching her arm or butt when we were in the kitchen together and making her lunch and including silly notes tucked somewhere in the bag. The past year had been rough, but it hadn't been all bad. I realized I wouldn't trade the love and levity I experienced hanging out with Portia for anything.

As I made the tea, I considered how I'd been operating in the world. Sometimes I used my introversion as an excuse to be alone, but I needed to get over myself and get better about communicating. I appreciated that Jasmine said she needed me. That made my heart overflow with gratitude for her and us. And I needed her too.

I brought tea, sandwiches, and sliced cucumbers upstairs since I didn't know if Jasmine had eaten lunch or not before leaving work at Leslie's behest. In the next two hours, we talked more than we had in the last two months. I apologized three more times for abandoning her, Leslie, and Portia. But I was tired of talking.

"Your toiletries and whatnot are where they usually are." I leaned over to kiss Jasmine's cheek. "Why don't you take a long, hot shower while I take the dishes to the kitchen."

Much to my surprise, she didn't hesitate or protest or make a snide remark. She was no doubt tired of talking too.

When I came back upstairs, Jasmine was lying on the bed face down wearing one of my t-shirts and running shorts, despite having her own clothes here. I took this as a good sign. Besides, if I had my way, there wouldn't be cotton between her body and my hands for long anyway.

After showering too, I didn't bother with clothes. Instead, I pressed play on the multi-disc CD player for continuous smooth jazz, slid her shorts off, tossed them on the floor, and straddled my knees on either side of her body, my clit pressed firmly on her butt, triggering my immediate arousal and slickness. I massaged her shoulders until I felt the knots loosen a little, giving me permission to continue relieving tension in the rest of her body.

I kneaded each of her butt cheeks and held my thumbs against pressure points in that soft crease where her butt met the back of her thigh. Her soft moans were a glorious sound that, until then, I didn't know I'd missed.

The way her backside rose to meet the rhythm of my hands, the wetness I felt when my hand found her opening, let me know she had missed us too. I spread her ass and put my tongue in places it hadn't been in far too long.

"Wait a second," she said faintly.

"Are you okay?"

"I'm better than okay." Jasmine got on her knees and put her face back on the pillow. Her essence was perfectly exposed for me.

"Tell me what you want."

"I want you to fuck me however you want."

Oh my god! Why hadn't we made up sooner? I spread her lips wide and inserted an index finger, then a middle finger. Soon enough, she was bucking back on three of my fingers, her body's physiological response making it easy to meet her body's demand for more friction. She came like that, me riding her from behind, pulling her closer so I could thrust harder, raw desire emanating from her to me. Not too long after, both of us collapsed on the bed with me snuggled next to her, one leg covering her and listening to her breathe heavy sighs.

Jasmine loved hard. After four years together, I knew she needed to process that amount of expended energy. But just when I thought she was asleep...

"Get on top of me."

I did. I laid on top of her and put my lips on hers.

"Let me be more specific."

I turned my head to the side to hear her better.

"Sit on my face."

I did as I was told. Between her tongue deep inside of me, while she simultaneously explored my ass with a finger, the sensations were intense. Even with the fading sunlight streaming through the skylight, I saw brilliant stars as I exploded, like a supernova.

It was impossible to make up lost time, but we damn sure tried.

CHAPTER FORTY-ONE

Jasmine

I dropped Leslie off at the hospital's parking circle. There was no way she would be able to ambulate without assistance to her treatment today. I asked her to alert one of the guards to bring a wheelchair so we would have an easier time getting upstairs for her appointment. She was sitting in the wheelchair by the elevator when I got inside. Leslie looked like she was in pain but denied it every time I asked. She was guarding her stomach and paused like each sentence was painful to utter. When I wheeled her up to the reception desk in the infusion center, the nursing staff looked confused.

"Hi, Ms. Sharp, we weren't expecting you today. Dr. Jordan cancelled your appointment."

"Really? She didn't say anything to me nor have I heard from her office," Leslie squeezed out.

"Okay, let me call upstairs." I appreciated the nurse's attentiveness. But the measured, one-sided responses I heard raised the hair on my neck. Something was wrong, and no one needed to tell me that. Leslie looked fragile. She was having difficulty walking, her appetite was non-existent, and she was sleeping most of the day and evening. "Yes, I'll send her to the office now."

"Ms. Sharp, Dr. Jordan's assistant asked that you come up to her office."

Leslie looked at me but didn't say anything.

When we got to Dr. Jordan's office, her assistant came out to get us, apologizing for the mix-up and escorting us to a space that was unfamiliar to me.

"We've never been in here before."

"I have," Leslie let me know. "It's the office that she generally uses when the whole treatment team gets together. The medical staff, supportive staff, and anyone else on someone's team."

"We've needed a whole team. I wonder why we haven't been in here."

"I suspect there's a complication." Leslie was too nonchalant for my taste. Yes, she had been through this process twice before with her mother and sister, so I tried to keep my voice even and neutral. "What do you think it is?"

"I don't know, I've not been feeling well though."

"How come you didn't say anything?"

"I thought it would pass, for one, and two, what good would that have done?"

This wasn't the time to fuss. "Alright, let's see what Dr. Jordan has to say." I tried to be reassuring, but my heart was pumping so hard it felt like my temples were reverberating.

A woman knocked on the door before entering and introduced herself as a registered dietician. Next came an oncology nurse from downstairs and then Dr. Jordan arrived.

"Hi, Leslie, I apologize for the confusion. I've already addressed the staff about the lapse in informing you of the change. We were supposed to tell you to come here instead of chemo today."

Leslie shook her head, acknowledging what the doctor said.

"Your recent labs show that you are neutropenic. Your neutrophils, a type of white blood cells, are significantly low and we need to delay treatment until your numbers increase. I'm hoping it'll only be a week, no more than two, which is why our dietician is here. You two have met?"

"Just now, yes."

"She'll recommend food and nutrition to support you."

Leslie nodded.

"Oncology is here too to review our IV infusion schedule and administer injections to help stimulate bone marrow growth. We'll also make sure your red blood cells aren't impacted." She paused, presumably to let Leslie ask questions. "I also recommend you limit your social contact to reduce the potential of infection."

This was a lot.

"The other reason I wanted to meet was I've been notified there are two studies accepting candidates for research. I need your signature to submit the applications on your behalf. What questions do you have for me?"

"Do you have a recommendation for which study would be the best?" I asked.

"Whichever one she gets accepted to."

Well, damn! That was where we were? At the extreme measure stage? I took the food recommendations from the dietician since I prepared most of the meals anyway while Dr. Jordan and Leslie left for a quick assessment. When Leslie returned, she had prescriptions for pain, nausea, and mouth sores that she hadn't mentioned before, and we headed back downstairs.

I pulled over into one of the parking spots in front of the hospital, where Leslie was waiting.

"What?" Leslie looked at me as I helped her into the car.

"You have got to tell me if there's something medically going on. If you have mouth pain, you aren't going to eat, and if you're in pain it's harder to deal with everything else."

"I didn't want you to worry. It's not like you aren't dealing with stuff too," she said as I hopped in the driver's seat.

"Yes, that's true and we still need to immediately take care of concerns we have some control over." I grabbed her hand. "Let's say the hard things. What do we need to do now that treatment is delayed for one or two weeks?"

She sighed, "Pray the tumor cells don't go wild and grow."

"Is that possible?"

"Yeah." Leslie stared out the window, making it harder for me to hear her. But I had heard enough. "I suspect there will be another chemo adjustment when we start back. Some of these situations with Angel didn't come up at all or for my mother it wasn't until the cancer returned that we were at this point. I don't understand why mine has to be so aggressive." She covered her face and started crying. "I don't know if I'll get to ring the bell. I'm really afraid."

Lord, I have absolutely no idea what to say to this woman, I prayed. I'm already mad at you and haven't had much to say lately. I want to help my friend with the right things to say and do. Please give me some guidance and direction.

"What do we need to do now?" I asked.

"We need to have a very hard conversation—I need to talk to you, T, and Paul."

"Let me know when."

"Now."

"Wait, what?"

Leslie pulled out her phone. I wasn't sure who she was dialing until she said, "You need to call me, we need to meet immediately to discuss *your* daughter."

CHAPTER FORTY-TWO

T

I had been downstairs in the basement folding laundry and preparing to return to school when I heard Jasmine and Leslie's muffled voices.

"Hey, you," I said to Jasmine after coming upstairs carrying a basket of clothes and kissed her on the lips.

"Hey," Jasmine replied rather solemnly and nodded her head in Leslie's direction.

I furrowed my brow at Jasmine and turned to speak to our house guest. "Hey, Leslie."

"How are you?" Leslie asked but didn't wait for a response. "I need y'all to meet me at the dining room table in ten minutes." She shuffled away down the hall.

I stared at Jasmine searching for a clue as to what this was about. As far as I knew, they had just come back from Leslie's routine chemo treatment.

In turn, she sucked her lips into her mouth and jutted her chin toward the dining room.

I took the basket upstairs to our room and returned to find Leslie sitting at the dining room table with a three-ring binder. Jasmine sat down and gave me a pained look. I responded by discreetly acknowledging my uncertainty.

"The next few weeks of chemo are on hold," Leslie started. "My recent scans showed no decrease in tumor sizes and also no growth. Short of being selected for a study and getting medication instead of a placebo, I may be facing a decision whether to continue treatment or focus on the quality of my remaining life."

Jasmine had her eyes closed, but her head was nodding side to side. I moved closer to her and took her hand.

"So, today is a good day to take care of this." Leslie patted the black binder in front of her. "I also figured I better take advantage of Paul spending time with his daughter for a few hours. It's a good time to speak freely. Well, not sure about the good time part, but I need to talk to you all sooner rather than later."

"I feel like I know where this is heading." Jasmine looked at our clasped hands.

"You know, you've heard me ask, pray, demand more time, and since I don't know if that's going to happen, we need to implement a possible Plan B."

"I'm just not ready for it," Jasmine barely whispered.

"I'm not ready for this conversation either, but I need to make sure you two are aware of decisions I've made and ask for your assistance in tying up loose ends." Leslie took a deep breath and slowly opened the binder. "This book contains bank information, my will, which has been filed in Baltimore City, and trust documents drawn up for Portia."

I sat perfectly still and held on tight to Jasmine's hand, which had started trembling.

"Okay," Jasmine nodded, "we're doing this today."

"You know the hospital is right next to the courthouse. There are also lots of attorney offices in that three-four block radius. I looked up estate planning and interviewed a few lawyers and I settled on a nice female attorney who listened to me and didn't try to persuade me to leave my family in charge because we're related by blood or my ex-husband since he's Portia's father."

"What?!" I shook my head. "Oh, hell no!"

"I know, right? He's going to be somebody else's daddy too? No, thank you. Anyway…," Leslie waved her hand dismissively at the mention of Paul's expanded paternal role. "The lawyer recommended the will for public record and the trust to transfer assets that don't need to be made public…like accounts for Portia. Jasmine, I made you the executor and T, you're the back up. Yes, I should have discussed this with you…" Apparently disbelief was splayed all over our faces. "So, if this is something you're unable to do, you gotta let me know now."

"Or what, forever hold my peace?" I asked nervously. Jasmine nudged me with her shoulder.

Leslie smirked.

"Sorry…I'm here for Portia." My palms were sweaty, and my right leg suddenly wanted to involuntarily jump up and down.

"I suspected you would be. My daughter adores you."

"Jasmine, my banking account information, 401K documents, and Portia's 529 plan details are in here." She pointed to the binder. "The estate attorney and I went through everything that I could think of. Jasmine, your name has been added to my bank accounts as payable on death."

Jasmine nodded, sucking her bottom lip into her mouth. She was barely holding back the tears pooling in her eyes.

"Just to be clear, Angel's and Paul's names aren't on a damn thing. I needed to be strategic to ensure Paul didn't have access to funds as Portia's father. I can't get around his custody as her father—believe me, I tried to see what I could do. You may have to go to court for partial or joint custody. The will makes my wishes clear that I want Portia to stay with you two. My attorney has my documented statements and is ready to assist you."

"Wow." I was at a loss for anything intelligent to say. Leslie had been busy. The fact that she trusted us even though we were a hot mess as of late was incredibly endearing.

"She will remain on retainer for three years should I pass away."

"Why three years?" I heard myself ask.

"Portia will be thirteen and I have no doubt that she will articulate where and with whom she would like to live."

"The kid is astute," Jasmine finally said.

"Quiet as it's kept, she already calls this house home. I know this is a safe, loving space for her to thrive. T, you've already taught her about business, fundraising, and you see how she cares for those that may be less fortunate. I was an adult when I lost my mother and even as an adult, I was perplexed with not having a mother figure to turn to. My daughter is not even a teenager yet. I need to make sure that, when she has questions or loses her way because I'm not here—"

I got up to get a box of tissues from the living room. Both Jasmine and I were sniffling and wiping tears away. My heart was heavy because of this moment and full because of the responsibility. I got us all water while I was up too. Maybe they didn't need it, but my mouth had gone dry half an hour before.

"I need you to help her, guide her, keep her safe, and continue teaching her how to be fierce in a world that would have her thinking otherwise."

Jasmine and I both nodded in agreement, still snorting and wiping away tears and snot.

"Alright, change of subject, kinda." Leslie closed her book. "You know I'm fairly frugal." She laughed at herself. "I had hoped to become part of the millionaire's club and be comfortable when I retired. Instead of expensive purses or shoes, I purchased insurance, funded my 401, and saved more than I made. There's a little over five hundred thousand dollars in the trust for Portia's schooling, a car, wedding, and a house down payment, in whatever order those events happen in her life."

Jasmine and I looked at each other in amazement but refocused back on Leslie when we heard the catch in her voice. She had kept it together, but now water gathered in her eyes too. She took a few breaths and pressed on.

"I hope you'll let Angel remain a part of her life. Although her behavior has said otherwise, I know Angel loves Portia. She's family and the only person left who's known me longer than anyone else. She has family pictures and knows the stories. T, I'm almost finished with the other photo album that you've helped me create. I haven't decided when the right time to share that will be and maybe I won't—It could be a decision you two will eventually make."

I downed the rest of my water and started sipping out of Jasmine's glass. If ever we had questions about parenting, we just needed to say to ourselves, "What would Leslie do?" Because sister-girl was an extraordinary model.

"I don't know how to thank you for everything you've done for the Sharp family. I would love to live long enough to tell and show you…but that, unfortunately, is not my decision."

Leslie paused again and swallowed hard. She reached for Jasmine's hand and Jasmine got up to hug her.

"I don't know what to say." Jasmine cried in the crook of Leslie's neck.

I watched the two of them hold on to each other for dear life.

CHAPTER FORTY-THREE

Jasmine

The previous two weeks had been busy getting Portia ready for the school year, which started the fourth Monday in August. She was headed to the fifth grade, meaning she'd have a new uniform color, but the pattern remained the same. I was thankful Leslie had given me the inside scoop to check the parent association website to find someone selling their kids' used uniforms. I had connected with one of those parents the week before and now Portia had enough uniforms for the school year. The clothes looked to be in good condition and were a fraction of what they would have cost if we had purchased them new. I was excited because the drop-off and pickup times for her grade were fifteen minutes later. The previous year had been a struggle, with everything so new to me and T. We had certainly been drinking from a fire hose back then. This year, however, we knew what to expect—I was ready.

Leslie rode with us on the first day back, then we headed to treatment. She had ultimately gone without chemo for three weeks, and when we arrived the staff let her know that Dr. Jordan had ordered a new set of scans to assess Leslie's status. A nurse added that Dr. Jordan would probably come to speak with her sometime during her appointment.

This wasn't completely out of the norm, but the doctor's news hadn't been great the last time, so I felt a sinking feeling in my stomach, but I tried to remain calm.

During the last hour of the infusion, Dr. Jordan came in, drawing the curtain for privacy—although really there was none. It was a curtain in an open bay of chairs. The doctor leaned in close to Leslie and spoke in such a low voice I had to pull my chair closer.

"I think you have a good chance of being selected for one of the studies we applied for," she began. "If you're selected, the study research team will lead your care. I must be honest, since they won't identify participants for a few more weeks, we need to decide what your treatment plan will be while we're in this holding pattern. Remember we talked before about future treatment versus maintaining your quality of life?"

"You think the scan is going to show growth?" Leslie asked.

"I don't know, I'm worried that it might. Three weeks is a long time for an aggressive cancer to go untreated. Even if there's growth and you make the study, there's a good chance that the antigen receptors growing with lab support and infused back into your blood to target cancer cell proteins may not attack enough or get in front of the multiplying cancer cells."

I jumped in. "I'm sorry, Doc, can you make it plain?"

"Sure. The team will extract good, fighting cells, give them extra support, and then put them back in her bloodstream to attack the cancer cells. In a nutshell, we need more good cells to fight the ones we don't want."

"Thank you."

"Of course," Dr. Jordan assured me. "I'm hoping the benefits of the research, along with additional interventions, begin to shrink the tumors."

"And if it doesn't?" Leslie wanted to know.

"That's where the discussion with the Palliative Care Department comes in."

"That's different from hospice?"

"Yes, they look at the whole picture to see what other resources you or your family may need."

"I'll still get chemo while I'm waiting?"

"Yes," Dr. Jordan replied. "And depending on the scan, we may do another two to three days of radiation and back to chemo. Hence, the importance of having a conversation with our palliative care specialists."

"Okay, sign me up. Where's their office?"

After our "black book" discussion, Leslie's decisiveness made a whole lot of sense.

Dr. Jordan smiled. "I'll put a consult in and someone from the department will speak with you here." She patted Leslie's arm, nodded at me, and left.

Leslie put her head back and covered her eyes with both her hands. "That wasn't totally bad news, was it?"

"I don't think so. At this point, we need all hands on deck. They'll look at your medical situation from all angles—support, advice, and the impacts of treatment on you and your family. Can't hurt."

We were still talking when Leslie's assigned nurse came back and informed her that Dr. Jordan had ordered a little anti-nausea medication to be administered after chemo, so it would be another twenty minutes or so.

"Okay, I'm going to close my eyes for a minute then."

Leslie was just about asleep when a gentleman came over, nodded a greeting to me, and sat down.

"Hello, Ms. Sharp."

Leslie didn't immediately respond.

"Ms. Sharp."

"Yes, hello." Leslie opened her eyes.

"I'm Dr. Singh, the palliative care physician rounding today. I wanted to introduce myself and see if you have any questions about palliative care in general. Would you like to talk privately?"

Leslie declined, introducing me as her daughter's godmother, and proceeded to ask questions about his role and how it factored in to her care. She asked again to ensure she wasn't entering hospice. He assured her the two areas were totally different. Much to my surprise, they even talked about family. He ended the visit by sharing that he had a ten-year-old granddaughter.

"My daughter is the same age, and I'd love to eventually have a ten-year-old granddaughter," Leslie admitted.

"I'd like that for you too." Dr. Singh gently touched Leslie's hand and left.

When we were about ready to leave, a nurse came over with a stack of papers.

"What's this?" Leslie took the papers in her hand.

"More information about today's treatment and a referral for home support from Dr. Singh. He thought having a visiting nurse would be helpful. Give the agency a call. They can recommend useful community resources for you and your family."

****

The initial palliative care home visit, which happened the first Thursday in September, was uneventful. I listened for the first fifteen minutes to the conversation between Leslie and the nurse about home care needs, then I stepped out so Leslie could have privacy and to answer my ringing phone. It was Angel, whom I hadn't talked to in a month of Sundays.

I wasn't thinking when I told her, "I need to call you back, the palliative care nurse is here."

When she said, "I'll talk to you soon," I thought she meant she was going to call me back. But the doorbell rang an hour later, and Angel was standing on my porch.

"What did you mean a palliative care nurse is here?"

She had gall to have both concern and indignation in her voice. Both prospects grated on my raw nerves.

I gave Angel the evilest stink eye I could muster. "The nurse just left. Your sister has been sick for an entire year. What do you think I meant?"

"I don't understand. What's happening?"

Maybe Angel deserved grace, but it wasn't in me to give it just then. I was waiting for the day I could tell her how I really felt about her actions, or lack thereof, toward her sister during this cancer fight. When Angel's tears started, I was not ashamed to say, I didn't care. Angel had operated throughout the past year like she only wanted the highlights, but not today. Today she would not have the luxury of absence. I provided every gory detail of what her sister had been going through.

When she muttered, "I didn't know," it grated my skin.

"You didn't want to know. You didn't take her to any appointments. Nor have you supported your niece, who asks about you constantly."

"What should I do?" Angel's pitiful expression made my core hotter than it already was.

"I think you need to go upstairs and tell your sister whatever you want her to know."

"I don't know what to say."

Why did people always say that? "Figure it out, Angel. I don't know what to tell you." I was restless and irritated and had to get away. I picked up Coco's leash and shook it. She heard the bell tinkling and came running.

"I need some fresh air," I all but spat at Angel. Coco and I left her standing at the front door.

We started walking along the Jones Falls Trail, which was only a short distance from home. I was at least fifteen minutes in before my jagged breaths slowed and I could formulate more rational thoughts. Two minutes after that, I was already at the corner of Pimlico and Cross Country Boulevard, a mile west of the house. I turned around like Forest Gump when he realized he was tired of running. The nerve! Now she was concerned? Is that what happened when you needed to have difficult conversations without the luxury of time?

I rounded the corner onto my street and saw T's car in front of the house. Any other time, that would have made me a bit gooey inside. But the endorphins I had produced walking under the green tree canopy—a canopy that would soon give way to orange, gold, and maroon falling leaves—and taking in God's oxygen supply threatened to immediately dissipate. Angel's SUV was still where it was when I left. I walked in—Coco didn't wait for me to take her leash off before running to find Portia. I heard Portia and Angel talking upstairs.

T rounded the corner from the kitchen. "You went for a walk?"

"Coco and I did, yes. We had unexpected company."

"She's not moving in, is she?" T deadpanned.

"Oh, you got jokes." I didn't know why that made me laugh, but I doubled over until tears were running down my cheeks.

"No, she definitely ain't moving in. Remember in *Imitation of Life*—"

"Never saw it."

I pursed my lips. I would have sworn T was dropped from another planet. "How could you not have? Anyway, in that *classic* movie, the daughter treated the mother terribly and at the end started screaming "Mama" *after* the funeral procession."

T lifted her eyebrows.

"Angel is the young lady screaming, except she's screaming for her sister."

"So, what do you think this means now?"

"I don't know. It's not my issue. They're having a family convo. No matter how this turns out, I have no regrets. We, you and I, have done the heavy lifting. I have no regrets."

"I'm with you. No shoulda, coulda, woulda on our part," T cosigned with me.

T pulled me by the waist to her. Her warm, sweet lips brought some of the endorphins back.

"Hmmm…how was your day?" I asked. "Where have you and Portia been?"

"You know your godchild always has an angle. She saw the butterflies I created for my next show, and she wants them on t-shirts for the breast cancer walk next month so we went to a print shop. The kid wants all of us to wear matching shirts," T said in a sing-song way.

"That sounds cute. You have a design that you don't mind using?"

"Oh, yeah. I have a few designs that I think could work."

"Wait a minute." I held a finger up to T.

Angel and Portia were coming down the stairs. "I'm going to get Aunt Angel some water."

Angel's eyes were bloodshot and puffy, and her face looked swollen. As angry as I was with Angel, I offered her the briefest smile. She was going to need to process her behavior—not my issue.

"Is it okay if I come back tomorrow?" Angel asked just above a whisper.

"I need to check her schedule. Leslie's chemo has been reduced to two times a week."

"If you can let me know, maybe I can take her one day each week?" She took the water that Portia offered. Portia hugged her and retreated into the kitchen with T to give Jasmine and Angel some privacy.

"That would be really helpful. I'll check the details and send you the information later tonight."

"Jasmine, I'm sorry, and thank you. I'm going to go now before I fall apart again." Angel stepped toward me with her arms outstretched. Although I wasn't a fan of hers right then, I also didn't want to contribute to her suffering. I held her close until she stepped back, her chin brushing her chest. "Goodnight."

"Well?" T asked, coming back into the living room.

"Ms. Butler, I believe we have turned a corner."

CHAPTER FORTY-FOUR

T

Jasmine and I were better together. When we were in sync there was little we couldn't accomplish together. Too bad it had taken us a year to figure that out. I had been uncomfortable the day Leslie sat us down to discuss her affairs and outline her wishes about taking care of Portia. Afterwards, I called my mother, once I got myself together. Mom was very supportive—she made me feel better and put things in sharp focus.

"Baby, Leslie is trusting you all to raise her child," she'd said. "I don't know her well, but I am a mother. She didn't just wake up that morning and make that decision. She selected you and Jasmine, that's an honor."

I wasn't sure I saw it as an honor rather than of immense responsibility, but we had accepted the task, and we didn't want to mess up.

And now that Angel had pulled her head out of her ass, things were a little easier. The three of us—me, Jasmine, and Angel—took turns with the St. Jo's pickup line, and Jasmine and Angel alternated weeks taking Leslie to treatment until she was officially accepted into a study.

I didn't fully understand the details of that process other than we wanted her to get medication and not a placebo. But Leslie was soon to be off to the research center, along with other participants. There, they would be divided into groups and, once the study was concluded, return home for further monitoring.

Jasmine was still nervous about the whole idea and ultimately what the future held, but we planned a small gathering to shower Leslie with love and things to take with her to the research center. I agreed to make a light fare and Portia volunteered to bake cookies. So on the night of the get-together, except for the veggies roasting in the oven, my part was done. I went to chill in our bedroom.

Jasmine was sitting on the bed and quickly wiped her face with a crumpled tissue.

"Hey, you okay?" I sat on the bed next to her.

"I'm fine." She looked at me.

My left eyebrow shot straight up.

She sighed. "No. No, I'm not fine. I'm worried." Her shoulders slumped. "I'm worried that we're not doing enough as Leslie continues to decline."

"Isn't that something you all discussed with the doctors?"

"Yes, doesn't mean I'm not scared though."

"Fair." I put my arm around her shoulder. "Can you put the worry away for the night and enjoy us getting together for a little cheer?"

"I'll be better by the time I go downstairs. I won't bring the mood down. Leslie wanted her core people around her tonight. I will take her tomorrow."

"So once Leslie gets there, she's officially in?"

"Yeah, they'll do an assessment and confirm she's agreed to all the research stipulations."

"Is Portia going tomorrow?"

"No, Stephanie said she didn't know if that was a good idea."

"Okay, I can drop her off at school before I go to work and pick her up."

"Thanks, baby. Now if we can just clear this last hurdle for treatment and recovery." Jasmine closed her eyes and sucked in air through her nostrils as I watched her chest rise for what seemed like fifteen seconds. "I'm praying so hard."

"Oh…you talking to God again?" I nudged her with my shoulder.

"We have our chats." She smiled.

"I think we're all chatting. Mom said they put Leslie's name on the prayer list at their church. Do you think I should tell Leslie that?"

"Yes, I think she'd appreciate it." Jasmine laid her head on my shoulder and sighed again.

"Let me check on the food." I gave her a quick peck on her forehead. "Folks should be here soon."

"I'm coming. I'll be down in a few minutes to light some candles."

"Are they scent-free? Remember Leslie said some smells are making her more nauseous."

"That's right." Jasmine snapped her fingers. "That didn't start until the last chemo adjustment. I'll just dim the lights, that'll be fine."

***

I was taking the vegetables out of the oven when the doorbell rang. To my surprise, Stephanie walked in with balloons when I answered the door.

She stood up a bit straighter. "What? It is a celebration, right? A celebration calls for balloons and ice cream."

"Yes, Stephanie." I reached to take them both from her.

"Everybody is a little sensitive," she said, leaning in to hug me. Stephanie throwing shade and snark? Yes. Hugs? Not so much. "I'm so glad you two are good again," she whispered.

"Thanks, that's two of us." Clearly, hell was freezing over.

Jasmine came out and saw Stephanie hugging me. "Oh, this is serious! You alright?"

"I don't know, but T was kind enough to give me a hug." She rapidly fanned her eyes.

I queued old-school R&B music on the radio while Jasmine and Stephanie embraced. "Girl, let me go before I start crying." Stephanie cleared her throat and Jasmine released her.

Leslie made her way gingerly down the steps. "Nope, no crying tonight. We're going to laugh, T has cooked! I've been smelling it for the last hour. We're going to celebrate life." Stephanie helped Leslie to the sofa and placed a few pillows behind her for extra support. The doorbell rang again, and Angel came in with festively decorated bags.

"What do you have there?" Leslie asked.

"You haven't seen these in a *loonnnng* time." Angel sat the bags on the coffee table and plopped down next to her sister. "Where's Portia?"

"She's coming, she was on the phone with her little friend Quetta." Leslie started to peek in a bag, but Angel pushed her hand away.

Once everyone got settled, Angel asked if she could do a toast.

I got up. "I need to get glasses."

"I have some." Angel passed the bags out.

Leslie opened hers first and squealed. "Where did you find these?"

"Girl, I gave the house a good cleaning and found these from Mom's party."

I opened my bag to find a wine glass decorated with fuchsia and pink tulle. *Not something I would use daily.*

"This is a good sign," Leslie declared. "Mom's glasses, my sisters, my daughter…my family is here." Everyone offered some acknowledgement of agreement. "Let's say grace."

We held hands and stood around the table and let Portia give thanks on our behalf. By the time she finished with her prayer, the music had changed to gospel. Kirk Franklin and God's Property were telling us the storm was over.

"When did you change the station?" I asked Jasmine.

Jasmine looked at me. "I thought you changed it."

"I didn't touch nothing." We both looked at the radio and back at each other. "Well, I guess we needed a reminder that we need to have a little faith."

"Right…more than George Michael faith." I winked.

Before everyone left, Leslie asked if we could all "touch and agree" again. We had all done very well masking our emotions bubbling just below the surface. But there was something about sharing energy with other human beings, so this was going to put everyone over the edge. By Leslie's third "Thank you," tears were glistening on Jasmine's cheeks, Stephanie was keenly focused on her feet, and Angel was outright blubbering. We held hands for a few minutes after Leslie stopped talking. Portia broke the circle first by hugging her mother. As Portia hugged her, Leslie looked around the room at all of us and said, "Take care of my greatest treasure."

Nobody wanted to disappoint this kid. "We will," we declared together.

***

After our guests were gone, Jasmine and I snuggled in bed listening to each other breathe and enjoying the stillness that permeated the house now.

"Could tonight have been any more emotional?" she asked and pushed closer, which I hadn't thought possible.

If I weren't delusionally tired, this comfortable position would have given me a second wind. Jasmine's butt was wedged snugly against my crotch. My arm was wrapped around her waist and our fingers were threaded together.

"I don't think so—I didn't know I was going to have to break out the tissues."

"That was best, wiping all that snot on the back of my hands would have been nasty."

"Ewww." I drew my hand back. That sentiment made me recoil.

She reached behind her and grabbed my hand and kissed my open palm.

It was my turn to take a deep inhalation. "You okay?"

"As okay as I'm going to be with my friend knocking on death's door."

"You know I have your back, right?"

"Yes, ma'am, I know." Jasmine's body relaxed against mine a bit more and her breathing became deeper.

I kissed her shoulder blade. "Just making sure you're crystal clear."

CHAPTER FORTY-FIVE

Jasmine

Leslie and I headed to Bethesda mid-morning to avoid rush hour and commuters heading to DC from Baltimore. Portia had a moment when she and T were leaving for school—understandably, she didn't want to leave her mother. I imagined that day at school wasn't going to be the best for her. T was a godsend though, talking Portia off the ledge.

I drove south on Interstate 95 and around 495 with Gospel Fest on blast. We needed all the positive energy we could get. The trees along the highway were headed toward peak fall foliage.

"Are you nervous?" I turned the radio down as we neared the Colesville exit.

"I am. I'm not really sure what to expect. The brochures mentioned numerous blood draws and scans. The other part I thought could be helpful was the therapy groups they offered." Leslie paused, staring straight ahead. "I really have a better understanding of why Angel acted like she did."

"Yeah?" I glanced over at her.

"I'm not excusing her shitty behavior by any means, but I imagine once you recover from this kind of fight, life looks different. Angel was living her life on her own terms…not yours and certainly not mine."

"I get that. I don't understand why she waited so long to get involved though. But you know what? That's water under the bridge."

"True. She said she's on standby for my discharge. I'm hoping the first round of data-gathering is done by the time of the breast cancer walk. I want to be there."

"From your lips to God's ears. Let's see how this goes."

We rode in silence the remainder of the way. I pulled up to the American Research Center security gate and stopped next to a guard in a military uniform. Leslie handed me a piece of paper, and I showed it to him. In return, he hurriedly spit out directions and waved us through.

"What else goes on here?" I knew they did research, but I didn't know much else.

The campus was huge, with mostly red brick buildings, a mix of old and new, and trees interspersed between them. Except for dude with the gun at the gate, the place felt more like a college campus than a stodgy government institution.

"The packet indicated this place serves military members, families, and research."

"Hmmm…that's rather vague, intentionally, I presume." I steered us to the building. The gentleman I spoke with on the speaker phone said I couldn't accompany Leslie inside, so I asked him for a wheelchair. "Keep us posted on your progress."

Leslie made a slow nod of her head and sucked her bottom lip into her mouth, trying to stifle tears.

"And let us know if we need to pick you up when you get your discharge order."

More head bobbing. We hugged each other extra hard.

"Will do. I love you."

"Love you more!" I waved as she was wheeled away. I hopped back in the car and kept my composure long enough to drive a half-mile off ARC's campus up Rockville Pike. I pulled onto a service road and wailed until I could pull myself together to make it back home.

***

I didn't know how long Coco and I had been asleep on the couch, but the sound of jingling keys woke me up. The achy crook in my neck told me I had been in one spot for far too long.

"Hi, Godmommy!" Portia dropped her backpack and sat next to me. I hugged her and kissed her temple.

"Hey, you." I wondered what I looked like. My eyes felt swollen, and my mouth was dry. No doubt I was dehydrated from crying so much. T came in behind Portia and our eyes met.

"Please go put your backpack in your room, change your clothes, and then you can get a snack before homework," T instructed Portia.

I appreciated her help so much.

"Once Portia had scooped up her stuff and disappeared upstairs, Coco hot on her heels, T looked back at me.

"What's wrong?" she asked. "Did everything go okay with dropping Leslie off?"

"Yeah, it went fine. I couldn't go in, so I turned around and came home."

"Okay, that doesn't explain why you look exhausted."

"I've been thinking about something." I patted the couch.

"What's that?" T sat down where Portia had been moments before.

"You said Portia wanted to make t-shirts for the walk, right?"

"Yep."

"I didn't want to say anything, but I don't know if we should make them *in honor of* or *in memory of*—" I couldn't say Leslie's name.

T gathered me in her arms, and I proceeded to wet her shirt with water leaking out of my eyes. Every time I thought I had made peace with whatever would happen, I realized that I was not there yet. I really would not be okay if Leslie died. Who would be?

Once I got myself together again, T disappeared into the kitchen. She came back with a cup of tea. "Seems like forever since we've sat with tea."

"It does, and that reminds me, there's a new tea shop on Eastern Avenue that caught my eye. Folks in the office have talked about it. Jason's assistant said it was so nice she went, drank tea, and read her latest copy of the *Urbanite* front to back. So much has changed since this time last year."

"And we've managed," T said. "Not perfectly, but we're not perfect. We've learned a lot of lessons for a reason. We've been caregivers and parents, and I still want to be your lover." T added a falsetto riff like Prince.

"You are silly!" I playfully poked her in the side.

"So, let's make the shirts 'in honor of.' We shouldn't claim anything before it happens. We're still lifting prayers, yes? For remission, for healing, for anything better than what's currently happening."

"But what if—"

"Uh-uh, nope." T put her hand up. "We're not going there. If we have to, we will, but let's not tell a story before it happens."

"Are you really going to use Portia's design?" I asked.

"Portia and I are collaborating on a t-shirt design," T replied, rolling her eyes.

"Yes!" The little person unexpectedly exclaimed. She had returned, now wearing a light-blue shirt and bite-sized sweatpants, and headed to the kitchen for her snack.

"You two are a lot! I mean that exactly the way it sounds." I smirked, I didn't know T and Portia working on another project was the good news I needed to hear at this moment. "What do you think if everyone comes back to the house after the walk in a couple of weeks? Maybe grill a little something, have a few different salads, keep it simple."

"That sounds nice. A good gathering for pictures with the t-shirts. Speaking of which, we need to order them. How many do we need?" T asked.

"I know the three of us and Stephanie, maybe Angel, I'll send her a text to ask."

"John said he'd walk too. So, maybe seven or eight shirts? We'll finish the design and get sizes from everyone," T said.

"You may want to check with Portia." I pointed toward the kitchen.

"Why?" T asked, as if she were thinking *Why do I need to ask the child?*

"Stephanie told me Portia asked for her t-shirt size a week ago and she wanted to know if Stephanie was coming back to the house for dinner."

T closed her eyes and shook her head.

"She said we may want to check and see how many people Portia invited."

"You gotta love the tenacity." T grinned.

"Hmmm." I laughed. "That's what we're calling it? This has become a production. It's a lot, Teresa Butler, a lot!"

CHAPTER FORTY-SIX

T

Jasmine was right—we were a lot. If we were going to do this, we had to do it right. I had several "Transformation" paintings that I hadn't decided what to do with yet. I thought about putting them on sundry objects like coasters or magnets, something else I could market. The smaller butterflies would look great on a t-shirt, and we could make them purple and pink as Portia suggested.

After our staff professional development day in late September, I stopped by my studio to work on Portia's idea. I played with the lighting when I took photos of the canvases and narrowed the choices down to three. I needed to keep a tight rein on the number of options Portia could have. I enlarged the photos and when I got home that evening, laid each of them on a white t-shirt on the dining room table so she could make her final decision.

I was sitting out on the back patio chilling with Coco and soaking up the last days of decent weather before old man winter showed up when Jasmine and Portia got home. I heard Portia's girly squeak inside the house and knew she'd seen the shirts. Coco jumped off my lap and started barking at the screen door when they took too long to open it. Finally, Portia slid the screen open and rushed out.

"I love them!" she bubbled.

Jasmine came out and kissed the top of my head.

"Hey, babe," I said.

"The designs are beautiful. No stick or crayon figures for you." She laughed.

"No, indeed. There will be thousands of people out there—never miss a marketing opportunity."

"Do you want Leslie to see them before making the final decision?" Jasmine asked me.

"I don't' think that's necessary. It was Portia's idea, so let's leave it to her. What's the plan for Leslie? She was supposed to be discharged today. Isn't that what I heard you say yesterday?"

"Yes, Angel volunteered to pick her up, and I was absolutely okay with that."

"Cool."

Jasmine continued. "There are two main events, one specifically for breast cancer survivors, the other for those of us who love them. Both events raise money and awareness about breast cancer. The day of, Angel and Leslie will meet us after the survivors walk. It'll probably take longer to find them in the crowd than the time it takes to actually finish the race."

"You think so?"

"Ah, that's right…" Jasmine snapped her fingers. "This is your first breast cancer walk. You'll see."

***

The day of the walk, on the second Saturday in October, survivors were supposed to gather an hour before the rest of us. Angel borrowed a wheelchair from the friend of a friend to push Leslie along the short route and they had left the house decked out in so much attire, including sashes with "Survivor" inscribed on them. Leslie wore a pink tiara and pink tulle bracelets. Angel said she would stay with Leslie until we finished the walk or take her home if she was too fatigued. They would play it by ear.

That morning, there was a sea of people as far as my eye could see. Jasmine wasn't kidding. I had never seen so many shades of pink or uses of it in countless ways. A softball team carried pink gloves and bats. Ladies wore fluorescent pink wigs and pink Chuck Taylors. Another group didn't adopt pink but sported their signature color on everything, red bedazzled cowboy hats and boots, red boas, red sweatshirts, just red with purple accessories thrown in for good measure. People on skates, with strollers, pushing folks in various stages of recovery—it was mass pandemonium, in a good way. And I knew the pictures from the day were going to be memorable.

Every industry was accounted for, car dealers, restaurants, hospitals, and schools, all with pink, logoed shirts. I kept hearing folks say they were trying to beat Baltimore's record from the year before. Local papers estimated that the 2005 walk had brought in more than 20,000 participants. As if their mere presence wasn't enough, people were stopping to take pictures near the massive arch of pink, white, and fuchsia balloons that marked the walk's beginning in addition to every local media outlet covering the event. Cheerleaders, folks walking with pompoms, and so many team "fill in the blank" t-shirts. And like us, folks wore t-shirts honoring loved ones. Even with all the designs and creativity, I had to admit, our t-shirts looked amazing.

Multiple folks took pictures of Portia in her t-shirt, with a pink ribbon painted on her face. She gave an interview to someone with a mic and camera. They weren't from a local outlet, but they were kind and attentive to the well-spoken little girl outfitted in a butterfly t-shirt and pink camouflaged pants who said she was walking because her mom was sick. She enthusiastically said she wanted all the money raised that day to go into research. Lord knows we were praying for the research part to come through for Leslie.

Every person out there had a connection to someone affected by breast cancer, whether it was a family member, friend, soror, or coworker.

I spotted a news anchor with a survivor shirt on and walking through the crowd hugging and high-fiving people as they crossed the finish line.

The event was also well-sponsored. There were swag bags and lots of food once the walkers finished. And since it was a health event, there was table after table of educational materials, support groups offering their services, hospitals sharing information about their breast cancer units, and tables providing community resources. All were represented in large numbers. We walked around for another hour or so checking out all the vendors. Jasmine asked a lot of questions, not about breast cancer support per se, but about vendor involvement.

"What are you conjuring up?" I asked her.

She laughed. "I'm trying to figure out how ReBuild can help."

"I knew you had ideas—I smelled smoke."

She laughed again and gave me a side hug.

Somehow, we finally found Angel and Leslie in the massive sea of humanity, so we took more pictures. Of Portia hugging Leslie from behind and some with Portia, Angel, and Leslie. Two-thirds of the people in this last frame had had to fight cancer. I said a prayer for the other third. Leslie was trying to manage, but we could see the fatigue starting to set in so Angel took her back to our house.

***

Inviting folks back to the house had been a good idea in theory but time was tight. Thank goodness for family, I thought. My cousin Kevin had volunteered to help, so I sent him a text about an hour before we were going to head back to the house. I'd given him a key so that he and Terrence could get things set up, and by the time we got there, everything was ready.

Although the day was chilly, it was still fairly comfortable outside. People sat in the house and on the patio. Angel had even decorated with puffs of the colors of the day and added a little orange for good measure. I wasn't mad when folks ate, chatted just a bit, and left. Between the logistics of the day, the intense emotions, and the throngs of people we had maneuvered among, we were beat.

Once everyone was gone, the house was quiet again, and I was just finishing up cleaning the kitchen for the night, Jasmine came in, sidled up behind me, and wrapped her arms around my waist.

"My god, what a day."

"It was a good day, right?" I dried my hands and turned around to pull my girl to me. "The weather was nice, the crowd was massive, and our folks turned out."

Jasmine just shook her head against my chest.

"I took pictures of Portia holding all our hands, even John's. He keeps teasing me about being a mother, but he looked like a proud uncle today."

"He did, didn't he? Terrence and Kevin did too. I heard Portia asking Terrence about his cobbler," Jasmine said.

"What did she ask him?"

"If there was nutmeg in it?"

"No, she didn't." I couldn't understand why that kid kept amazing me.

"Yes, she did," Jasmine confirmed.

"You know what that means?"

"Yep, we're making cobbler next week."

CHAPTER FORTY-SEVEN

Jasmine

The morning after the breast cancer walk, T and I were enjoying our much needed Sunday morning coffee while the energy in the house was mellow. She was reviewing a list of things to do before her gallery event that afternoon. I was reading both of our horoscopes for insight into how our day was going to go when Portia ran into the kitchen.

"Godmommy, Mommy is really sick!" Portia said in a rush of words and rocking from one foot to the other.

"She's sick?"

"Yes. She's been sick all morning."

I inappropriately smiled. "Yessss!" I left the kitchen and ran upstairs with T right behind me. "Leslie, Leslie!" I found her hunched over the toilet and glistening from sweat. She looked terrible. "You're sick!" I beamed.

"Yes, Jasmine, I am sick." Leslie managed to hold her head up, but her eyes were closed. "I've been puking since about three this morning. And you sound pleased about this," she added dryly.

Portia and T were standing in the doorway looking confused.

"I *am* pleased, and you should be too." I grabbed a washcloth from the linen closet and wet it for her.

"Umm…" she started gagging, dry heaving this time.

"Do you know what this means?" I asked a bit too eagerly.

"Bitch…sorry, baby." Leslie flicked her wrist in Portia's direction. "Your godmother has clearly lost her mind."

"Don't be snarky, Leslie Sharp." I didn't like being called out my name, but a snarky Leslie meant she was still very much herself. "No, ding, ding, ding…" I tapped my temple. "You're sick, you look terrible…"

She shot me a look.

"I'm sorry, but this means you must be getting medication and not a placebo."

Leslie's eyes grew wide. "Oh, my god, I'm sick! I haven't been this sick in a few months. I feel horrible."

"This is great! Wait, remember the staff said if you get sick, you have to call the unit? Portia, make sure your mother stays cool with the damp washcloth. Leslie, where's the packet of information you came home with?"

"Do you need me to do anything?" T asked.

"No, baby, I just need to call the research center."

"The research stuff is on the desk in the room," Leslie said. T helped her off the floor to the edge of the tub. They stayed with her while I went to her room.

There, I rummaged around the piles of paper. Every organization gave patients reams of treatment information. Did people ever read all of it? I wondered.

"I found it," I screamed. "I'm going to call this number and see what's next."

I dialed quickly and got a response right away.

"Good morning, Center for Cancer Research, this is Cheryl speaking. How may I help you?"

"Hi, I'm calling for Leslie Sharp, a patient in your breast cancer study. She's vomiting, probably has a fever, she's sweating…"

"Does she have stomach cramps or a change in taste?" Cheryl asked.

"Hey, how's your stomach?" I called to Leslie.

"It hurts."

"Do you have anything going on with your mouth?"

"I taste metal."

I relayed Leslie's comments and Cheryl told me to get her to the research center by two that afternoon.

"Today? I have to bring her today? Uhh, okay." I hung my head and let out a breath. Dammit, T and I were getting back to a good place again, her art show was from two to five. The likelihood that I was going to make it around 495 and back to Baltimore before her show ended was close to impossible.

"What they say?" Leslie asked.

"You need to pack a bag for fourteen days and I need to get you to the research center by two today."

"What about T's show?" Leslie pointed at her.

"Girl, an art show is the last thing you need to worry about right now," T tried to assure Leslie.

"Maybe we can leave early enough so I can be back before the show is over."

"Let's see if we can find someone else to take me."

"Maybe. But you know both Angel and Stephanie are out of town." I knew Stephanie would be back that day, but Angel was away for work all week. Thoughts were churning in my head faster than I could process them. "Do you have someone else in mind?"

Leslie shrugged.

"Portia…," I turned to her. "Help your mom pack for a hospital visit. T…," We locked eyes and I nodded my head toward our bedroom.

Just inside, I closed the door and looked at T who was waiting patiently for me to speak.

"I'm thinking if I leave here shortly, by like twelve-thirty, and drop Leslie off at ARC, I can get to the gallery before you wrap up. Is that okay?"

"Baby, it's fine. You've been to a show, and Kevin will have staff there to assist."

"I know." I moved into her personal bubble. "I also know women like to swarm around."

"Girl, please. Is that what you're worried about? I'm old and domesticated."

"And you're still a catch." I leaned in and brushed my lips against hers. "But yeah, okay, thanks, baby. I'll be there as soon as I can."

"What about Portia?"

"She's old enough to stay here a few hours alone. I'll let Meg, Sarah's mother, know she's here in case Portia needs something."

"Nah, you don't have to do that…Lil Bit can come with me."

"Are you sure? You don't have time to watch Portia," I countered.

"Portia may have needed watching when she was three years old. But the Portia I know can help me sell paintings."

"You have a point." I kissed T on the cheek and went to retrieve a small suitcase from the basement.

Back in Leslie's room, I handed her the suitcase. "This is good news."

"News that I've prayed for," Leslie replied.

"Me too. Safe to say we all have. You want some soup?"

"Girl, I don't want any more soup! What's with you and soup?" Leslie laughed. "Owww, my stomach."

"See, soup would make you feel better," I giggled. "Okay, we'll leave here as soon as you're ready to go. My plan is to get you checked in and I'll get back to Baltimore, fingers crossed, before T's show is over."

T

Finally, good news. It sounded odd to say I was glad Leslie was sick, but lord knows, I was glad Leslie was sick. Mr. Charles and Leslie leaving 'way from here in the same year wouldn't be good. I had mentally prepared myself for the worst-case scenario. Not because that was a desired outcome, but because my relationship needed strength. Jasmine and I didn't need any more strain to test our bond. Whatever happened, happened. Our destiny was up to the Creator, but I wanted to be with Jasmine, we were a family with a huge village. This had been on full display during the breast cancer walk.

That afternoon, Portia and I headed to Gallery 54. It felt good to get ready for a show again. I had dropped my paintings off a few days before so that the gallery staff could hang them for maximum viewing and marketing effect. I wasn't sure about the "Transformation" series—it was truly a departure from any work I'd created before. These pieces were much more ethereal, at least that was how I thought of them. They had been born out of all the time I had spent contemplating life and its cycles, twists and turns, ups and downs. How things and people fit together for no other reason than the Almighty's grace and mercy.

We got there around one-fifteen to find an associate putting the finishing touches on the track lighting and Kevin rearranging promo materials for upcoming events.

"Hey, Uncle Kevin," Portia greeted him.

"Hey, there, I didn't expect to see you here," he said to her while looking at me.

I mouthed, "I'll tell you later."

"Let's go see how we can help Uncle Terrence." Kevin guided Portia with a gentle hand on her shoulder.

I put my hands into a prayer posture toward him as I backed away, wanting to check out how things had come together for the show. This was such a beautiful space. I was a little nervous—it had been a minute since I'd done this. I was taking a risk that people currently had disposable income to even buy art. The U.S. economy was headed in the wrong direction, with people losing their houses and jobs, not to mention gas prices were way too damn high. But life's craziness over the past year had given me inspiration to create a different style of art. I was hoping to add some beauty in the world.

Even if Jasmine didn't make it back to Baltimore in time, it was okay. She needed to take Leslie to the hospital and hopefully everything would work out. But then a half hour into the event, I was stunned as hell when Stephanie walked through the door.

"Hey, thanks for coming. I'm not sure if you know, Jasmine took Leslie back to ARC. She was sick this morning, and they wanted her there for further observation."

"Oh, I know." Stephanie nodded, looking around with her bag in the crook of her elbow. "I just came back into town and was told I needed to get here."

"Really? How come?"

Stephanie rolled her neck. "To keep the bees away from my best friend's honey." She cackled and hit my shoulder lightly.

"Are you serious?" My eyes widened.

"I'm here, aren't I?"

"Y'all are too much." I found the effort annoyingly cute. "Okay, I'm going to circulate with potential buyers. By the way, Portia is here somewhere."

"Oh, good. I'm going to look around too. Oh, wait..." Stephanie grabbed my forearm.

I looked down, the unexpected contact startling me.

"You need to let me know if someone named Nia comes in."

"Nia?"

"I think she said Nia, or was it Mia? I don't remember. What I do remember is Jasmine saying Ms. Thing was flitting about being a nuisance at another show."

"Stop! Nia is no concern for Jasmine. We've been up to our necks in family responsibilities, and she brings up a trick from four years ago?"

"I know she's of no concern, 'cause I'm from ova west. She don't want none of this." Stephanie threw up Baltimore's westside hand signal.

"That's right, Doctor Stephanie. A scuffle would look great on WBAL's evening news." I waved her off. "I can't with you two."

I was so glad when, a little after four o'clock, Jasmine arrived. I couldn't help thinking about the difference four years and several art shows had made with her standing as my partner. She was very comfortable hosting and answering questions about my work. She also made a few inside jokes that I was only authorized to hang art at home—anyone else needed to call a handyman.

But Jasmine could certainly hold a grudge too. A few years back, Nia Bostic had been a bit brash in making her presence known at the first ever art show Jasmine attended to see my work. As a matter of fact, Nia's antics almost resulted in a straight-up cat fight and Jasmine had never let me forget it, even though at the time we were far from being a couple.

Fortunately, though, we saw no sign of Nia as the show went on. And promptly at five, Kevin and I were standing by the gallery door as the last guests filed out.

I thanked the few remaining customers as they completed their purchases, then turned to Kevin.

"How did we do?" I asked him.

"Wonderful! I'm so glad you're painting again, T. I must admit, I wasn't sure about this new direction, but patrons loved it. All this pollinator and environmental justice talk, let's see what you can do with bees next." He playfully bumped me with his shoulder and we both laughed.

And I couldn't help wondering myself what might come next. Maybe more inspiration with Portia's help, the little muse I didn't know I needed.

CHAPTER FORTY-NINE

Jasmine

I made good time getting back around the Capital Beltway. It was only three-fifteen when I started heading north toward Baltimore. I parked and was inside the gallery less than an hour after dropping Leslie off at the research center. I waved to Kevin and saw T, who looked like she was talking to a customer. Not wanting to interrupt her, I scanned the gallery and saw Stephanie across the room.

I had a brief flashback to an ugly scene from a few years before, when one Nia-something tried to push me out of the way, purring to T about hanging some art at her house. That incident almost ended my first date with T, right there in this very gallery. It was also the first time I met John, Kevin, and Terrence. John was instrumental in refereeing the commotion that came from that scene. Over the previous four years, he had told that story countless times, each time embellishing my response to being pushed out the way. I did a quick glance around, no pixie fairies in sight, thank goodness. I was glad to put that memory away and went straight for Stephanie.

"Hey, chica, any bees buzzin'?" I asked, hugging her.

"Nope, I've been watching for them." She cupped her hands like a telescope.

I laughed. "How's the turnout been?"

"I don't know what a good turnout is for T, but there's been a constant stream of folks through here. How did the drop-off go?"

"It went fine, I couldn't go in. I literally left Leslie at the front door. She said she'd call when she could."

"Good. She's where she needs to be. I've learned something new today…"

"What's that?" I could only imagine what would come out of my friend's mouth.

"I certainly didn't realize how much T's paintings went for, phew! Teaching may need to be T's side hustle."

"That's where you two are similar in doing what you do. You love your pro-bono work with the underserved kids and need the swanky clientele to fund your ability to donate and practice freely. Teaching, and ultimately a pension, does the same thing for her."

"Got it. She's been talking up the folks in here today. I didn't know she had it in her."

I tapped Stephanie's arm with the back of my hand.

"On another note, we're all glad you two are okay again," she added.

"That means a lot coming from you."

"I heard about Leslie's shenanigans to get y'all to act like adults. Cheers to her! Look, I was happy to help today but I'm heading out, I'm beat."

"Well, I certainly appreciate you guarding my honey pot." I hugged her again.

Stephanie really laughed, "Yep, no bees buzzing around here—or none that made it apparent."

"It's been a good day, let's keep it going." I crossed my fingers.

"Fingers and toes crossed."

We bumped crossed fingers, a throwback to junior high school.

CHAPTER FIFTY

T

By Halloween, I had decided not to go to Savannah for Thanksgiving. I knew if I pushed, Jasmine and I could have made it happen…but why? Life was much better this year than this time the year before even though we were still pretty busy.

One afternoon, during a phone call with Mom, I got her to agree that she and Dad would come to Baltimore for Christmas.

"We had such a delightful time last year," she said. "But we'd like to make new memories this year."

I sensed a tad of snarkiness in my mother's voice. "So you'd be okay staying at the studio again?"

She agreed. "That was fine. Everybody had plenty of space, and we weren't in anybody's way. Are you all going to host Thanksgiving since you'll be home?"

"I'm not sure. I need to see what Jasmine wants to do. I'd be okay if we did absolutely nothing or maybe just a simple celebration."

"Baby, I don't know if you all can do simple," Mom heckled. "And you're certainly teaching Portia to celebrate life in a big way."

"What's that mean?"

"She's gotten the chance to see how precious life is, you all have. How's her mama doing?"

"I'm trying not to be too excited or jinx anything, but she's doing well. Jasmine said Leslie's recent scans are showing much smaller tumor areas. She's not out of the woods, but it looks like she's heading in the right direction."

"Amen to that! We've been praying for her recovery."

"Thanks, Ma. You and all of us."

"What kind of award did you win?" She asked now, changing the subject abruptly.

"How did you know I won an award? I planned to call and tell you this evening." Through all the challenges of the past year, I completely forgot Jasmine said she was going to nominate me and Portia for some kind of community service thing. And apparently the muckity-mucks in her company agreed that our fundraising for their children's program was noteworthy."

"Portia told me. She called because she was thrilled."

"Well, I didn't know she would beat me to telling *my* mother about exciting news." *How did she get to tell my mother my good news?*

"Oh, don't be like that."

"Like what?" I said an octave higher than I meant to. "I'm not, I'm not jealous." I was pouting but only slightly.

"Okay, you're not jealous. Well, let me talk to her before we hang up, it's getting late."

"Didn't you just talk to her earlier this week?"

"I did, and I want to speak with her tonight…if you don't mind."

"Fine! Portia!" I yelled upstairs.

"Jealousy isn't like you," she scolded.

"I'm not jealous. Portia, pick up the phone. Bye, Ma."

Jasmine snickered when I placed the phone on its base.

"What?" I asked her.

"Ohh, you're a bit salty 'cause your mama wanted to speak to Portia."

"I am not. I was just surprised that I didn't get to tell her about the award first."

"Awwhhh, it's okay. I'm proud of you." Jasmine patted my arm, but it felt conciliatory. "You and Portia, along with Gus and the kids at your school, really did a wonderful thing and…again, like the family picture albums, partnerships like yours are going to be replicated at other ReBuild agencies across the country. That's big doings!"

"It is, which is why I wanted to share the good news. Anyhoo…I'm over it. Are you looking forward to the ceremony?"

"I'm excited 'cause the awards dinner is going to be at the new Reginald F. Lewis Museum that opened last year. I've wanted to go ever since reading about their interesting African American art and history exhibits, but I also wanted to wait until the crowds died down to visit. I was surprised to hear the museum was the location for the event. I suspect Ruth had something to do with that."

"That's pretty cool. I've been wanting to check the museum out too. I was thinking we could have a date night there—we have been a little busy this year."

"We *have* been a tad preoccupied. Meanwhile, it sounds like your folks are coming for Christmas?"

"Yes. What about your mom?"

"I'm going to extend an invitation, and she can decide where she wants to spend the holiday. The support group that she finally started going to last month is helping with Dad being gone. Her being here alone with us, and without the buffer of my father, may be a bridge too far. I think it's a long way off before she accepts us. If she can't, okay. She also knows I'm no longer going to just be tolerated."

"Yes, ma'am." I clasped my hands together to signal the end of the discussion. *I wasn't getting in the middle of that family drama.* "I know two things—you've been clear about your boundaries and the Butler-Charles family is doing Christmas again!"

CHAPTER FIFTY-ONE

Jasmine

The awards dinner was scheduled for a Friday in November. The Reginald F. Lewis Museum had been open less than two years, so having the gala at Baltimore's newest museum was a huge win, but it wasn't free. Ruth had worked every angle she had to ensure the venue price was affordable for our guests. She especially kept in mind people whose financial constraints prevented them going to the museum on any day, as well as those who wouldn't go for any number of reasons. She was determined to have these folks included in ReBuild's event there. I had seen the guest list—a mixture of politicians, our board of directors, construction staff, and families who lived in ReBuild homes.

On the night of the ceremony, T and Portia both looked so good. Before we left we sent a picture to Leslie, who was still at ARC, but we expected her to be discharged before Thanksgiving. T wore a fitted navy suit and Portia wore a honey-colored dress with a sash. She had taken to wearing a pink cancer ribbon on most of her outfits. I smiled thinking about the unsuspecting adults who might dare ask her about the ribbon and get a lengthy talking-to about the need for more cancer research.

Quetta's uncle brought her to the ceremony, we had agreed to bring her home. Having Quetta there would make it easier to keep Portia engaged in children's activities. And it would be a nice full circle moment—some of the pictures from the slide show would have Quetta and her family included.

Once we arrived, I checked out the swag bags and especially loved that they were full of local charm. I noticed that many of the national guests kept pulling things out of their bags, marveling at them, and asking about this or that. But no one from Baltimore needed an explanation about the crab mallet, Utz chips, mini-can of Old Bay, or the small pack of Berger cookies.

The highlight for us was the moment Jason presented the award to T and Portia for their efforts to raise money for ReBuild's children's program. I loved their acceptance speech. T recognized Gus, the Industrial Arts program, and his woodshop kids. Our slide show included happy customers with their mountable clothes racks. Portia honored T for her help with the idea. She even said, "I hope we can sell more next spring." T was good-natured about being put on the spot.

Jason closed the gala by thanking everyone in attendance and made a fundraising appeal to support organizations helping those in need during and after the holidays. Afterward, he made his way to me and whispered, "The suits gave me a verbal for filling a new VP position. I hope you'll consider throwing your hat in the ring."

"That's a surprise and sounds like a great opportunity." I broke into a smile.

"I think it will be." He pointed to Portia, "Too bad she's not fifteen years older—we'd already have our next Director of Community Engagement. She's something, isn't she?" He hooted.

"Oh, you don't know the half of it." I waved goodbye to Jason and caught up with my bunch. The girls skipped ahead of us as T and I walked back to the car. I was so proud of my family. We dropped Quetta off and headed home.

"We make a good team," Portia announced from the back.

"We do make a great team," T co-signed.

"Yes, we do," I agreed. It had been a lovely evening.

CHAPTER FIFTY-TWO

T

The days leading up to Thanksgiving couldn't have been better. Suffice to say, the span of events over the past year along with the gratitude season had all of us feeling more emotional and sensitive about the fragility of life. There had been an increased impulse to recognize and honor those we loved. Since we weren't going to Savannah, we planned a Jasmine-style Thanksgiving Day. That meant watching the Macy's Thanksgiving Day Parade on TV, enjoying the dog show, and ordering a prepared meal from a local grocery store—it still needed to be heated and plated.

Jasmine joked that she would make the presentation pretty and we really didn't want her cooking a turkey. Her mother had chided her in the past for getting a box meal with a turkey and fixings, but I was fine with all of it. Whoever else came to dinner could bring sides or dessert.

Jasmine was excited to stay home, forego going to church, and staying in pajamas until dinnertime. I was so onboard with her plans, if for no other reason than to prove to my mother that we could do simple. But Leslie called on Tuesday to say she was being discharged and asked us to pick her up on Wednesday.

Nobody in their right mind living in the surrounding DC, Maryland, or Virginia area wanted to get on the road the day before Thanksgiving. Except in this case, Jasmine and Portia got up early, made their way to Bethesda, and were back home by two in the afternoon—and with a healthier-looking Leslie. She had gained weight, had a bit of peach fuzz on her head, and her skin glowed. She looked better and apparently was feeling better and pretty sassy too. When I marveled how good she looked, she pranced around the living room with a few twirls.

"I feel good," she responded.

Wednesday dinner was pizza. It was easy and didn't take up any space in the otherwise packed refrigerator. Once Portia and I cleaned up the kitchen from dinner, Leslie said she was going to head upstairs to talk with Portia before she went to bed and then we could catch up downstairs. Jasmine and I were chatting in the living room when Leslie returned.

"Who's coming tomorrow?" she asked as she sat down.

"Just the four of us, very low key. Stephanie's away. You can see if Angel wants to come. Does she know you were discharged?" Jasmine asked.

"Yeah, she knows. Angel has a new boo. Sounds like a nice guy. I have something for you. Do you want to try a new blend of tea? One of the other research participants turned me on to it."

"I won't pop positive, will I?" I asked suspiciously.

"No! It's to help lower stress and calm you."

"And it's legal?" Jasmine asked before Leslie went to put the kettle on.

When the kettle whistled. Leslie went back to the kitchen.

"She's really feeling much better. Do you see how she's moving?" Jasmine whispered.

"I can hear you!" Leslie laughed. "And I really do feel much better." She came back with a tray and three piping cups of tea. "I didn't see any cookies."

"Your daughter is on strike. We didn't give her extra screen time, so she didn't make us any tea cookies this week.

"Is she getting catty?" Leslie scrunched her fingers into claws.

"Her personality is strong. I wonder where she got that from?" I asked and we all laughed. I sipped the tea. "Ugh. This tastes like what I imagine tree bark would taste like."

"I put a little honey in it," Leslie said defensively.

Jasmine tasted hers and pinched her lips together like she had sucked a lemon. "This tastes like dirt."

"It's earthy." Leslie laughed again. She was clearly feeling alright.

"That's about right. What is this?" I put my cup down and pushed it away.

"It's called Ashwagandha. It's very good for several things, most importantly stress. I've been drinking it for a couple weeks now. Drink up and wait an hour, you'll feel calmer."

I glanced at Jasmine.

She lifted her cup toward me. "Cheers."

I scrunched my nose and lips at her.

"I have to check in at Charity," Leslie said. "I have an appointment on Monday with Dr. Jordan." She quickly caught us up on her treatment plan, then added, "She came to see me, and we've had video conferences with the research team. Technology is amazing, it felt like the Jetsons in there sometimes."

"So, what's next?" Jasmine wanted to know.

"The infusions have really targeted the cancer cells and not made me as sick. Bonus! There may be one more chemo adjustment on the horizon, but it's looking good, family." She raised her arms triumphantly.

Jasmine got up to hug Leslie. "We have a lot to be thankful for."

They hugged and hugged—I knew their tears would start soon. And I could barely see them through my own.

CHAPTER FIFTY-THREE

Jasmine

I started planning a night away after I overheard Ruth mention to another staff member that schools were going to be closed the next day for professional development. That meant T had a little flex time before she needed to be at school in the morning. Leslie was able to drive again so she would do the morning drop-off and then I'd get Portia as usual after school.

I called in a prepared food order from the gourmet grocery store down the street from St. Josephine's. I could pick up my order and place it in a picnic basket before T got home. Lastly, I sent T a text that said, "Date night begins at six. Be dressed to impress." She was almost dressed by the time I got home.

"You look nice, smell good, you clean up real well, Ms. Butler," I said, walking into our bedroom and moving closer to her.

"That's my name, don't wear it out." She leaned in to kiss me on the cheek.

"You are so silly."

"So where are we heading on this very impromptu date night. Who's going to be here with Leslie and Portia?"

"I think they'll be okay overnight."

"Overnight? What do you have planned?"

"You have a professional day tomorrow, right?"

"Yeah?" She was skeptical.

"So, you have a little flexibility in getting to work. You'll see. We're going out for the evening."

"Do I need a toothbrush?"

"I have everything you need for a memorable evening, ma'am." I dropped my voice to a sultry octave.

"Don't write no checks you can't cash, Ms. Charles. You've been tired a lot lately."

"True that, and I had a large coffee around two o'clock. So…" I winked. "Let's go."

"Well, well, I'm following you."

By the time I took the familiar roads heading to Bolton Hill, T was more than curious as to what was going on.

"Are we going to the studio? Jasmine, what are you up to?"

"I thought we could have a little picnic and talk or something." I blew a kiss before getting out of the car in front of T's studio. I went to the trunk for the overnight bags I'd packed and placed in there earlier. The bags were loaded with all our favorites, seafood entrees, crab dip, spinach and avocado dip, feta and blueberry salad, and more snacks and flavored lemonades than she would drink.

T came around the car to help carry the bags. "Oh, my, look at you. What's in here?"

"I told you, everything you'd need for the evening."

"Alrighty, let's get this party started." T did a little dance.

I hadn't seen that smile in a long time, not one that was easy and unburdened. T headed up the steps, unlocked the door, and had turned off the alarm by the time I finished pulling the remaining bags from the trunk. I told T to go up and get comfortable with what I had packed in the bag for her, then made quick work of setting a tablecloth over a blanket on the living room floor. I lit candles around the room and lastly threw a few pillows on the floor for support. By the time T came back downstairs, I had glasses out for drinks with cheeses and crunchies.

"What can I do to help?"

I handed her the remote to find us some music. She selected some hard rap with lyrics that started with "Hit it, hit it" and started laughing.

"Really, that's what you see here?" I gestured to the floor.

"If I'm lucky," she said, wiggling her eyebrows and grinning.

"Seriously, give me that." I found a slow Grover Washington, Jr., tune. "Let's start here. I'm going to run upstairs and get comfortable too. I've set a few things out for your pleasure."

"Yes, ma'am. I see that. I'm looking forward to your return."

I gave T a long slow luscious kiss on her lips, sucking the bottom one into my mouth, traveled to her cheek, and stopped at her neck.

"Oh, my." She swallowed. "Yes, please return soon."

I palmed her ass. "Be right back."

It took all of fifteen minutes to take my clothes off, hop in the shower, and put on a new two-piece lingerie set. I giggled as I pulled the tags off. I couldn't remember wearing anything sexy the entire past year—this would be a nice change of pace. I took a last look and did a quick figure eight with my hips. If she played her cards right, I would be doing a little more of this motion. I chuckled to myself and headed back to the kitchen to take the remaining food to the living room.

"Hmmm, looks good," T said as I came back and joined her.

"I know, right? All our favorites."

"I wasn't talking about the food."

My face hurt from smiling. We needed this. We had been drinking water from a firehose since Leslie's diagnosis. T and I lounged, snacked, and kissed for what seemed like hours.

"Thank you."

"You are welcome. My pleasure." I kissed T again.

"This was nice and much needed."

"Baby, thank you. I couldn't have managed any of this last year without you. You've been there even when people related by blood came up short. I know it wasn't easy."

T listened.

"I understood…mostly…when you needed time away," I continued. "Trust, I didn't sign up for the care we gave either, but I'm glad we did. Our chosen family was wonderful. Your cousins, your parents, Stephanie, and John. I'm grateful for all of them. I'm thinking Christmas will feel a bit more hopeful this year."

"I think so. It seems like either we've become veterans at this caregiving thing, or the situation just doesn't feel or look as bleak."

"I agree. We've been taking care of everyone else. I thought tonight we could take care of each other."

"Do tell, what do you have in mind?"

"I can show you better than I can tell you. Follow me." I started walking to the steps leading upstairs to the bedroom.

"Following you, yes, ma'am…immediately. I'm blowing out these candles."

CHAPTER FIFTY-FOUR

T

One afternoon before Christmas I got out the pictures I had taken of Leslie over the past year and began to review them. The difference a year made! You could see the worry and illness despite feigned smiles. I loved some of the more candid pictures of her with her head wrap off. There were at least two dozen pictures taken since Leslie's discharge the previous month. You could see the sparkle and joy in her eyes. She looked more relaxed and the shots with her looking lovingly at Portia were some of the best photos I'd taken in a long time. And I'd been glad to hear from Jasmine that Dr. Jordan hoped Leslie would get to ring the bell signaling the end of her treatment by next year.

The pictures I'd taken of Portia really showed how much she had grown. The year before, she had been maybe chest-high to Jasmine and now in recent pictures, she stood as tall as Jasmine's shoulders, making it clear she was going to take height from her father. I had taken snapshots of basketball games, of Portia making the wood racks, vending at the farmers' market, as well as shots of her at the ReBuild holiday party and the breast cancer walk.

A few days later, after going through all my photos, I had one of them enlarged on canvas—the light and balance were perfect—to give to Leslie as a future housewarming gift when she returned to her condo. It felt good to be back in a creative frame of mind, participating again in Kevin's monthly gallery exhibits, getting requests from other nonprofits needing photography services, and fielding interest calls from my "Transformation" series. With all this, life was busy. One of the organization tables we had visited during the breast cancer walk had also contacted me about using a few butterfly pictures for their magazine. Things were looking up.

***

Before my parents arrived for Christmas, Mom called to discuss their travel itinerary. They hadn't been fond of their flight the year before since they had to make connections through Atlanta, one of the busiest airports in the world. So this time they were coming to Baltimore by train. "Hey, baby."

"You all were serious about not flying, huh? That train ride is over ten hours." I glanced at the arrival and departure times she had sent me in an email.

"It's thirteen and we'll be fine. By the time we got up early, got to the airport, made connections, and got to you, there wouldn't be much difference. Plus, it's cheaper, and I can pack us a nice cooler of food for the ride. You just be ready to pick us up from Penn Station."

I smiled, remembering my childhood road trips. "Yes, ma'am. That cooler will probably have pound cake, slices of bread, and fried chicken, huh?"

"That's right, and some fruit." Mom laughed.

"I won't be mad if you save me a slice of cake."

"I'll make a fresh cake once I get there."

I silently pumped my fist yes!

"Are we staying at your place, at the studio?"

"Yes. Leslie and Portia move back to Leslie's after the holiday," I replied.

"I'm so happy for that little girl. Baby, I'm telling you, we've been praying for her mama."

"Prayer works. Wait until you see how good Leslie looks. She's glowing."

"Oh, that's good news. But I need to go now—my book club will be here soon."

"I didn't know you were in a club."

"Yes, we do more socializing than reading, but it's good. We have a few widows in the group, they like the company. Speaking of which, how's Jasmine's mama? Is she coming over for Christmas supper?"

"Got it, book club that may or may not read the book." I chuckled, then addressed my mom's last question. "She's okay. Jasmine said she finally agreed to going to a support group and has been making friends. But some of her church friends haven't been calling as much. Between us…it was Mr. Charles that folks liked."

"I can see that." My mother, ever the diplomat. "Okay, gotta go. Love you."

"Love you too."

CHAPTER FIFTY-FIVE

Jasmine

On Christmas day the house was packed. Aside from T's parents and the four of us who lived there, the usual suspects were in attendance as well. Kevin, John, and the rest of the crew. I felt like we were celebrating our own Christmas miracle 2006. Our laughter was louder, hugs longer, and smiles were deeper. It was truly a holiday so different from the one before. The heaviness was gone from the atmosphere—there was a lightness—and we touched each other with an intensity and warmness fueled by the human need to be connected.

When my mother arrived, we all paused. She hadn't been to our house in months, since dropping some of my dad's mementos off. I watched her tentatively greet everyone and I listened as she apologized, in her own way, to T.

"Thank you for supporting my daughter and her goddaughter. I know it wasn't easy. I'm glad she has someone who…umm…helps her."

T was cordial though, and I didn't expect anything else. I had to keep from laughing as Ms. Mary moved quickly and stood right behind her daughter. T's mother had her back and I didn't think T even knew her mom was in such close proximity. I was glad my mother had said something decent because Ms. Mary did not tolerate foolishness. It may have been my imagination, but I was sure I heard everyone exhale.

I had loved watching my goddaughter grow over the past year. We all had. Portia was such a kind and insightful child. I saw her showing my mom her journal, which contained the list of books she had read for the year.

My mother told Portia, "Jasmine was a great reader when she was your age."

I didn't realize she had remembered that. Clearly, my mother's harshness had softened, her edginess was muted—grief looked different on everyone. I could tell folks were still a little hesitant in their interactions, rightly so, but they gave her grace. In turn, my mother shared during the meal that, "Robert would have loved the atmosphere here this Christmas." Her voice caught when she looked at me and said, "He loved this Motown Christmas album playing. That's what we wrapped all of you all's gifts to each year."

I stood to embrace my mother and hugged her from the side. The real surprise was when she looked around the room and added, "Words can hurt and have consequences. I'm hoping to make amends in the new year." I later saw Ms. Mary and my mom in the living room talking quietly together.

Dinner was plentiful. Terrence's love language was food, and he loved us deeply Christmas day. His affection was evident in his warm gingered yams, savory tender meats, and butter-kissed homemade rolls. And he had let his aunt make a few desserts. When we thanked her for the pound cakes and banana pudding, Ms. Mary responded, "He allowed me to help. I've stopped trying to add to the menu. I simply ask him now, what should I prepare?"

Once dinner was over Leslie stretched. "I'm going to head back upstairs to rest a bit."

The guys were headed to the basement to watch football.

But before anyone could get away, T stopped them all from retreating to their corners and cliques. Leslie returned to the couch.

"Hold tight, can everyone gather in the living room?" she requested. "Jasmine and I would like to say a few words." She motioned for me to get gift bags we'd put together as well as a special gift for Leslie.

I sat them on the coffee table, handed T the larger gift, and T waved her hand as if to say I had the floor. I gently smiled at my wonderful girlfriend and cleared my throat a few times.

"I hope I can get this out. We want to say to everyone in this room, thank you. To our family, both biological and chosen, this journey could not have been possible without your wonderful support. You all made love a verb and put caring into action." I wanted to keep it light—I thanked Stephanie for helping me keep my mind and John for helping T with hers. I thanked Terrence and Kevin for the endless supply of food. I thanked T's parents for their prayers and for embracing us. I thanked Angel for recognizing we needed help. I even thanked my mother for raising me to step up to a challenge.

T passed the bags out. "These are a little something from us to remind you of what Jasmine said."

All the bags contained framed pictures of events that took place during the last year. Leslie's bag was a little different. It contained an album with a year's worth of pictures that T had taken of her, Portia, and all of us supporting her journey. There was even a picture of Dr. Jordan and the staff. She turned it toward T.

"How?" Leslie asked, holding her hand to her heart. The day had been joyful with few tears, but having seen memories beautifully frozen in time, threatened to change that.

"I know people and I'm charming." T chuckled. "Wait, there's one more." T handed Leslie a three-foot square gift wrapped in pink paper and suggested to Leslie they hang it in their condo when they moved back.

Leslie ripped the paper off revealing a gorgeous portrait of Leslie and Portia sitting on the little bench in my backyard garden. Portia was lying in her mother's lap with her eyes closed. Leslie's eyes were closed too and her hand rested on the side of Portia's head. It was the first time I was seeing the picture just like everyone else. The vulnerability that was captured on canvas caused tears to flood my vision. The sniffles I heard without looking around the room let me know I wasn't the only one moved by the image.

Chief among the snifflers was Leslie. "T, I can't thank you and Jasmine enough." She stood up and hugged both of us. "I could not have asked for better support. You all loved on Portia and you literally loved me back to life."

***

When our guests had all left, I took a shower while T drove her parents back to the studio. I popped into bed to wait for her, but I apparently drifted off to sleep because I didn't hear her return. I did, however, smell lemongrass soap when T nestled behind me and woke me up. To my delight, she was bottomless.

"Could this day have been better?" I asked her.

"Maybe?"

"Hmmm…what would make it better?"

T whispered while tracing her fingers along my thigh, awakening nerve endings that hadn't been awake very much lately. Ordinarily, I would have protested because we still had house guests, but I wanted her. I wanted to physically express how much she meant to me and our relationship, especially over the past year.

I pressed my butt into her center, to which she replied by returning the pressure. She used one hand to explore the rest of my body and climbed on top. I pulled her mouth down to mine and ran my tongue along her bottom lip before meeting hers. I never wanted this feeling to end. Our lips were still locked when she moaned, having discovered how wet I was. She took her time, quietly, methodically, patiently bringing me to an orgasmic cliff.

I enthusiastically returned the favor, bringing her to her own climax sometime later, sucking her clit until I felt her rhythmic contractions subside. I returned to lie on top of her. "That, Ms. Butler, made it a perfect day."

CHAPTER FIFTY-SIX

T

We weren't asleep but we hadn't really stirred enough to get out of bed either the next morning when there was a child-sized knock at the door.

"Come in," Jasmine answered as she inched further away from me, as if the kid didn't know we were a couple.

Portia popped her head in the door. "Are you up? Mommy and I are making breakfast."

"Oh, nice. How long do we have?" Jasmine tried to sound excited.

"Mommy said she'll pour the batter in fifteen minutes." The little chef closed the door, not sticking around for commentary or protest.

"O-kay. Fifteen minutes it is then," I said, kissing Jasmine's lips briefly.

Jasmine pulled the comforter up to her neck. "Any chance they're going to bring the cooked batter, pancakes, waffles, crepes, whatever they're whipping up down there, up here to us in bed?"

"I don't think so." I gave her a slight smile and half-hearted shrug.

"Okay, would you like to bring my pancakes to bed?"

One of my eyebrows lifted. "No, ma'am. This is the last breakfast before they go home. We are going to sit at the table, enjoy the delicious vittles they're serving, and take them home."

"Do you realize we've had someone here, other than us, for almost a year and a half?"

"Yes, Jasmine. I am aware and that's why you're going to get dressed, have breakfast, and then we'll help them move back home." I kissed her lips a bit longer, this time to reinforce the point.

"Then it's just us again."

"And Coco. Though she may want to leave with them. Coco is going to miss Portia."

I got dressed and headed to the dining room. True to form, Coco was in the kitchen hoping for a piece of bacon to fall—or in Portia's case, to fall on purpose.

Jasmine came to the table just as Leslie set down a platter of pancakes, bacon, and eggs. Portia provided a quick prayer and didn't stop talking until we finished breakfast. She made mention that she didn't need to take everything as she would be coming to visit often and probably spending the night. Oh, joy!

We toyed with renting a van to take all of Portia and Leslie's accumulated clothes, books, and things back to Angel and Leslie's condo. Waiting until the last Saturday before the end of the year wasn't an optimal time to rent a van. In the end, we decided to just fill our cars and make multiple trips.

We both drove, taking Leslie and Portia home on the first run. That gave them the opportunity to get settled while we packed the cars again and made a second run. At the condo, Angel provided a warmhearted surprise, with fresh flowers, balloons, and a welcome home banner hanging in the living room. Angel purchased foot-long subs and snacks for lunch. Once we all finished our meal, Jasmine and I offered hugs, discussed tentative scheduling plans, and returned home.

Back home, I had to balance feeling emotional about the past year and seeming too eager to have the house back to ourselves. We had done it, with a team approach. Working together had helped us get to this point. And now, I almost felt like carrying Jasmine over the threshold of our next chapter.

More than four years before when Jasmine and I started dating, I had whined to John about being part of a family, as if that were the worst thing. I'd made "family" sound like a four-letter word. But only a few months ago, I'd been sad at the possibility that the family I had come to know and love might fall apart. I thought about all this as I walked in the door, where I found Coco waiting and heard nothing but the hum of the refrigerator. It had been a long minute since the house was this still and quiet.

***

A month ago, when life had started feeling less chaotic, I made hotel reservations for a suite downtown. I thought it would be a grand surprise to see the New Year's Eve fireworks from a suite overlooking Baltimore's harbor. Portia and Leslie agreed to keep Coco since I hadn't made kennel reservations, and the young lady had laughed—she laughed out loud—when I called the previous day to ask if they had any space for Coco on New Year's Eve. I told Jasmine all she really needed was her toothbrush. We would only be gone overnight and would be home by noon. I packed a little bag with a little something special—candles, massage oil, stuff to have fun.

I dropped Jasmine off in front of the hotel and asked her to wait in the lobby while I parked and got us checked in. An extremely polite young man showed us to our suite and left.

I turned to her once in the room. "You like?"

"Oh, my god, a suite? The view!" She peeked in the en suite. "Look at this bathroom." Jasmine did a three-hundred-and-sixty-degree turn in the room. With a smile wider than I'd seen in a while and her hair pulled back in her signature bun that said *I'm confident and sexy without much effort.* "I love it!"

"You, me, and someone else could fit in there."

She raised an eyebrow. "Hmmm…I keep asking you if you're into the menage scene now."

"You've never asked me that and no, I only need you to fulfill all my unadulterated thoughts and pleasures."

Jasmine laughed. "This was an excellent idea and the best surprise. I'm not sure where I thought we were going." She whistled. "This was a pretty penny for New Year's Eve."

"We're worth it. Listen," I whispered and pulled her close to me.

"What?" Jasmine tilted her head, whispering too.

"It's quiet, just you and me."

"I know, right?"

"No family, no kids, the dog isn't even barking." I nibbled her ear.

"Phew!" Jasmine let out a long slow breath. She didn't say it, but in my mind I knew she was releasing everything we had been through. "How did we survive this?"

"We leaned on each other," I said.

"Yes, we did. It was hard. And I really didn't know how this was going to turn out."

"Yeah, it got scary. That conversation with Leslie about her estate?" I shook my head trying to erase the memory.

"Thankfully we avoided that mess, and Portia is home with her mother. They're probably still unpacking as we speak. Leslie is excited to be home and looking forward to a new start. I'm happy for them."

"Me too," I agreed.

"Portia especially. Thank you, baby. We did well by them."

"We did. Portia's a good kid."

I thought about my long and intense journey from wondering "Why us?" to resolutely believing "Why not us?" It felt good. We'd been there for Leslie and Portia, like family should be.

"Okay, enough of the past," Jasmine said, interrupting my thoughts. "What about next year?"

"What about next year?" I asked her.

"Let's talk about you and me." Jasmine started twisting her hips and humming the first few bars of an old Salt-N-Pepa tune about relations between consenting adults.

I joined the hip movement when Jasmine dipped to the right. "Alright now. Get it girl! Still in sync, you and me."

"Baby…"

The first fireworks exploded bright amber over the harbor, drowning out Jasmine's words so I pulled her to me again and kissed her deeply. This was indeed a great way to start fresh.

Happy New Year!

BOOK CLUB QUESTIONS

1. How do the dynamics between Jasmine and T evolve throughout the story, and what are the key moments that define their relationship?

2. What role does the setting of Baltimore play in shaping the characters' experiences and the overall narrative?

3. How does the theme of family manifest in the book, particularly in the relationships between Jasmine, T, and Portia?

4. How does the author address the topic of illness and its effects on both the individual and their loved ones?

5. How does Portia's presence in Jasmine and T's home influence their relationship and daily routines?

6. What are the significant turning points in Leslie's journey, and how do they affect the other characters?

7. How does the author use humor to balance the more serious themes in the book?

8. What role do secondary characters, such as Paul and Angel, play in the development of the main characters and the plot?

9. How does the author portray the theme of resilience in the face of adversity?

10. What are some of the ways the characters support each other, and how does this support evolve over time?

ACKNOWLEDGEMENTS

There's something to be said about writing a second book. We know a bit more about the herculean task of transforming words on a page into a tangible book and yet, we still want to tell more stories.

Thank you to our editor, Pamela Dell. Your attention to detail, insightful feedback, and knowledge of which rules to break and which ones to follow made this project exponentially better. Our Beta readers, K. Thompson, Precious H., and S. Wright—thank you for your time helping us craft a better story and developing well-rounded characters. Eddie Pierce, Jr. of Rainbow Room Publishing, thank you for answering the call whenever we have questions. Griselda Togobo, we cannot thank you enough for providing the creative space and encouragement. And public relations extraordinaire, Cherrie Woods, you're the cheerleader we didn't know we needed. We knew we found the right person when you said, "I'm your machine."

Thank you to readers and bookstore friends who asked for a second book. And to those who have already slyly mentioned a third story…

We hear you!

CONNECT WITH NAOMI

WEBSITE

naomiriversbooks.com

EMAIL

naomiriversbooks@gmail.com

FACEBOOK

@naomiriversbooks

INSTAGRAM

@naomiriversbooks

We would love the opportunity to participate in your book club and/ or for you to join our VIP reader team.

Subscribe to our newsletter for updates at naomiriversbooks.com and follow us on Facebook and Instagram.

ABOUT THE AUTHOR

Naomi Rivers is a wife writing team who believes in romance, fairy tales, and happily ever after. Their first novel, *THIS: A Simple, Complex Love Story*, was written over twenty years to maintain their connection during multiple deployments. They are both retired U.S. military veterans and reside with their two rescue dogs on the east coast. Naomi's work has appeared in I Heart SapphFic's anthology *Favorite Scenes from Favorite Authors* and *From a Black Perspective: The Homeland* published by Rainbow Room Publishing.

9 798987 329733